WARDEN'S
REIGN

ESSENCE OF OHR
Book 1

PARRIS SHEETS

WARDEN'S REIGN
Essence of Ohr – Book 1
Copyright © 2020 by Parris Sheets

FIRST EDITION SOFTCOVER
ISBN: 1622536533
ISBN-13: 978-1-62253-653-5

Editor: Darren Todd
Cover Artist: Samuel Keiser
Interior Designer: Lane Diamond

EVOLVED PUBLISHING™

www.EvolvedPub.com
Evolved Publishing LLC
Butler, Wisconsin, USA

Printed in Book Antiqua font.

BOOKS BY PARRIS SHEETS

DEDICATION

For Matthew, who gave me the courage to pursue my dream.

WARDEN'S REIGN

ESSENCE OF OHR
Book 1
PARRIS SHEETS

CHAPTER 1

When the sun set and the moon dominated the sky, the ramblers walked. Their trunks towered over Kole, carried aloft by thousands of roots as they crawled across the underbrush like giant insects. The massive trees stumbled into one another, knocking about as if intoxicated by the silver moonlight which fueled their nightly gala.

Kole eyed them greedily. Bringing one of these back was sure to please his mentor. *I'll have my shepherd title by morning.*

"Whoa... I've never seen ramblers this big," Niko said beside him, his weariness to follow Kole apparently forgotten at the sight of the gargantuan trees. His quill, a sharpened twig, scratched furiously along the wad of parchment he used as a notebook. Though stained and torn from years of use, Niko treated it like the finest treasure. He even slept with the damn thing.

Kole glanced sideways at the page where he could just make out Niko's sketch of the massive trunks in the soft moonlight, quickly scribbling guesstimated measurements next to each specimen before the ramblers scurried out of view.

"Two hundred meters tall," Niko murmured as he jotted his note down. Apparently the trees were more important than Kole at the moment. "Just look at the width of that trunk. Thirty?"

"Sure." Kole's pointed look seemed lost on his friend. "Told you it'd be worth it."

As Niko finished his drawing, an uncertain tone shaded his voice "Yeah, well, let's not do anything stupid. I'd prefer *not* to get trampled tonight."

He patted his reluctant friend's back. "We'll be fine."

Niko grumbled. He formed Kole's opposite in every way: tall and athletic with dark hair and deeply tanned skin. A shadow of stubble poked from his chin even though he was a year younger than Kole.

Kole always felt scrawny next to Niko. Next to anyone, really. He stood a full head shorter than average, and, at fifteen, still retained the puffy cheeks of a child half his age.

"So what's the plan?" Niko dipped his quill into the portable inkwell at his waist. "No one's going to hear the horn way out here."

Kole scrunched his nose. Niko was right. They couldn't count on the other hunters to help wrangle the rambler back to camp. And the two of them would be no match for a tree this size. But he refused to go back empty handed. Again. Six nights he and Niko had gone out to hunt, and six nights they'd returned to camp with heads hung low. The only thing more embarrassing than a week's worth of failure was the thought of Dya capturing a rambler before him. She wasn't even trained. How ridiculous would he look if the runner-up for his apprenticeship caught a rambler before him? He refused to give his mentor a chance to second guess his decision. It *had* to be tonight.

"We'll ride it back," Kole decided.

Niko stared open-mouthed at the trees. "Are you sure you can steer one this big?"

He shrugged. "Can't be much different than the smaller ones."

In truth, Kole was guessing, but no way would he admit that to Niko. It had taken a good hour to persuade him to come out this far in the first place. Kole had enticed him with promises of unique ramblers to add to his sketchbook. If Niko sensed even the slightest doubt, he'd abandon the hunt.

"Russé's okay with it? I thought you weren't supposed to do this stuff without supervision."

Kole rolled his eyes and whispered though his teeth, "He doesn't have to know."

"What?"

"It's all right, Niko. I'm a shepherd. I'm trained for this kind of thing."

"*Apprentice.*"

Kole winced at the word. "I know how to steer a rambler, Niko," he said, heat rising to his cheeks. "Every night that we come back with nothing gives Dya another chance to one up us. She'll rub it in my face forever. Do you want to beat her or not?"

Eyes squinting, Niko stared, as if weighing the argument in his mind.

"You'll get a real-life demonstration just like I promised." He gestured to the ramblers. "It'll give you an advantage at the next Shepherd's Trials. Knowing this stuff will get you to the final round."

"Fine," Niko relented. "Just be careful."

Kole craned his neck back and lifted his eyes, sizing up the ramblers. Their branches reached like long fingers toward the sky, as if they meant to touch the stars with their leaves. They easily stood twice the size of any rambler back at camp.

He grinned, picturing Dya's jealous pout when he and Niko paraded one of these beauties through the outpost. Russé would praise him and, once hollowed out, he and Niko would have one of the finest homes in all of camp.

Unhooking the twisted vine rope from his hip, Kole scrutinized the ramblers. Dozens of tall, fat trees walked by, perfectly suited for a new, spacious home. Maybe he'd pick a white oak; he had a particular fondness for their wide, round canopies. A flash of maroon swept by in the distance. Kole gave a secret smile when he spotted the red maple. Though the trunk looked a bit thinner than the others, it would still make a fine house. How grand those red leaves would look among the green trees back at camp. As it neared, though, his inflated confidence wavered. It stood tall above the others, and its roots stomped the ground with an air of primal edge.

Kole stepped back. The lanky maple might prove too hard to coerce. He reined in his greed and looked for something more manageable.

Through the horde of trees, Kole noticed a rambler with an uneven gait. Instead of gliding gracefully over the forest floor like the others, it hobbled. He sighed. Not as impressive, but it would do.

"Take notes." Kole trotted away. As he ran, he untangled the vine rope and circled the knotted loop above his head. His wrist flicked faster and faster until the vine blurred green and whistled. Approaching from the side, Kole found the cause of the rambler's limp. A group of damaged roots hung like dead snakes from its trunk.

Kole raced up next to it, careful to stay at a safe distance. Eyes set on a low-hanging branch, he released his rope. The lasso hit its mark, slipping over the bottom bough. He tugged, tightening the rope securely around the branch.

Green grass raced below him as the rambler unknowingly carried a stowaway. Kole climbed up the vine, leery of looking down until he reached the bough. Once he'd laced his fingers over the bark, he climbed the length of the branch to the trunk and descended to the damaged roots.

During his training, squeezing the root had proven enough to coerce ramblers into submission. But those had been saplings. The harmless act made the rambler think it was in danger. He figured his bare hands posed little threat to a rambler this big. How could he make it aware of his presence? He slipped his hunting knife from his belt and rested the blade on the root, then paused and glanced up. "Sorry, big guy." He plunged the knife into the root.

A deep shudder ran down the trunk, and the rambler swayed to a stop.

Fight or flight? His eyes scanned the roots for any hint of reaction. When it didn't move, he frowned. *Neither?* Odd, but not unheard of. Russé had mentioned times when a rambler would give itself willingly. A smile touched Kole's lips, and he stood, chest puffed at his success.

"Not so big and bad, are we?" he said to the rambler. Kole returned his knife to his belt. "We got him!"

With an astonished grin on his face, Niko pocketed his notebook and jogged up. "I don't know. That seemed a bit easy. Are you sure?"

"For Soul's sake, man, give me some credit." He patted the trunk. "Just look at it. Still and responsive like Russé says. Might want to write that down."

Niko cautiously pulled his notebook out, one eye on the tree while he wrote.

"I can't wait to see Dya's face. C'mon, get up here. I'll show you how to steer it." With a heave, Kole pulled up one of the dead roots on the rambler's injured side. It took two hands to hold it steady.

As Niko climbed the rope, a shudder shook the tree. He hesitated mid-climb, eyes wide.

Kole waved him on. "It's all right. It's just—"

His words halted as the rambler charged. He fell forward, arms flailing. Catching the trunk, he steadied himself, then turned his attention to Niko, who clung to the swinging rope. His friend's mouth hung open in a silent cry as the roots slammed into him, batting him back and forth like a bird in a windstorm.

"Hang on!" Kole's heart raced as the rambler picked up speed, clipping the surrounding trees. Each collision threatened to knock him off, but he held firm. He pulled his knife and stabbed the lame roots.

C'mon. Stop, you overgrown weed! When the rambler didn't slow, Kole focused on what his mentor had taught him. *Think. Think like a shepherd.*

Jump.

Kole glanced down. The grass rushed by with a blur of green. If Niko slid down the rope, he could probably land without much injury.

But landing addressed only the first problem. Even if they made it to the ground, they'd be trampled under the rambler's roots. *What would Russé do?* A quick glance to the lightening eastern sky told him dawn neared. They could ride it out until the tree anchored itself at daybreak. They'd just have to hang on until then.

He looked back at Niko, who helplessly slid further down the vine. Time worked against them. He needed a plan and fast.

A muted roar pulled his attention away. He lifted his head, looking up the path. A knot twisted his stomach. Ice shot through his veins as he stared at the very reason shepherds never ventured out this far.

Fire. Not orange or yellow like fire should be but black.

Kole shuddered, tightening his hands around the roots. The stories their camp leader told of the black fires always ended in death and destruction. It always ended with the Black Wall. And their rambler barreled straight for it. They had to dismount. Now.

"Niko," he cried, daring to peel a hand from the trunk to wave down. He shouted again to no avail. Niko, clenched up in a ball, desperately gripping the spinning rope, couldn't hear him. If he could, he was too scared to acknowledge it.

With the rambler showing no sign of changing course, Kole took a deep breath and climbed. He scurried up the trunk, ignoring the bark scratching his skin, and made his way to the bough where his rope still hung. The rambler's jerking stride threatened to buck him off. Kole gripped the rope and slid down to his friend, who startled at his touch. "We have to jump."

Niko's gaze flicked from Kole to the ground, and he balled up again, shaking his head.

"C'mon, Niko. We *have* to." He didn't dare point out the flames ahead for fear Niko might faint at the sight. He lacked the strength to keep them both on the rope.

The heat of the radiating flames warmed his cheeks. They had perhaps a minute before it would swallow the rambler whole. If Niko wouldn't jump, he'd have to make him.

Kole climbed over him, positioning himself as low on the vine as he dared. He whispered a quick prayer to the Seven Souls, hoping his grip would hold out, then unhooked his feet from the vine and pumped them back and forth, further jostling the already swinging rope. Satisfied with the momentum, he climbed back above Niko and pulled out his knife.

His eyes darted from the Black Wall to the thrashing roots below. He'd have to be careful—patient—to pull this off. His heart pounded in his throat as the smell of charred wood found his nose. Kole waited until the path of the vine carried them to the top of the pendulum and swung back the other way, behind the rambler and, more importantly, away from the black fire, then sliced the vine.

Kole's stomach rose to his throat as they fell safely past the rambler's roots. He clenched up, bracing for impact as the ground rushed up to meet them. Air shot from his lungs when he hit the grass.

Adrenaline kept him from feeling the true pain of the impact, but he knew he would wake up tomorrow sore and bruised. While still able, he pushed to his feet and hurried to his friend.

Niko lay on his side. His jaw twitched, eyes large, but he wasn't looking at Kole: he stared at something over his shoulder.

Kole turned in time to see the flames of the Black Wall lick hungrily at the oncoming rambler. The tree plunged its roots into the soil at the last second. Chunks of grass and dirt lifted as the rambler tilled through in a desperate attempt to stop. That's when it dawned on him: the rambler had never intended to run into the flames. It had been a scare tactic to get the boys to dismount. *Outsmarted by a tree.*

The rambler's leaves shook. Kole tilted his head. He'd know that sign anywhere. The rambler was frightened. It wasn't slowing fast enough and still closed in on the Black Wall. His eyes fell to the roots. They strained, buckling against the earth to lose speed, but the clump of lame roots slid uselessly along, unable to contribute. Without its full strength, the rambler had no chance.

The moment the black flames brushed the canopy, the leaves and bark turned to ash. For a moment, the tree held its shape, the rambler's roots still scrambling away from the wall, though Kole knew it no longer held any life. Like a ghost still going through the motions, unaware of its own demise. The ash floated to the base of the wall, and the mighty rambler Kole had hoped to make his prize was no more.

He gulped. A few more seconds and they would have shared the same fate. Gone in an instant. He looked back at Niko, whose face, even in the darkness, shone glaringly pale.

"That's the... the...." Niko's jaw slacked, unable to form the words.

"Yeah." Kole craned his neck, letting his eyes follow the height of the wall. It soared above the forest. He couldn't tell where the flames ended. The wall seemed to go up until it blended into the night sky.

Something felt off. He knew the forest well, and he knew how far they'd strayed from camp. Sure, he'd taken Niko out of bounds, but they hadn't gone *that* far. The Black Wall sat well beyond the boundaries. And yet, here it stood, miles closer than it should have.

A touch on his shoulder pulled Kole from his thoughts.

"Let's get out of here," Niko croaked, nodding to the gray smoke seeping from the base of the licking flames.

Neither of them spoke on the way back. They ran, eager to distance themselves from the wall. The pain of dropping from the rambler caught up to Kole by the time they reached the outskirts of camp. He found himself hunching over to relieve the cramp traveling up his back. He expected to wake black and blue in the morning. Despite the discomfort, Kole pushed his legs faster, the weight of discovering the Black Wall giving him strength.

A horn echoed above them, signaling their arrival. They passed between the first set of anchored trees, which marked the outer rim of their small encampment.

Bridges hung from tree to tree throughout camp. From a distance, it reminded Kole of a large web. The vines, strung through each plank of the bridges, shone silver in the glow of dawn, like spider's silk. Small platforms wrapped around the top of the trunks, where the bridges connected with the next anchored tree, and rope ladders dangled from the platforms, leading to the forest floor. Each trunk had a door carved into the bark, which opened to its hollowed interior.

These trees had once been ramblers, too, before the shepherds anchored them. Now they served as houses and watched their kin from afar, unable to join in the nightly dance. Kole often wondered if they were doing the right thing by anchoring them – if the ramblers felt chained up like prisoners. Normal trees, those outside Solpate forest, never moved. In a way, the shepherds merely restored them to their original state. The thought sat better with him, but Kole never could shake the feeling that they were stripping the magic away from them – the magic that made Solpate so dazzling. But the refugees did what they needed to survive. Nothing more, nothing less. The ramblers only moved at all, Kole kept reminding himself, because of the power of the Great Red.

Three more safe havens resided in Solpate, all built in a similar fashion, but Kole's home, the northern camp, only housed children. Once a child came of age, they transitioned to one of the other camps to make room for new children coming over from the city. Kole and Niko still had a few years until they moved on themselves.

Another horn sounded.

"We have to tell them," Niko said between breaths.

"I know. I'll handle it."

They followed the sweet scent of Goren's rabbit stew, but instead of the camp leader laboring over breakfast, they found Dya. She stood on her toes circling the large wooden paddle around the rim of the cauldron. Though she may have been the oldest girl in camp, her height said otherwise.

Dya's twitching frown betrayed her foul mood, probably from the failed hunt. Her brown eyes snapped to them. "Well it's about time. Goren called off the hunt nearly an hour ago."

"We didn't hear it," Kole dismissed. "Where's Shepherd Russé? I need to—"

"You didn't hear it?" She clicked her tongue. "How far did you two go, exactly?"

"Why does it matter? It's not like we caught anything," said Niko. "Just tell us where Russé is."

"It *does* matter," Dya snapped. "Going out of range is cheating."

"Hunting with a *shepherd* is cheating," Niko shot back.

"So Russé helped us a bit. Big deal. Did us no good. Besides," she folded her arms, "you had a shepherd with you, too." She gave Kole a once over. "Well, *shepherd in training.*"

"Not the same," Niko said.

Kole winced. Everyone seemed so quick to point out his apprenticeship status. He'd be lying if he said it never bothered him, but he let the blow roll of his back. No time to argue when the Black Wall was on the move.

"You're just jealous Russé didn't pick *you* as his apprentice," said Niko, taking a step closer to her.

Her eyes darkened as she advanced, their noses mere inches apart. "I could say the same to you. At least I made it past the first trial."

The shepherd's trials had become a rough spot for all of them. Kole had only barely beaten Dya in the last test and, in turn, earned his right to apprentice under Russé. She was a natural when it came to communing with the ramblers, unlike Kole, but no one matched his navigation skills. A shepherd needed an innate ability to find their way through the ever-moving forest above all else. No doubt she would earn her apprenticeship at the next trial. But Niko? His performance at the trials was particularly embarrassing; he never made it past the first test. Sure, Niko had smarts and strength, but he never took risks. His skills seemed better suited for a less dangerous calling. Kole would never tell him that, though. It would break his friend's spirit. All Kole could do was help him train and hope he had a better shot next time.

Before the argument heated further, Kole tugged Niko's shirt, dragging them apart. They huffed but relented. He stepped between them and turned to Dya. "Russé?"

She rolled her eyes with a sigh. "He went out looking for the both of *you* half an hour ago. I imagine he'll be back soon because of the horns."

"Then Goren. Is he here?"

Dya jerked her head toward the edge of camp. "A rambler charged the outpost. He's untangling the canopies. Leave him be. It's a feisty one; the horns didn't scare it. That rambler charged right back to the post after he'd chased it off. I swear these trees are getting more daring by the night."

"This is important. It can't wait," Kole said with a sideways glance at Niko, who's body looked as rigid as a trunk.

"What did you do now?" Dya cast an accusing glare at the both of them. Her eyes lingered on Niko. After looking him up and down, she shook her head, a few strains of black hair falling loose from her bun. "On second thought, never mind. With you two, the less I know the better." She shooed them away from the cauldron and returned her attention to the stew.

"Relax," Kole whispered once they'd moved out of earshot. He patted Niko on the back. His muscles tensed under his hand. "Maybe you should sit down. I'll find Goren."

"No need for Goren." Niko nodded past him. "The shepherd is back."

Kole turned. His mentor strode from the outposts wearing a particularly unpleasant scowl and clutched his staff with white knuckles. The old man's blue eyes locked on Kole. Niko, apparently taking Kole's advice at this *particular* moment, retreated to the fire pit as the shepherd neared.

"Where have you been?" Russé barked.

He gulped. "We found —"

"No. *Where have you been?*" Russé demanded. "I blew the horn half an hour ago!"

"I know," Kole said, shoulders sagging forward. Lying would get him nowhere. Russé was too keen for that. "We went a little... out of range."

The lines around Russé's mouth deepened. "How many times will you put Niko in danger? It's one thing to go out alone but to put his life at risk, too?" He sighed. "He doesn't know the ramblers like you. He could have been trampled. It's these kinds of things that keep me from naming you shepherd. You need to consider the consequences *before* you act."

"I know, Shepherd Russé. I messed up. But it's not just the ramblers we have to worry about." Kole peeked over to Niko, who sat across from the fire, staring into the flames, jaw clenched. Kole lowered his voice and stepped in so only Russé heard his next words. "We saw the Black Wall."

Russé opened his mouth, eyes widening as he scanned Kole's face. "The Black Wall," he repeated steadily.

Kole gave a quick nod. Russé didn't speak—only stared.

He had seen the Black Wall once before with Russé, maybe a month ago, as a part of his training, but he had never drawn that close; they had traveled the better half of a week north just to get a glimpse of it. The Black Wall, his mentor had told him, had no end. It stretched around the entire continent of Ohr, encasing it like a ring, put there by the gods for a reason no one really understood. The wall had been around for centuries, slowly advancing, devouring the world one country at a time. Only recently had it slowed to a halt, un-moving for the last decade.

It seemed its hibernation had ended.

After what seemed like a minute with no response, Kole began to think Russé doubted his word.

Finally the old man said just what Kole had expected. "That's impossible. The wall is—"

"Almost a week's ride out, I know. But it was there. I saw it—we both did. It turned a rambler to dust."

A scrutinizing eye still on Kole, Russé pursed his lips. "How far?"

Kole shrugged. "An hour's run north. Maybe less."

Russé's eyes set on Kole, but they became distant, as if he was looking right through him. "After all of these years I thought it had stabilized...."

"Shepherd Russé?" Kole said quietly. Once Russé focused back on him, Kole asked, "What do we do?"

"Does anyone else know about this?" his mentor pressed.

"Well, no. Just me and Niko."

Russé nodded and stepped around him.

"Wait." Kole grabbed his elbow. He immediately released his grip when Russé turned on him.

A flash of irritation passed over the shepherd's eyes. They softened. "The only thing we can do is run."

The words hit Kole in the gut. He knew what the shepherd meant, but he needed to hear him say it. "Run? You mean...?"

His gaze drifted to Dya stirring the camp's breakfast, a smile on her face as she wiped her forehead of sweat. Above to the bridges to see the older kids, who had finished their nightly watch, hung their horns over the small branches outside their doors, and headed down the rope bridges in hopes of claiming a front spot in the breakfast line. Some of the younger kids, the early risers, creaked the doors open and peered out, waiting impatiently for the morning horn to mark the end of curfew.

The shepherd's jaw flexed. "Abandon camp."

CHAPTER 2

Kole sat next to Niko. They exchanged a brief glance. He wanted to tell his friend everything; that after ten years, they were leaving, but he couldn't bear to be the one to do it. Never, in all that time, had Kole thought of leaving. Not like this. Often, he would fantasize about life back in the city. He'd think of his family—his parents, whoever they were. But the fantasies stopped there.

Being alone in a city like Socren meant nothing good for an orphan. Without a family—without protection—they became prime targets for Savairo and his men. If not for the Liberation smuggling the orphans out of the city, Niko, Dya, Kole, and all of the children here would have become soldiers in Savairo's army. Or worse, test subjects in his perverted experiments.

Niko remembered everything from his old life back in the city; his parents, brothers, and sisters—all up until the day of their murder. Like the others, Kole had lost his family, too. Only he didn't remember them. Part of him hoped they'd died like Niko's family. Strange as it may have seemed, it comforted him more than the chance that they'd left him, unwanted. After years of wishing and hoping, urging his brain to conjure a face or recall a name, he accepted that any memories he possessed lay locked in the depths of his mind.

Kole adopted the forest as home. Leaving wasn't preferred, he'd miss this camp, but there were more trees in the forest to anchor. As long as he had Niko—as long as they stayed together—he'd be home.

As Kole stared at the ramblers beyond the outposts, the sun rose.

The groaning and creaking of wood echoed through camp as the ramblers settled down for the day ahead. They plopped their trunks on the ground and drilled their roots deep into the soil like giant, wiggling earthworms. Sunlight touched the rambler's branches and, one by one, they grew rigid as if turned to stone. In a matter of seconds, the entire forest had stilled, save for the morning songbirds flitting through the canopy. Kole gazed fondly at them.

Like the trees, the animals had been affected by the strange magic of the Great Red. Instead of feathers like most birds donned, these were covered head to talon in vibrant petals. In spring, the birds blended in with the blooms on the branches. You wouldn't know you were looking at one until it sang. They fluttered away as Dya blew the breakfast horn.

Above, the doors of the trunk houses slammed open, answering her call. Three-dozen feet pattered over the swinging bridges. The children funneled down the ladders and formed a line behind the cauldron.

"I could use a little help," said Dya, one hand on her hip while the other jabbed the ladle at Kole and Niko.

Kole rose without complaint. He welcomed the work, as boring as it was, to take his mind off things. He handed out bowls and spoons in a daze, his head swirling with thoughts of the Black Wall. Kole wondered how the children would take the news. He hoped it wouldn't cause any of them to relapse.

Long nights awaited him, Niko, and Dya. Being the oldest of the bunch, they tended to the children. Kole could handle their nightmares easily enough. He'd tell them everything would be all right, and the few young ones who couldn't quite shake their fears, he allowed to sleep in his bunk until dawn. Each passing year had helped the orphans adjust. Fewer and fewer nightmares plagued the little ones these days. With any luck, by age seven or eight, they would shake them completely. Only the new children, freshly smuggled over the mountains, posed a challenge, but that number had dwindled over the years.

It was the night terrors Kole worried about. Dreams so vivid, it woke their bodies but not their minds. They saw things — horrible things from their past that drove them from their beds. A few orphans had wandered off after dark under the trance of a night terror and perished in the forest, trampled by a rambler. Since then, Goren, their camp leader, took care of those succumbing to such dreams. Only he could wake them. As extra precaution, they also established a night watch to ensure no one left the outposts during the rambler's walking hours. Kole sighed. *So much for taking my mind off things.*

Kole took a bowl of porridge and joined the children around the fire. He slumped on the log next to Niko and shoveled in a bite as Russé and Goren appeared.

Goren, sporting fresh cuts and bruises on his arms and legs, likely from the feisty rambler Dya had mentioned, rubbed his shiny bald head as he called for everyone's attention. "Good morning, my children," he said, his usual cheeriness seeming rather forced.

"Good morning, Goren," the children replied, all huddled by the warm flames, spoons paused to listen.

Kole and Niko exchanged glances as they mumbled their greeting.

"I'm afraid Russé and I have some—um, well—unfortunate news." He looked over the group, mouth pursing, as if avoiding what came next. "After breakfast, I need everyone to go back to their bunks and pack. Only bring the things you brought from Socren that can't be replaced. We'll be relocating to one of the other refugee camps in Solpate until the shepherds can anchor new houses for us."

Gasps and groans circled around the fire pit.

Niko stayed unnaturally still next to Kole.

"Relocating?" Dya put down her bowl. "What's going on? Why are we leaving?"

Goren sent a nervous glance to the shepherd, who stepped forward.

Russé leaned into his staff and turned to address the orphans. "We've had some issues with the ramblers around here. I'm sure you've noticed. They're growing more aggressive and are no longer deterred by our horns. It's in our best interest to move to a safer location before they cause another accident."

Kole's mouth fell open. "What?"

Russé's eyes snapped to him, narrowing in warning.

Kole's cheeks warmed. Russé was lying. Purposely. Was he trying to spare the children? Maybe he was concerned about their relapses, as well. Kole understood it was a sensitive subject, but the orphans weren't stupid. They would learn the truth eventually. And now, more than ever, they needed to know the dangers in their home and cope with it, even if it meant Kole stayed up every night dealing with bad dreams.

"They deserve to know," Kole said.

"Kole," Russé barked.

"Niko already knows. There's no point in hiding it."

"Hiding what?" Dya asked from across the fire pit.

Kole waited for Russé to respond. The silence lengthened as the children glanced between him and the shepherd, waiting for someone to speak.

"The Black Wall," Kole answered. "Niko and I found it during the hunt. It's moving again. *That's* the real reason."

"The boy is right, Shepherd Russé." Goren sunk down to a log. The morning sun shone off his bald head. "It's foolish to lie."

Russé turned on him. "And how far does it go? How much will you tell them?"

Kole looked back and forth between the camp leader and his mentor, whose eyes were locked in a silent argument.

Goren lifted his chin. "I'll answer whatever questions they have. We'll deal with the repercussions as they come."

Russé shot Kole a glare. Different than the ones he'd received time and time again. Not borne of anger or frustration, instead... discerning? The look writhed Kole's stomach.

"So be it," said the shepherd.

Kole leaned back so Niko's broad shoulders blocked him from Russé's view. He would be reprimanded at the end of this. Kole only hoped his retaliation hadn't cost him his apprenticeship.

"If there *are* any questions, that is." Goren scanned the group of orphans.

Dya clutched her bowl. "Is the fire actually black?"

"It's just as Goren described in his stories," said Kole. "We saw a rambler walk through it. The flames ensnared it... engulfed it...."

Goren nodded.

"Why is it moving again?" asked Kole.

The orphans' heads snapped from Kole to Goren.

"I don't know." Goren leaned forward and sighed. "The Black Wall is the greatest puzzle our world has ever known. It's a merciless force. A destroyer. It has razed cities. Hundreds of thousands of lives lost in a single breath. Which is why we need to relocate. As long as we stay within range, we're not safe."

As powerful as the wall may be, running couldn't be the only answer. Kole refused to accept that. In the past, they had always done so: fled. But the wall always followed, herding the people of Ohr further from their homes. Eventually it would catch up to them. Eventually the wall would consume so much, they would have nowhere else to run. Everything had a weakness; they just needed to find it. "There must be some way we can stand against it."

Goren pulled his mouth to the side. "Fire like this doesn't need fuel to burn. Nothing, no matter how big, can stop its advance. And water...." His eyes darkened. "When I first came to Solpate forest, I performed many experiments on the trees and the creatures to make sure it was safe before the Liberation brought you all here. The Black Wall was no exception. I have tried to extinguish its flames with water. Suffocate it with earth. Snuff it with wind." He shook his head. "The moment anything comes within the wall's reach, it turns to ash. *Water turned to ash.* Not vapor. *Ash.* That's when I realized it's unlike any fire we know. This magic resembles nothing I have ever seen. It's the magic of the gods."

"The Souls?" Kole whispered, but the orphans had grown so quiet, it sounded as if he'd yelled it.

Goren nodded. Behind him, Russé shifted uncomfortably. The way the shepherd tapped his fingers on the top of his staff told Kole he disliked where the conversation was heading. His mentor looked as if he was holding back the urge to clamp Goren's mouth shut the next time he spoke.

Goren pulled a metal chain from his tunic. A crudely made symbol dangled from the links. A large, circular stone rested in the center of the pendant. Seven iron prongs sprouted from the edges, creating a sunburst shape, and at the end of each prong sat a smaller stone.

The symbol of the Seven Souls.

Each colored stone represented the different Souls and what they created. Blue for Issira, the goddess of water. Green for Risil, creator of plants and trees. Braxus' deep yellow portrayed the earth. Vara's crimson stood for the changing seasons, and Caradin's smokey brown was for the animals. Two final stones rounded out the symbol: orange for Obell's fire and gray for Aterus, who'd forged the human race.

Their creations, though vastly different, all held a beauty. Kole found it hard to believe the Souls would create something with such a dark purpose as the Black Wall; something that could destroy a mighty rambler in seconds.

Goren rubbed the pendant as he spoke. "It's speculated that the Black Wall was created when the Souls ascended. But I'm not sure why. I tested the wall thoroughly when I came here because I believed, at the time, there had to be more to it—something undiscovered. A good in it." A frown. "I found nothing of the sort."

Goren cleared his throat and tucked away the necklace. "This is where the world is divided. Some believe the Black Wall was put here as a test to determine our worth as creations. If we survive and prove ourselves, the Seven Souls will return for us. Others think the Souls are trying to wipe us out so they can create a new world. But I don't believe any of that nonsense."

"What do you believe?" Niko whispered next to Kole.

The corners of the bald man's mouth drooped. "I think it's a result of something truly terrible."

"A mistake?" Kole asked.

Goren confirmed with a nod.

"Why is it still here, then?" Kole asked. "Why didn't they cast it away?"

"Perhaps they couldn't, under the circumstances." Goren's hand clutched the symbol on his chest. "I think something caused an imbalance in power. I think one of them died."

Kole shook his head, certain Goren had misspoke. "But the Souls are immortal."

"That they are. It would take immense power to kill one."

Kill. Kole's gut twisted. He knew what Goren was trying to say, but he seemed to tiptoe around the word for the children's sake. Murder. Goren thought one of the Souls had been murdered. But the only thing he could think of that possessed the power to do such a thing was....

Kole's jaw tightened. A Soul had been murdered by one of their own.

At first it sounded absurd. Gods were creators. They were benevolent. Moral. That's what he'd heard in the stories. Goren often told them tales of the gods gifting man with knowledge, power, and healing. Then again, Kole had never actually met one. Few had. And stories were just that: stories. They were old. Contorted and embellished through the generations. Even Goren was guilty of it. In reality, maybe the Souls could act every bit as corrupt as man and as brutal as beast.

"How could—" Kole stopped himself from saying 'murder' for the sake of the orphans. "How could an imbalance create the Black Wall?"

Goren eyed the orphans, probably wondering if he had gone too far—said too much. He continued despite their wide-eyed stares. "The Seven Souls are powerful beings. Their powers remain in check because of the others, perfectly balanced like a scale. If one were to die, I believe that shift in power could create a catastrophe such as the Black Wall... among other things. But this is only speculation," he said softly to the children.

"What do you mean, *other things*?" Kole asked.

Goren raised a brow at him. "Can you not think of another anomaly? Something that, by all sense of reason, can only be explained by other powerful magic?"

When Kole didn't answer, Niko did. "Ramblers." He clutched his notebook in one hand, the other furiously scribbling away, putting each of Goren's words to paper.

Goren nodded. "Trees are not meant to walk, and yet here in Solpate forest, they do."

"I thought the ramblers got their powers from the Great Red," Kole said.

Goren nodded. "How do you think the Great Red got its magic? It all comes back to the Souls. They are the source of all things terrible and fantastic." Goren glanced at Russé and added, "Their powers can even have an effect on certain peo—"

"Enough," Russé barked, slamming the end of his staff into the soil. "None of this helps us with the Black Wall. You wanted an explanation, now you have one. This is what we are facing. This is why we are leaving. We can do nothing against it. We can only move before it surges through camp and kills us all."

At that, the orphans broke out in nervous whispers.

Goren raised his hands to hush them. "It's quite all right, children. We won't let that happen." He shot a glare over his shoulder to the shepherd.

Russé's hard expression softened slightly, though he still held a grimace. "I suggest everyone go to their bunks and pack."

Goren straightened himself, jaw setting. "As Shepherd Russé says, my children. Finish breakfast and go."

Before Goren had finished, Russé stalked off, his staff jamming into the ground with every stride.

"What was up with Russé? He seemed tense," Niko said as he closed the door of the tree trunk.

Kole shrugged. "I've seen him angry, but never like that. Something Goren said got under his skin."

Inside, the tree was completely hollow from trunk to canopy. Small holes cut from the bark served as windows. They dotted the tree, letting the warm morning sun pour in. Kole took the spiraled stairs carved along the outer walls of the trunk, circling along the tall, cylindrical room to where his hammock hung below Niko's.

As the boys packed in silence, Kole's thoughts wandered back to Russé.

His mentor had seemed so on edge. Kole knew the Black Wall was dangerous—the image of the burning rambler still haunted him—but he couldn't rid the squirm in the back of his head telling him something more brewed.

Of all people, Kole never thought Russé would keep things from him. He must have had a good reason to lie to the orphans. If it had been only about that, Kole might have excused it, but the way Russé reacted when Goren spoke of the Souls—cutting him off when he mentioned how they affected some people... the mere thought sent a nervous chill down his neck. Russé was his mentor. He was supposed to teach Kole everything about the forest. So long as Russé kept him in the dark, Kole felt useless to the refugees.

"You all right?" Niko asked, picking up a pair of small, wooden bear figurines his father had carved for him back in the city; the only thing left of his family. He placed them in his hammock.

"Fine." Kole wished he had something of worth to bring with him. Something from his family. Save for a change of clothes, he owned only his bow and arrows. Kole unhooked his hammock and tied the ends together to form a sack. "What did Goren mean about the Souls affecting people?"

Niko shrugged. "He might've meant sorcerers."

Goosebumps rippled over Kole's arms. "Really?"

"Yeah—I mean, it goes hand in hand with the ramblers, right? And the animals, too. They all sorta, I don't know, evolved, I guess, because of the magic. I think it'd be something similar. Normal people turn into sorcerers? I don't know. That's what I got from it."

"Right." Kole placed his sack on the stairs and shouldered his bow and quiver.

Sorcerers. It seemed plausible, and yet, he didn't want it to be true. Worry gripped him. He chewed his lower lip, keeping the bubbling feeling at bay. He had never met a sorcerer, only heard about them in Goren's stories, but one in particular made him leery of the title: Savairo. He reigned as the current Warden of Socren and was the reason they'd gone into hiding in the first place. Kole knew little about him beyond that. He was, however, familiar with the warden's experiments.

Savairo created abominations. The refugees called them Kayetans— dark creatures bound to the shadows with long, sword-like claws. Their forms appeared when the moon dominated the sky. The morning banished them until the following night. Kole had seen them before, during his shepherd's training. Every season Savairo sent a Kayetan into the forest in search of rebels. The shepherds went into high alert then. Though the shepherds controlled the ramblers on the daily, their primary duty meant keeping the camps safe and unseen from Savairo and his Kayetans. Savairo's abominations had yet to discover them, but they had managed a few close calls.

Kole shuddered to think what else a sorcerer could do. He wondered if he could tell a sorcerer by sight alone. Maybe they looked different, like the animals in Solpate or the ramblers. Magic had changed *their* nature. Would it work the same with a person?

"Do you think Russé is a... you know...?" Goosebumps crawled over Kole's arms again, dreading the answer.

"A sorcerer?" Niko's hands paused as he tied up his hammock. "Never thought about it. Guess he could be. He's quite good with the ramblers, but the other shepherds are just as skilled. Except you. 'It can't be much different than the smaller ones,'" he mimicked Kole's voice two octaves too high. "Says the guy who almost got us killed."

Kole gave him a pointed glare. "There's no way I could've known." He sighed at Niko's raised brow. "Fine. I probably should've been a bit more careful. Thought it out more. But I *don't* sound like that."

Niko chuckled and patted Kole's shoulder. "Sure you don't." After a moment his brow furrowed. "Honestly, I've never seen a sorcerer to know the difference."

"You've seen Savairo."

Niko lugged his pack over his shoulder. "Not in person. I remember watching the guards raise a statue of him in the city square with my family the night before—" Niko caught himself. A pang of sorrow flashed behind his eyes.

"I'm sorry. I didn't mean—"

"It's fine." Niko shook his head. "I'm fine, really."

Kole grabbed his bag and they climbed down the spiral staircase, passing the other boys hurriedly packing their own hammocks.

They exited the trunk and stepped onto the platform. Kole leaned against the rail, letting his eyes take in the beauty of his home for the last time. They landed on Dya, who stood on the platform at the opposite side of the bridge, pulling the dried clothes from the branches of the tree. After folding them neatly, she piled the extra tunics and pants in a leather bag. Her head turned as the door behind Kole and Niko slammed shut.

"Oh, good. I wasn't looking forward to doing all this on my own. Grab the boys' clothes, will you?" She tossed them a sack, which only made it halfway down the bridge, then returned to her work.

Kole retrieved the bag. "This is what we get for being the first one's done." Niko shrugged and they got to work taking down clothes. The cloth hadn't quite dried and still retained the scent of sweat. Not bothering to fold them, Niko and Kole balled them up and stuffed them inside the sack.

Shoving the last pair of shorts inside the leather bag, Niko turned to Kole. "I think we'd know if he was a sorcerer—Russé, I mean. He'd be more evil, wouldn't he? More like Savairo?"

Kole slung the sack over his shoulder and they crossed the swinging bridge toward Dya. "Are all sorcerers evil?"

"Never heard of a good one."

Kole hoped Niko was right about Russé. But the shepherd still held a secret, and the incessant itch in his core would only cease when he uncovered it.

"Here," Kole said, plopping the bag of clothes next to Dya's feet.

After folding a shirt and sorting it into its proper pile, she straightened, a skeptical eye set on Kole. "Did you fold them?"

Kole shifted his body to cover the small, open hole where a wrinkled sleeve poked through the drawstring closure.

"They weren't dry," Niko said, "so we'll just have to wash them again, anyway. We'll fold them then."

"As long as you're volunteering."

As Niko tried to talk himself out of washing clothes, Kole leaned over the rope bridge and scanned the encampment. He spotted Goren fiddling with the cauldron down below, desperately trying to move it.

"Need a hand?" Kole called down.

"Much appreciated, young shepherd," said Goren.

"C'mon." Kole grabbed Niko's arm and pulled him to the rope ladder. They slid down the vine and rushed over.

"Careful, boys, it's still a bit warm," Goren said as Niko and Kole grabbed the lip.

Even with three people, the cauldron proved heavy. They couldn't lift it outright, so they rolled it through the coals and tipped it down in the grass.

"What are you doing with it?" Kole wiped his soot-stained hands on his shorts.

"Bringing it with us, of course. The Liberation sacrificed quite a bit when they smuggled this out of Socren. It's much harder to hide a three-hundred pound cauldron than a few bags of grain. They'd be much displeased if they have to do it again. I'll be damned if I'm going to leave it here to rust."

The Liberation had been providing food, seeds, supplies, and anything else the refugees couldn't make themselves, to the camps for years. Kole remembered getting small shipments twice a season when he was younger, but now the Liberation only seemed to come when the refugees fell in dire need of something. Seeing as how the refugees had grown more independent—establishing a small garden in each camp and learning to hunt and scrounge the forest to supplement their diet—they relied on the Liberation less and less.

Niko, hunched over, his hands on his knees, eyed the cauldron. "I hope you don't expect us to roll it the entire way."

"No need to worry about that. I still have the wheelbarrow they used to transport it," Goren answered.

Kole smirked. "Of course you do."

Goren lifted his chin as if he'd received a compliment. "Everything needs to last out here, boys. What we can't replace or make ourselves needs safekeeping. There are thousands of trees for bowls and spoons, but metal we do not have. I'll get the wheelbarrow. Wait here," he said as he retreated to his house.

Kole spotted his chance and moved to follow him.

"I can't lift this thing by myself," said Niko.

"Calm down," Kole hushed. He glanced back at his friend who, with both hands on his hips, looked irked to have Kole ditch him. "I'll be back."

Kole slipped through the door of the trunk, mouth open, questions of sorcerers and Russé on the tip of his tongue, then he clamped it shut.

Russé stood on the far side of the room, hunched over a wooden chest.

The door squealed behind Kole as it closed and hit his backside.

Russé glanced up at the noise.

"I can handle it myself, lad." Goren removed what looked like junk, scrapes of wood, and broken ropes from a pile near the wall, revealing a worn down wheelbarrow.

His mentor held his gaze then glanced between him and Goren. "Finished packing already?"

"Uh, yeah. Not much I really need besides my bow." Kole reached around and dug his nails nervously into the wood of his bow.

"Good." Russé motioned to the chest. "Then you can help carry the larger things." He shut the lid, locked it, and, after tucking away the key in his tunic, gripped one of the handles and waited patiently for Kole to come over and take the other.

"Uh, well," Kole began, trying to think of an excuse. "I'm kinda helping Goren—"

"Oh, for the love of Souls, boy, how weak do you think I am? I can steer an empty wheelbarrow." Goren tossed out the last of the garbage and pinched the wrinkly skin on his arm. "I might look old, but there's still some use left in this body." Kole stepped out of Goren's path as he steered the wheelbarrow past him, clipping the table and staircase before reaching the door. "Just be a lad and get the door for me."

Kole did as he was told. His eyes lingered on the bald man's back as his chance to get answers walked out the tree. He locked eyes with Niko through the doorway, pleading him to come inside; Kole didn't want to be alone with Russé after calling him out at breakfast. Niko gave an apologetic smile in return and moved to help Goren as the door swung shut.

Kole turned around, facing his inevitable punishment.

Russé gestured to the chest again.

With a heavy sigh, he crossed the room, feet reluctantly shuffling against the worn floor of the trunk. All the while his mentor eyed him. Kole could hardly bear the silence. If Russé meant to scold him, he'd rather have it out of the way, quick and clean like the cut from a blade.

"I'm sorry I went so far out with Niko," Kole blurted. "But I'm not sorry about letting the camp know the truth. There's no way I could lie to them. We have a right to know why." His words came out more defensive than he'd intended.

Russé nodded.

A nod? Is that it? Kole bit down on the inside of his cheek. He had prepared for the anger—the frustration his mentor had shown by the fire nearly an hour ago. He hadn't just imagined it. Niko had seen it, too. But Russé seemed distracted. Maybe he was more worried about the Black Wall than he let on.

"You're not going to drop my apprenticeship?" he pressed.

"Why would you think that?"

"Because I didn't go along with your lie."

Russé sighed. "I know why you did it. And as for your little adventure with Niko. If you hadn't broken the rules, perhaps we might not have noticed the wall until it was too late. So no, I will not be dropping you from your apprenticeship. Unless you desire as much."

Kole stared at him, slack jawed. "N-No."

"Good. Now, will you help me lift this blasted thing?"

Kole grabbed the handle. A small inner voice dared him to ask Russé if he was a sorcerer, but he ignored it. Kole chewed his lip. His knees wobbled as he lifted. "What's—in—this—thing?" he breathed.

"Books."

Kole's face grew warm as he struggled to keep the chest at waist level. He hurried along to the door with Russé, who didn't have a drop of sweat or strained vessel anywhere in sight. His mentor's face remained calm and relaxed, as if he were plucking a pebble from the creek.

The old man had always been strong. Kole had seen him wrestle rambler roots and had never given it a second thought. But was he *abnormally* strong? Now that he thought about it, Russé could probably lift this chest on his own. Kole peered at him. So why had he asked for help?

Then it dawned on him. Russé knew what Kole was up to, purposely tailing Goren in case his apprentice came snooping around for answers. If so, getting Goren alone would prove far more difficult than Kole had thought.

They squeezed out the door and dropped the chest next to the cauldron, which Niko and Goren, with the help of Dya, had already loaded into the wheelbarrow.

Kole arched his back. His spine popped in relief.

"Ah, my journals," Goren said.

"You wrote all the books in here?"

The camp leader nodded. "I've been keeping track of everything since I led the first Escape out of Socren. Writing keeps me sane."

Russé returned the key. "We should get moving."

Goren looped the key around his cord, where it dangled next to the Seven Souls pendant, then took up his horn, sending a blaring note through the canopy.

The orphans emptied from the trunks, flooding the bridges and ladders. All the while, Kole eyed the necklace. Maybe he could bypass Goren altogether. Those journals surely held something of use.

With the Black Wall on the move, Goren would lead them as far south as possible. It would be at least a week before Kole could catch Goren alone. He refused to wait that long; his curiosity would drive him mad. He needed to get his hands on that key—tonight—but he'd need help to do it.

Kole slipped away as Russé and Goren rounded up the children.

"Hey," Kole said, nudging Niko's back. "What do you say to helping me steal one of those journals?"

Niko glanced over Kole's shoulder and pointed at the chest.

Kole slapped his hand down. "What are you doing? Don't point at it! I did say *steal*, didn't I?" Kole shot a quick glance at Russé and Goren, who were both herding the children into somewhat organized lines.

Convinced no one would overhear them, Kole turned his attention back to Niko. "So will you help or not?"

"Why do you want one of Goren's old journals?"

"Didn't you hear him? He writes everything down in those things—since his first years here. Maybe there's something about the Seven Souls or the Black Wall. Maybe even something about Russé. Come on, think about it. If anyone knew he was a sorcerer, it's Goren."

Niko perked at the word sorcerer. "All right, what's the plan?"

Kole gave a sly grin. "*You* are."

They discussed their strategy as everyone organized. Once the camp was ready to move, Kole returned to help Russé with the chest. He staggered with every step, but with the plan on his mind, he kept any complaints to himself. With luck, he'd be reading Goren's journals by nightfall.

As Goren led them under the final bridge marking the edge of camp, Kole looked back. He spotted his treehouse in the distance. It had been the first tree anchored in Solpate. The image of it being brought down, wrangled by Russé, had imprinted on his mind. Seeing him take down that rambler had sparked Kole's interest in the shepherds. Ever since, Kole and Niko had spent nearly every waking minute training for the shepherd's trials.

A loud crack resounded through the forest.

Kole jumped. The chest slipped from his hands and cracked as it hit the ground, giving him a peek inside. He held back a grin. Maybe he wouldn't need the key, after all.

"Rouge rambler!" Dya called ahead as she ushered the children behind a trunk.

Kole snapped his attention to the forest. Every tree stood perfectly still, as they should, and yet, running toward them, speckled in morning sunshine, was a sapling rambler.

"Get back!" Russé commanded, striding forward to meet it.

The only other time a rambler had uprooted during the day like this was when a sickness broke out in the forest. It affected the trees much like rabies affected an animal. To his relief, Kole spotted no sign of peeling bark or wilting branches.

Goren and Niko corralled the remaining children while Kole caught up to Russé.

"How is it moving?" Kole reached for the rope at his hip but found it missing. He cursed. He had forgotten to grab another after he had lost his to the Black Wall last night.

The shepherd shook his head. "Not sure."

"I don't have a rope," Kole confessed.

Eyes fixed on the rambler, Russé cocked his head. "I don't think we'll be needing it," he said in a curious tone.

Immediately, Kole knew what he meant.

The rambler slowed as it neared the shepherds. A few meters away, it stopped. A sapling this size couldn't have been more than a year old, yet it stood three times taller than Kole, and its trunk seemed too thick to wrap his arms around. The tree's roots wriggled — trembled — like Kole had when he stood in front of the Black Wall, betraying its fright.

Russé approached it. One hand outstretched toward the sapling, he leaned in, stroking the sapling's bark with his fingertips. Calming, is what the shepherds called it. Kole had often seen Russé do this with the more agitated ramblers — ones with a reputation for stampeding the outer walls of camp. Russé had taught Kole how to do it, but he had yet to master the skill. Calming took patience to perfect. Kole didn't bother with such tedious skills when wrangling produced the same effect..

When the rambler didn't still, Russé pulled his hand away.

"Why won't it root?" Kole asked.

"It's a messenger," said Russé. "Something's happened. Goren," he called.

Goren poked his head out from behind a trunk, his toothless mouth agape.

"There's been a breach. We have an intruder in the forest," said Russé.

Normally news of a breach would fail to surprise Kole. But one Kayetan had already come this summer. It seemed odd for another to come so soon.

Unless....

Kole's eyes slowly moved north.

The timing was quite suspicious. First the wall. Now the extra scout.

"You can't leave us here. I know the forest well enough but moving this many...." Goren glanced back at the orphans. "The Black Wall is too close."

"I understand. I will stay, but I can't let this go. I'll need to send word to—"

Kole stepped forward. "I can do it." Like hell he would stand back and let another shepherd take this. He was just as capable as any of them. And if he did this right, it might earn his shepherd's title.

Russé turned to him and dipped his head. "This requires an *experienced* shepherd."

Kole gulped. His cheeks warmed. He expected some to doubt his skills, but coming from his mentor, the words cut deeper. Kole pushed his chest out, preserving a small piece of his pride. "By the time another shepherd receives word, the intruder could already reach one of the camps."

Russé's blue eyes pierced Kole's for a moment, as if searching for another option.

"I can handle it," Kole said before Russé set his mind against it. He figured Russé would hesitate letting him go, but this is what he had trained for.

Russé came in close so his words only reached Kole. His voice sounded urgent. "The Kayetan has the ramblers spooked. I fear it may have something to do with the Black Wall."

Kole nodded. They both feared the same.

"Are you up to it?"

Kayetan. Urgent task. Danger. Finally a *real* shepherd's mission. "Yes."

Russé's eyes dulled for a moment as he looked down his long, thin nose. "We can't let the Kayetan find the camps. I don't know why it's here, but we must keep the refugees safe at all costs. Lure it out of the forest—use the ramblers if you must—but if things go sour, get out of there. Don't be a hero. Promise me, Kole."

Kole chewed his bottom lip. His definition of a hero differed from his mentor's.

"Kole," he warned.

"Promise," Kole said, figuring what the old man didn't know wouldn't hurt him.

Seemingly content with his answer, Russé returned his palm to the trunk. The young rambler twitched at the touch.

Kole climbed the roots and braced himself.

"Don't be seen."

Kole nodded. Russé tapped the quivering roots, and the rambler took off with a burst of speed.

CHAPTER 3

It had crept into late afternoon by the time Kole reached the southern border of the forest. The trees had thinned, revealing the base of the mountains beyond, draped in the orange light of the sinking sun.

The rambler slowed to a stop and drilled its roots through the carpet of grass, stiffening. Apparently, this was as far as his ride would go. Kole hopped off and closed in on the mountains. He took care to keep low as he moved, using the underbrush to cover his presence when he could.

Once he reached the edge of the forest, he approached the nearest tree. Kole placed his hand on the trunk and closed his eyes, focusing his thoughts on the Kayetan. He pictured the shadowed creature. Imagined it slithering down the mountain and past the trees. The bark under his palm warmed in response, then the sensation faded. Kole let his hand fall. It offered little to go on, but it was all he needed. Kole flicked his eyes up to the oak's canopy. "Which way?" he asked, hoping the rambler would cooperate. *If only I had paid a bit more attention to those Calming lessons.*

Leaves rustled from the oak's western-facing branch despite the breezeless evening. Kole dipped his head in thanks and bounded west.

As he ran, something made him slow. He couldn't figure out why his gut told him to stop, but something felt off. It occurred to him when the intense aroma of sickly sweet sap filled his nose. The scent was normal enough in Solpate, but this was no airy waft of sap; it hung thick in the air, as if a tree was bleeding out. He followed the scent deeper into the forest until he spotted a tree with a massive gash cut from its trunk. Kole didn't need to commune with it to know it was suffering. The wound looked smooth and clean as if made from the single swipe of a blade—a sharp blade. Sap oozed from the laceration. This smacked of the Kayetan's work. Kole felt certain of it.

His eyes followed the dripping sap down the trunk, where a small piece of fabric, no bigger than his palm, lay suspended in the sticky substance. He plucked it out. It was black and thick, the kind of material one used for a coat or a cloak. The Kayetan hadn't come alone. It was following someone.

Smearing the sap off on his pants, he pocketed the scrap and turned north. Whoever the Kayetan chased, if they still lived, Kole needed to reach them before nightfall. Once dusk, the Kayetan would reform and continue his hunt.

Maybe Russé was right. Maybe this hunt was greater than Kole could handle. He pushed down the growing fear in his stomach and scolded himself. No time to turn cowardly. Someone was in danger. They needed a shepherd. *I am a shepherd. Keeper of the trees. Guardian of the refugees.* He repeated the mantra in his head as he ran north.

Moving from trunk to trunk, he kept his eyes to the floor, searching for anything that could tell him where the Kayetan's victim had gone. A glimpse of discolored moss caught his eye, and he swerved toward it.

Kole pressed his hand into the darkened moss engulfing the tree trunk. Blood. The quarry must have passed by here. No. Not passed. They had stayed here for a time. Long enough for the moss to soak up the blood. Hiding, he guessed. Glancing to the floor, he spotted a drop of blood on the grass. Kole scrutinized every flower, stone, and trunk until he found another and another stain of red.

The trail grew easier to follow as the injured person continued to bleed. Soon Kole was following a dense, dotted line of blood. He couldn't imagine someone running much farther in such condition; surely they'd collapsed close by.

A whimper up ahead made him halt. He waited until it came again, then lowered into a crouch and closed in on it.

As he followed the noise, Kole came upon a clearing, and he immediately knew where the trail had led him. He crept behind a trunk for cover as he surveyed the glade ahead.

The Great Red stood before him. The tree looked unlike any other in the forest: a red ruby among a sea of emeralds. Its bark, leaves, and branches lived up to its name — all varying shades of red, from scarlet to burgundy. Kole always thought of it as the heart of the forest.

One leaf from the Great Red could blanket a grown man, and its trunk spanned so wide, it could've held all the orphans in camp if hollowed out. A massive hole darkened the trunk. Jagged splinters pointed outward, as if something had erupted from its center. No one knew what caused the chamber. It had been there since he could remember. Kole couldn't tell how deep the tree's wound went; the fading sunlight failed to illuminate the entire cavity. The whimpering seemed to emanate from inside the tree.

As he leaned around the trunk, the canopy above shook its leaves at the Great Red as if to say, *They went that way.* "I know that already," Kole snapped. As soon as he stepped out from behind the trunk, the whimpering stopped.

Kole froze. Whatever lurked inside the trunk had seen him. He put his hands up and slowly approached, hoping the gesture would convince whoever lay hidden inside that he posed no threat.

Near the hole, he opened his mouth to speak, but a pair of arms shot out. One wrapped around his back while the other pressed over his mouth and dragged him inside.

Kole kicked, his muffled cries echoing inside the dark space of the hollowed trunk. A body pressed up against him. Warm breath tickled his ear. "Be quiet! He might hear you." Kole relaxed at her voice. Her clothes reeked of dirt and iron—the smells of the city. She was the one the Kayetan had chased into the forest. The girl released him and scurried to the back of the trunk, her form completely disappearing into the darkness.

"How is she?" he heard her say.

"She needs help," came a second, desperate voice. By the rasp, Kole guessed it came from an older woman. "We need to get out of here."

The girl who had grabbed him returned to his side. "You have to get them to safety, shepherd."

"How many?"

"Two. But the child is badly wounded."

Kole noted the dark amber sky through the canopy. They had maybe an hour before sundown. If they moved fast, they could make it to the southern camp before the ramblers awakened and the Kayetan appeared. "Follow me."

She caught his arm as he moved to climb out. "We need a distraction first."

Kole tilted his head. "For what?"

"The Kayetan."

"Don't worry, it won't be back until dusk." He pulled from her grip. "C'mon, we need to hurry."

The girl pushed him against the hollowed trunk and turned his chin so he was looking to the east. A tingle passed through him as she leaned into him, her cheek grazing his own as she pointed to a trunk barely in view. "There. Between the trees."

He struggled to focus on anything other than the girl's body pressed into his, but he followed her finger to a small cloud of smoke lingering around the base of a trunk. He blinked, thinking his eyes were playing tricks on him. Then a set of long, black claws appeared between the trees. "Impossible! They can't walk in daylight."

"Normally, yes." She pulled away, sitting across from him, her face still shrouded in shadow. "His name is Idris."

"They have names now?"

"This one does."

"How can he—"

"There's no time for a history lesson. Lily will die soon." A short cry carried from the back of the trunk. "Now that we have a shepherd, we can move. I can distract him long enough for you to get out of here. Take Lily and Etta to safety. Understand?"

"I can't leave you here. Idris will kill you."

"I can handle myself."

"Why don't I—"

"It's not up for debate. This is the plan." She fumbled with her belt then pushed something hard into his hand. "Just in case."

He thumbed the item. A dagger. "But I already have—"

"A sunstone blade?"

"Sunstone?"

"It's the only thing that can take him out. If things go sour, use it on his heart. It won't work unless you strike the heart, got it?"

Kole nodded, looking back out to where he last saw Idris, but the Kayetan had vanished. "If Idris can walk in daylight, why not come in after you?"

"I'm not sure. When he saw the tree, he stopped his pursuit."

"What does he want with the Great Red?"

The girl shrugged. "If I weren't being hunted, I think it would entrance me, as well. But we can use his distraction to our advantage." She moved to the side of the hole, her face finding the light for the first time. Vibrant green eyes stared back at him. Straw-colored curls fell on either side of her face, and her nose, cheeks, and forehead were covered in dark freckles. "Are you ready?"

Kole nodded.

"Etta, it's time," she called back, and a plump, red-haired woman emerged with a small body cradled in her arms. Lily, Kole guessed. Both Lily and Etta wore bloodstains. Something else caused his breath to catch, though. A quick look and he gauged Lily was no more than five or six years old. He gritted his teeth, a new hatred for the Kayetan bubbling in his gut.

"Stay here," the girl urged Etta. "I'll lead him away. Once I'm out of range, go with the shepherd."

"Be safe, Vienna," Etta said.

Vienna nodded and climbed from the Great Red. The last light of day doused her golden waves as she strode under the canopy.

The Kayetan appeared instantly as if a wolf waiting for a rabbit to dash out of its hole. Its faceless shadow stood between two trunks. The body appeared fluid, like swirling smoke, and two sunken indentations rested where his eyes should have been. And his hands.... In place of fingers were long, sickle-like claws, reaching well below the creature's knees.

Idris turned his head to the trunk. His eyeless face seemed to stare directly at Kole through the shadows. Kole shuddered and scrambled backward, deeper into the cavity.

"Finally come to face your death?" The Kayetan's smooth, deep voice sent a chill up Kole's spine, raising the hairs on his neck.

Vienna crouched down, a dagger steady in her hand. In the light, Kole noticed its odd appearance; a white blade made of what looked like quartz. A pulse in his hand made him look down at his borrowed blade. Dim light radiated from the material, flickering like fire.

Sorcery. He let the blade clang to the floor of the trunk.

Birds flew from the canopy as a gurgling noise erupted from the creature. It took a moment for Kole to realize the Kayetan was laughing. "A brave face, dear girl." Idris flexed his claws. "But you have no chance against me without your Liberation. I'll kill you just like the girl. An agonizing, slow death."

Vienna lunged forward. She slashed her blade at the shadow, but he vanished before her attack came near.

The Kayetan reappeared behind her. Vienna spun, bringing her dagger in for another attack, but Idris dodged it like before. A frustrated grunt escaped her.

"It would be fitting—dying next to the Souls you so desperately cling to."

Vienna kept her dagger pointed at the Kayetan. Her eyes, betrayed with confusion, shifted between Idris and Kole, who waited anxiously in the red tree, but she said nothing.

"When I'm done with you, I'll deal with the hag," Idris growled.

Vienna dashed for the edge of the clearing. Kole dug his nails into the trunk. Once she reached the edge of the clearing—time to move.

A stream of smoke shot out from the Kayetan's hand and caught Vienna by the neck. She cried out and dropped her dagger as the smoke solidified. Five dark claws curled around her throat.

Kole fumbled to collect his discarded dagger as her face reddened. His fingers curled around the cold metal hilt. Once Idris had dealt with Vienna, he'd come after them. Kole peered to the back of the trunk, where Etta and Lily sat. With Idris' attention focused on Vienna, Kole spotted their chance to escape. Yet he hesitated. His fear stopped him; a little for himself, but he feared more for the refugees. Would this risk drawing the Kayetan toward camp, exposing them? But he couldn't sit and watch Vienna die, either. He'd have to fight.

"Stay here," he said to Etta, then launched himself from the trunk and charged the Kayetan. He brought his knife down toward Idris' back. Before it could pierce the shadow, Idris shot away, and Kole's blade harmlessly sailed through the empty air.

Vienna dropped to the ground. Her hands patted the grass in search of her dagger. After taking it up, she jumped to her feet, her free hand massaging her throat.

"Are you al—" A blow hit Kole's back. He fell forward, head striking the ground with an audible thump. A stab of pain shot down his spine.

"Another child for me to kill?" Weight pressed into Kole's back, pinning his chest to the grass.

Vienna raced toward them. She ducked under the Kayetan's first swing, retaliating with her own. Her attacks seemed careless, less about accuracy and more about regaining Idris' attention.

It worked. The pressure lessened on Kole's back and he rolled free, pushing up to his feet. His head spun, but a guttural moan from Vienna sobered him up. Kole caught a glimpse of smoke lash out at her stomach. The force sent her flying into the canopy, and her back hit a branch with a crunch. She yelped and slammed into the ground so hard that Kole felt the impact through his boots.

Kole bared his teeth and ran at the Kayetan, blade raised. He slashed wildly. Idris dodged his onslaught with ease; his shadowy form proving more agile than the nimblest of birds. A jet of smoke hit Kole's hand, and his dagger tumbled into the grass. He froze.

Idris' eyeless face appeared in front of him. He bore down on Kole, who stumbled backward.

A glint of stone caught the corner of Kole's eye. The dagger lay a few feet away. If he dove for it.... *Then what?* Even if he could reach it, Idris moved too fast. He'd never get the chance to use it.

"Ah, a shepherd. The runt of the litter, too." A tendril of smoke drifted from Idris' claws.

Use it on his heart. It won't work unless you strike the heart. Vienna's words rang through his head. No wonder his strikes had met only air. He needed to hit Idris' heart. Kole flicked his eyes to the creature. Did he even *have* one? Kole saw only the swirling smoke and shadow.

Kole let out a frustrated grunt and rolled toward the dagger. Just because he saw nothing like a heart didn't mean none beat in that creature's chest. His fingers grazed the sharp stone, but the smoke lassoed his torso and pulled him back. The shadow elongated and coiled around his body, pinning his arms to his sides.

Kole wriggled against the ethereal restraints as Idris lifted him off the ground, but it seemed pointless: he'd only go free if Idris willed it.

The Kayetan took a step toward Vienna.

"Don't touch her!"

Idris looked back at him. He kept his sunken eyes on Kole as he sent a stream of smoke from his other hand. A gaseous sphere engulfed Vienna, lifting her like a rag doll.

Vienna's eyes snapped open. She pounded against the sphere, but it refused to budge. Smoke shot into her nose and open mouth. Her body stiffened, and the veins in her neck swelled as she struggled to breathe. All the while, Idris kept his attention on Kole as Vienna suffocated.

"Leave her alone!" Kole thrashed, but the tendril around his torso only tightened.

Vienna's eyes glazed over.

"No!" Kole's scream came out as a gasp. *Please. Don't let her die!*

Amid his rising anger and frustration, something in Kole's mind shattered. A splitting pain erupted in the back of his brain. It felt shallow at first, as if someone held a nail against his head, driving it into the bone with a hammer. Then, the pain tore past his skull and sunk further and further into his head until he knew only searing agony, and all he could do against it was scream.

Bright, white light enveloped the forest, blinding him. He couldn't see Vienna in her bubble of smoke or the Great Red towering above him. Even Idris disappeared behind its intensity. He was alone in a vast expanse of pure light and pain.

The pressure lessened around his chest. The Kayetan had dropped him. Still screaming, he landed on the grass. Kole clawed the base of his skull where the pain seemed to originate. Through his screams, a whisper swept by his ear. He couldn't tell who was speaking or make out the words—couldn't focus on anything besides the violent throb threatening to implode his head.

Then, just as suddenly as it had appeared, the light faded, and with it, the pain.

Gasping, he rolled into a ball as the forest returned.

Kole sat up. His head spun at the quick movement. He fingered the back of his head to find it untouched. No blood or wound, only smooth skin. Blinking hard, he steadied himself and scanned his surroundings.

Idris. Where was he?

Kole clumsily staggered to his feet, a dull ache still pounding in his head.

Vienna lay motionless in the grass, a small puddle of blood forming from the wound on her arm. He hurried to her side and rolled her over. Her chest rose and fell, if only slightly. She was alive.

The light... he thought it had come from Idris. Some attack. But the Kayetan had gone and Kole and Vienna were alive. If not Idris, then who?

Kole shook his head and immediately regretted it, as the throbbing rose like a swelling wave. He took in a slow breath, waiting for it to subside. He could figure out the light later.

The trees creaked and moaned, anxious under the fading sun. Kole quickly tore a piece of cloth from the bottom of his pants and wrapped it around Vienna's arm. Anything more would have to wait until he got her to camp.

He pulled Vienna to his chest. The vague scent of honey wafted from her locks. Kole lifted her carefully from the floor as the first few ramblers broke free from the soil.

"Etta," he called. Etta's face poked from the trunk. "Are you all right?" She gave him a nod and climbed from the tree, Lily still whimpering in her arms. "Follow me."

As they crossed the clearing, he heard a voice.

"*Kole.*"

He stopped. Thoughts of Idris swept through his head at first, but this voice sounded different. Feminine. Soft.

"*Kole.*"

He looked down at Vienna, unconscious in his arms. She lay perfectly still except for the rise and fall of her chest. Then, he turned to Etta, who hummed softly to Lily, rocking her back and forth like a baby. His head spun, searching for the source of the voice, but only the Great Red with its empty cavity and the waking ramblers surrounded him.

He shook his head. Maybe he had been hit harder than he thought.

For a long moment, he stared at the red tree, watching. He pursed his lips, dismissing it, and set out for camp.

CHAPTER 4

Back pressed against the trunk of the small sapling, Kole gripped a root in either hand and steered the rambler west. He checked on Etta, whose arms were wrapped tightly around the trunk, eyeing the sapling warily as it carried Lily and Vienna aloft. A root gently coiled around each girl's body, since neither of them had the strength to hang on themselves. Etta protested the idea at first, but Kole had promised her it offered the fastest way to travel now that night had fallen and the ramblers moved about. And they had to act quickly. With Lily's paling skin and shallow breathes, her condition worsened by the minute. The sooner they reached Charlie, the better her chances.

After ten minutes keeping the sapling at a grueling pace, Kole finally spotted the bridges. They had reached the southern camp. Usually Kole avoided Darian's territory, but only one herbalist resided in Solpate. Kole had no choice.

"Signal Charlie. We need aid," Kole called up to the startled scouts and halted the sapling.

A horn blew and, within the minute, three forest stags galloped toward him. Thick moss, draped over their wooden antlers, cascaded down their backs and over the twisting vines of their rumps. One carried a rider. The long black beard and pot belly gave the camp leader away: *Darian*.

Kole's mouth twisted. He stepped off the rambler and helped Etta dismount.

Darian pulled the reins and stopped just short of Kole. "What is the meaning of this? Where is Russé?"

"Busy." Kole rushed over to the nearest stag. The rambler followed and lowered the girls onto the animal's back. The stag stamped its polished wooden hooves uneasily, nostrils flaring.

Darian's stern gaze dropped to the unconscious bodies. "Who are they?"

"No time to explain." With a final wave of his hand, Kole dismissed the rambler, and it scurried off into the forest.

Darian scoffed. "This is not how things work, *apprentice*. Your master will hear about this."

Kole ignored his threat and mounted the stag. "Take Etta with you. I'm riding ahead."

"Now wait just a min—"

Kole kicked his heels into the stag. Wind whizzed by his ears, drowning out Darian's protest as the animal bounded forward. He squeezed his legs tighter around the animal's belly, one hand clutching a fistful of the stag's moss-laden neck. Using the crook of his elbow, he secured Lily while the other prevented Vienna from sliding off. Lily whimpered at the stag's bouncing gait. "Hold on. It's not far."

The stag carried them to Darian's house, a fat willow tree situated in the middle of the southern camp. Kole leapt off before the animal halted and pulled Lily from its back, leaving Vienna behind.

The herbalist burst from the door of the willow. "This way, shepherd." He ushered Kole through the doorway. "On the table." Charlie cleared the surface with a sweep of his arm, sending bowls and cups clattering to the floor.

Kole laid Lily down. The blood from her cloak seeped into the grain of the wood.

Charlie rummaged through the open drawer of a dresser, stacking odd tools—a vial of yellow liquid, a long roll of cloth, stitching string—into his arms. He tossed a blanket at Kole. "Put pressure on the wound."

On catching the blanket, Kole turned to the girl and pulled back her cloak. The front of her dress, from collar to hem, had soaked through with blood. Without the long slash on her bodice, Kole wouldn't have known where to start looking. "Chest wound. It's long and it's deep." He wadded the blanket and held it over the lesion. "Sorry if this hurts." Kole pressed down on the wound. The girl coughed in response. Her eyes rolled behind her lids, though she didn't wake.

"How was she injured?"

"Kayetan."

Charlie's hands paused over his equipment, mouth opening as if he meant to speak, then he snapped it shut and returned to his frenzied search. He pulled out the last few items and rushed over. Upon seeing her, he dropped his equipment. He removed the blanket and pulled back the bodice and cursed. "This is far beyond anything I've handled. It's all the way to the organs...."

"But you can do it, right? You can help her?"

"She's lost so much blood." He gauged the length of the wound.

"You have to try."

Charlie nudged Kole out of the way and lifted the blanket to reveal the laceration. "I'll need to wrap it."

As Kole propped the child up for him, the door burst open.

"Lily! My dear Lily!" Etta cried.

Darian followed her inside, Vienna in his arms, and kicked the door shut. "What in the name of the Seven Souls is going on?"

Etta ran to Kole and took Lily's hands in hers. Charlie poured the vial of yellow liquid onto the wound then unrolled the cloth and wrapped his patient's torso.

Darian laid Vienna's unconscious body in a hammock then came back down the spiral staircase. When no one answered him, he narrowed in on Kole. "You bring strangers into my camp without questioning them? Did you even exchange the pass phrase?"

"Oh, shut it, Darian. You know I am no stranger!" Etta snapped.

The stubby man pointed an accusing finger at Kole. "But *he* doesn't! He very well could have led one of Savairo's men straight to us." He glared at Kole. "You put every refugee in danger with your carelessness. I'll have your apprenticeship for this."

Kole clenched his fists, rage swelling in his chest. How could Darian care more about protocol than the girl dying on his table? "You want my apprenticeship? Have it! I'd do it again a hundred times over if it means saving them." The moment the words left his mouth, his heart skipped a beat. Had it come to this: choosing between doing what was right and keeping his title? Well, then, he had made his choice.

"The safety of a hundred is more important than one," Darian retorted.

Their heated glares met for a long moment. Kole tore his eyes from the camp leader when Charlie let out a nervous groan.

"Oh, no—come on, little one, hang in there." Charlie's voice shook as badly as his hands.

Lily's skin was ice cold. Kole held her shoulders tight, keeping her upright despite her limpness, and rubbed her arms in hopes to warm her up.

"Please, Lily. Don't go. Not yet," Etta said. Bowing her head, she whispered something unintelligible as Charlie desperately pulled the cloth tighter around Lily's chest.

On contact, each new layer of the bandage bloomed red. Kole swallowed the hard lump in his throat.

Lily's chest stilled.

Charlie let the bandage fall to the table and grabbed the girl's wrist. They waited.

It seemed like hours as Charlie searched for a heartbeat. The room filled with a thick silence.

The herbalist shook his head.

"No! Lily!" Etta wrapped her arms around the girl. She sobbed into her chest; her face pressed against Lily's limp body, not caring that the blood transferred to her cheek.

"I'm sorry, Etta. There's nothing more I can do," Charlie whispered.

Kole backed away in a daze.

He had failed her. As he backed up, Kole bumped into something firm. He turned to see Darian, his beady eyes burning into Kole from over his beard. Kole saw no remorse—no sadness in those dark eyes.

Charlie put a hand on Etta's back. "I can have a grave ready for you if—"

"No," Darian barked. "She stays in the willow. Once the refugees are asleep, you can take her to the hill to be buried, but not before. I don't want to cause a scene."

"A scene? My baby is dead and you don't want a scene?!" Etta cried.

"We don't know what happened out there. Best we keep things quiet until we do."

"It was a Kayetan," said Etta.

"Now hold on." Darian waved a hand. "We can't assume until we investigate. It could've been a bear or—"

"It wasn't a bear," Kole cut in. "I saw it. We all did."

"That wound is not from a bear," Charlie confirmed.

Darian's jaw clenched at the herbalist's words. "It still doesn't mean it's a Kayetan. They cannot walk in daylight, they are—"

"Bound to the shadows, I know," Kole finished. "That's what I thought, too. *This* one isn't."

"There is no reason to panic until we know the facts. If word carried around that a Kayetan is roaming free in the forest, we'd have an uproar."

"It's dead," said Kole.

"You killed it?" said Darian.

"I-I don't know what killed it. There was a light, and then it was gone."

"Dead and gone are two different things." Darian turned to Etta. "What happened out there? Why are you here? We weren't expecting the Liberation to send a new group until next season. They never sent a messenger."

Etta eased Lily onto the table. She stroked the girl's arm as she spoke. "I don't know anything about a messenger, but we'd planned the Escape for weeks on our end." A pause as she smoothed Lily's tattered dress, slick with blood. She intertwined her fingers with Lily's. "Everyone arrived at the meet-up point on the mountain without any trouble. Things looked good, as scheduled. We didn't make it halfway up the peak before the Kayetans ambushed." She spat the creatures' name.

"Then Savairo knew. He must've intercepted the message. Which means he knows about everything: the Escapes, the Liberation, *us*. Dammit." Darian's fist slammed the wall. Smoothing a hand through his greasy black hair, he nodded for her to continue.

Etta's voice trembled. "They slaughtered us. The Liberation tried to fight back, but they were outnumbered." Her eyes turned wild as if she were reliving the moment. "Everyone split up. I don't know what happened to the others. I took Lily and ran." A fresh wave of sobs shook her, and she crumpled over Lily's body.

Kole moved over to her. Unsure what else to do, he placed a hand on her heaving back.

"What happened next—once you arrived in the forest?" Darian asked.

Etta lifted her reddened face, cheeks tear-streaked and puffy. "Idris must have followed us down the mountain. If not for Vienna, we wouldn't have had a chance. She's one of the Lion's recruits."

So Vienna is a member of the Liberation. That explained how she knew so much about the Kayetans and Idris and where she got her hands on those odd blades. The Liberation were Kayetan killers. The only defense Socren's people had against Savairo's abominations.

"After Lily and I escaped, Vienna caught up to us. We thought we were safe when dawn came, but when we crossed into the forest, Idris cornered us. He slashed Lily through the chest. We couldn't run after that. Vienna had us hide until the shepherd came to lead us to camp."

Kole stared up at Vienna, who lay still in the hammock above. She had made the right call. The location of the refugee camps remained a secret to everyone but the shepherds. Even Darian didn't know where the other three camps resided, which might have explained his bitterness when new apprentices were taken—jealous that a kid knew more than he did. The fact remained, no one wandered Solpate without a shepherd. If Vienna had taken the chance and tried to find the camps on her own, they would most likely have been trampled by a rambler before Kole had found them.

First the Black Wall, now Idris. Not to mention the Liberation's botched Escape Etta mentioned. What were the chances it would all occur within the same twenty-four hours? This was no coincidence. Something strange bloomed. He needed to find the roots of it before anything else happened. This mission had been a close call. They couldn't afford to be surprised again. "I need to get back to Russé."

"You will stay here until this mess is cleaned up," said Darian.

"I need to report back."

"You are in my camp. You abide by my rules."

Kole narrowed his eyes. "You have no authority over the shepherds."

"Did I miss your shepherd's ceremony, *apprentice*?" Darian spat. "Without the title, you can't act on your own accord. And seeing as Russé isn't present, or any other shepherd for that matter, you are required to follow the next in command like every other refugee." Darian folded his arms. "Once we've searched the camp's borders and deemed them safe, then you can go off and do whatever you like."

"And how long will that take?" Kole said through gritted teeth.

"A few hours."

"*Hours?*"

"We will take as long as we need to ensure our safety," Darian said. He nodded to Charlie, who had been cleaning the blood from Lily's face and arms in silence. "You are in charge of these two. No one leaves until I return. Understood?"

Charlie dipped his head. "Understood, sir."

After Darian left, Charlie set down his bloodied cloth and checked on Vienna. "Passed out. She'll be fine."

Kole sighed, relieved. His eyes trailed back to Etta, who slumped over Lily. "We can't leave her here, Charlie."

"You heard Darian. Strict orders." The crack in Charlie's voice signaled his turmoil.

Kole moved in and kept his voice low. "I must leave. There is more going on than Darian realizes. Not that he'd believe me if I told him."

"Believe what?"

"The Kayetan may not be our biggest concern. I *have* to get back to Shepherd Russé. He can't demote you, Charlie. You're the only one with medical skills in this camp."

"Maybe so, but there are worse things than being demoted."

Kole didn't want to raise alarm, but if Charlie refused to budge, he had no choice. Barely above a whisper, he said, "The Black Wall is on the move."

The blood drained from Charlie's face, and he backed up into the table, pulling Etta's attention.

"You will let us leave," said Kole.

A shuddering mouth answered. Twitch-like, Charlie nodded.

"Etta?" Kole crossed the room and laid a hand on her shoulder. She peeked up at him, eyes soggy, and leaned from the table, letting Kole take Lily into his arms.

Etta seem unfazed by the ramblers. She kept close to Kole, the weight of her stare on his back, and mimicked his every step as they passed under the bridges. The scouts had left their posts to gather at the willow's entrance. While Darian briefed them on the situation, Kole and Etta slipped out the back window with Charlie's hesitant aid. Lily in his arms, Kole set out for the burial grounds.

The earth steepened underfoot as they made their way up the hill beyond camp. The wild ramblers never set foot on the gravesite. Kole liked to think they knew the importance of this place; understood it as a place of peace, and out of respect, left its soil untouched.

Flowers of white and yellow crested the soft curve of the hilltop. Their petals held a velvet sheen in the cool moonlight. Here, no canopies blocked the sky. The stars shone so brightly for miles in every direction. But nothing compared to the light of the fireflies hanging in the air, drowsily skimming the tops of the flowers—their wings giving off a dull hum as if singing to the dead.

In that very moment, Kole thought, if the sun never rose again, it might not be so bad.

Kole carefully stepped around the graves. Most of them were old enough that the flowers had overrun them, but a few still appeared darkened with overturned earth. A young boy named Fredrick had passed a month ago. He had been seven years old when he fell ill with a fever. Kole stopped at the foot of his grave. He hadn't been there when Fredrick died, but he remembered him. The boy had traveled in the first group of refugees that Kole helped Russé guide through the forest. Fredrick had kept pretty quiet—frightened mostly—but Kole remembered the awe on his face when he first glimpsed the ramblers. Kole's mouth pressed in a sad smile. He wished he had known him better.

Kole lowered Lily to the ground. She would rest next to him. A friend for Fredrick. A friend for the afterlife.

Etta's eyes moved over the graves. "How many have passed?"

"A few dozen."

Kole strode to the hill crest, where a single sapling stood, rooted into the earth. It swayed its tiny canopy back and forth to the hum of the fireflies. Kole unhooked the ropes from the stakes anchoring it down and stepped back.

The tree shook as if stretching from a long rest, then rose up and followed Kole to Fredrick's grave. He guided Etta out of the way as the sapling got to work. The rambler's small roots churned the soil, tearing out clumps of grass and flowers until it became soft enough to sweep aside.

"I'm sorry about your daughter." Kole said while the sapling worked.

Etta kept her eyes on Lily as she spoke. "She was *like* a daughter in every way. But I did not bear her." The blood had dried on Etta's face, making her skin look like rust. "Just as all of the orphans in Socren were. I had so many sons and daughters, but they were never my own."

Kole's eyebrows drew together. "You cared for the orphans?"

"Yes, dear. I kept a house full of children whose parents were taken or murdered by Savairo," she said gloomily. "I was their caregiver for a time, but they all eventually left in the Escapes. The Liberation picks the orphans first. Socren is no place for a child right now."

"That's how you know Darian?"

She nodded.

"How long did you run the orphanage?"

"A good twenty years or so. You'll have to forgive me, though. At my age, I can't remember too much before the last decade. Most of it gets blurry... but I *never* forget my kids. I know every orphan who's come through here."

"All of them?"

"Aye. Every name, every freckle, birthmark or scar... and if they were a troublemaker...." Her mouth twitched as she tried to smile. "*Especially* if they were a troublemaker. Those are more permanently branded in this head." She sighed. "Yes, I remember them all." She knelt down to Lily, her voice growing hoarse. "Living and dead."

Kole frowned. As he stared at Lily, a seed of hope bloomed within him. Had he been like her? A child in Etta's orphanage? Etta must remember him—maybe not his face; it had been ten long years since he left. But his name? She was the one person who might be able to tell him about his past. His family.

Once Kole finally mustered up the courage to speak, the rambler had finished with the grave. It reached its roots over to Lily and picked her up.

Etta moved to stop the tree, but Kole held her back with a touch to the shoulder. They watched as the young rambler placed Lily in the grave, then crawled back and waited.

Etta stepped in next to Lily, placing the child's pale hands delicately over her torso, one atop the another as if she were sleeping, and brushed the tangled hair from her face. She licked her thumb, stamped it into the loose earth, then brought it to Lily's forehead and drew a familiar sunburst shape between her brows. "May the lost find their way." Etta closed her eyes and held her hand to the stars. Kole did the same, muttering the phrase softly under his breath. Then, Etta gave Lily a final kiss on her cheek and sobbed.

Kole studied Lily's face. All he could think about were the terrible things she had seen leading up to her death. It seemed the worst way to die: overwhelmed by fear. She had drawn so close to freedom only to be killed before she could grasp it.

His heart swelled. He had failed her. The guilt wrenched his stomach.

Kole offered a hand and helped Etta out of the grave. She leaned against him as the sapling slid the first pile of dirt over Lily.

Before long, Lily lay another lump of raised dirt on the hillside. Kole left Etta to say her final words as he returned the rambler to its spot atop the hill.

He sneaked a glance back at Etta as they returned to camp. Her swollen eyes were cast down as if vaguely aware of Kole's presence. She moved in a sort of trance. Remembering how her eyes lit up when she had talked about her children, Kole tried to distract her, saying, "You said before that you remember all of your orphans. Every one, right?"

Etta looked up for a moment, then nodded.

"Do you remember me?" If she was surprised by the question, she hid it well. Her silence, though, sent a wave of anxiety through him. "I was an orphan in Socren ten years ago," Kole nudged. Perhaps grief left her distracted. "Niko and I made the trip together."

"Niko? Yes, I remember him." A quick jet of air, which Kole thought was a laugh, escaped her lips. "He was a curious lad, that one. Always getting into trouble, too, now that I think of it."

"Then you have to remember me. We were inseparable. We still are."

"Oh, no, dear, Niko was quite the loner."

"Loner?"

"He came from a big family. Six siblings, if I recall." Etta frowned. "Savairo had his parents killed when he discovered they were working with the Liberation. Niko had a rough time in the orphanage. Didn't make any friends, unfortunately. That's why I picked him for the Liberation's next Escape. He needed a new start. How is he doing?"

"F-fine. He's fine."

"That's good to hear." Etta must have seen the disappointment on his face. She took his hand and squeezed it. "Is there something wrong?"

"No, I... I just thought you would remember me."

"You? Did you... you mean you weren't born here in the forest?"

"No."

"Oh, well you look so young, I just assumed.... Sorry, dear, but I don't."

"I came over in the Fifth Escape with Niko," Kole added, trying to jog her memory, but the more he spoke, the more his hope deflated. "I was only five. I don't remember much," he admitted.

"Are you sure it was the Fifth Escape? The Fifth was a small group, you know. The first Escape that the Liberation allowed children to go. I know every single boy and girl I sent on it."

"I'm sure you just forgot me. I was there. Maybe the memory is just blurry, like you said."

"My children do not get blurry," Etta said firmly. "I take great pride in keeping their names and faces in my head. So long as they stay in here," she tapped her temple, "they will have someone who cares for them. They will never be forgotten."

Kole's face burned. He turned away from her. How could she remember Niko but not him? And Niko a loner? Nonsense. Goren told them many times how they lived in Socren as orphans and traveled the mountains with their group to the refugee camps. That's how it had always been.

He moved his attention to the forest. The ramblers always seemed to calm him.

"Kole." The firmness in her voice disappeared. "Five years old is not as young as you think. You should have some memory of your life before Solpate. You would remember me, your parents, your friends...."

She grabbed his shoulders and squared him off to her. "Look here. Do *you* remember *me*?"

Kole tried so hard to go back in his mind—to think of anything that he could trace back to her, the orphanage or Socren. There had to be a face he remembered. Maybe a voice? A name? His mind came up blank, as usual. "No." Frustration gripped him once more. "I don't remember anything," he snapped. "There's just... Solpate."

"Did you ever think there is a reason for that?"

Kole cocked his head. "What do you mean?"

"Listen, Kole, I don't know about your past, but I do know it wasn't with me in the orphanage. If you really want to know what happened to you, I'd start by asking whoever fed you this lie."

Lie? But it was Goren. *He wouldn't lie to me. Not about this—never about this.* Goren knew how envious Kole felt every time a memory came back to one of the orphans. How he had cried himself to sleep some nights wishing tomorrow would be the day when his past returned to him. No. Kole didn't believe it. There had to be another explanation.

Kole led Etta silently back to camp. He needed to get back to Niko—to the chest—to Goren's journals. They had to hold the answers.

As they passed under the first outpost, his thoughts were cut short by a scream.

He grabbed Etta's arm and pulled her behind him. More screams joined the first. Kole hurried Etta up the nearest anchor tree. Her frail arms shook as she climbed the ladder to the canopy.

"Stay inside," Kole called up to her as she reached the platform. She looked down to him with empty eyes, as if her mind was too preoccupied with thoughts of Lily to register the chaos around her. "Don't come out until you get the all clear," he said, then sprinted away.

The refugees filled the bridges above, scrambling into the treehouse doors. He ran from trunk to trunk toward the center of the chaos and found the willow. Something dark shifted behind the curtain of leaves.

Kole slipped between the dangling vines and dove behind the trunk. His back pressed against the bark, he leaned around, catching a glimpse of Darian standing statue-like outside the willow's door. His face shone as white as a stroke of lightning, and he stared at something just beyond Kole's vision.

The silky voice he heard made the air catch in his throat.

Idris was alive. He had found the southern camp.

CHAPTER 5

"Where is he?" Idris asked.

"Where is who?" Darian squealed. Any other time, Kole would have gotten a bit of satisfaction watching Darian squirm.

"The god! Where is the god!"

"I don't know what—"

"I saw the tree. He's been released." A clawed hand wrapped around Darian's neck. His face purpled.

Kole shrugged his bow from his shoulder. He aimed carefully and fired. The arrow whistled through the air and sailed straight through the Kayetan's shadowy form. Kole knew it wouldn't hurt him, but the distraction made Idris loosen his hold on Darian's throat.

Idris' blank face turned to him before Kole could slip back behind the tree. "Ah, the little shepherd. My master is pleased to know where his people take refuge. I am in your debt, young one, for leading me here."

The blood drained from Kole's face. "No... " he breathed. "I didn't. You were... I didn't."

The Kayetan released Darian, who dropped to his knees in a coughing fit. "Oh but you did." Idris floated toward Kole.

Kole wanted to run, but his feet refused to move. He stood there, bow drawn, frozen in fear.

"You led him here?" Kole felt Darian's daggered gaze on him, but Kole's stare never strayed from Idris.

"You're lying." His fingers wrapped tighter around the wood of his bow. Part of him knew Idris would say anything to distract him, to make him doubt himself. He tried to resist, but a small voice inside him believed the Kayetan.

"I knew someone would come after them eventually. I just needed to wait it out. It's amazing how quickly you dismissed my absence when that girl was hurt. I thought it would take a bit more convincing, but you ran straight for camp."

"I...." Kole's hands shook on his bow. The tremor spread up his arms and down his torso until his entire body surrendered to its mercy.

"You little brat. I told you to stay put," Darian wheezed from the base of the willow.

"Quiet." A jet of smoke shot from Idris' hand. Darian flew back into the trunk. His stubby body hit the ground in a crumpled pile.

"Stop!" Kole yelled.

The Kayetan turned back to him. "As you wish." He dropped his clawed hand back to his side. "I do owe you one, after all. Not only for bringing me here but for confirming my suspicions about the god." Idris circled around him. His voice slithered into Kole's ears. "Maybe you know where he is."

"I don't know what you're talking about."

"Seems to be the theme." Idris put a hand on Kole's bow, forcibly lowering it. Kole's arms fell limp at his side. "But I know what I saw. That light.... He has been set free. And how interesting that they would respond to a child like you."

"They?" Kole swallowed as Idris slid a claw threateningly across his chest.

The Kayetan laughed and pulled away from Kole. "No wonder you are such a horrible shepherd."

The light. That splitting headache. Was that what he meant? If Idris hadn't caused it, then who? The only other person present was Vienna, and she had been passed out cold. Then he remembered the voice calling his name. It had seemed to be coming from....

The Great Red.

Was *that* what Idris meant? The tree was a god? A Soul? No, not the tree. Something *within* the tree, inside that strange cavity.

"I will not leave until the god is in my custody," Idris said. Darian groaned from the ground. "Do you hear that, Darian? I have orders to bring the Soul to my master. I know you are harboring him. Best turn him over sooner rather than later. Savairo lacks for patience. I'm sure you remember how he gets when he's angry. You have until morning to produce the Soul, or I will find him myself. I don't think you'll like my methods." Idris' body swirled into a cloud of smoke and vanished through the willow leaves.

Darian lurched to his feet once the Kayetan had disappeared. "What have you done, Kole?" he said, gripping the trunk to keep him steady. "You led him straight to us."

Kole staggered back, shaking his head. His whole body numbed. "I thought he was dead. I didn't know."

Darian scoffed. "You ignorant little brat. He will come for us, now. *Savairo* will come for us. He will kill us for what we've done. You've doomed us. All because you couldn't follow orders!"

Kole's mind blanked. If he would have followed orders, Vienna — Etta — might be dead. He had only tried to save them. To save Lily. He'd never sought to play the hero; he just didn't want anyone to die. Now everyone was at risk. What had he done? Oh, for the love of Souls, what had he done?

Darian spoke true. It *was* his fault. *He* had led Idris here. *He* had outed the camp. A decade of secrecy — of peace — and he'd thrown it away in a single night. He'd been careless, and the refugees would pay for his actions.

The only way out was to make a deal. The Soul for their freedom. Only, he had no idea where the god was or how to find him.

Russé. If anyone could make sense of this, it was him. He could undo this. Sorcerer or not, Kole needed him. Russé offered the only hope the refugees had left.

Kole turned and ran.

"Where are you going? Get back here." Darian called after him.

Kole didn't stop. He wrangled a sapling at the edge of camp and rode it north.

CHAPTER 6

It neared midnight when Kole spotted the campfire through the ramblers. He pulled back on a root, forcing the sapling toward it. His gaze held steady on the fire in the distance as he weaved through the gallivanting trees.

Forms of sleeping bodies lay huddled around the fire. He jumped from the sapling and sprinted toward the two standing silhouettes of Russé and Goren.

Kole grabbed his mentor by the elbow and dragged him away from the sleeping orphans.

"What's wrong?" Russé asked.

Once he deemed that they moved out of earshot, Kole snapped around. "The Kayetan—it killed a girl. I-I led... I led it to camp. It was an accident. I had no other way."

"Whoa, Kole. Slow down. Start from the beginning."

Russé waited, stone faced, as Kole told him what had happened since he left. By the time he finished, Russé's bushy brows had joined together at the center of his forehead.

"I messed up again—I know—but I couldn't... I couldn't let them die," said Kole. The weight of his guilt shook his hands. He clenched his fists attempting to still himself, but the tremble moved up his arms— pierced his heart.

"No. You did the only thing you could."

Kole's mouth hung open. Words meant to lessen his burden only offered more confusion. "I did—what?"

"In time, Savairo would have discovered the refugees' hideout anyway. He's been sending scouts into Solpate for years."

"But I led that thing to camp."

"True or not, the camps were compromised the moment the Escape suffered an ambush. It seems Idris spared his prey to follow them. You were right in what you did." Russé put a gentle hand on his shoulder. "Never second guess yourself when it comes to helping another."

His mentor's words lifted a small weight from Kole's chest, but he didn't think he'd ever shake the guilt. "What do we do about Idris? He said he wouldn't leave without the god. What does that mean?"

"Forget about that for now."

"It can't wait!" Kole glanced to the sleeping orphans and lowered his voice. "Idris talked about consequences. We have until dawn. He's watching us."

"Did he follow you here?"

Kole froze. "I don't... I don't know."

Russé turned his eyes to the surrounding forest. "Then we must move while we can. Hopefully Idris has his eyes on the southern camp. That'll give us the chance to escape."

"Where will we go?"

"East, toward the coast. As far away as possible."

"What about the others?"

"I'll send word to the other camps. They can act on their own accord. Once the children are safe, we can come back and aid them."

"We're just going to leave?" Kole protested.

"We'll save who we can before Idris makes another move. If he thinks we are conspiring an escape... who knows what he'll do?"

His heart ached for Etta, Vienna, and the other refugees, but he knew Russé was right. They had to save the orphans while they had the chance. Still, it felt wrong. Nothing Russé said would convince him otherwise.

Kole found Niko snoring next to the fire. He shook him awake.

Niko sat up with a start. "Back already? That was quick. How'd it go?"

"Bad."

"Huh?"

Kole shook his head. He had no desire to tell the story again, and he was grateful Niko didn't push him further.

"Oh, hey. I got a book, like you wanted," Niko said, rubbing his eyes. "You know, one of Goren's journals. Since the chest was broken, I didn't need the key. I slipped one into my pants when no one was looking." Niko pulled a tattered, hide-covered book from his waistband. "There's a lot in there, so I grabbed the biggest one I could find. Figured the good stuff would be in the big one."

Kole took the journal from him. With everything else, he had forgotten about his plan.

"Aren't you going to open it?"

Kole tucked the book in the back of his trousers. "Later. Help me wake the others."

Niko must have sensed the urgency in Kole's voice because he jumped up without another word. The boys woke the orphans one at a time, instructing them to stay quiet as they gathered their things. Most of them were so tired, they didn't protest and sleepily obeyed.

Goren normally would've used the horn when waking the camp, but Russé decided against it and Kole agreed; better to keep quiet in case unwelcome ears hovered around.

Once everyone was on their feet and ready to move out, Goren doused the fire, leaving the full moon as the only source of light, and huddled the kids close together. They walked, shoulder to shoulder and chest to back, arms outstretched, holding the shoulders of the person in front of them, to keep their ranks as tight as possible in the low light. Niko, Dya, and the older orphans stood on the outsides of the group, linking arms, creating a snug ring around the kids.

Kole helped Russé calm a large rambler. They leashed it with a rope and herded the children through the roots so they could march safely beneath the trunk. Russé urged the rambler forward.

After the camp was well on their way, Kole fell back, slipping in next to Niko. He linked his arm in his.

"What's going on?" Niko whispered.

Keeping his voice from carrying to the kids, Kole leaned in and whispered, "There was a Kayetan."

Niko's mouth dropped open. "Here?" he said a little too loudly. A few of the kids stared up at them curiously.

Kole narrowed his eyes in warning.

"What's going on?" Niko mouthed.

Kole shook his head. This seemed a bad time and place to explain.

Russé led them east through the forest, zigzagging their escort like a trained horse between the wandering ramblers. Traveling the forest during the walking hours presented enough danger, let alone alongside three-dozen children. Progress was slow.

After carrying on for what seemed like an hour, a rogue rambler collided into them from the side. Splitting wood erupted from the canopy, and a mighty bough hit the ground. The children screamed as the roots of the rouge rambler tangled into their own.

Russé tugged the rope he'd tied to the trunk taut.

The rambler towered over Kole, and the group groaned as it leaned away from its entangled side. Most of the roots slipped free, but a few stubborn ones held strong. Their rambler continued to twist until the strain proved too much. The roots snapped.

"Move!" Kole yelled.

A root lashed through the middle of their formation. Kole grabbed sleeves and shirt collars of any orphan he could reach and pulled them down. He dove at the last second, the root whizzing overhead as he hit the forest floor, then he peeked his head up. At least a dozen kids had been hit. They lay on the floor, whimpering and groaning. Most seemed like they had only fallen over, but a few, Kole could tell, nursed broken bones.

Russé pulled their rambler a stop. Another tug and it drilled its roots partially into the soil, creating a protective cage around the group. Russé sped toward them. "What's the damage?"

"Doesn't look good," Goren said.

"You all right?" Kole asked the orphans beside him. The four he had managed to get to safety nodded, though their large eyes were full and frightened. "Niko? Dya?"

"Never better," Dya replied, her arms wrapped around two smaller girls from the middle of the wreckage.

Niko lifted up from the grass. "I'm good." His eyes moved to the girl by his side, who clutched her arm to her chest and let out a cry. "She's not."

"We'll be safe as long as they behave," Russé eyed the ramblers beyond the cage of roots.

"On your feet," Goren called to the children.

"We can only spare an hour. Splint the worse cases. We'll have to carry the others." Raising his voice, Russé spoke to the group. "You heard me. Take up the injured."

Kole, Niko, and Dya harvested a handful of branches and giant leaves. They stripped the veins from the leaves to use as twine and helped construct slings for two orphans with twisted wrists and ankles. Only one had a broken leg. Dya volunteered to carry him and Kole strapped him to her back with the remaining twine. After tending to the final few, most of whom had received minor bruises, Kole and Niko herded the injured to the center of the formation, then took up their positions on the outside once more.

"Hey... do you see that?" Niko said, his eyes fixed on something over Kole's shoulder. He slipped his arm from Kole's and took a trance-like step closer to the cage of roots.

"We have to go." Kole turned and followed Niko's gaze. He spotted only ramblers for miles, scurrying about the forest.

"I thought I saw something... moving between the trees. Like smoke. Like a...."

"Kayetan?" Is what Kole meant to say, but the same deep-seated pain he had felt in the back of his skull under the Great Red had returned and transformed his words into a scream.

Kole's legs gave way beneath him. It felt as if a knife slowly twisted into his brain. He pulled at his hair, hoping it would relieve the pressure as a buzz of jumbled whispers slithered in his ears. Their tones sounded harsh and sharp, like arguing—all of them talking at once.

The voices grew louder. They shouted at him. Screamed.

Then, they stopped.

Kole had a brief moment of clarity in the silence. He focused on his breathing, slowing his heart. Then, a single voice rang through him as if the speaker's lips were pressed to his ear.

"*Run.*"

Kole opened his eyes. The children, Dya, Goren—even Niko—stared at him in horror.

"Run." Kole said quietly. But the words were not his own. His mouth moved involuntarily, like a puppet's.

"Run!" Kole screamed again. He cupped his jaw, forcing it closed, but it flew open again. "Run! Run! Run!"

The words finally stopped when the ground began to rumble.

Once he regained control of his mouth, he snapped it shut. Fear washed over him, wondering what had just happened, but he had no time to seek answers. His eyes flicked beyond the cage of roots in search of the source of the quake. The Ramblers were on the move. They stampeded south, trampling over one another, their canopies clipping the rambler protecting Kole and the orphans.

The cage of roots sank further into the ground, bracing itself against the onslaught. It held for now, shielding the refugees. Collision after collision, the roots grew weak, quivering as they sunk further into the earth. If they stayed put, they would all be crushed by their own rambler.

Kole looked desperately to Russé, but his focus was drawn to something behind the stampeding ramblers. The blood drained from Kole's face.

Idris stood only a few dozen meters away among the chaotic ramblers, and behind him towered a wall of black fire. Idris held up his arm. A gale swept through the forest, and to Kole's horror, the Black Wall surged forward.

Black flames licked out, swallowing ramblers by the dozen. Thick clouds of ash formed from the disintegrating trees, clearing the way as the wall moved toward the refugees.

"Run!" Russé yelled over the thunderous quake.

The children screamed and darted in every direction.

"This way. Stick together." Kole reached out to catch the fleeing children. Some slipped away, but his hands found purchase on two boys. He ran them toward the cage of roots. Dya did the same, pushing the children out from the rambler's protection, then ran ahead and led them through the stampede. Kole glanced around, expecting to see Niko following, but he was nowhere in sight. He turned his gaze behind him. Niko stood, trance-like, staring where Idris had appeared.

"Niko!"

No answer. He cursed. Never a worse time for him to freeze up. "Go," Kole told the children. "Follow Dya. We'll catch up." Kole sped over to Niko and grabbed him. "What are you doing? We have to move."

"It moved the wall. How did it do that?"

"Doesn't matter. Let's go." Kole dragged Niko a few feet before his friend shook the trance and they slipped through the cage of roots.

They ran, hand in hand, following Dya and the orphans as they made their way through the stampede. Goren and Russé flanked the orphans, shouting out warnings to Dya to veer left or right when a rambler ventured too close.

Then, sheets of ash billowed through the canopy like a blizzard of black snow. The wind carried it overhead, masking the light from the night sky, and covered the forest in a blinding darkness. Kole lost sight of the orphans.

"Where are they?" Niko said next to him.

Kole strained to hear Russé's commands through the roaring wind. "This way." His hand tightened around Niko's and pulled him faster.

The raging gale battered Kole's chest. No matter how hard he pushed his feet, he couldn't keep his pace. A yell on the wind gave him hope that he and Niko were closer to the group than he thought. Then, a dark shadow shot from the ash.

A root slammed into his chest and ripped his hand from Niko's. He flew back. Air rushed from his lungs as he hit the ground.

With a groan, he lifted to his elbows and sucked in a shallow breath. His lungs fought against him. He felt a sharp pain in his chest, and he knew he had cracked a rib. Kole gritted his teeth and rose to his hands and knees. He winced. *Shallow breaths,* he reminded himself. "Niko," he cried weakly into the fierce current. Hot ash sprayed into his mouth. He gagged and coughed, sending a fire into his lungs.

Through the wind and quake he heard a faint response. Kole crawled toward Niko's voice.

"I'm... here," Kole said between gasps. His hand found flesh. An ankle. Niko.

Niko crouched down and helped him up.

"I can't... breath," Kole wheezed, leaning against his friend.

Niko wrapped an arm under Kole's shoulder and took his weight. "Which way?"

Kole's head spun. He'd lost them in the darkness.

On their next step, the gale proved too strong. It blasted them head on and forced them to their knees.

Kole twisted his fingers around the long grass, keeping his other arm securely around Niko.

The swirling wind came down on their backs like a constant wave. It took all of Kole's strength to stay grounded, leaving him drained.

Kole felt his feet go up first. He clung desperately to the soil — to Niko — but the wind was relentless.

The current pulled him free. The only thing keeping him down was Niko's fingers laced in his own. Another gust and they both joined the current up.

Kole grabbed onto Niko as they tumbled through the ash, their bodies clipping the canopy as they traveled up to join the storm of ash and wind.

The current took them higher and higher. Kole's stomach lurched as they spun. He couldn't tell up from down, but he knew where they were headed. The swirling gale was pulling them in, toward the booming noise — the source of the wind and the ash: the Black Wall.

A sudden crosswind ripped between Kole and Niko and yanked them apart.

Kole clawed at the air, catching Niko's arms.

"Hold on," Kole screamed. His fingers slipped. Kole dug his nails into Niko's forearms as they spun.

The wind whipped. It swirled and tugged.

His nails filled with skin and as they dragged down Niko's flesh. His friend gave a faint cry and warm blood trickled over Kole's hands. Kole squeezed tighter but found no traction.

Kole felt Niko's wrists pass through his.

Past his palms — his fingertips.

And then.

Niko was gone.

"Niko!" Kole's body tumbled through the wind. It shook him. Tossed him.

Kole felt the heat of fire. Not the nice warmth when the sun tanned his skin but the icy burn when he would venture too close to the bonfire. His skin prickled and bubbled. He could feel the blisters swelling over every inch of his body.

His skin burned. Melted.

And Kole screamed. Not for the broken rib pressing into his lungs, or his boiling skin, but for Niko.

He screamed because he had let go.

A pressure formed around his ankle. It tightened and, with a sudden jerk, the heat lessened. Something dragged him away from the fire. Little by little, he escaped the vicious gale and into calmer winds. Out here, the current was too weak to keep him aloft, and he fell.

As he dropped, the tendril around his ankle slithered up his leg and wrapped itself around his limbs. It covered his torso, arms, and shoulders, until it encased his body completely. Finally, it curled gently around his neck and over his eyes, bringing with it the rich scent of soil. Kole only glimpsed it for a second before it pressed over his face.

A branch.

His descent slowed.

The root loosened its hold on him and pulled away, but before he fell, a new tendril curled around his body and cradled him like before. Again, it loosened and dropped him, but another limb waited right underneath him, always catching him in a gentle manner, yet the state of his blood-slicked skin left him wincing at every impact.

As the ash thinned, he saw he was being carried by the arms of the stampeding ramblers. They passed him off through the forest until the Black Wall shrunk from view and he heard a familiar voice.

"Kole...." Russé whispered.

Kole turned his head, his burned skin ripping open as he moved. Warm blood flowed from his neck, down his soot-covered back. He tried to speak but found his lips had melted shut.

When he reached the ground, the root pulled away, laying him on the crunchy grass of the singed forest. Each blade felt like a dagger stabbing into his burned flesh.

"Kole?" Russé knelt over him, his own face powdered in ash. His eyes held a terror—a panic Kole never thought he would see from his mentor. "You'll be all right—you will. I can... I can fix this."

Kole only blinked at him. With his adrenaline fading, the pain of his wounds became unbearable. His body convulsed; reckless uncontrollable movements that tore open his skin. The fissures spread up his sides. New warmth oozed from the wounds.

Kole passed out with one thing on his mind.

Niko....

CHAPTER 7

"Kole."

Kole opened his eyes. Sunlight speckled his face as the canopy swayed in the wind overhead.

A shadow loomed over him. "Do you see that, Kole?"

Relief washed through Kole as he recognized the voice. Niko. He was alive.

Niko pointed a finger north. "Do you see it?"

Kole sat up and followed his finger. "See what?" When he turned back, his friend was gone.

"There's something out there. Out in the forest." Niko's voice echoed around him. "I see smoke."

"Where are you?"

Suddenly, Niko was standing in front of him, his eyes fixed north.

Kole shook the fogginess from his head. "What... what's going on?"

"Did you see the smoke?" Niko's glazed eyes turned to Kole. Something seemed off about them. The usual spark behind his brown eyes had gone.

Kole sunk back. "You-you mean the Black—"

"No," Niko snapped.

"Niko, what happened? How did you escape? The last thing I remember... the wind—it tore us apart. I thought you were—"

"Dead?" Niko cocked his head. "But I am dead, Kole." Kole gasped as the skin on Niko's face began to ripple. "You let go. You let me die." Niko's skin sagged and melted from his face, revealing a gleaming-white skull. His eyes fell back into the cavity, leaving hollow pits staring at Kole. Niko's jawbone bounced up and down as he spoke. "Why did you let go?"

Kole fell to his knees. "I didn't. It was the Black Wall. I couldn't hang on." Kole watched in horror as the skin peeled away from the rest of Niko's body until only a skeleton remained. "I'm sorry, Niko. I'm so sorry," Kole cried up at him. "I'll find the smoke for you. I'll find it and kill it."

"Wake up." Niko's teeth fell from his mouth as he spoke. They bounced off his ribs and landed on Kole. "*Wake up!*"

Kole tore his eyes open.

Russé stood in Niko's place, a waterskin in his hands.

"Niko... " Kole said weakly.

Russé hushed him, then bent down and pressed the spout to his mouth. "Drink," he insisted.

Kole found that his mouth was no longer melted shut, but his lips felt wrinkled and raw as the water passed over them. He choked on the liquid and coughed.

Blood spattered onto Russé's face, but the old man seem unconcerned. He tipped the waterskin again. Kole drank it greedily. The cool stream of water stung as it ran down his throat and filled his belly. Russé slowed the stream to a stop and walked away.

Kole shifted focus to the clearing around him. The forest was coated in a dreary gray. A thick layer of ash dusted the trees and grass. The ramblers had anchored, which meant the sun had risen, but the sky hung so thick with haze, only a small glow of dull light pierced through.

Russé placed a hand on a large trunk. The tree groaned, and a bough lowered from the canopy. Its leaves lightly brushed Russé's cheek as in greeting, then placed one of its branches over the uncorked waterskin. An amber liquid formed at the tip of the branch and dripped into the water, then the bough ascended, rejoining the canopy.

Russé brought the waterskin to Kole. "Drink."

Kole eyed it wearily.

"This is what's making you better." Despite Kole's grunts, Russé poured more into his mouth.

He swallowed hard. The water tasted surprisingly sweet, of maple and citrus. A spark ignited within him as the sugary water passed over his tongue. Warmth filled his core, and his skin began to itch. He lifted to his elbows. Naked. The wall had burned the clothes from his body along with his bow, quiver, and Goren's journal.

As he examined his skin, he found it less charred than he remembered. Small black burns lingered, but most of his body had reverted to blisters. They shrunk before his eyes, then disappeared completely, leaving angry red skin in their place, spotted with deep wells and thick cords of tissue like a skinned animal.

"What's happening to me?" Kole asked, voice hoarse.

"The ambrosia is doing its best to heal you." Russé's face retained its grimace. "But the process is slowing."

Kole stared again at his chest. Some of the texture had smoothed, though less a transformation than just a moment before. The ambrosia's effect was diminishing. His eyes darted over his mutated skin. Fear rumbled through his core. Every bone in his body ached with dread. Not this. Never this. If it didn't keep up, he'd be like this forever. Scarred. Maimed. Another drink. He needed *more*.

Kole snatched the waterskin after Russé refilled it, gulped it down, then tossed it aside and waited.

Though the warmth again radiated inside him, his skin remained half healed.

"I'm sorry, Kole. I think its run its course."

"No." Kole touched the skin of his chest, fingers following the braided cords and lumps of flesh covering his entire torso. His hands moved up his neck to his face. The former velvety feel of peach fuzz had been replaced with a slick veil, like the fresh skin beneath a scab that had fallen off prematurely. Kole gritted his teeth. Tears fell from his lashless eyes. A quick sweep over the top of his head told him his hair had gone, too. Beneath his fingers, though, a carpet of fuzz seemed to be sprouting. His gripping fear shifted—bubbled and rose.

Russé knelt next to him. "You're alive. That's all that matters." The relief in his mentor's bloodshot eyes hinted that the ambrosia's effect had been a gamble.

"I need more." The words slithered through Kole's teeth like a hiss.

"It won't do anything."

"Get me more!"

Russé's eyes weighed heavy on Kole as he walked away.

Kole flexed his hands. Stiff. He opened his mouth and found the same resistance, as if his body were fighting every movement. And yet, remembering the root that had slammed into his ribs, he twisted his torso. No pain.

Russé returned with the flask. "What is this stuff?" Kole poured the draught into his mouth, coughing as the undiluted liquid rolled down his throat.

"It's made from the sap of the tree, and the nectar of its hibernating flowers and fruits. It heals, but at a cost to the tree." Russé shook the ash from his shirt, pulled it over his head, and handed it over.

Kole tied it around his waist. "What cost?"

"Death." Russé gestured to a group of trees Kole only now noticed. They looked like skeletons next to the surrounding forest, and they sagged as if every ounce of moisture had left them. Kole had never seen a dead tree. The Great Red kept them alive. Even the ones they used as homes still grew and shed their leaves with the seasons.

Kole stared at the oaks and bowed his head toward them in thanks. He *was* grateful for being alive. *Alive.* His dream rushed back to him. "Where's Niko?"

Russé's lips tightened to a thin line. His blue eyes locked with Kole's, but he kept silent.

Kole stared at his mentor, whose silence sparked a flash of anger. *"Where is Niko?"*

Russé cast his eyes down as he spoke. "The Black Wall overwhelmed us. No one else survived."

"No one... survived?"

Russé offered him an open hand. Something metallic reflected in his palm. Goren's necklace. Kole took the pendant and thumbed the crude iron. Goren was....

No.

Kole squeezed the symbol and rose to his feet. His head spun from the sudden rush. He steadied himself on Russé's shoulder. They couldn't be gone—not everyone. There had to be survivors. Niko could be out there, burned and calling for help. He had to find him.

Kole tried to run but only managed a limp.

"Save your strength," Russé said.

He didn't listen. Niko had to be out there. If he and Russé had managed to survive, he surely would have, too. They were only apart for a moment. The wind couldn't have taken him far.

"Kole!" Russé called him back. "He's gone. Niko is *gone.*"

He couldn't accept it. He wouldn't. Kole followed the thickening layer of ash, searching for footprints. "Niko!" he yelled as he hobbled along. His voice echoed off the trunks. Not even the morning birds responded.

"Kole, stop," Russé said, somewhere behind him.

"Niko." Each passing moment of silence sent a new pain to his heart, and tears blurred his vision.

"You *must* stop!"

"I'm not leaving without him." Sounds of feet closed in behind him. Russé grabbed his arm and pulled him back. Kole tried to twist out of his grip, but Russé held firm. "I need to find him."

"There is no one to find. Niko is dead. Goren, Dya... all dead."

"How do you know?" Kole wailed, fighting against Russé's hold.

"Because I found them," Russé roared. His grip lessened slightly, and his voice softened to a meek whisper. "I found them."

"Liar," he screamed. "He's alive. He has to be."

"Nothing survives the Black Wa—"

"*We did.*"

"The trees saved you." An apologetic tone lined his words. "They pulled you from the wind. Before you passed the fire. A moment longer and you would've shared the same fate."

"And you?" He eyed the shepherd: tattered clothes, unruly hair, but his skin... not a blemish. "How did you get out?"

"The ramblers grabbed me before the wind took hold. I stayed clear of the fire."

Kole remembered the root twisting up his leg, pulling him free of the wind. They must have tried to save Niko and the others, too. "The ramblers probably carried him too far away. Somewhere you didn't look. There was a whole stampede. They're probably scattered out there."

"You and I are shepherds. We share a connection with the ramblers that the refugees do not. The trees recognized you. They sensed your pain."

Kole looked around in a daze. The trees had saved him—pulled *him* from the mouth of the Black Wall—but not the others? His gratitude quickly flipped to resentment. Kole glared at the trees. The ramblers had stood by and watched his family be slaughtered. He wished the ambrosia out of his system—wished for the pain to return. He didn't deserve to live. Not like this. Not in their place.

"Please," Russé said, "stop now. The end of this path would break your spirit forever. I don't want you to see them like that. I want you to remember them for who they were, not for what the Black Wall has done to them."

A glance to the razed land over his shoulder and Kole shuddered. He couldn't begin to imagine what horrors lay in the aftermath. As much as he hated it, Russé spoke true: He didn't want to see it. But his heart still urged him forward. Even the slightest chance of finding a survivor justified trying. "What if—"

"No one is alive out there," Russé's voice quavered slightly.

"I have to try. I owe them that."

"The Kayetan is still out there. He could move the wall again. We need to keep our distance."

So Idris *had* moved the wall. That's what it had looked like, but Kole had been so far away, and everything had happened so quickly, he'd doubted his own judgment.

"If I find him, it's me he should be scared of," Kole spat and spun on his heel. Before he could take a step, Russé tackled him to the ground. Kole kicked and writhed, but Russé held on.

The uncontrollable hate — the anger — swelled inside, smothering him. He forgot about the forest, about Idris and the Black Wall. He held onto his anger. Held on because if he let it go, the truth he wanted so badly to ignore would sink in. He wasn't ready to face that loss. He needed something to focus on — something to direct his frustrations onto — and right now, it was Russé. The shepherd flinched as Kole's fists came down on his back.

Soon, Kole's body grew tired. He willed more anger to rise, to block the grief from crashing down, but he couldn't fight it anymore. He surrendered.

Kole didn't know how long he stayed there, sobbing into the old man's shoulder, but Russé just let him. His mentor sat calm and still and patient until his eyes couldn't muster another tear.

Pulling away, Kole stood. If it had been any other day, he would have been embarrassed to let Russé see him like this, but he felt so drained, he didn't care.

Niko was dead, and it was *his* fault. If only he had been more careful, Idris —

No.

Idris. This was *his* doing. *He* set the wall on them. *He* was responsible. If not for him, Niko would still be alive

Kole turned his face to the canopy. Warm sunlight peeked from the haze and soaked his scars. The forest was demolished, littered with broken and overturned trees, half buried under the banks of ash.

"Where is it now? The Black Wall," Kole croaked. The further he cast his gaze, the more barren the forest became, but the Black Wall was nowhere in sight.

"It retreated," Russé said grimly.

"And Idris?"

"Gone for now."

CHAPTER 8

Back at the southern camp, Kole tugged the shirt Charlie had given him over his head. The hem of the tunic fell past his knees, looking more like a dress. Cursing his child-like height, he tucked the extra fabric into his pants and pulled the drawstring taut. Then, he got to work on rolling up his pant legs. The lost elasticity of his skin made every move, twist, and turn more restricted. Bending over sent an uncomfortable tug up his back. It felt as if he were wearing clothes two sizes too small. Trapped in his own body. His fingers fumbled for the hem of his pants, but he couldn't quite reach. He pulled the material up from his knee instead, but his hands paused when he caught a glimpse of the ravaged skin on his calf. With a growl, he yanked the fabric over his ankle and let it pool around his feet to hide his scars.

Looping Goren's necklace over his head, he leaned against the windowsill of Darian's willow tree and stared out at the forming crowd of refugees beyond the curtain of leaves. Everyone had come for the vigil, it seemed. When Russé had brought him back to the southern camp a few hours ago with news of the orphans' destruction, Kole had been on full display: naked save for Russé's shirt wrapped around his waist. The refugees had stared—whispered—faces pale with terror. Kole's stomach twisted. They'd stopped looking at him as a shepherd. He was a freak now. A magnet for pity. An abomination like Idris.

He backed away from the window so his face would be obscured in the darkness in case one of the refugees grew bold and glanced into the willow.

Russé and Darian stood by the campfire, wearing matching grim expressions. Two people, a man and a woman Kole recognized as Harlow and Lucca, the leaders from the eastern and western camps, sat silent behind them.

"Shouldn't you be on your way?" Etta asked from the spiral staircase.

Kole moved his chin over his shoulder, trying to keep his full face from her view. "Shouldn't you?"

Etta gave a weak smile. She sat next to the hammock, where Vienna still lay unconscious, a wooden comb in her hands. "My place is here." She took the comb to Vienna's locks.

Etta had a moment of shock when Kole first walked in. Since then, she had remained neutral, as if trying not to make his appearance a big deal. A part of him appreciated it. The other part felt that ignoring it only made it more apparent.

"How is she?" he said, playing along. If she meant to pretend that nothing had changed, he could at least get an update out of her.

"Charlie said she's fine, and yet...." Etta's mouth fell to a worried line.

Vienna lay motionless, save for the steady rise and fall of her chest under the deer hide blanket. Her blonde curls dangled in one of Etta's hands while the other pulled the comb through them. The waves bounced back into place after each gentle stroke. Kole remembered how soft her hair had felt on his face.

"She is strong. She'll wake up," Etta said firmly, as if saying the words aloud would make them true. "I wouldn't go anyway, even if she were all right."

"Why not?"

"I suspect you know why." Etta eyed him. "The same reason you're biding your time at the window. So much death... it isn't easy to process. I'll grieve in my own time. Until then, I have other things to occupy me."

Kole let out a frustrated sigh. This went beyond grieving; it was about his burned skin and what he'd done. Hiding seemed like the last thing he should be doing. "I need to get out there. They were *my* family. I knew them best." He swallowed back the rising lump in his throat. "I just...."

"I know. And no one expects you to. There's no need to relive it."

The longer he looked at her, the more the lump swelled. He turned back to the window.

"Why don't you get some air? Clear your head."

He did need to get away. He had no desire to talk—to explain himself and be put on display. Staying here would only make him recall the last, painful memory of Niko, and Kole wasn't ready to accept it—to let him go. Not until Idris was dead.

Pushing from the window, Kole glanced to Vienna's sunstone blade on the table. While Etta was distracted, fussing over a tangle in Vienna's hair, he walked over, swiped the weapon, and tucked it in his pants. "You're right," he said after it lay safely hidden. "I'll get some air."

Etta smiled. "Good lad."

Leaving through the front door would draw attention. If he exited through the canopy, he had a better chance at sneaking out. Kole climbed the spiral stairs leading to the top of the house. Careful to stay hidden, he creaked the door open and slipped through, then rounded the trunk and bounded down the swinging bridge as a horn bellowed to mark the start of the vigil.

Kole tread lightly on the wooden planks to the edge of camp and descended to the floor. He strode into the forest, following the sounds of babbling water to a nearby stream.

As he knelt by the water, a new reflection stared back at him. His chubby cheeks looked hollow now, and the soft curve of his jaw had grown taut. Red, blotchy skin, riddled with thick cords of scar tissue, stretched across his face and neck only to disappear under the collar of his tunic. The skin under his left eye drooped, giving weight to the features below, and set one side of his mouth in a permanent frown. And his eyes. Still a dull gray-blue, now something about them made him feel like they belonged to a stranger.

As he tore his gaze from his reflection, he caught sight of the pendant dangling at his neck.

The Seven Souls.

That was who Idris was looking for—well, one of them, anyway. Idris had mentioned a Soul to Vienna under the Great Red. And for some reason, the Kayetan thought one was here in Solpate, hiding among the refugees. The notion was ridiculous. The seven gods had abandoned Ohr long ago. Even if it was somehow true, the shepherds knew every inch of the forest; they would know if someone else was hiding out here. A god wouldn't go unnoticed.

Kole had always been fond of the stories Goren told of the Souls. But now, after all that had happened, he began to doubt if they were as great as Goren had led the orphans to believe. They had created the very monstrosity that had slaughtered his camp and maimed his body. Goren had said that the Black Wall was a mistake. *Intentional or not, they're responsible.*

Kole wondered how many more had died from the wall. He remembered the worn map Goren had shown him on occasion, depicting the old world. Most of it had been scribbled out, updated with each move of the Black Wall, leaving only a portion of the southern hemisphere intact. Only Ohr remained. That blood — that scorched land — was on the Soul's hands. They were just as guilty as Idris and Savairo. All of them had played a part in taking Niko from him. Kole hated them for it. And he hated himself, too, because deep down he knew the harrowing truth. The small, accusing voice, no matter how hard he tried to silence it, kept creeping up in his conscience. *He* had led Idris to camp. The blame was his to share.

He squeezed the pendant so tightly it threatened to rupture his tender skin. He wanted to throw the necklace into the water and let the stream carry it far away from here. Arm stretched out, he readied to drop it, but he couldn't bring himself to do it. After all he had lost, he couldn't fathom tossing away the last piece of his former home.

Warm pink light filtered through the leaves of the forest as the sun set. Howls replaced the birds' melody around him, and the flickering of fireflies slowly emerged between the trunks.

He wasn't ready to go back and face sorry smiles. Some of the refugees would offer their condolences and support. Others would gawk at his scars and blame him as much as he blamed himself.

His eyes scanned the banks. Before he knew what he was doing, he gathered a handful of pebbles near the stream and piled them at the water's edge. Then, he dragged his finger through the mud and spelled out the dead: Goren, Niko, Dya. The list continued with every child who had perished. Kole whispered their names into the breeze as he wrote. When he reached the last, his heart grew heavy. A final drag of his finger and he wrote his own at the bottom.

Goren was gone, and with him, the only hope at unraveling Kole's past. He had lived his whole life thinking he was an orphan like the rest of the children — like Niko. Kole didn't know what to think anymore. If he wasn't an orphan, maybe he still had a family living in Socren. A mother. A father. *Real* siblings. He felt guilty for thinking that way. It didn't matter if he had a blood brother somewhere in the wide spaces of Ohr. Niko had been his *true* brother. And he was dead.

Kole pushed the sprouting hope aside as he caressed the rippled skin of his face. No one will claim me now. *Not like this.* He slammed his fist into his own name written in the mud. The lump in his throat returned, but he didn't bother holding it back this time. Instead of tears, his voice ripped from his throat, and he yelled into the evening air until his lungs gave out. He sat back, eyes up to the canopy as he slowed his breathes. A sharp pain came from his waist as his belly expanded with each breath. Hand caked in dirt, he touched his waistband where he had tucked away Vienna's odd, pulsing dagger.

Idris. That *abomination* had been following him around the forest ever since their encounter at the Great Red, using Kole as his pawn. He had been too stupid — too distracted to notice he was acting as the Kayetan's personal guide. It was time to use that to his advantage.

Kole gritted his teeth and stood. Any fear creeping up Kole's spine drowned in his growing rage as he strode from the stream and into the dense forest of sleeping ramblers. "I know where he is." Kole spun, his eyes darting for any sign of smoke. Only the trickling steam answered him. "Come out. I know where your god is." Kole touched the lump of fabric hiding the dagger. "Do you want your Soul or not?"

A tendril of smoke lazily weaved through the trunks. His hand instinctively went to the hilt, but he released. He had to stay calm or he would waste his chance. *"Aim for the heart. It's the only thing that will kill him."* Vienna's words calmed his twitching hand. He took in a slow breath as the creature formed before him.

"It was foolish to come alone," Idris said.

"If you kill me, you won't have your god."

"Kill you? Why would I kill you? It's a great feat to survive the Black Wall. I wouldn't want to deny you the infamy. So many will come to see your face. The mutilated shepherd."

Kole swallowed. This was all a game to the Kayetan, and for whatever reason, Kole seemed to be Idris' favorite pawn. The only upper-hand Kole possessed sat tucked away in his waistband. *Be calm. Be smart.*

"I see right through you, shepherd. You don't have what I seek. So I wonder... why have you called on me?"

"You know why," Kole spat.

Idris' dark form glided around Kole, circling him like a wolf eager to pounce. "Have you come to kill me, young shepherd?" He pointed a claw into his churning black form where his heart should be. "Do it. Stab me right here. I'll make it easy for you. I won't even move."

Kole shuddered. It was a twisted ruse. But a part of him felt tempted. His legs twitched beneath him, urging him to charge; to kill Idris as savagely as the Black Wall had killed Niko, to repay every ounce of agony he had cast on him and the refugees. But Kole wanted more than just to kill the Kayetan. He wanted to make him suffer.

"Avenge your family. That's what you want, isn't it? Justice?"

"Why did you kill them?" Despite his best efforts to sound confident, Kole's voice betrayed him, cracking as Niko's image from the dream—skin melting away from his body—found its way to the surface.

"*I* didn't kill them. The wall did that."

"You moved it!"

"Yes, well, Savairo's orders. I told you he was an impatient man. Besides, I have found people are much more eager to talk after seeing what *could* become of them. It holds more power than a mere threat, don't you think?"

Kole sneered. Idris wasn't just talking about the orphans, he was talking about *him*. Kole refused to let Niko and the others be reduced to a bargaining chip. Their death and Kole's... mutilation, wouldn't be used to scare the others into submission. "You took everything from me."

Idris floated forward, bringing the swirling smoke of his body inches away from Kole. "Do it. I deserve it."

With a cry of rage, Kole gave in to his instincts. He pulled Vienna's dagger from the folds of his pants, his stiff hands awkward around the hilt, and stabbed Idris square in the heart.

White light flashed in the darkening forest, followed by a shrill of pain, and the Kayetan burst into a cloud of smoke.

Then, silence. A minute passed. Kole's shoulders slumped forward. A heaviness lifted away from him, and he took in a slow breath. But his relief was short lived as a deep-throated laugh erupted from the trees.

"No." Kole glanced around, then scrutinized the sunstone blade. He hadn't missed. He hadn't. *Why didn't it work?*

"You think a hunk of rock can kill me?" Idris reformed next to a nearby tree. A pillar of smoke encapsulated the Kayetan's body. He grew within it, becoming as tall and wide as the surrounding trees. His claws extended to the length of broadswords.

Kole's heart pounded against his rib cage. He stepped back, afraid to run—afraid to take his eyes from the gargantuan Kayetan.

"That sorcery may work on those filthy half-breeds," Idris bellowed, "but you'll find I am much more resilient. Only my master is both creator and reaper."

The smoke pillar faded. Idris loomed over Kole, claws twitching, then the Kayetan stepped forward.

Kole ran. His legs pulsed, but his stride was smaller than before. The scars—his skin—prevented him from reaching his former speed and made his gait uneven, more of a hobble than a run.

As the silver moonlight poured down on the forest, the trees slowly began to awaken. Kole wrapped his arms around the root of a rambler as it sprang from the soil next to him and half-climbed, half-scooted himself up to the trunk. It wasn't the fastest tree, but it moved far quicker than his new legs could, and he lacked the leisure of waiting for something more manageable. Kole grabbed hold of a root and sliced it with his blade, spurring the rambler to action. The tree paused and waited for his command.

He risked a look over his shoulder. Idris gained on him, his shadowed body passing through the scurrying trees like a thick fog. Kole pulled back on the root and his rambler lurched forward.

A horn sounded behind him: three long notes. A signal. Someone was calling for a retreat. Kole ignored it at first, assuming a scout had spotted the Kayetan's smoke and raised the alarm, but the horn sounded again: the familiar, unwavering draw Russé or Goren used as a signal for curfew. It seemed meant for Kole. Russé was calling him back. He tugged the root and veered the rambler toward camp.

The canopy crunched above. Kole hugged the trunk as his rambler quaked. Wood and leaves plummeted past him like an avalanche. He peeked up, eyes following the trunk, to see a jagged stump. The rambler's canopy was gone, slashed clean off by the Kayetan's massive claws. The bald tree trembled. Kole grabbed the roots and urged it faster as Idris drew back for another swipe, but the rambler seized up, too distracted from its injury to follow commands.

Kole threw himself to the ground. His legs buckled, and he rolled onto the tender skin of his back. He winced. A shadow overhead cut the pain short and brought his attention to Idris, who tore his claw through the rambler's trunk, where Kole had stood a second earlier, and split it in two. Kole clambered to his feet and pushed his way through the crawling roots of the nearest tree. He tried to position himself directly under the thick trunk to stay hidden from Idris' view, but he struggled to keep pace. His body would soon fail him. The exhaustion had already taken hold. But the camp outposts came into sight, less than a hundred meters away. Normally, Kole would have thought little of the distance—he had always been a fast runner—but as he limped beneath the trunk, falling behind the rambler by the second, he knew it now came with great risk.

Now or never. Taking in a deep breath, Kole zigzagged through the veil of crawling roots and darted for the bridges.

Another long draw of a horn sounded. He glanced up.

Russé stood on the bridge, horn to his mouth, and waved his staff at Kole.

Kole's feet pounded hard over the grass as he closed the distance, his stride as quick as his racing heart. Black smoke swirled in the corner of his eye, but his focus locked onto Russé. He didn't need to look back to know that Idris was gaining on him.

A whoosh, like the sound of an arrow whizzing through the air, swept overhead, drawing louder as it closed in on him. Kole dove, eyes squeezed shut, anticipating the strike of the claw on his back.

It never came.

Instead, the Kayetan shrilled.

Kole flipped to his back. His dive had brought him to a stop beneath Russé's bridge. A root, sprouted from the ground by Kole's feet, held Idris' claw like a shackle and halted the creature's attack.

Russé pointed his staff at the enlarged shadow. With a wave of the gnarled wood, the root tossed the Kayetan's arm away and receded into the soil.

Idris stumbled back, gave a low growl, and charged again. Before the Kayetan could take his second step, a slam came from above — the knock of wood hitting wood.

The ground rumbled. Roots shot up around Kole, showering him in dirt. He scrambled back in horror as a living, squirming fence of vines and roots rose up to his mentor. They continued to grow, arcing overhead until they tangled themselves together at the top. With a sweep of his head, Kole realized the entire refugee camp had been encased in a dome-like cage.

Through the gaps in the woven vines, Kole saw Idris' attack ricochet off the root wall. The Kayetan stood there for a moment — silent — as if planning his next move. Then, a deep gurgling laugh thundered through camp. It shook Kole's bones.

"I wondered how many I'd have to kill before you'd show your face." Idris shrunk to his original size as he spoke.

Russé stood tall on the bridge.

"You couldn't hide forever. You will drain yourself before long, Risil, and when you do, I will be waiting." With a jet of smoke, Idris retreated into the forest.

Risil. The name rang clear in Kole's head. He narrowed in on Russé.

Risil, the Green Soul. One of the Seven. This was him? Russé was the god of nature? The Kayetan must be mistaken.

Kole froze as Russé crossed the swinging bridge and descended the vine ladder to the forest floor. As Russé approached, his eyes caught Kole's.

Kole recoiled. In that instant, he didn't recognize the person striding toward him. Though the man had the same thin, wrinkled skin, and the same puffy bags under his eyes as his mentor, something rippled under the surface of his blue eyes that Kole had never noticed before: a depth—an alienness that made the hair on Kole's neck stand on end.

Russé stopped in front of the crowd of refugees that had formed under the bridge behind Kole.

Darian stepped forward. "How did you—who are you?"

For once, Kole was relieved Darian had opened his mouth, because it drew Russé's eyes away from him.

"I would like to speak with the camp leaders in the willow." No one uttered a word as Russé walked to Darian's house. "You, too, Kole," he said, then disappeared inside the trunk.

CHAPTER 9

"Is it true? You're a Soul?" Though his body ached from running, and his fall off the rambler had left the skin on his back raw, Kole refused to sit. His fingers fiddled with the loose fabric of his shirt, keeping it from touching tender skin, as he leaned against the wall of the trunk and waited for the answer.

"Yes," Russé said from the table.

Kole's hand moved to Goren's necklace hidden beneath his tunic. What little awe he felt quickly morphed to anger. He glared at the Soul. "You let them die."

Silence weighed on the room.

Russé avoided his gaze.

"Didn't think I'd figure it out, did you?" He stepped toward the Soul. "You had the power to summon a barrier around the entire camp, but you couldn't save Niko? You could've saved the orphans. You had the power. You *still* do. You just refused to use it."

"Kole." Russé reached out a hand. "It's not that simple."

He slapped it away. "They died because of you. Just say it. You and your ramblers let them burn!"

Horror struck the three camp leaders' faces.

"Is this true?" Darian's raspy voice came quiet.

"No," Russé roared. "The Black Wall is beyond my power. I had to choose. There was nothing I could do for them. I could only save one. Everything has its limits."

"He *did* save us from Idris," Lucca said, dipping her head to the window, where the sliver between the closed curtains allowed a glimpse of the dome of roots outside.

No matter what the Soul said, nothing could simmer the pain in Kole's heart or redeem his faith while the screams of the dead played fresh in his mind. "You should've told me what you were."

Darian's face reddened. "*You*? He should've told *us*." He pointed a stubby, accusing finger at Russé.

"I didn't find it necessary at the time," Russé said. His voice sounded firm, but his back sagged as if the encounter with Idris had exhausted him.

"Necessary," Darian scoffed. He looked to the other camp leaders for support, but Lucca and Harlow sat quietly by the window, their eyes hard on Russé. "What proof do we have that he's a god? He could very well be a sorcerer trying to fool us. Savairo can create demons with his magic. Surely a sorcerer could summon nature as easily," Darian said, shooting a suspicious gaze at Russé.

"I have a feeling you will dismiss any proof I offer, and I have neither the desire nor the strength to dance for you. Believe what you want, Darian, but Idris is out there waiting for the slightest falter in my defenses. And falter they will," Russé said.

Kole thought back to what Idris had said to Vienna during their battle. He turned to Russé. "You were imprisoned in the Great Red, weren't you?"

Something passed over his mentor's face. It disappeared before Kole could pinpoint it. "Yes."

"By who? How did you escape?" asked Kole.

Russé stayed quiet.

Kole let out a quick breath and shook his head. "Always evading questions." Why hadn't Kole seen it? But how could he? A god? That answer remained absent on the list of any possibilities. More than that, Kole had been so wrapped up in becoming a shepherd, trying to impress and reach the level of skill Russé held when it came to shepherding. All a scam. Everything. *What a fool I am.* No wonder his mentor held such extraordinary talents with the trees. The Soul made the very creatures he controlled—held a bond Kole could never hope to possess. He must have been such an easy target, too; gobbling up everything Russé had to say; living by his advice. And why shouldn't he? The old man was his mentor. Russé was supposed to have been someone he could trust.

Russé straightened. "I know you all have questions, but right now we need to discuss our situation with the Kayetan."

"*Our* situation? Oh, no." Darian waved a hand at him. "*You* are the one he wants. *You* are the one who brought this 'situation' to us. If not for you and your 'apprentice' the Kayetan never would've found us."

Kole wound the fabric of his oversized shirt around his fingers to keep his temper at bay. Normally, he'd snap back at Darian, but he held his tongue, partly because he agreed with him. Though Kole knew he held some responsibility, Russé deserved blame for the rest. He had every opportunity — and power — to stop this. Darian had a point: Idris wanted *him,* not Kole.

"Kole is not to blame," said Russé. "I take full responsibility for my apprentice."

Kole's eyes narrowed. "I'm not some child with a night terror. I don't need your protection."

"Then accept the consequences." Darian sneered and raised a hand. "I move to have Russé and Kole banished from Solpate."

Kole pushed from the wall. "Why are you banishing *me*? Idris only wants him. If we give him up, we might be able to bargain his release for our lives." Russé sent him a sharp look. Kole folded his arms, glaring in return.

"Need I remind you, our camp was discovered under your watch, *Shepherd* Kole," Darian spat. "Banishment is a merciful sentence."

"Hasn't he been through enough?" Lucca gave Kole a sympathetic frown, then adverted her gaze.

Kole stared at his feet, a fire in his cheeks. The last thing he wanted was sympathy. He could handle this on his own.

"Consequences don't alter because he's been...." Darian paused. Kole could've sworn he heard the beginning sounds of 'mutilated' leave his mouth. " ...injured." Darian turned to the window. "But the kid is right. We could make a deal with the creature. Hand the Soul over in exchange for a truce."

"A deal with Idris is a deal with Savairo," Russé said. "Do you really think he will honor an agreement with those who have fled from his rule?"

Darian stepped forward. "Idris said —"

"Think of the words you are about to say," Russé scolded. "You are putting your trust in one of Savairo's engineered experiments. The creature who wiped out the northern camp. Why would he not lay the same fate upon you after the deal is made?" His blue eyes cast over them. "If you think Savairo will let you continue to live here without repercussions, you are all fools. He will come for you."

Darian folded his arms over his chest, looking very much like a reprimanded child.

"Then what do you propose we do?" Harlow asked from the window.

"We do what should have been done ten years ago," said Russé. "We fight."

Kole rolled his eyes. The Soul used the word 'we' as if he counted as one of the refugees—as if he understood the danger they faced. They had no all-powerful magic to defend themselves. Not against Idris or the Black Wall.

Darian's lip stiffened. "You want to go to *war* with Savairo? The refugees know nothing of battle. We'll be slaughtered."

"Not if we join forces with the Liberation. With their help, we can rally the peoples of Socren," said Russé. "There is strength in numbers."

"Numbers isn't the problem, skill is. Half of them have never held a sword," Darian snapped.

"Then we play to our strengths. These people are skilled hunters. Many are keen with a bow."

The interior of the willow fell silent for a long moment. Kole could hear Darian's heavy breaths from across the room.

Could they go to war? Kole never thought of the refugees as fighters, not soldiers at least. His only experience came from the few practice bouts he'd had with Niko, but that was all for sport, and they had used fallen branches. Kole held no chance against someone in a real match, much less a soldier. Especially not now with his... limitations. As much as Kole hated to agree with Darian *again*, he was the only one making any sense.

Finally, Lucca stood, her wiry gray hair standing on end. "I agree with Russé. We have grown cowardly here in the forest. Hiding— running from our problems. What did we expect? Savairo won't go away. And what about all of our people still living under his tyranny in the city? They deserve freedom just as we have."

Darian threw his hands out, gesturing to the walls of the willow. "You call this freedom?"

"It's damn well better than Socren," Lucca said firmly.

Harlow's hulking form stepped next to Lucca. He gave her a strong pat on the back. "Aye. It's about time we acted. Let's make a stand."

"How can you blindly agree with the Soul? Need I remind you, he's been hiding his identity from us. How can you trust him?" said Darian.

"He is a god, Darian," Lucca answered. She lifted her sleeve, exposing a black tattoo on the soft side of her forearm. The symbol matched the one hanging around Kole's neck. "If I can't put my trust in a Soul, then there is nothing left in this world worthy of it."

Kole could think of a thousand things more worthy. He had always liked Lucca. Though she acted a bit odd at times, she was intelligent and kind. Still, how could she so easily forgive Russé's treachery? He had betrayed them. Stood by while dozens were slain. How could she not see it?

Kole's gaze fell to his pendent. All his life he had believed the Souls were real. He prayed to them in his times of need. Now one stood before him, and he didn't know what to think. His mentor hardly matched what he'd envisioned a Soul to look like—to act like. It seemed strange, but somehow *seeing* a Soul made him believe in them a little less.

Russé massaged his temples. "We must reach a decision before Idris grows impatient and decides to set the Black Wall on us again."

"Well, I believe him," Lucca said.

"As do I," Harlow agreed beside her.

Kole held his tongue as Darian's cheeks turned a peculiar shade of purple. "Are you trying to manipulate me with threats of the Black Wall? We don't even know if he was the one who moved it."

"He did," Kole croaked, trying not to replay the scene in his head. He'd avoid giving weight to Russé's argument, but he couldn't lie when the lives of every refugee hung on the line.

"Coming from a truly reliable source," Darian said through his teeth. He turned his attention to the group. "We need evidence—proof of his command over the wall. We can't risk uprooting the refugees for hunches and maybes. Word alone won't cut it."

"You're more willing to endanger everyone?" Lucca stepped forward, fire in her eyes. "If you weren't such a stubborn ass—"

Harlow held her back with a strong arm. "He'll come around."

"Convincing you isn't my priority," Russé said, voice weak. "Goren is dead. His vote falls to me. As long as Lucca and Harlow agree, you are outnumbered."

"The northern camp no longer stands. It gets no vote," Darian fumed.

Harlow turned to Kole. "Kole lives. The camp remains."

Lucca dipped her head.

Russé collapsed into a chair with a wheeze. "My energy is waning. Make a decision or we will be at Idris' mercy."

Harlow peered out the window. "How long do we have?"

"Half hour. Maybe less." Russé sagged against the wooden table still stained with Lily's blood.

"War is the best plan we've got," Lucca said.

"It's the *only* plan we've got," Harlow said.

"We must find a way to agree on this," Lucca said. "Think about the refugees, Darian. Put your prejudice aside and act the title you were given." Darian sneered, but Lucca held his gaze. "They are *all* counting on us. We'll never get a chance like this. We have a *Soul* on our side. He's going to help us win back our city."

Russé flinched at her words.

A minute ticked by. Finally, Darian said, "And just how do you propose we go about this with the Kayetan keeping watch over our every move?"

"Leave him to me," said Russé. "Kole and I will lure him out, then make our way to Socren."

"What?" Kole dropped the hem of his shirt.

"Take him," Darian said. "I don't need any more trouble."

"I'm not going with him," Kole said fiercely. "I'm sure a *god* is quite capable of delivering a message on his own."

"I need someone to accompany me," said Russé.

"Then take a shepherd." Kole motioned to his body. "I'd only slow you down."

"I can help with that."

He didn't know what Russé meant, and he didn't care. "No."

"Please. I need someone I can trust."

Kole forced a laugh. "Well, so do I." *Someone you can trust? The gall.* The real question was if he could trust Russé. How could he believe anything his mentor—no—this *Soul* said? He'd had every opportunity to trust Kole with this. Ten years of opportunity. *Some mentor. Some god.* And even now, no matter what the Soul said, Kole sensed he was still holding something back.

"Do you wish to stay here?"

Kole winced at Russé's question. He hadn't thought that far ahead. If he'd been asked that a week ago, he would have said yes. Solpate was home. The only one he remembered, anyhow. But Niko was dead. And the ramblers... they weren't home anymore. When he looked at them, he no longer saw the magic that had driven him to become a shepherd. He saw their roots wrapped around his body. He saw them dragging him from the hands of death while his friends burned below. Every second he spent here reminded him of the screams, the ash and fire.

If Kole stayed, he would be prey to every accusing eye in camp. Rightfully so. The refugees would stare at his scars. They would whisper and question what he had done to stop Idris, and Kole would have no excuse because none existed. Why had he insisted on dealing with the Kayetan alone? His desperation to prove himself as a shepherd had put them here.

Grief and guilt made his chest ache. He wanted to sink into the floor and forget any of this had happened. Go back in time and change things. The only thing keeping him functioning was the deep-seated fury blooming from his belly, calling him to Idris. *That abomination will pay for every life he took. For what he did to me.*

And like that, his heart hardened. Kole knew where he wanted to be—what he wanted to do. He clenched his jaw, wondering if this had been Russé's plan all along. Despite an inner voice screaming at him that he was playing right into Russé's hands, his mind was set. He would see to Idris' death, even if it meant risking his own.

"Fine." Kole stared the Soul in the eye. "But the trust isn't mutual."

"Are you ready?" Russé asked, his hand on the base of the towering wall of roots.

Kole nodded and entangled his fingers in the forest stag's mossy neck.

Three days. That was the time Russé and the others had agreed upon. On the morning of the fourth, they would march on Socren and take their city back from Savairo. The details remained obscure—they had no time with Russé's waning strength. Even now, the old Soul shook, though he tried his best to hide it. But their job was simple enough: travel to Socren and convince the Liberation to join the refugees' rebellion. They would agree. They had to. The refugees' survival depended on it.

A crowd of refugees had formed behind them, some eyeing the Soul in wonder and curiosity while others held accusing, suspicious expressions. For a moment, Kole felt a twinge of relief as their gazes were drawn away from him; not that they could stare at his face any longer, as Kole had wrapped Charlie's extra bandages around himself in a makeshift balaclava. But his hands were still exposed. He'd pulled the sleeves down as much as he could, balling the fabric in his palms to keep them from view.

Kole shifted on his steed. Only the thin layer of his pants protected his inner thighs from the animal's rough back. It pained him, but he stayed quiet in lack of any other option. At least Charlie had taken care of his back. The herbalist had insisted on cleaning and wrapping it before Kole and Russé departed.

"Idris will be right on our tail once I bring down the wall. We ride hard and fast straight to the mountains. If anything goes wrong, run. *I'll* deal with the Kayetan. Understand?"

Kole turned back to his mentor, avoiding his gaze, and nodded.

Russé removed his hand from the roots and mounted his own stag.

They had picked Darian's most prized animals from the corral: Nali and Alon. Forest stags proved agile beasts to begin with, but these two were magnificently bred. If nothing else, Darian had done well creating the perfect mount for a place like Solpate. Strong muscles rippled beneath their bark skin, giving their powerful legs the strength they needed to make quick turns and high jumps at a moment's notice. They had been bred for speed—for agility—and it showed.

Kole patted Nali's barky neck. *It doesn't matter how fast Darian bred you to be. You just need to be faster than Idris.*

The pair traveled light, packing a few pieces of dried meat in a small saddlebag on Nali's rump, to keep from meddling with the animal's natural balance. Aside from food, Kole carried the borrowed clothes on his back and Vienna's sunstone knife on his belt.

Cool air hit his face as the mess of roots and vines above parted to reveal the velvet-black sky. Moonlight poured down on them like a pitcher of cold creek water. Goosebumps crawled up Kole's arms, either from the breeze or the anticipation bubbling in the depths of his gut.

Russé inched his stag forward.

Nali's heart quickened under Kole. Could he sense it too? The danger lurking beyond Russé's wall.

The earth sucked up the last of the roots, and Russé kicked off.

Nali's nostrils flared as he sprang after Russé and Alon. Tensing at the sudden burst of speed, he curled his fingers around the thick vines on Nali's neck, hoping it would be enough to stay mounted. The ramblers rushed by in a blur as Kole bobbed violently atop the stag, who stayed tight on Alon's tail. They synchronized, weaving back and forth among the walking trees, their strides fluid and effortless despite the terrain.

Minutes turned to an hour and still no sign of the Kayetan.

The cramping in Kole's legs, flexed tight around Nali's belly, made every passing moment feel longer, and the constant bouncing of the stag's stride, no matter how gentle, sent fire to his skin. Kole worried he couldn't last much longer. Gaze fixed on the stag's neck, covered in plush moss, he willed his skin to stay intact. He'd rather not add bloodied legs to his list of injuries.

A shadow rolled over him. Kole looked up to see a jet of smoke trailing overhead.

"Go!" Kole yelled. The stags bleated in response and turned west, quickening their pace.

The Kayetan rolled up next to Nali. Kole leaned left, leading the stag away. He turned in time to see a tendril of smoke wrap around the animal's back legs. Nali let out an agonizing bleat and stumbled, sending Kole into the air. Before he landed in the grass, a root caught him around the waist and tugged his body in the opposite direction, toward Russé's racing stag. The next thing he knew, Kole was sitting on Alon's back in front of Russé, where the root had dumped him.

Russé gave the animal a brisk pat. "Come on, Alon. Show me what you were bred for." The stag bleated and lengthened his stride.

The Kayetan came up fast on Alon's side. Kole clung onto the speeding stag as the forest streaked past. He could feel Alon's muscles twitching beneath him. The animal's body shuddered as his breaths turned to labored grunts. Alon had reached his limit, and Idris gained on them.

"Hold on," Russé shouted as a rambler stepped in their path.

Kole's fingers grew numb from squeezing. He pressed his face into the animal's neck, and Alon kicked off the floor. They soared up, landing on the rambler's roots with a jerk and galloped around the edge of the trunk. Another rambler came in range, and the stag leapt again, hopping from root to root until they made their way to solid ground. Kole looked back, hoping the maneuver had thrown Idris off their tail.

It hadn't.

Idris raised one long, sickle-like claw, and slashed the stag's back leg. With a sickening cry, Alon collapsed, and Kole and Russé tumbled into the grass.

Russé got up first. He dragged Kole to his feet and pushed him into a run. Kole only noticed the ground vibrating beneath him once it grew so strong, it nearly sent him to his knees. Ahead, the surrounding ramblers dropped to their trunks and raised their roots. Any confusion vanished when Kole saw Russé pointing his staff at them. The ramblers linked together, creating a road of twisting roots before them. Kole slowed as he approached, but Russé put a hand on his back and shoved him forward.

"Trust them!" Russé shouted as he jumped on.

Kole reluctantly followed. When his shoes touched the tangled roots, they rolled forward and swelled like an ocean wave. The trees up the path joined their roots to the hill, retracting them as Kole and Russé passed by. All the while, the shepherds ran at the crest, feet pounding over the uneven path.

Kole caught a toe between the churning vines. He lurched forward. A root seized his waist, propping him back up before he missed his next stride. Trusting them to keep him upright, Kole quickened his pace as much as his scarred skin and creeping exhaustion would allow, despite the throbbing wound on his back fighting against him.

Idris screeched behind them. It sounded more distant than before, but Kole was too scared to check.

They closed in on the mountains, which were minutes away at this speed, but it wouldn't matter. He saw no use trying to fight the Kayetan: Vienna's knife did nothing, and they couldn't outrun him. Kole hoped Russé had a plan.

As the trees thinned, dawn broke.

Reaching the tree line, the hill of roots rose and thrust the shepherds into the air. Kole flailed, blinded by the harsh morning sun, and landed on the rocky base of the mountain.

A shrill of pure hatred pierced the air.

Kole's eyes flicked back to the forest. Idris hurled himself at them. The moment his form left the shadows of the trees, he exploded into a cloud of smog and reformed in the shade cast down by the last row of anchoring ramblers.

Kole scrambled to his feet and lunged for the slope, but Russé grabbed his elbow.

"Wait."

Kole turned, the panic coursing through his own body clearly lost on the old shepherd, who stood his ground, a curious eye on Idris. "Wait for him to kill us? Are you crazy?"

"Look."

Though reluctant, Kole followed the old man's gaze. He flinched as Idris charged for them once more, but the Kayetan burst in a dark fog at barrier of the shade. *He can't cross it.* It seemed Idris had a weakness after all: direct sunlight. Kole's body sagged in relief. "Bound to the shadows."

"Seems that way," Russé said weakly.

Idris hissed and paced the tree line.

Russé rose and slouched into his staff, his forehead pressed against the smooth wood as he struggled to slow his breaths.

"You all right?" Kole asked, less out of concern and more because he wasn't too keen on carrying the Soul up the mountain. Despite saving his skin back there, Kole had yet to forgive. Far from it.

Russé nodded and turned to the mountain. "We'll need to be swift. If night falls and we haven't reached Socren...."

Idris will catch up to us. Kole turned south and took in the only obstacle standing between them and Socren.

The Poleer mountain range jutted through the rich earth like a row of giant, rotten teeth, spanning east and west as far as Kole could see. They were steep and bare like the bones of a scavenged animal. Uneasiness swept over Kole. They could no longer count on the protection of the ramblers.

CHAPTER 10

The ascent pushed Kole's limits. Hours had gone by, yet they barely made it halfway up the mountain. The climb had taken a toll on his new body. His thin skin rubbed raw in his boots, and the insides of his arms and legs stung with every swipe against his clothes. Dread filled Kole as the gradual slopes came to an end. Perilous cliffs soared high above them toward the clear cerulean sky, some reaching as high as the summit, while others were short and sharp like the tip of a blade.

"It looks like we climb from here," Russé said, hands on his hips. Kole could tell from his set jaw that his mentor was dreading the ascent as much as him.

Kole approached the cliff and held out a hand to test his mobility. The skin under his arms pulled. Similar to his limited stride, he couldn't stretch out completely like he used to. He stepped back and cursed himself. "Unless you mean to leave me behind, we should take another route."

Russé wordlessly approached the cliff and pressed the smooth tip of staff against the rock.

"What are you doing?"

"Helping."

A dozen roots sprouted from Russé's staff and bore into the sheer rock face. They wriggled into the stone, sending a web of micro fractures up and down the wall. Little by little, the staff shrunk as the wood disappeared into the mountain. The roots looped and tangled within the rock. Kole stepped back from the wall and realized they had formed a lattice of new holds.

"Grab on. They'll do the rest."

Kole swept a finger across a root. "Your staff is gone."

"Not gone—changed."

"It's enchanted?"

"No. I shaped it from a fallen branch years ago."

"How does it work? Your magic."

"In my current state, I can only shape plant life, not create it."

Kole looked him up and down. "You have other... states?"

Russé sent a worried glance toward the afternoon sun. "Something like that. As long as I have a piece of wood or leaf, I can use my power."

"So, you—"

"Grab hold. We haven't much time," Russé said. "I will answer your every question when we get to Socren. I promise."

Kole frowned. "You never change," he muttered, then gripped the roots peeking out from the cliff. The moment he touched them, the roots at his feet jutted out and flattened into a wide platform big enough for his foot. He stepped onto it, surprised that it held under his weight. Another root widened above it, forming a makeshift staircase.

Russé climbed beside him the old-fashioned way. After Kole's foot left the bottom root, he understood why the old man took to climbing. The root sank back into the rock and another sprouted around his knee to present the next step. Two steps at a time. Enough for one person only. Kole kept his hands on the side of the cliff for stability. Though far easier than traditional climbing, an hour of this left his palms raw and hot. With the sun beating down on him and the constant, slow trudge up the cliff, Kole's body grew uncomfortably warm. Out of habit, he moved to wipe the sweat from his brow but found the balaclava bone dry. Kole glanced to Russé, whose body was drenched, then examined his own arms. Not a bead of water.

The bandage over Kole's forehead, loosened by his touch, fell into his eyes. He jerked his head back and missed the next step. Vision obscured, he blindly reached for the wall as a sense of weightlessness crept into his stomach. A deafening crack sounded from the cliff and something coiled around his waist and pulled him forward. After regaining his balance, Kole pushed the cloth from his eyes. The staff had shot out a root to keep him from falling. Kole sighed and forced himself not to look down.

"Are you all right?"

The incident had pushed his already racing heart to its limit. "I have to stop."

"There's a landing maybe twenty meters up. We can rest there."

Kole closed his eyes. Forehead pressed into sun-heated rock, he took a deep breath and nodded.

The shepherds pushed on for another five minutes until they reached the landing. They still had a good hour's climb before the summit, but Kole appreciated the brief respite. He stretched his stiff muscles, then unwrapped the cloth over his face so the wind could cool him. Lowering himself to the edge of the cliff, he dangled his feet off the rocky shelf while Russé propped himself up against their next endeavor. Kole drank deeply from his waterskin, then drenched his bandages and re-wrapped them over his head. His skin cooled on contact. Though his entire body stung like an open wound—especially his back, where the agitated scabs had reopened—he appreciated the small relief the cool water granted.

Kole cast his attention to the forest. A green ocean spread out before him. From this height, the trees looked no bigger than blades of grass. In the distance, Kole could just make out a patch of bald, gray land where the Black Wall had swept through two nights ago. He recalled the heat of the flames. The feel of his fingers on Niko's wrist. His throat twitched, still raw from the moment he'd learned Niko's fate. He swallowed, fighting against the water collecting in his eyes. The sooner they made it over the peak, the faster he'd be free of the constant reminder. His eyes fell to his hands, raw and mangled with scar tissue. He would never be free of the memories. Not when the biggest reminder covered his entire body.

"I think there's a clear path to the top." Russé glanced to the sun, whose bottom curve floated above the horizon.

Kole could see the worry on his face. The Soul knew just as well as Kole that they'd never make it to Socren before nightfall. Soon Idris could escape the confinement of the shadows and follow them up the mountain. Kole only hoped they could reach the summit before dusk. They'd be easily slaughtered hanging from the mountain.

"Are you ready?"

"Do I really have a choice?"

Grueling. It was the only word Kole could think of to describe the climb. His muscles cramped, and his skin burned from the constant movement.

"Only a little further," Russé wheezed from the cliff beside him, though it seemed like the Soul was speaking more to himself.

They reached a small plateau at the top. Russé and Kole both collapsed onto the rock. He examined his hands: torn and angry, almost as if he had stuck them in boiling water.

Russé gripped the lattice. It shook at his touch, and the roots sucked out of the rock, reshaping into his old, worn staff. "We won't make it."

"What do we do?" Kole panted.

"I don't know." Russé stood, a pensive look on his face. "Get as far as we can. Find a place to hide."

A warm breeze rolled over the southern side of the mountain, carrying with it a caustic odor. Kole gagged. He could tell by Russé's contorted face that he smelled it too. "What is that?"

Russé wandered to the southern edge of the plateau. His jaw twitched as he stared down.

With a wince, Kole pushed to his feet.

Russé turned, face pale. "*Don't –*"

Too late. Kole stared down on a horrific scene.

At the end of the plateau, the mountain took a drastic dip, sloping into a wide, shallow basin, no more than fifteen meters deep. It wasn't the basin itself that made Kole's blood run cold, but rather what it contained. Hundreds of men, women, and children lay within. Their dull eyes stared up at him – bored into him. The bodies lay tangled together, all in various stages of decomposition. Some looked fresh and well preserved, mummified by the sun, while others had turned black and rotted away; their stained bones peeking out beneath weathered skin.

Kole's stomach convulsed. Quickly unraveling the cloth around his face, he turned away from the basin, scene still burned into his mind, and retched.

Stomach drained, Kole spoke in a whisper, "Savairo did this?"

Russé bowed his head. "A dumping ground."

"He killed all of those people?" Kole had heard the stories: the rumors of Savairo's sadistic nature. He thought he knew what they were getting into when he agreed to come to the city. Kole had always guessed the camp leaders withheld certain stories, watering the others down for the little ones. Now he understood why.

"I'm sure they're not the only ones." Russé leaned into his staff.

Kole clenched his fists. "How could he do this? How could anyone?"

"You'd be surprised of the evil that exists outside of Solpate. Worse, I don't think they had a quick death."

"What do you mean?"

"The markings on the bodies. Those wounds alone wouldn't be enough to end a life, and they're too precise for torture."

Kole ground his teeth. These people – these children – were used as fodder. Children the Liberation had been unable to save. Niko's family.

His family. Is that how they ended up? A life Savairo deemed so worthless that when their use was spent, he robbed them of a proper burial. No one deserved that.

May the lost find their way, he thought, unable to bring the words to his lips. "This is what's been happening while we've been in the forest? Why were we hiding? They needed our help."

Kole buried his head in his hands. He had been so content in Solpate, living with the shepherds and the orphans, that he never felt the need to come back to the city for anything. But if he had known what was happening—that others suffered in his place....

He scolded himself. Of course he knew. Kole had heard the stories. But never in his darkest nightmares could he have imagined this.

"Not everyone can be saved," Russé said softly.

"Maybe more would have lived if the refugees stayed and fought instead of cowering away behind the mountain," Kole snapped.

"We can't know that."

"You raised us blind. We could've helped—done *something*—but you never gave us the choice! The shepherds never *helped. You did nothing*!"

A shadow passed over the Soul's face. He blinked it away. "We're helping now."

Kole thrust a finger at the basin. "I'm sure *they're* thrilled to hear it."

Russé opened his mouth as if he was going to argue, then closed it.

"We have to stop him. Savairo and his Kayetans have taken too much. It's time we took something from *him*." Kole walked to edge of the northern cliff. "We start with Idris. Here and now. This was you're plan, wasn't it? To fight? So do it. Use your power, Risil." Russé flinched as Kole said his true name. "Kill the Kayetan before he hurts anyone else."

"I am drained. I couldn't defeat him alone even if I wanted to."

"You won't be alone."

Russé's face hardened. "I will not allow you to put yourself in such danger. I won't make that mistake again."

"You won't *allow* it? Is that what this is coming down to? I am not yours to control. If you were never a real shepherd, I was never your apprentice. I have no loyalties to you anymore."

How could Russé possibly not understand the weight of what he'd done? He'd betrayed Kole. And with that came consequences. Kole wasn't Lucca. He wouldn't excuse Russé's behavior because he was a god. If anything it only made it worse. "It could've been different. I could've helped you. If you only told me before... more might've survived."

Russé's lips drew back in a taut line. "The past cannot be changed." Something flashed behind his blue eyes. Remorse? Guilt?

Kole ignored it. "You think I should be grateful you saved me? You should've let me die with Niko." Kole clenched his jaw at his friend's name. The tears came despite his efforts to subdue them. "What gives me the right to live over him? Over all of them. You have this weird obsession with keeping me safe, and I've never understood why."

"Because you are the only one who can take down the Black Wall!" Russé broke from his glare and turned away.

Kole paused, repeating Russé's words in his head, trying to make sense of them. "What?"

A terrible screech echoed up the peak. Kole and Russé had grown so engrossed in their argument, neither had noticed that the sun had set.

"We need to hide." Russé ran to the edge of the plateau.

Kole pushed his confusion to the side. "We need to fight."

"We would both die."

"Then we die fighting."

Russé crossed the distance between them and grabbed Kole by the arm.

"Let go." Kole dug his heels into the rock, resisting his pull. Struggle as he may, Russé dragged him to the edge of the cliff. The Soul's eyes drifted from Kole to the pale corpses, and Kole realized what he was planning to do. "Don't you—" A shove to his chest cut him off.

As Kole fell back, the silhouette of the Kayetan appeared on the plateau behind Russé. Kole's anger vanished in an instant. He shouted a warning, but Idris was already at the Soul's back.

The world seemed to pause. Kole fell slowly, watching it all unfold. He was helpless. Powerless. Useless to stop it.

Idris thrust a claw into his victim. Russé arched his back as the tip erupted through the front of his chest. A mortal wound. Blood dribbled from Russé's mouth. A last knowing look at Kole—one of warning—then Russé staggered back and dropped out of sight.

Kole landed hard among the stiff corpses. The wound the herbalist had patched up reopened with a soft rip, but adrenaline fueled him. He rolled to get up and found himself staring straight into the eyes of a man with scraggly black hair and dark, clouded eyes. Everywhere he turned, more eyes met his gaze; some rotted and soggy like overripe fruit, others only empty holes, giving Kole a glimpse of the decomposed flesh beyond. He couldn't escape them. Kole clambered over the pile of bodies, flesh ripping and tearing under his feet and hands as he crawled to the sloping wall of the basin. With each step and kick, the disturbed bodies unleashed a fresh wave of rotten stench so strong, Kole's lungs burned.

"Russé?" Kole pounded his hands on the rocky wall, gagging against the overwhelming odor. *Please don't be dead.* He had been angry—furious—at the Soul, but he never wished *this* on him. What about his powers? Why wasn't he using them? He called again.

No answer.

A hiss circled the basin.

Back against the wall, Kole scanned the open sky above, tracking the sound. The shadowy outline of the Kayetan formed on the northern ledge where Kole had fallen a moment earlier. His blank, featureless face titled down and let out an ear-splitting shriek. Then, Idris shot forward.

Kole pulled Vienna's dagger from his belt, stumbling over the bodies as he tried to keep his feet. He knew he had no chance against the Kayetan—not with a blade, no matter what it was made of—but if he was going to die tonight, he'd die fighting.

Kole fell back as roots sprayed out from the rim of the basin. They wove themselves together, creating a web over the mouth of the giant pit.

Appearing just as stunned as Kole, the Kayetan halted.

One of the roots lashed out, hitting Idris square in the chest. He flew backward with a wail.

Kole waited. Listened. The shadow returned to the ledge, peering at Kole through the slits in the roots. "It seems your master has enough energy to save his runt." Idris raised his claws threateningly and let out a throaty laugh.

Movement stirred in the corner of Kole's vision. The bright moon revealed it to be a hand dangling over the rim. It was holding something.

"Russé," Kole breathed. He scrambled back to the basin wall. As he moved over the bodies, cold slime coated his arms and legs. Fumbling, he caught himself on a swollen leg. His hand sank into the soggy skin like mud, stopping when it hit bone. He flinched away and vomited as he smeared the decomposed flesh from his skin as best he could on the wall.

Stomach drained, he glanced up. A small, dark object fell from Russé's hand, bounced off the cage of roots with a firm knock and landed somewhere among the corpses. Kole stared back at Idris, who hadn't seemed to notice.

Idris floated over to the Soul. "Shall I end it?"

"Don't touch him," Kole shouted.

"It looks like I won't have to. These human forms are so frail. He'll bleed out soon. Pity."

"Russé. Get up. You have to get up." Kole listened earnestly for a response: a gasp, a groan — anything to tell him the Soul was alive.

Silence.

"I'll kill you," Kole whispered. "I'll kill you!" His throat grew raw, screaming with every ounce of breath his lungs could muster.

Then, a familiar sharp pain pierced his head. The same grueling sensation he had endured under the Great Red. The splitting ache lasted only a moment this time, then faded as the soft, feminine voice echoed inside his head.

"*Shh, Kole,*" it whispered from the back of his mind. The voice calmed his racing heart.

Kole pushed her away. He didn't want to be calm. He wanted the rage — wanted to kill.

Idris' sinister laugh deepened at Kole's threats. "Big words for a runt. I thought you'd *want* him dead. He lied to you all of these years."

"Shut up!"

"There are secrets, you know. Secrets you couldn't even fathom. Horrible, terrible things he hasn't told you. What he's done...." Idris' smoke-like body swayed side to side in the air.

"I'm not playing your mind games." He covered his ears, but Idris' smooth voice slithered through his fingers.

"The Soul's been lying to you. About your past. About who you are."

Curiosity piqued, Kole lowered his hands. "What would you know?"

"All of it." The Kayetan moved closer to the roots, swaying above him in the night sky.

"*He's luring you,*" the feminine voice echoed in Kole's head, louder this time.

"I know what you're trying to do," Kole said. "It's not going to work."

"And what am I trying to do?"

"Bait me."

"I thought you wanted answers," he hissed.

"Not from *you*."

The Kayetan swelled. "When you lurk in the shadows you *hear* everything—*see* everything. No one knows the truth better than I."

"He's lying."

Kole recoiled as her voice crashed down on his conscience like rolling thunder.

"Enough!" Kole willed them both to stop.

"As you wish." The Kayetan floated over to the edge of the great pit. "Don't say I didn't give you a chance." He reached toward Russé. A small tendril of smoke snaked from his claws and lifted the Soul's limp body. "Say goodbye."

"Put him down," Kole snarled.

The Kayetan floated wordlessly from the basin, Russé in tow.

"Where are you taking him?" Kole jumped onto the wall—arms screaming at him, hands madly searching for holds.

"Can't you see it's a trap?"

Kole ignored her. He'd lost too many people. He couldn't lose Russé, too. Not to that devilish creature. Kole climbed recklessly. He pushed his body, letting his skin stretch to its limit. The reopened gash on his back throbbed, but he ignored it.

"You must stop."

He didn't slow.

"You leave me no choice."

Reaching for the ledge, Kole felt a strange chill spread in his body. His right arm was extended, ready to pull himself onto the plateau, when it numbed. It grew heavy and stiff as though it had turned to ice, but his skin looked no different. Then, he felt her presence grow within him. Whoever it was—whatever it was—had moved from the confinement of his mind and crawled down his neck to his limbs. Everything it touched numbed. Kole tried to climb—to move—but no matter how much he urged, he couldn't command so much as a twitch from his fingertips. He was a puppet at the will of his handler.

She repeated over and over in his head, *"Forgive me."*

"Let me go. I have to help him."

"No."

"Who are you? Why are you—" Kole didn't get to finish. The presence within seized his jaw and slammed it shut.

"I will watch over you," the woman answered.

Still unable to control his body, Kole watched his hands and feet push off the wall on their own. He fell back into the depths of the pit. Bones snapped and rotten flesh shifted beneath him as he landed among the corpses. His shirt soaked through with cold sludge.

"Stay until daylight."

The warmth returned to his limbs. As soon as he had control over his body, Kole crawled over the dead to the basin wall. Every touch was cold, wet, and vile. He focused on the rock, and when he finally reached it, he peeled of his shirt and sullied bandage Charlie had wrapped around his torso, sleek with slime, and tossed them aside. The chill air stung the open wound, but the pain didn't register through the rush of nerves. An icy finger trailed over his conscience as he gripped the wall to climb.

"Daylight," she warned.

Any move he made to escape met with numb limbs. She forced his body back down. After his third attempt, Kole curled up next to the wall. His body shook uncontrollably and his bottom lip quivered against his breaths as if he was sitting in a snow drift. But Kole felt no cold at all. His blood ran hot with anger.

The full moon crested in the night sky when Kole finally calmed. And with it, the full pain of his agitated wound overtook him. He thought back to this morning when he'd received it, landing on the ground trying to escape Idris back in the forest. Then he'd failed to best the Kayetan, and again now. Lingering on the memory boiled his blood. He ground his teeth to pass the time. His nose had grown accustomed to the stench, but his eyes would never get used to the scene spanning over his shoulder.

He peeked out, eyeing the bloated body of a young man whose skin was tinted gray. Welcoming any form of distraction from his back, he studied him. Russé had mentioned strange markings on them. Up close, he spotted it: a thin continuous incision traced around the edge of the corpse. They were meticulous. Scanning the bodies, he noticed, on the fresher ones at least, that they all matched that delicate precision.

His thoughts returned to Russé. What had he meant when he said Kole was the only one who could take down the Black Wall? Russé seemed to think Kole had some advantage over it. Last he checked, the wall burned him same as anyone else. What could he possibly do against it that a god could not?

Kole perked up, remembering that the Soul had dropped something into the pit before Idris had taken him. Crawling around the curve of the basin, he put as much weight as he could against the wall so his hands and knees wouldn't disrupt the corpses. Alas, he found that no matter how delicately he moved, it proved impossible. He peered into the nooks and crannies between the piled bodies, trying to avoid their faces.

Wedged between the elbow of a corpse was a small book. He grabbed it. Even in the darkness he recognized it: Goren's journal, the exact one he and Niko had stolen. The last time Kole remembered having the book was right before the Black Wall swept them up.

Impossible. It had been wedged in his belt. The journal would have been destroyed in the flames along with his bow. Kole thumbed the spine. Perfectly intact. It made no sense. Then again, not much did at the moment.

He opened the cover to the first page. The full moon gave enough light to discern black runes, unfamiliar to him, written on the parchment. Kole riffled through the book, searching for anything he could understand: a phrase, a word. Page after page, scribbled in every corner of open space, held the same odd language. The book was filled to the brink, and yet, it seemed as worthless as if it were blank. When he came to the last page, he paused. A crude drawing of the Seven Souls symbol stared up at him.

If Russé had felt the need to keep it away from Idris, then he must have been able to read it. There was something important here, hidden among the runes. Something about the Souls? But how had Russé got his hands on it in the first place? It had flown right into the Black Wall with Kole. He was missing something. Kole rolled his tongue as he thought. Could it be sorcery? Could magic be *that* strong? Russé admitted that his powers failed to compete with the Black Wall—and he was a god. Kole ground his teeth. There he went again, blindly believing whatever Russé spewed. Habit, he supposed. One he needed to break.

Perhaps the journal held some kind of magical protection. Something to help it survive. Still, though, it didn't explain how Russé had it.

With no way to decipher the text, Kole tucked the journal into his waistband and leaned back against the lumpy crags of the basin wall.

But he found no peace. How could he hope to distract himself surrounded by corpses?

The children bothered him most. He avoided them as best he could, but as his eyes scanned the bodies, they came to rest on a small frame. Kole bit his tongue against the rising wave of bile. The boy couldn't have been much older than ten. Since the body lay face down, hiding his foggy eyes, Kole felt a little better about examining him. He crept closer.

On the base of the boy's neck rested a small tattoo of a distinct sunburst. Kole let his eyes wander. How had he missed it before? Like Lucca, the Souls' symbol marked each body. The tattoos were all small, located in places easily concealed. A woman to his right had it drawn behind her ear. One man was branded on the front of his neck under a long, bushy beard, which hung to the side. Kole saw it on ankles, shoulders, palms—even one on the heel of a naked foot. They were everywhere. A common link. Was that why Savairo targeted them? Because they believed in the Souls?

Fools, he thought. He looked to the sky partially masked by the web of roots, wondering if these people would still revere their gods if they knew they were nothing more than powerless impostors.

Kole watched the moon slug its way across the night sky, willing it to move faster. When the first sign of light spilled over the rim of the basin, he tentatively climbed the wall. To his relief, the woman's voice didn't return. He sped up the remaining cliff to the plateau and heaved himself through the entangled roots.

Without even searching the plateau, he knew Russé was gone. A pool of blood sat at his feet, slowly soaking into the rock until it would be nothing more than a small stain on the mountain. The only other remainder sat a few meters from the drying blood—the remnants of Russé's staff.

As Kole approached, he noticed most of the staff was embedded in the rock, as if Russe had slammed it so hard that the earth had cracked beneath it and swallowed it up. Kole moved to tug it free. The staff vibrated. A deep rumble shook the basin as the roots which had sprouted over him hours ago slithered back into the mountain. The staff popped from the rock and rolled to Kole's feet. He leaned over, hand hesitant for a moment, then picked it up.

Digging his nails into the grain, Kole looked out over the basin. He felt numb. Not his body but his brain. His heart.

Standing at Poleer's peak, Kole observed the drastic differences between her polar sides. The familiar, emerald green forest spread north, his true home, and at the base of her southern slope outstretched the plains and hills leading to the center of the continent. Kole had seen it drawn out in elegant detail a few times before on one of Goren's maps. His camp leader would bring it out after dinner on occasion to teach the children about the coastal cities to the east, the looming volcano of the south (home to the metal makers Socren used to trade with) and the marshlands to the west rumored to have entire cities built on stilts to avoid sinking into the swallowing swamp. He wondered how much of it still survived. The Black Wall could have consumed them long ago.

He could still turn back. Return to camp and....

And what? The forest was unsafe so long as Idris lived. Soon the Kayetan would report to Savairo. Even if Kole could catch up to Idris, what could he do to stop him? He had to continue with the Soul's plan and find the Liberation. It seemed the only option the refugees had. But he didn't know where to begin looking, let alone how to convince their leader of the need for aid. Once he had done his duty, he'd find Russé and put him to rest. He owed the old shepherd that, at least.

One last look over Solpate made his heart swell. He re-wrapped the cloth over his face and neck, though there was nothing he could do about his exposed chest (he wasn't about to put the grime-soaked shirt on again), then stabbed the staff into the gravel and took an unwavering step down the southern side.

He was destined for the city, cloaked in the shadow of the towering mountain.

CHAPTER 11

By mid-morning, Kole had made it more than halfway down the mountain. The sun finally climbed high enough to crest the peaks and bathed the city in light.

Gray stone rested at the base of the mountain. Socren dwarfed all the refugee camps combined, with buildings ranging from tall, lofty towers, like needles pricking up through the soil, to small, stout structures, crowned in muted stone. Houses formed neat rows adjacent to the narrow streets. From this high up, its people looked like ants bustling along. Thick stone walls encased the crowded capital, almost acting as a shield from the rolling yellow fields beyond.

Outside the city walls, small houses nestled between squares of brown farmland. They lacked the meticulous placement of their stone counterparts in the city, looking as though they had plopped down wherever they could fit.

As Kole contemplated how he'd find the Liberation in such a massive place, a faint voice carried on the wind. He took cover behind a small boulder.

"How do we always get stuck with disposal duty?" Kole heard the nasally male voice say.

"Maybe it has something to do with your complainin'," came a second gruff and husky voice.

"Complaining?" The first one scoffed. "I tell you what: if I do complain, it's about you. We'd be at the festival right now if you hadn't missed your shift."

Kole slipped to the side of the boulder and peered down the mountain. If he waited until they passed, he could make a run for it. Staying quiet enough to avoid detection remained the problem. Back in the forest, it would've proven all too easy. The ramblers provided an abundance of cover, but the mountain lay bare. Gravel refused to absorb the sound of his footsteps, unlike grass, and he could only hope to move as quiet or fast as before with his body's new limitations.

As he weighed his chances, an odd, low squealing piqued Kole's curiosity. He brought his eyes to the top of the rock.

Two broad-shouldered men came up the path, adorned in worn leather armor with the double lion head crest of Socren embroidered on the breast. One sported a scruffy brown beard while the other stood barely over five feet, but he was built like a bear. Swords hung from their belts, and in their hands, dragging through the dirt behind them, were long whips.

Soldiers.

He meant to hunker down behind the boulder while they passed, when the bear-like man spun on his heel and lifted his whip. "Hurry up."

Three men, dressed in ragged loin cloths, lagged behind the guards. Bare skin stretched thin over their rib cages. The men hunched over large wheelbarrows filled with corpses. *More bodies for the basin.* Kole bit back a growl.

The slaves dug their heels into the loose gravel and pushed forward at the sight of the guard's raised whip. Straining and sweating, they struggled to move the heavy loads.

"That means all of you," the short man barked and strode over to one of the slaves who had fallen behind. He looked the most sickly of the bunch, with sunken cheeks and ribs so prominent, it reminded Kole of a scavenged carcass. The guard grunted as the slave's cart teetered. "Get it together, mutt, or I'll have your labor extended."

The slave looked up in dismay. He pushed his feet faster, but the rocks slipped out from underneath him and he fell. His chin clipped the rim of the wheelbarrow. The load tipped as he landed in the gravel, bodies spilling onto the mountain. A loud crack, and the whip came down on the slave's back. He didn't scream.

"Get up." The bearded guard cracked his whip again before the slave could scramble to his feet. "Useless animal."

Kole dug his nails into the boulder. It took all his will to keep from intervening.

As the slave turned to reload the barrow, Kole caught a glimpse of his back. A fresh wound bloomed across his skin, joining the scars of his past whippings. There were too many to count. Kole wished to tear the whips from the guard's hands and repay the beating. But finding the Liberation took priority, and with no proper weapons, he was sorely outclassed.

The wounded man continued rolling the limp corpses back into the wheelbarrow while the other slaves glanced nervously between him and the guard's twitching hand.

"Come on. Hurry it up. I've got a pint waiting for me, and I'm not about to miss anymore of the celebrations 'cause of you lazy lot," said the short guard. He walloped his metal-tipped boot into the slave's stomach.

Kole winced and squeezed his eyes shut, picturing the forest—the trees—anything to calm the temper swelling in his chest. Then, the bearded guard said the worst thing possible, words that made Kole's spine crawl.

"He's been slowing down for months now. Put him out of his misery," he ordered his comrade. "He can join the others in the pit."

The sound of a drawing sword awoke something in Kole.

He didn't remember pouncing from the rock or dashing across the gravel. He ignored the look of confusion on the first guard's face as Kole ran past him toward his comrade. Kole's senses only returned when the vibration of Russé's staff colliding with the guard's head ran up his arms.

Bewildered, the bear-like guard staggered back. Kole tossed the staff aside and jumped on him, his mind too clouded to reconsider picking a fight with a man twice his weight. They rolled down the slope, struggling against each other. Slowing to a stop, Kole found himself pinned under the heavy man.

The guard pulled himself up. A dazed, horror-filled expression contorted his face as he looked down to Kole.

At that moment, Kole felt the cool air caress his face. His bandage had fallen off in the tumble. He fought his instinct to cover his scarred skin and took advantage of the distraction. Wriggling his legs free, he wedged his knees under the guard's torso and launched his body off him.

The guard rolled to his back. Kole crawled on top of him and punched the only exposed skin he could find: his face.

"What the—hey, kid, what are you doing? Get off him," the bearded man called, clambering down the slope after them, sword in hand.

Kole kept his attention on his prey. Blood poured from the guard's broken nose, but Kole kept punching. The image of the basin fueled him, consumed him. Kole hit him for every corpse lying in that pit, for every time he'd brought his whip down on that helpless man, and every other horrible act Kole's mind fabricated in his rage.

His next punch stopped mid-strike. Despite the blood pouring down his face, the guard had snagged his forearm. Kole's fury sobered in an instant. The brief moment of hesitation gave the guard an opening to catch his other arm. Kole sat frozen, arms locked in a vice grip, as he stared down at the bloodied man beneath him, who had him locked into place like a pillory. He tried to wriggle free, but the guard held strong.

The bear-of-a-man spit a mouthful of blood, along with a few teeth, into the dirt. He grinned up at Kole and said, "Take his head off."

Kole's heart pounded against his rib cage. He was alone, helpless and overpowered. What had he been thinking? He should've stayed behind the damned rock.

The sound of metal whizzing through the air made Kole look up. The bearded comrade's sword arced toward him. Kole shook as he stared, wide-eyed, at the oncoming blade aimed for his neck.

Then, a clear note rang in the cool mountain air. A small, silver ball ricocheted off the guard's armor and fell to the gravel beside him.

Kole and the guard stopped and stared at each other, confused.

Another tiny ball hit his armor. Then another. They kept coming, littering the ground as they harmlessly bounced off. The guard lowered his sword and looked around.

A figure, dressed head to toe in black, vaulted out from behind the boulder where Kole had been hiding moments before. The eyes and nose lay hidden behind a black mask. Only the mouth was left exposed. It held a wicked smile.

"Not you again." The guard frowned behind his beard and moved his attention from Kole, who still sat atop his comrade, to his new opponent.

Slingshot in hand, the black-garbed figure continued launching pellets at the guard. This time they were aimed more carefully, striking the guard's hands until Kole swore he heard the crack of a bone, and the guard dropped his weapon with a shriek.

With the guard's attention drawn away, Kole kneed the guard beneath him in the groin, ripped his hands from the loosened hold, then darted away.

The stranger in black tossed Russé's staff back to Kole. He caught it and brought it down on the bloodied, swelled face of the guard who had set him up to be slaughtered. One swing to the forehead was all it took, and the stocky man's eyes rolled back.

A scream made Kole turn. The bearded man held out his hand in agony, his fingers crooked and twisted from direct hits of the slingshot.

The stranger seized a large rock from the gravel and smacked it into the guard's head, cutting his cry short with a sickening crunch.

He let the blood-stained stone fall to the ground, then turned to Kole. "You all right?"

Kole's head spun, shrouded in a fog of adrenaline, but he managed a nod.

"You're in for some trouble, mate." The boy wedged the handle of his slingshot into his belt beside two stout daggers.

"Trouble?" Kole asked as they walked back to the slaves.

"Do you have any idea what you've done?" The tallest slave said, protectively stepping over his injured companion as Kole neared.

Kole lowered his staff. "I'm not going to hurt you."

"Hurt us? You've done much worse than that." The slave walked right up to him, face inches away, unflinching at Kole's burned face. "Our heads are marked, now."

"The guards won't give you any trouble. We took care of them." Kole nodded to the stranger in black.

"Not *we*, mate. Don't bring me into this. That was *all* you," the boy said with a step back, waving his hands innocently.

Kole glanced to the boy. If not for him, Kole would be without a head right now. Why was he giving *him* all the credit? Kole looked back at the slave. "You're free."

The slave loomed over Kole with a deepening frown. "Free? From what?"

"Th-the abuse." Kole furrowed his eyebrows, bemused as to why they weren't happy.

The man brought his face to Kole's, his rancid breath smacking into him as he spoke. "What would you have me say? *Thank you?*"

Kole stepped back, and the slave closed the distance once more. "I, uh, no. I just thought—"

The strange boy whistled and tapped his foot impatiently. "Here it comes," he said out of the corner of his mouth, then puckered his lips and continued his whistling tune.

"You just thought you would play hero and save the day, did you? Well let me tell you how this will all play out. When the guards come to, *we* will be the ones to suffer the consequences." The slave sneered. "My five years would've been up by the end of the week, but you show up and decide to be brave—to save the poor, beaten men. My body has taken years of beatings. All to earn my freedom. Now, so near the end, and it's robbed from me by a foolish boy. A gracious punishment for something like this is an extension of labor; the harshest, death. I can't survive another extension. You have most certainly killed me, either way."

Kole felt the blood rush from his face. "I didn't—I didn't know."

"Wouldn't expect ya to." The boy walked up and nudged Kole with his elbow. "Let me handle this, will ya?" He turned to face the slave. "All right, big guy, tell ya what. You three can't stay here anymore 'cause of the kid, so—"

"The guard was going to kill him." Kole gestured to the injured slave on the ground, who was still clutching his stomach where he had been kicked.

"Hey," the strange boy held up his hand, "I got this, all right?" He returned to the slave with a serious tone. "Go across the mountain—you know the way. Stay at the tree line, and someone'll find ya. Don't go in alone, got it? The trees have a mind of their own over there."

The slave gave the black-garbed boy a grimace then called to his companions. "We have no other choice." He looked down his long nose at Kole.

Kole clenched his jaw and dropped his eyes to the ground as the men left the wheelbarrows and trekked up the mountain, aiding their injured kin between them.

He stared at the unconscious guards. His hatred for them exploded like a raging wildfire. These guards—Savairo—they had no right to treat people like this; keeping them under control through fear and violence. He had only meant to help yet had somehow made things worse for the slaves. His gut twisted.

"So you're from the camps, eh?" The boy lifted the fabric from his face. Wild, curly brown hair sprang from the cloth, framing sly green eyes. He had a small nose and a soft jawline, hinting he was near to Kole's age.

"Uh, yeah," Kole said hesitantly. "How did you know?"

"You're kiddin', right?" The stranger pulled out a small flask. He twisted the cap off and poured it into the mouth of the unconscious guard. "Everyone livin' on this side of the mountain knows about the immigrant labor laws. Been in effect since before I was born. Which means you don't live here in Socren. And seein' how you're hikin' *down* the mountain and not the other way 'round—well—it really isn't much of a puzzle there, Blondie."

Kole touched the patchy peach fuzz on his scalp self-consciously.

"Plus, a face like that is hard to miss."

Kole snatched the bandage from the rocks and looped it around his head, but without a shirt, his scars were apparent.

"The real question," the boy continued, unfazed, "is why you're here."

"I'm looking for the Liberation. It's urgent. I need to speak with—"

"Whoa!" The boy glanced around nervously and lowered his voice. "You can't go askin' stuff like that, Blondie. You're gonna get yourself killed." He stepped to the next guard and poured the clear contents into his mouth, as well. Finished, he returned the flask to his pocket.

"What is that stuff?"

"Taliroot extract. Makes the memory a bit fuzzy. Supposed to use it beforehand, but we don't have that luxury today, now do we? Just hope it confuses 'em enough they don't remember your face, eh? *If* they wake up." He gave Kole a once over, shaking his head. "You really are sheltered out there, aren't ya? Look," he folded his arms over his chest, "I think I can help ya out."

"You know where the Liberation is?"

The boy smirked. "I know a guy."

Kole squeezed Russé's staff uneasily.

"Don't worry, mate, I'll get ya there. But first," he pulled a long, black strip of fabric from his pouch, "I need ya to put this on."

Kole took the fabric, examining it.

"It's a blindfold," the boy said plainly. "Put it around your eyes— no peeking now. Can't have anyone knowin' my little secret."

"What secret?"

"Exactly."

Kole eyed him up and down, unsure whether he should trust him.

The boy clicked his tongue impatiently. "I get it. Strange place. Strange person. But I can't wait around forever. If we linger too long, someone's gonna come lookin' for these guards, and I can tell ya, they won't be as friendly as me. So what do ya say, mate?"

Kole frowned. If this boy *did* know how to find the Liberation, Kole could make up for lost time. But if he didn't....

He had to risk it. If things went sour, he'd just have to get himself out. He nodded.

The boy smiled and jabbed an open hand at Kole. "The name's Felix."

Kole stared at it.

"Not use to handshakes—got it. No worries, Blondie."

"My name isn't Blondie. It's Kole."

Felix squinted at Kole for a moment, then shook his head. "I'll stick with Blondie. Can't get too acquainted—just in case."

"In case of what?"

A sly smile crossed his mouth. "I thought your business was urgent." Felix turned around, put his fingers to his lips, and let out a melodic whistle that reminded Kole of the morning bird calls back in the forest.

Felix's unusually happy demeanor felt off-putting in a place like this. And that he popped up out of nowhere from the very spot where Kole had been hiding made him wary. Had Felix been watching him? He certainly seemed eager to help.

Felix must have sensed Kole's doubt, because he took the blindfold from him with flashing green eyes. "Looks can be deceivin', Blondie. Put on the 'fold or we'll have ta leave ya here."

"*We?*" Kole asked.

"You don't think I'd attack Socren guards without backup, do ya? Relax." Felix brought the blindfold up to Kole's head. "Nothin' personal, just protocol."

Felix had saved his life. Could he trust in that? Then Kole saw it—a small tattoo drawn on Felix's right earlobe: the symbol of the Seven Souls. The tattoo eased his nerves, and he relented.

"Atta boy," said Felix as he came around and tied a knot in the back.

"Is he ready?" The voice didn't come from Felix but from a different boy with a deeper tone. Older, if Kole had to guess.

"Aye," Felix confirmed.

"All right, grab 'em," the boy commanded.

"Don't I call the shots?" Felix said.

A strained silence.

"Sorry, Felix, only trying to help," the voice grunted.

Felix laughed. "Lay off the serious, people—I'm only kidding. Let's move out."

Footsteps crunched near Kole. He jumped as a pair of soft hands touched his right arm. They squeezed tight at his movement and forcefully led him forward. Another pair, large and rough, seized his left, bringing along the scent of sour sweat; the kind of stink that can only be achieved by refusing to bathe.

They led Kole up a steep slope. The sun warmed his right cheek, which meant they were heading north, back up the mountain.

After a short climb, they stopped him.

"Want me to get it?" The throaty voice came.

"No," Felix heaved. "I got it. Just—need—some leverage—and—"

Metal whined. Then, a cadence of slow clicks. They hastened, and the ground rumbled beneath him until it sounded like a purr.

"There! You see? Not everyone needs your bulky muscles to function."

The clicks ceased and a hand guided Kole onto what felt like a platform. Kole stomped his foot on the floor. Wood. Its dull echo resounded, carrying far below his feet until it faded away.

"Whoa, Blondie, don't want this thing snappin', do ya?"

"No funny business," said the sweaty boy on his left.

"This is... safe?" Kole asked.

"Of course! Leo made it himself," Felix replied.

"Who's Leo?"

A snort answered him.

"Off we go," said Felix.

Another whine of metal and more clicking.

Kole braced himself as the platform jerked down, then steadied itself into a gentle descent. Soon, the warmth of the sun faded from his face, replaced by cool, moist air and the bitter smell of soil. They were heading underground.

"Hatch is closed. Take it off," Felix ordered. Rough hands tugged at Kole's blindfold, yanking his head back and forth until the cloth came free. They stood in complete darkness.

"Put a light on, will ya?" Someone grunted across from Kole.

"Who's got the lamp?" asked the reeking boy.

"I thought you had it, Boogy."

"Huh? What lamp?"

"What do you mean 'what lamp'? We literally carry it everywhere." Annoyance crept up in Felix's voice.

"Oh, will you all shut up?" A girl spoke. Her soft hands fell from Kole's arm. "It has to be somewhere on the rig. If you'd just look instead of arguing, we'd have already solved the problem."

"Yeah, well, I distinctly remember puttin' one of ya in charge of it," Felix grumbled as the sound of shuffling feet crept along the length of the platform. There was a thud, and the platform wobbled. "Found it." His voice came from Kole's feet. With a click, light spilled forth from the small glass lamp, illuminating the cavity. Felix quickly hopped to his feet and glanced around with wide eyes, as if trying to convince the others he hadn't just face-planted.

While everyone shook their heads, Kole took in his surroundings. He had guessed right. They'd moved underground and were sinking further into the mountain by the second. He glanced down. The platform was crudely made, with cracked wooden planks crisscrossed over one another and patched in several places. Through the cracks, Kole could see the dirt tunnel continuing far beyond the light of the lamp. The rig swayed at the slightest movement and gave Kole a jolt when it scraped the side of the tunnel.

"Rules!" Felix paced back and forth along the rickety wooden platform. "No names, as instructed by Leo."

"You told him *your* name." A muscular boy with a neck as thick as Kole's leg grunted at Felix.

"And you used my name a little bit ago," another boy accused. Kole did a double take. A tad pudgier, this boy looked identical to the thick-necked one. Both were built solid, like tree trunks, and had a sort of distant airiness to their gaze.

"Yeah, you said Boogy, remember?" The other one said with a frown set on Boogy.

"All right, fine. Forget the name thing. But we don't get attached," Felix reminded.

"Hello there, I'm Criz." Criz nudged his pudgier look-a-like beside him. "This here is my brother, Boogy."

"Hey, I can introduce myself, ya know." Boogy dipped in an awkward bow. "I'm Boogy."

"Hello," Kole muttered.

"This here's gonna be Blondie," Felix pointed to Kole, "until we get the okay from the boss. Now ya know these two morons." He gestured to the brawny boys. "This here is Pipes." Kole followed his finger to a girl with bright, auburn hair.

"Pip-*er*," The girl, clearly annoyed, corrected. She tucked her long hair behind her ears.

"And Thomas," Felix finished.

Kole turned his head toward the smell. Before him stood a handsome, dark-haired boy with distinctive angular brows. Thomas was a whole head taller than Kole, which made him look much older than his boyish physique suggested. Thomas rolled his eyes at Felix's introduction.

"Rule two!" Felix clasped his hands behind his back. "The intruder—uh, *guest*—is not to know the location. Done that," he boasted, making a check in the air with his finger, then tucked the blindfold away in his pouch. "And three. Uh...."

"Strip them of weapons," Piper said irritably. "You did that, right?" Her eyes fell to Kole's staff, and she shook her head. "You didn't." She grabbed it.

Kole tugged back, noting her surprising strength. Everyone moved their hands to their weapons. He eyed them for a moment, then released his hold.

"It's just a mangled piece of wood." Piper passed the staff to Criz, which made the weapon look more like a twig in his paw-like hands, then patted Kole down. Her fingers stopped at his waist. Kole flushed at her touch as she grabbed Goren's journal.

"Aww, let him keep his book, will ya? What's he gonna do, bore us to death with a story?" Felix said.

"Some words are deadlier than blades." Piper tucked the journal under her arm. "You'll get these back when Leo clears them." She patted the legs of his pants, then slipped her hands to the base of Kole's back. The side of her mouth twitched as she pulled Vienna's dagger from his waistband. Piper's jaw fell open. "Felix."

"Hmm?" Felix snatched the dagger from her hands and put the weapon up to the light. When the blade hit the lantern's glow, Kole noticed the stone had changed from its previous white to a dull black. Felix's head snapped back to Kole, and the happy-go-lucky expression morphed to suspicion. "Where did ya get this?"

His glare made Kole step back, but Thomas put a firm hand on his elbow, squeezing it in just the right place to send a jolt of pain up his arm. "A girl gave it to me. Vienna."

"She gave it to ya, huh?" Felix tucked the blade in his belt.

Kole nodded.

"And why would she do that?"

"We were up against a Kayetan. She gave it to me to defend myself."

"Where is she now? Is she alive?" Felix's voice switched to desperation.

"Yes. At least I think so. She was hit by Idris—some kind of smoke bubble." He shook his head. "She fell unconscious and was still asleep when—" Kole stopped himself, wondering if he should mention Russé, "—when I left." Kole's eyes moved from face to face. He could tell that he hadn't convinced them. "That's all I know, I swear."

"We'll see about that," Thomas said as the platform lugged to a stop.

Carved into the dirt wall was a tall archway leading to a tunnel.

Felix stepped off first and blew out the lantern. As the fire in the lamp snuffed out, an eerie glow ignited ahead. Once they all exited the platform, Felix took the lead, followed by the brothers, while Piper and Thomas pulled up the rear behind Kole. The tunnel was wide enough to accommodate Criz's and Boogy's frames and tall enough where Thomas didn't have to crouch. Nailed to the tunnel walls were small lanterns unlike Kole had ever seen. They looked like perfect clear globes from afar and glowed bright and steady as opposed to the flickering flames he'd grown accustomed to.

He reached out and touched one. It felt smooth and hard under his fingers.

"Moonstone," Piper said behind him. "They only work when surrounded by complete darkness."

The smell of sweat reached Kole's nose as a pair of hands roughly steered him away from the wall. "Keep it moving," Thomas grumbled. Kole wondered if his frown was permanently fixed to his face.

Piper walked up beside him. "Have you heard of it?"

Kole shook his head.

"Well, it's not from the moon, and it really isn't a stone at all. They're pieces of wood cut from the trunks of the crystal trees in the west. I've never seen them myself, but they're said to glow when the sun goes down. Supposedly an entire forest of them extends up the west side of Ohr."

Kole looked on in wonder, noticing the grains in the crystal looping around, resembling the rings in a tree trunk. "How did they get down here?"

"Leo has his ways," Piper said, smirking.

"Who's Leo?" Kole pressed, hoping she'd give him some sort of clue.

"You'll see soon enough," Thomas snapped, putting an end to their conversation.

The group walked in silence until the tunnel split. Four tunnels lay ahead, each lined with moonstone spheres. Kole peered down them. As far as he could tell, they were identical, and further down, the tunnels split again. It didn't look like a place Kole would want to get lost in. Uneasiness flitted through his stomach. If this went sour, an escape would prove difficult.

"Welcome to The Cobwebs," Felix said, swooping his hand toward the paths.

"Don't make it sound so dramatic. It's just an abandoned mine," Thomas said.

Felix jabbed a finger toward Thomas. "Not *just* a mine—a maze!" His shout echoed down the tunnels. "An unsolvable labyrinth."

"Yeah, people have died down here," added Boogy.

"It's pretty dangerous." Criz nudged his brother in agreement.

Felix's face held a satisfied smile. "These tunnels lead nowhere unless you know the secrets of The Cobwebs. If you do, you'll find they lead you anywhere you wanna go."

Piper folded her arms. "It's a giant maze that loops back on itself with hidden doors along the walls. Find the right door and you find your way out. Now, can we get going, Felix? I'm starving."

"Hey," Felix deflated. "Why'd ya do that? He was falling for it. You were gettin' scared, weren't ya, Blondie?"

"Not really." Kole tried to sound casual despite his feet yearning for the mountainside. At least up there he knew where he was going. The moment he stepped into the tunnels, he was at the mercy of these strangers.

"It's serious stuff, 'member that time I got lost? Thought I was a goner for sure," said Criz.

"You wouldn't be able to find the exit if it smacked you in the face," Thomas said through his teeth.

Criz's face reddened. He puffed his chest and marched toward Thomas, hands balled into fists. Boogy caught his brother before he could take another step and held him back, whispering something Kole couldn't hear. Whatever it was seemed to calm him, and his face reverted to its normal color.

"Can we please stop bickering? We have a job to do." Piper pushed her way past Felix and headed down the right-most tunnel. "Are you coming?"

Kole tried to memorize the path, but after ten minutes of walking, he had completely lost his bearings. Eventually, Piper slowed her pace. She dragged a finger up and down the wall as she walked. At first Kole thought she was biding time, but then she halted and pressed her hand into the dirt. It passed through with no resistance, and the illusion faded, revealing a knob. Kole blinked as Piper gave it a twist. Metal clicked somewhere behind the tunnel wall and, to Kole's amazement, a crack emerged in the earth. It ran up the tunnel, then arced back down until it had traced the outline of a door. Piper leaned in and it creaked open. "Ladies, first," she said, a dark twinkle in her honey-colored eyes.

The boys filed through the door, grumbling as they passed Piper's smug face.

When Kole stepped through, his jaw dropped.

A giant, dome-shaped room lay before him. The gray ceiling towered overhead, streaked with wide veins of milky stone, spreading out like forked streams down the roughly cut walls. A massive moonstone sphere, bigger than Boogy and Criz combined, hung from the apex. Its light reached every nook of the dome. When it hit the veins of white rock embedded in the walls, they pulsed with an eerie light.

"I'll go get him." Felix swung open two large doors at the far end of the room and disappeared.

A gray stone table sat at the middle of the floor, adorned with a carving of the Seven Souls symbol at its center. Eight chairs lined the long, rectangular table and a taller chair sat at the head.

Piper, Thomas, Boogy, and Criz all took a seat while Kole stayed back near the exit. His eyes moved to the doorway as Felix returned, a tall man at his side. The man's eyes locked onto Kole—an intensity in them that made Kole reach for the doorknob behind him.

CHAPTER 12

"Look who I found comin' down the mountain. Says he's from the refugee camps." Felix lowered himself into the chair next to the head of the table.

"Is that so?" The tall, middle-aged man with sleek, black hair, a short, dark beard, and piercing eyes, stared curiously at Kole. A billowy black coat, covered in pockets of various sizes, draped over a plain tunic, and a familiar tattoo peeked out from his collar. "Please, sit." Leo gestured to the empty chair beside him as he took his place at the head of the table.

Kole's fingers relaxed on the metal knob behind him, and he took a shaky step forward. As he approached, he noticed the fine wrinkles around Leo's mouth. He sat without a word.

"I would ask you to remove your coverings," said Leo.

His jaw clenched at the request. "I'd rather not."

A strained silence.

Leo leaned back and let out a sigh. Kole couldn't tell if it stemmed from impatience or surprise that he had refused his request. "If you cannot trust us, we cannot trust you. It is your choice."

His bare chest already stood on display, what would his face matter? The moment he unraveled the fabric, he wished it back on as a low gasp came from where Thomas sat. The others remained quiet.

"What is your name?" Leo asked.

Kole flicked his eyes up to see that Leo's pupils had expanded, overtaking his irises. Kole blinked, wondering if his eyes were playing tricks on him, but when he looked again, he was sure: they were completely black, like a total eclipse. *Sorcery.* Shifting nervously on the cold stone, he answered, "My name is Kole."

"You are from the camps, yes?"

He nodded.

"I need you to speak it."

His eyes flicked around the table. Everyone stared at him expectantly except Felix, who'd leaned back, propped his feet up on the table, and was picking at his nails.

"Are you from the camps?" Leo asked again.

Kole swallowed. "Yes."

"Very good."

Felix looked up from his fingernails. "Congratulations, you're tellin' the truth — we don't have ta kill ya now."

Leo threw a sharp glance Felix's way, and he returned to his grooming.

It *was* sorcery. A sort of truth magic, it seemed. And with Leo quite adamant at voicing his answers, Kole guessed it only worked on the spoken word. He would have to choose his phrasing carefully.

"What are you doing so far from home, shepherd?"

Kole didn't remember telling anyone he was a shepherd. Was it another part of the spell? He shook his worry away. What would it matter if Leo knew? The priority was finding the Liberation. The faster he accomplished that, the sooner he could search for the Soul. "I have urgent news for the Liberation. Felix said he'd take me to them."

Leo raised a brow. "Did he? And is that *all* he told you?"

"Yes, sir."

The man turned to address the group. "I have to admit, I am slightly disappointed that you five chose to lure the boy here without speaking the phrase. It is a good thing we found him first." Leo's black eyes landed back on Kole. "You have found the Liberation. You really should not be so trusting, Kole. It is extremely fortunate you fell into the right hands. I know it is not what you are used to back in Solpate, but Socren is a dangerous place. If Savairo had found you first...."

Kole scanned the kids around the table. They couldn't be much older than him. *This* was the Liberation? Surely there were more members. *Older* members.

"Well, technically he did," Felix said. "I found Blondie here attackin' a pair of guards."

Leo frowned. "I trust you handled it."

"As best I could. A little Taliroot was all I had."

"Taliroot," Leo grumbled. "I told you not to rely on that."

"If they make it back to Socren, at least their memories'll be all screwy."

"We can only hope." The Liberation leader turned back to Kole. "What news would force a shepherd from Solpate?"

Before Kole could open his mouth to speak, Felix slid Vienna's dagger across the table. "I'm guessin' it has somethin' ta do with this."

"You found Vienna?" Leo grabbed the dagger. "Is she alive?"

Kole nodded.

"Say it," Felix snapped, jabbing a finger in Leo's direction. "Say it to *him*."

Kole shot a glance between Felix and Leo. "Yes. She was alive when I left."

Leo's black gaze bore into him for a moment, then he nodded to Felix. "He speaks the truth."

A wave of relief washed over the room.

"We have ta go get her," Felix demanded.

"Your sister will be fine in the refugees' care. You know that if she were here, she would call you a fool for such a notion."

"Can I do it for her?" asked Boogy, who sunk back in his chair when Felix shot him a glower.

"So this has to do with the Escape the other night." Leo leaned back. "I think you should start from the beginning."

Kole had only just begun recalling the breach when Piper interrupted.

"Etta? You found, Etta?"

"Her and Lily."

"Thank the Souls!" Piper whispered.

"Lily didn't make it." Kole looked down to his hands. "We were too late."

Her face paled. She reached for the symbol on the table and closed her eyes, mouth moving in silent prayer. Thomas put a hand on her back, but she flinched from his touch.

"Etta will not have taken that well." Leo closed his eyes, too, for a moment and bowed his head.

Kole told them everything: the encounter at the Great Red, Idris moving the Black Wall, the death of his people, and the Leaders' plan to rebel. As he spoke, he found himself avoiding any mention of the Soul. All the while, everyone leaned in, eagerly listening, except Leo, who gave no hints to what stirred behind his black eyes.

Once Kole had reached the end of his story, Leo spoke. "Idris is the most powerful of his kind — a product of blood magic, I presume — but moving the Black Wall... it would take a great deal of power."

"It coincides with Savairo's claims," said Piper.

"No sorcerer possesses the kind of power to harness the Black Wall. Not even creations rumored to be cut from his own skin."

"Cut?" Kole asked.

Leo tilted his head. "Kayetans are abominations made from dark sorcery. They are shadows," he said, lifting a hand into the light of the moonstone lantern. The penumbra of his hand cast down on the table. "Our very own shadows, removed from the body. When created, they are bound to their master and will act out his every wish. The hosts from which they were taken, I am afraid, do not survive the experiment."

"The basin," Kole said. The silence around the table confirmed his suspicions. Those bodies were used to make Kayetans. Used then discarded.

"The majority of the Kayetans came from normal, non-magic folk," said Leo. "As such, their powers have more limitations. These Kayetans only appear after sundown. Idris, though, is different sort of creature. I believe his unique abilities come from the host of which he was cut."

"What kind of host?"

"A sorcerer. Their blood has magical properties. As we have seen, that plays a role in the type of creation that is produced in the experiment. I fear that if Idris is his first Kayetan from magical blood, it would make him a prototype. He would be at the lowest form of his potential. If Savairo perfects his experiment, there is no telling how powerful the species may become. Sooner or later we will face an army with Idris' powers... or something far more terrible."

An army of Idrises. The thought chilled Kole. If it came to that, the refugees would be no match for Savairo, no matter how many allies they recruited. "How do we kill him?"

Leo nodded to Vienna's blade. "I have enchanted the obsidian with fire essence. Once the material is charged, it turns into sunstone. The enchantment only lasts for a few days before it fades and returns to its natural state. You can also charge the blades in the sun, but it takes time, and it is less potent. Sunstone seems to be their only weakness other than actual fire. A stab to the heart will kill a Kayetan."

"It didn't work."

Leo cocked his head, a curious gaze on Kole as if he had misheard him.

"Vienna told me about their hearts. I got a good clean shot on him, but nothing happened."

"You have used the sunstone on Idris?" Leo asked, leaning forward in his chair.

Kole gave a curt nod.

"The blade was still charged—still white? You struck true?"

Another nod.

Leo's hands curled into fists. "What exactly happened when Idris was struck? Tell me everything—every detail you remember."

Kole gnawed his bottom lip as he thought. "There was a flash of light. He screamed." Leo nodded, urging him to continue. "His body spread into a cloud of smoke and disappeared, but he reformed."

"Is that all?"

"Yeah." Kole dipped his head. "It was odd. I've never seen anyone *want* to be stabbed."

Leo's eyes flashed. "What did you say?"

"He wanted me to stab him." Kole glanced around the room. Every set of eyes bore into him, as if the members were debating whether Kole had gone crazy. "He provoked me, like he had some sort of death wish." He only realized how outlandish it sounded once he said it aloud: an enemy asking to be killed. "I thought it was a trap."

The tension in the room thickened as the Liberation looked from Kole to Leo. A heaviness weighed down on Kole's shoulders, and he sunk back into his chair hoping someone would speak.

"It *was* a trap," Leo said in a low voice. "I think Idris was conducting his own experiment with you. He wanted you to use the blade on him like we have on his kin. It sounds like he was testing his strength." Leo straightened. "The blade did its job exactly how it was intended. The fire I imbue in the stone creates an effect similar to when a Kayetan is caught in the sun. Shadow cannot survive in direct light. When exposed to it, they die. If it failed to work on Idris, it means...." His fingers tapped the stone table as he thought.

"It means Idris has a power source of his own," Piper said.

Leo looked to her, mouth twitching as if the thought forming in his head was the last one he wanted to believe. "Then he *must* have sorcerer blood in him."

"Or something stronger," Piper said darkly.

A frown formed as Leo rose from his chair and paced the far side of the room. "I should have foreseen this." He mumbled something unintelligible to himself then paused, head snapping back to Kole as his pupils enlarged once more. "How is it that your friend was taken but you were not?"

Kole opened his mouth to answer then snapped it shut, unsure whether to tell the Liberation about Russé. Could he trust them? Would they even *believe* him? Even though Russé was dead, it wasn't his secret to tell. If the camp leaders wanted the Liberation to know, they could tell them when they arrived. Kole felt sure of his decision, but it didn't help his current situation. If he lied outright, Leo would pick up on it. Forming his words carefully, he said, "Russé pushed me in the basin before Idris saw me. He tried to hide me. I couldn't see very much from down there. I'm not sure what happened exactly, but he didn't come in after me." Kole fiddled his fingers under the table, hoping Leo would take the bait. His words were true. Every last one. And he would get away with his secret as long as Leo abstained from too many questions.

"Hmm." Leo's eyes narrowed. "So, you were left in the basin while your friend was captured. Is the shepherd familiar with the arts?"

Kole cocked his head.

"Sorcery," Piper said across the table.

Kole's insides ran cold. The images of the Soul manipulating the forest to his will and reshaping his staff on the mountain flashed in his head. Was his power the same as a sorcerer's? His mind raced to find the right words to answer. Ones that would be truthful without revealing too much. "I don't know."

Leo's mouth twitched as if unconvinced.

"I've seen him do... odd things. I thought it was a shepherd's skill at the time."

Any warmth Leo had shown before vanished from his face.

Kole swallowed. He fought against the urge to squirm for fear it would give him away.

"What did you say his name was again?"

Risil. The name resounded in his head as he spoke, unable to control the crack in his voice, "Russé. The shepherd's name is Russé."

The Liberation leader frowned, and Kole knew he had been caught. "This is important, Kole. If he uses magic, I must know about it."

"Yes," Kole breathed, "he uses magic."

Leo rubbed his beard. "Then there is a possibility your friend is still alive."

"What?" Kole squeezed the arms of his chair. "How do you know?"

"Even the strongest magic cannot bring the dead back. He had to be alive when Idris took him, if only just. There would be no reason to take the body unless Idris had use for your shepherd. Seeing how non-magical blood is quite easy for his master to get his hands on in the city, I assume Russé was collected for experimentation. I know it sounds bad, but that is his best chance at survival. Savairo will keep him alive as long as he is useful. But he cannot stay in the Warden's possession for long, or I fear we will have another advanced Kayetan on our hands."

"He's going to turn Russé into a Kayetan?" His heart beat fast as it dawned on him. Russé had sacrificed himself to spare Kole. Maybe the Soul thought his powers would protect him. By gods was he wrong. Those powers were a curse. Idris would tell his master who the shepherd truly was. If Savairo turned the Soul.... Kole refused to think about the type of monster Savairo could create from *god's* blood. No doubt it would result in his most deadly Kayetan yet. Kole had to get the Soul out of there.

"We will not let Savairo turn your friend." The tension in Kole's back released as Leo's pupils retracted to their normal size. "Thomas."

"Yes, sir."

"After we are finished, go to the city and find out what you can. It might be a more guarded secret than you are used to. I doubt the townspeople will know anything about it. You will have to dig deeper. We need to know where they have taken him."

"Yes, Leo."

"I'll go with you," Kole said.

Thomas gave his scars a once over and scoffed. "You'd blow my cover before we got into the city."

Kole slammed his fists on the table. "*I'm going with you.*"

"Your heart is in the right place." Leo placed a hand on his arm. Kole pulled away. "But Thomas is right. You draw attention as it is. And after what happened with the guards... I am sure they are on high alert. Thomas can handle this on his own. He will inform us of any leads."

"You don't understand. I *have* to be the one to find him." Russé had kept his secret all this time for a reason. Looking around the table, Kole started to understand, if only slightly—and most reluctantly—why the Soul had lied to him. It was impossible to know who to trust with something like this. He debated telling Leo the truth, but he was afraid what might happen if he did. Would Leo hold Russé as a bartering chip like Kole had wanted to do when he first found out? Leo couldn't know. None of them could. He needed to be the one out there looking for him. Once Russé was free, the Soul could do with his secret as he wished, and Kole could let go of his guilt.

"Thomas will gather the information. When we have what we need, you may accompany him for Russé's retrieval."

Kole ground his teeth and sat back. Arguing was getting him nowhere. He eyed the door to The Cobwebs. He'd have to act on his own.

"Now as for the refugees, we have two days to make this happen." Leo scratched the wiry hair on his chin. "We are not ready for this. Despite our dwindled numbers, we will not stand by and watch our people be slaughtered. We have to act."

"Is this is the whole Liberation?" Kole asked. Scanning the room, his confidence in them wavered. Everything was supposed to have taken a turn for the better when he reached the Liberation. He had expected to be greeted by hardened soldiers, not five kids and whose oldest member couldn't manage to control his own body odor. They could never hope to defeat Socren's forces with a few teenagers and a group of untrained refugees.

"I am afraid so. We lost what little numbers we had when the Kayetans ambushed the Escape the other night. The Kayetans outnumber us ten to one. Savairo creates them at such a staggering rate, we are doing our best just to stay alive. And we have more to fear than his army of shadows. We will be up against the full strength of Socren's army. Guards, sorcerers, not to mention Savairo himself. Strategy alone will win us this fight."

"What are you proposing?" Piper asked. Her hard demeanor returned despite the red cast over her eyes from the news of Lily's death a few moments prior.

"We lure them to Lilith's pass, where their formation will bottleneck. This is where you come in, Felix."

Felix's lips curled into a mischievous smile. "Traps."

"We will need fertilizer from Bowen. Retrieve it so I can get to work. I will craft as many explosives as time allows," said Leo.

"We can flank the sides of the pass, too—use bows, tip boulders," Thomas added.

"Yes. With that, we need numbers. Criz. Boogy."

"Aye," the twins said.

"Recruit the farmers and anyone else we can trust outside the city walls. Call in all of our favors."

"Sure thing, boss," they grunted, maintaining their odd unison.

"Even then, our odds are bleak." Leo paced again. "Two days... separate the army...." He mumbled as he passed behind Kole's chair. Then, he held up a hand. "We will plan our attack for dawn to avoid Savairo's Kayetans. It will be a more even fight, then. I will have the refugees arrive a night early to assimilate them into our ranks."

"I'll grab Fiona." Piper stood and rushed through the double doors.

Leo plucked a feather quill from one of the many pockets in his coat and pulled up his sleeve. He poked his forearm with the sharp point. A bubble of blood ballooned on his skin. Twirling the tip of the quill in the red liquid, he lifted it up to the height of his face and began to write. At least, it looked like he was writing.

Leo swooped and curved the quill through the air, shifting down every so often when he ran into the edge of his invisible paper.

Silvery words formed mid-air. Each letter drifted up and down like they were floating underwater. With a final flick of his wrist, Leo finished his message and stashed his quill. He swiped his hand through the middle of the paragraph. The words bounced and broke apart until they were a jumble of silver letters.

Piper returned with a small, rust-colored hawk perched on her arm. The bird tilted its head, casting a round eye at Leo.

Kole admired Fiona's feathers. He was used to the extravagant birds of Solpate adorned with vines and petals, much like the forest stags, but he found beauty in Fiona's plainness.

Leo dug into his breast pocket and presented a tiny, silver ball no bigger than a thumbnail. It popped open with a press of his finger. Like a miniature tornado, the scrambled letters swirled into a funnel and sucked into the ball. Once the final letter slipped in, it snapped closed.

Leo moved to Fiona. She nuzzled her beak against his arm as he attached the ball to her leg with a small leather tie. Her wings ruffled as if anxious to take flight.

"Patient, now," Leo soothed. "You do not know where you are taking it, yet." Then, he lowered himself so his eyes leveled with the bird. As he spoke, she stayed unnaturally still, as if she understood every word. "Solpate forest. Southern camp. Darian. Urgent. Now fly."

Fiona gave a final chirp before pushing off Piper's arm and zooming toward the ceiling. Kole gaped at her as she circled the room three times, picking up speed with each lap, then shot up through a narrow tunnel he only now noticed, carved into the roof of gleaming stone.

"She should return in a few hours. In the meantime, you all have a job to do." Leo's gaze landed on Kole. "I will have Felix scrounge up some food for you and show you to a bed."

A gurgle from his stomach erupted at the mention of food. He couldn't remember the last time he'd eaten.

Leo's eyes shifted to Felix. "No funny business."

"You got it, boss." Felix sent a wink Kole's way once Leo turned.

"You may return his personal items to him. He means us no harm," Leo directed at Piper.

She pursed her lips and handed back Kole's staff and journal. "Oh, and Piper?" Leo stopped next to her. "I need a word."

"Of course."

Kole overheard Leo mention something about 'keeping records up to date,' but the rest was drowned out by the twins.

"What did he tell us to do, again?" Boogy looked strangely at his brother.

"We're going to the festival," Criz said.

"No, you knuckleheads," Thomas scolded. "You're supposed to recruit the farmers."

"Oh, ya, I remember now."

Boogy scowled at Thomas' insult. "C'mon Criz, maybe when we get done we can sneak into the festival."

The brothers exited the door leading to the tunnels while rambling about the sweet pastries they wanted to eat in the city.

"I always wonder how they don't get lost in there." Thomas shook his head skeptically.

"It's 'cause I drew the directions on their arms," said Felix.

Thomas' brows raised. "They can read?"

"Don't be stupid. I said I *drew*—arrows, ya know."

Thomas chuckled then disappeared into the tunnels. Kole made a note of which way he turned and hoped the dank tunnels held his odor. If Kole could make it out the door, he could follow his nose and navigate The Cobwebs.

"Looks like it's you and me, Blondie. Ya hungry?"

Kole's stomach roared. "Not really. I'm pretty tired."

"All right. I'll show ya to your room."

Kole followed him past the double doors. All he needed was a moment alone. He had to find Russé, and he wasn't about to put his faith in Thomas to get it done.

Three halls sprouted from the domed room. The two to his left and right appeared to be plain walls made of solid stone with a single exit at the end. Nearly a dozen doors and moonstone fixtures lined the hall ahead. Kole put the layout to memory. "What's behind these?"

"Bunks." Felix nudged open an ajar door and held his hand out, gesturing for Kole to enter.

Flat, stone ledges jutted from the walls, creating human-sized shelves. It seemed they were carved straight from the rock. The proximity reminded Kole of the trunk-houses back home. Only one held any bedding. Crumpled on the lowest bunk in the corner sat a pile of blankets and a flat pillow.

"Leo said every bed was filled at one point. The Liberation used ta be a few hundred strong." Felix shrugged. "Before my time, though. Got it all ta myself now. Leo wants ya ta stay in here so I can keep a close eye on ya."

Kole moved to a nearby bunk and laid down the journal. He propped Russé's staff against the wall as he mustered a fake yawn.

"There's a bath at the end of the hall you can use. Guess I'll play maid and getcha somethin' ta sleep on. Souls know I'm not sharin' mine."

Kole waited for Felix's steps to fade. Once quiet, he hid the journal under the bottom bunk where it would be safe from unwelcomed eyes, grabbed his staff, then moved to the door.

The hallway lay empty. If Thomas and the twins had already left, it meant he only needed to give Felix, Piper, and Leo the slip.

He tiptoed into the hall.

Piper and Leo had turned left out of the domed room, so he'd have to keep an ear out for them. And Felix... which way had he turned? Kole shook the concern away. With any luck, he would be long gone before he returned.

He hurried down the hall, slipped through the double doors, passed the great table, and reached the door leading to The Cobwebs. But the knob refused to turn. He shook the handle. Pulled and pushed. Both hands this time. He grunted in frustration as a jingle of metal sounded behind him.

"Locked," came Felix's voice.

Kole spun, grip tight on his staff. Across the room, Felix leaned against the door frame, a ring of keys spinning around his index finger and a wad of blankets tucked under his arm.

His green eyes flashed. "Where do ya think you're goin'?"

"Nowhere." Kole bit his tongue.

"Yeah, yeah, save that crap for Leo." Felix pushed from the frame and walked over. "Thought you could give me the slip, eh, Blondie?"

"No."

Felix waved a hand at Kole's answer, uninterested in his excuses. "Think you're gonna go after your friend, huh?" His lips thinned. "I wouldn't trust Thomas with somethin' like this either. He's good at layin' low, I'll give 'em that. But somethin' like this ain't gonna be talked about on the streets. I, on the other hand, am very good at gettin' into places where I shouldn't be. And that's the only kinda places they'll be talkin' 'bout your friend, I reckon." Reaching past Kole, he unlocked the door.

Kole stared, stunned. "You're letting me go?"

"Not alone. You'd be behind bars in a matter of minutes," Felix laughed. Putting away the key, he swung the door open. "We gotta get you some clothes first. People tend ta stare at scars. One sec." Felix jogged out the double doors and turned down the hall. When he returned, he held a pile of black clothes with him. "Put this on."

Kole did as instructed then stepped into the tunnel alongside Felix. "Why are you helping me?"

"Guess I know what it's like. Bein' forced to step aside while a friend is in danger."

"You mean the Escape," said Kole.

Felix's jaw flexed. He turned right, down the tunnel. "*And* I'm a little pissed Leo didn't give the job to me."

"What happened? With the Escape."

No response.

"She's your sister, right? Vienna," Kole pressed. "Did you know Idris was chasing her?"

Felix stopped. "Tried to stop her. Told her to come with me. That we could lure the Kayetan away." He lowered his head. "But she's stubborn."

"She left you."

He nodded.

"Why didn't you go after her?"

Felix turned around, his eyes on the floor. "There were too many Kayetans. Somehow Savairo found out 'bout the Escape. When the Kayetans ambushed, everyone scattered. Vienna and I went after Etta and Lily, but we were overrun. I remember fightin' off a pair of Kayetans, and when I turned around, she was gone. I tried ta catch up, then Leo came along. Said Vienna had made her decision and she could take care of herself. Guess he was right."

"Yeah." The image of Vienna fearlessly jumping from the trunk to face Idris surfaced in Kole's head. She never so much as flinched. He hoped she had awakened by now.

"You comin' or what?" Felix called.

Kole hurried after him.

CHAPTER 13

"I don't know about this." Kole pulled the black hood low over his eyes. Felix had nixed the head wrap, claiming the hood would be more inconspicuous in the city. Though Kole's face was cast in shadow, he felt exposed as the tunnel's stale air passed over his scars.

"You'll be fine." Felix swatted Kole's hands away from the fabric. "Stop messin' with it, will ya?"

They went left at a fork and followed the tunnel to a stop. Felix walked to the very end, hands searching the ceiling.

"Maybe we should rub some dirt on ya. Might cover the red a bit."

Kole chewed his tongue to keep from snapping back. It seemed insulting to think that rubbing dirt on his face would distract less than his scars. Instead, he shook his head at the idea.

Felix punched through a thin layer of hardened soil, exposing a small, brass knob.

Chunks of earth fell into Kole's eyes. "Thanks for the warning."

Felix smirked and, with a turn of the knob, pushed up the door like a hatch. Sunlight rushed into the tunnel, extinguishing the moonstone lights behind them.

"As long as ya follow me and stop touchin' yer disguise and, ya know, don't mention the Liberation, we'll be fine." Felix pulled himself out of the tunnel.

Kole peered through the hatch. A cloudless blue sky stared back at him, trimmed with the dull-brown roofs flanking either side of their secret hatch.

Felix's head popped into view. "Oh, and don't say anythin' 'bout the refugee camps." He held a hand down to Kole. "Just don't talk, really."

"So be invisible." Kole grabbed his forearm and climbed out.

"Not invisible, blend."

A buzz of voices reached Kole's ears as he wiped the dirt from his pants. Felix slammed the door shut and Kole peeked out from under his hood, surveying his surroundings. "This isn't exactly my favorite terrain. I'm used to trees, remember?"

The tunnel had spit them out in a quiet alley between two short, stone buildings away from the main street. A pile of broken wooden crates surrounded the hatch. Some sort of trash pile. Though he'd just pulled himself from it, the door was barely noticeable. The top had been painted to mimic the pattern of the cobble road. Only on closer inspection could he spot the thin seam.

He glanced over his shoulder. The wall encasing Socren's inner city towered over the buildings only a few blocks away. From a distance, it had made the city look like a fortress, but now, seeing it up close, he noticed the wear and tear of crumbling and cracked brick. It looked as though one carefully placed strike of a mallet might bring the whole thing crumbling down.

"Keep low and you'll be fine. Stay close," Felix warned, then bounded down the alley.

Kole rushed after him, and they weaved in and out of the alleys, ever nearer the sounds of the festivities. Felix stopped him at the edge of the main street.

Vibrant banners of red and yellow strung, roof to roof, between the houses of the city. Hundreds of people crowded the cobbled road. Some huddled in small groups, engrossed in conversation with the occasional outburst of laughter. Others strolled along, streaming in and out of the various shops and houses, arms filled with their prizes. The buildings looked to be in better shape than the wall, if only barely.

The scent of cooking meat sent Kole's stomach into a frenzy. His mouth watered as he took in the marvelous smell of sweet root, cloves, and garlic. The lively strumming of a guitar drifted on the wind, too, periodically drowned out by a chorus of indistinguishable lyrics.

"What are they celebrating?" Kole watched a group of children chase one another about the street, joyously unaware of the vexing stares cast their way when their game of tag disrupted the crowds.

"Savairo's reign." Felix pointed to a statue in the center of a large courtyard further down the road.

The statue stood twice the height of the surrounding buildings and, although he could only see the back of it, Kole could tell it was of a muscular man: legs chiseled into a wide stance with arms held firmly on his hips.

"I only come for the food," Felix smirked. "And the occasional coin. If ya follow a drunk long enough, he's bound ta drop a few."

"How can they celebrate him? Don't they know what he's doing?" Kole frowned at the smiling faces.

"Only the people beyond the walls seem ta have their head on straight. In their eyes," Felix said, dipping his head to the townspeople scurrying around them, "Savairo's the reason Socren hasn't been consumed by the Black Wall. He takes credit for keepin' it away from the city. Reminds them every chance he gets."

"What about the basin? The Kayetans? He's killed innocent people!"

"Not so loud, Blondie," Felix hushed.

Kole chewed his lip, trying to get his anger in check as Felix peered around the corner of the house, making sure no one had heard his outburst, then turned back.

"Savairo's pretty open 'bout those deaths," said Felix. "He pawns 'em off as rebels tryin' ta bring about an uprisin'."

Savairo's right about the rebellion, all right. Little did he know, it was coming from over the mountains, not the people of his city.

"Savairo says they threaten Socren's safety. No one questions him when he talks of the Black Wall." Felix held a sour look on his face. "If ya follow Savairo—support him like these hollow heads—you're rewarded. Anyone who speaks against him ends up workin' the farmlands or face down in that basin."

So he threatens them with hard labor and death. He thought back to the slaves on the mountain. He'd handed them their freedom, yet the only thing they could think about was the repercussions of crossing Savairo. No wonder these people didn't revolt. Believing Savairo meant safety, even if it was all a lie. Blissfully ignorant, like Kole'd been in the forest.

"Enough talk. We gotta get what we can and return before Leo notices we left. C'mon." Felix nudged his curly locks over his tattooed earlobe then jumped into the street and snaked his way to the middle of the flowing crowd toward the courtyard.

Kole tailed him, though not nearly as graceful. He bumped into several people, who cursed at him. After muttering his apologies, he slipped past to avoid their chiding glares. Self-conscious, he tugged his hood down lower over his face.

"Don't apologize," Felix prompted when Kole caught up. "Push your way through. Don't look back."

Kole nodded, and they continued up the road. He did as he was told, pushing his way through—not even looking back when he collided with a young woman carrying a bouquet of wildflowers. They dropped to the ground. A pair of feet trampled them. Kole bit down on his bottom lip to keep his 'sorry' at bay. Thinking it best not to linger, he ducked his head and sank into the crowd.

Felix stopped at a small stone building decorated in red banners. In the window hung a painted sign which read: Ruby's Tavern.

"Ya like dumplins'?" Felix asked.

"Huh?"

"Dumplins'. Ya know, meat and pastry?" Felix pointed at a small cart next to the tavern.

A chubby man stood behind an array of scrumptious-looking food. Jerky, golden-crusted breads, and dumplings sat displayed on the many shelves. The divine smell of caramelized pork skins made his tongue swell.

"Yeah, sure."

Felix grinned. "All right then, you go keep the big guy busy while I snag a few."

"We're stealing them?" Kole grabbed Felix's arm and pulled him back. "We can't *steal* them!"

Felix blinked at him. "Why not?"

"It's wrong." Kole scratched his head. "Isn't it?"

"Look." Felix set his hands on his hips. "This festival's held every year near the end of summer. Suppose' ta align with the harvest, but it ain't much of a harvest anymore. Did ya see the farms from the mountain?"

"They looked dead."

"That's 'cause they are. The farmers have been forced ta run the land into the ground tryin' ta keep up with Savairo's crop tax. The land is worn out. It's got nothin' left. The farmers do all this work just ta stay outta prison and end up with nothin' left for themselves after they pay Savairo's tax. They starve out there."

"Still—we can't just take it." Kole looked around the crowd anxiously. "It'll draw attention."

"Only if ya get caught." Felix winked. "Don't think of it as stealin'. Think of it as takin' back what's ours. Well, you don't live here—so mine." Felix jammed his finger into Kole's chest. "They stole from me, Blondie, and I want it back."

Kole lifted a brow. "They stole your dumplings?"

"Would it help if I said Yes?"

"Let's just focus on Russé first. Worry about food later."

A deep sigh and his shoulders caved forward. "You're missin' out, mate."

Kole rolled his eyes. He got the feeling *this* is why Leo had given Thomas the mission over Felix.

They continued down the road toward a tall stone tower he guessed was the prison. As they neared, the density of guards increased. They wore the same armor as the two he'd met on the mountain. Felix led him through the backstreets until the line of shops ended. "This is about as close as we can get without pullin' attention. Take a look."

He switched places with Felix so he hugged the corner of the shop. One hand keeping the hood low on his face, he brought his eyes to the edge of the bricks.

Halfway between them and the prison stood a small, circular structure littered with posters. Kole squinted, but the lettering was too small to read. A little ways beyond was the main entrance of the prison: a rusted, wrought-iron gate, flanked by two heavily armed guards. They stood so still, he thought them statues, until one of them lifted a hand at an approaching man. After a brief inspection, the guards waved him through and returned to their rigid stance.

"The ones at the gate. They'll know, won't they?" Kole asked.

"I wouldn't be so sure about that. The guards change shifts every few hours. Just 'cause they're there now doesn't mean they were on duty when Russé was brought in."

His lips thinned over his teeth. "Then we need to find out who *was* on duty last night. We need to ask around."

"Askin'? No. Questionin' a guard is a sure-as-hell way ta get your ass in a cell. The only time you can risk askin' a guard is when they're at least two ales in."

"So what now? I thought you knew what you were doing."

"I do," Felix snapped. "I've gotta plan. Follow my lead," Felix said, then stepped out from the alley.

Kole moved to follow, but stopped as a man next to the stone structure in their path unrolled a scroll and punctured it onto a nail protruding from a crack in the rock. The face sketched on the parchment looked all too familiar. Kole waited for the man to leave, then rushed over to the poster.

"Where are ya goin'?" Felix protested.

Kole's breath caught in his throat when he realized that he—his face—was on the poster. It read:

Disfigured youth. Suspected of collusion with the Liberation. Wanted for crimes of assault, aiding a criminal, and murdering freedom workers. Detain on sight.

"Murderer? Like hell."

"Guess the Taliroot didn't work, then," Felix groaned.

"I didn't kill anybody!" A hand clamped down over Kole's mouth.

"Shut yer trap."

Kole glanced back to the guards. Though the helms covered their eyes, the heads had turned their way. His voice had pulled their attention. *Damn.* Kole dipped his chin, knowing a gust could catch his hood and expose them. Felix grabbed him by the sleeve and hurried back into the safety of the festival crowd.

"Leo was right, I need to lay off the Tali." He put an arm around Kole and guided him to the alley saying, "We gotta get outta here before anyone recognizes ya."

Kole shrugged him off. "We can't leave. I have to find Russé."

"I hate ta say it, but we gotta leave this to Thomas."

"I can't."

"He's your friend, I get it, but—"

"You don't understand," Kole snapped.

"All right, Blondie, calm down," Felix said, his palms stretched out before him. "I know it's not what ya wanna hear, but we can't stay in the city. If we're caught, you can bet we'll both be thrown in a cell just like your friend. We're his only chance at gettin' out, but we can't do squat if we get ourselves locked up, too." Felix brushed the dark curls from his face.

Kole refused to leave. They'd come too far. And though he hated to admit it, he couldn't do this alone. He didn't know the city. Acting alone meant certain capture. If Felix had retracted his aid, Kole would have to convince him. So he put on his best face and gave a long, hefty sigh. "Yeah, you're right."

"'Course I am."

"I guess Thomas is just *better* at this than we are." Kole let the disappointment seep into his words and dramatically pushed his shoulders forward. He risked a glance to see if Felix had taken the bait. He held back a grin as Felix's freckled face contorted.

"Better? Thomas isn't better. He's just a smooth talker. Gettin' information is more than talkin', it's about blendin' in with your surroundins. Bein' unseen, ya know?"

"Not really. But I'm not familiar with this kinda stuff. I guess Leo knows who's best for the job."

Felix's eyes darkened. He chewed his lip for a moment, then pulled Kole down the lane to the back of the building and took a right toward the prison. A smile touched Kole's lips as he followed.

The massive stone construction towered over the city, casting a dark shadow down the central road. Kole thought it strange that the townsfolk were so merry and engrossed in the festivities while the prison's shadow weighed on their backs. They knew what atrocities went on behind those walls, and yet, it seemed no one cared. Perhaps they had grown desensitized to it by now. Or perhaps they really did buy into Savairo's crazy notions.

Felix pulled him behind a low wall encasing a small garden and studied their target. "You wanna get in? I'll getcha in," said Felix.

Kole examined the tower. The few windows, scattered along the south-facing wall, looked barred. *No use climbing.* What did Felix have in mind?

A few guards strolled along the perimeter of the prison, and they were headed their way. Felix must have noticed them, too, because he darted off saying, "Stay here."

"Where are you going?" Kole whispered after him.

Felix crawled around the corner, grabbed a broom and a thick washing cloth, then he laid the cloth open on the ground and started pounding his palm on the street cobbles.

Despite how ridiculous he looked, Kole refrained from intervening. Maybe Felix knew of another tunnel. But then why hadn't they taken it in the first place?

Stopping over a particular stone, he jammed the broomstick into its side. The rock popped free. After tossing the broom aside, he heaved the skull-sized stone onto the cloth and tied the four corners together, then dragged it back to Kole.

"What is that?"

"Our distraction." Taking up the ties of the cloth, Felix lifted the rock and turned in a circle. The wrapped stone rose with each spin. He released, and it soared up. Before it struck home, Felix grabbed him by the elbow and pulled him into a run.

Kole stumbled into the open road after him, looking up in time to see the makeshift cannonball slamming into the structure where his picture hung. Guards yelled from the courtyard. One hand on the brim of his hood, Kole pumped his legs, tailing Felix, then dove behind the prison wall as shouts called out, "It came from over there!"

Armored boots beat over the cobblestone. Kole and Felix followed the prison's perimeter to the north side and slipped around the corner. Felix leaned, a quick check, then straightened. A toothy smile greeted Kole. "We're clear."

No thanks to you, he wanted to say, but held his tongue. "Warn me next time before you go catapulting rocks into buildings."

Felix shrugged. "It worked, didn't it? C'mon, this way."

They crept along the back wall of the prison in search of another entrance. Nothing but hard dirt lay between the prison and the city wall fewer than a dozen meters away. Kole was used to being surrounded by massive trees, but something about the gray stone sent a pang of claustrophobia through him. The edge of the building came up fast and still no way in.

Rounding the corner, Kole froze at the sight of a group of people garbed in red cloaks. He backpedaled and bumped into Felix, who let out a grunt of annoyance. Kole signaled him to be quiet and mouthed, "We have company."

Seconds passed without an alarm, and he relaxed against the stone. They hadn't noticed him. He moved to the edge, allowing one eye beyond the wall.

Felix came up behind him, probably taking his own peek. "Red Cloaks," he whispered. "Don't look 'em in the eye."

"Why?"

Felix made a circle with his finger around his temple. "They mess with your thoughts. Make ya see things."

The five figures wore capes of deep crimson. Long hoods hid their faces from view. All fairly small in stature, their curved posture hinted that they were several decades older than Kole. Surely they had no place in combat.

The whine of an un-oiled hinge reached his ears, and the cloaked figures stepped through the back door. Except one.

The cloaked figure stood facing the door as if waiting for something. Then, as Kole leaned in, eyes squinting for a better view, the hood turned.

The man's face was obscured by the shadow of the hood, save for two glowing, gold eyes. They stared at him. It sent a cold rush through his bones. The icy sensation shot into his head. A foreign voice resounded in his skull.

"Who are you?" it asked.

Kole's name involuntarily spelled out in his thoughts as if the Red Cloak was siphoning out the information. Then, pictures of his former face—round cheeks and smooth skin—entered his head. It morphed to the moment he first laid eyes on his scarred face.

Felix shook him. He blinked, and the ice in his veins thawed.

The cloaked figure took a step toward him.

"We gotta get outta here!" Felix pulled on his shoulder again, but Kole, still in a daze, lost his balance and tripped. "Don't look him in the eye!" he scolded, dragging Kole to his feet.

The Red Cloak strode forward, only a few paces away.

Felix dragged Kole, who was still recovering his bearings, back the way they had come. Step by step, his head steadied until he could run without assistance and matched his pace to Felix's.

When they made it back to the courtyard, the guards still huddled around the vandalized structure; the poster with Kole's face plastered over their shoulders.

Felix pulled him into a slow walk. "Look ahead. Slow your breathin'. Smile like yer two pints deep."

He forced a goofy smile and breathed through his teeth as Felix led him into the festival crowd.

"Hey, stop," a guard yelled.

Felix grabbed his wrist and pulled him into the mass of people. They zigzagged through the mass of cheerful faces, bumping into shoulders and sending large cups of ale splashing to the ground. Kole kept one hand on his head, trying to keep his hood from flying off. Felix swerved toward an alley as the crowd's song and chatter broke into yells of anger and alarm.

"Keep up!" Felix yelled over his shoulder as he dropped Kole's wrist and dashed behind a row of shops.

The scar tissue in his groin and behind his knees fought against him. It refused to stretch, to let him lengthen his stride enough to keep up, and sent a shooting pain up his legs when he pushed his limits. He fell behind with each twist and turn down a different alley. Panic overtook him, but he kept going. If he lost sight of Felix, he'd be caught for sure.

Finally, after the guard's shouts had faded, Felix slowed, giving Kole enough time to regain lost ground. Felix led them back into the crowd, his head swinging back and forth as if searching for something. He must have found it because he darted into the street and closed in on a large cart filled with potatoes. A single horse stood at the front.

With a sagging back, paper-thin skin and cracked hooves, Kole wondered how the horse was able to stand, let alone pull a cart. As sickly as the animal looked, nothing could have prepared Kole for the state of the woman holding its reins. A skeleton was the only thing Kole could compare her to—a living, breathing, moving skeleton.

As her gaze turned to meet them, her youthful eyes narrowed. "'ello, Felix." She turned toward the sound of urgent voices up the road and raised a brow. "In trouble, are we?"

"Always." Felix winked and she giggled. "Can we get a lift outta the city?"

"What do you have for me?"

To Kole's surprise, Felix produced a handful of fresh, steaming dumplings from his pouch. "When did you take those?"

"Don't worry, Blondie. I didn't get caught." More shouts from up the street. "Yet."

The woman gave a yellow grin and pocketed them. "Who's yer friend?"

"New recruit," said Felix.

She gave Kole a once over. Instinctively, he lowered his face, keeping his features in the safety of the hood's shadow, but his hands were still exposed. The woman tipped her head toward the cart. "In the back."

"Thanks, Anna." Felix and Kole climbed onto the pile of potatoes.

Anna gave a click and the cart rolled, bouncing over the uneven road. Kole lay as flat as possible. He pulled the dirty potatoes over his body, but they kept rolling off and bumping into the side of the cart with a drum-like rumble.

"What are ya boys doin' back there?" Anna whispered over her shoulder.

Felix shot him a glare. "For the love of Souls, stay still, will ya. You're makin' a ruckus."

He followed Felix's lead and wriggled his body into the small nook between the lip of the cart and the spuds. A few minutes passed before he saw the top of the city wall come into view.

After they rolled under the gate, Felix popped up. "Oh, man, Blondie. That was close!"

"Caught stealin' again?" Anna said over her shoulder.

"Not exactly." Felix crawled up the cart and took a seat next to Anna, leaving Kole to sit alone among the spuds. "Got spotted by Red Cloaks."

Anna's face paled as if she regretted asking. She turned her eyes to the road and urged her lame horse faster.

"I told ya not to look them in the eye," said Felix. "What'd they get from ya?"

"My name," Kole said. "My past."

Felix exhaled. "Could've been worse."

He hadn't meant to, but something about their gaze made him *want* to look. "Who are they?" Kole asked.

"Savairo's sorcerers," Felix said, pursing his lips as if he had smelled something foul. Anna shifted uncomfortably beside him.

Kole glanced back and forth between them, noting their uneasiness. "Why do I get the feeling they aren't just sorcerers?"

"It's not who they are, it's who they *were*. The Red Cloaks are the reason Leo started the Escapes." His mouth twisted. "Ten years ago, Savairo raided Etta's orphanage. He took the kids and taught 'em blood magic."

Kole remembered the curve of their backs under the cloaks. "Ten years ago... but that would make them—"

"Not much older than us," Felix said. "Leo says blood magic cripples the body. The more ya use it, the faster ya age or somethin' like that. You'd have ta ask him. Savairo uses his sorcerers ta do most of his dirty work so he doesn't suffer the effects."

"Enough—please," Anna said. The reins shook in her hands. "No more talk of those *things* on my cart." She leaned over, patting her horse on the rump, and cooed, "It's all right, Honey. No reason ta fret."

The horse limped along. It favored its front right leg, barely putting weight on it as it struggled to keep pace. The prominent, forward lean gave Kole the impression the horse felt the weight of its added passengers. His heart sank for the poor beast.

He turned his attention to the barren land as Felix and Anna talked of more pleasant matters. Fields of shriveled crops lined the dirt road; their hollowed stalks poking from the soil like diseased fingernails. The parched earth kicked up under Honey's staggering gait, leaving the trio shrouded in a brown fog of dust. Hand over his mouth to keep from coughing, Kole peered through the veil of dirt for any sign of life. No trees graced the horizon or any shade of green for that matter. It truly was a dead land.

"Honey is lookin' well," Felix said, bracing the frame of the cart. Kole decided to steady himself, too, after a dip in the road made him come down painfully on his tailbone.

"Her leg pains her a bit. Got a good swipe a few weeks back from a—" she stopped herself and sighed. "Anyway, she's put on some weight. All in all, her health is improvin'. Still in high spirits, too. That's all I can ask for, really. Long as she's able to work, they won't take her." Anna looked at her horse fondly.

"They're serious about that, then?" Felix lay back and propped his feet up on the railing.

"Yeah." She pursed her lips. "Herald's mare was taken two days ago. He's torn up about it, but he's gotta make payment somehow, else they'll put him to work at the prison."

"He couldn't make payment? I thought Herald managed an acre of potatoes."

"He did. Someone robbed him nearly a week ago."

"Why didn't he tell us?"

"You know Herald, stubborn to the core."

"Sounds familiar." Felix gave her a suggestive glare.

Anna looked sideways at him and lifted her nose. "I make good on my own."

"For now," said Felix.

Anna pulled the reins and Honey slowed. "Better get out here, or else you'll have a long walk ahead of you."

Felix gently tugged Anna's earlobe. She smiled, and he hopped from the cart. Kole followed suit after thanking Anna for the ride.

"If ya need anythin' send word ta the Liberation, all right? Don't be stubborn like Herald," Felix called to her.

She nodded then whistled Honey into a canter. The horse's hurried hooves hammered into the road, leaving behind a cloud of rising dust.

CHAPTER 14

Piper sat at the stone table, hunched over a large, archaic-looking book, quill in hand, scribbling away at the pages when Kole and Felix returned.

"And where have you two been?" Her eyes never lifted from her task.

"Out," said Felix.

Piper licked her thumb and turned the page, her mouth set in an unconvinced line. "Does Leo know about this?"

"He doesn't have ta."

Piper's amber eyes bore into Felix. "He already knows. I was instructed to send you to him when you returned."

"What are ya, his lap dog?"

Piper's fingers twitched around her quill as if she was debating whether to stab it into Felix. Her eyes darted back to the page, and she continued her work. Felix stomped out the double doors, leaving Kole alone with Piper.

Kole moved for the door when she spoke. "Are you all right?"

"Fine."

"You don't need to wear that in here." She licked her finger and turned the page.

"I know."

When Kole kept his hood in place, she said, "Heard report of an incident in the city. I'm assuming that was you two."

"Yeah."

She glanced from her book, eyes peering past the shadow covering his face. "May I ask you something?"

Out of habit, he dipped his head lower. "Sure, I guess."

Piper motioned for him to sit. After he settled in, she asked, "What was it like? The Black Wall, I mean." She pulled on a piece of auburn hair, waiting for him to answer.

Kole's throat tightened. The faces of the dead leapt from the deep chasms of his mind, shining crisp and pure in his eyes. Niko. He could see his friend—picture every detail of his face. His hands tingled as the sensation of gripping Niko's arms returned. The slip. The separation. He closed his eyes and bit his scar-ridden lip.

"I'm sorry. I'm sure it's still fresh in your mind. It's only been, what? Three days? It was wrong of me to ask."

"Two. It's been two days." Kole tugged his sleeves down over his hands. Forty-eight hours ago, he'd have been staring at smooth skin. Niko would still be alive. At this very moment, he'd be around the fire, a bowl full of hot stew cupped in his hands with the orphans at his side while they listened to one of Goren's stories. But two days felt like a lifetime in his new body. "The Black Wall took everything from me. It's all consuming... it's...." He tried to think of a word to describe the blistering heat bubbling his skin; the raging wind tossing him like a ragdoll through the sky. But the only word that came to mind was, "Evil. Pure evil."

Piper pursed her lips. "I know it killed a lot of people you loved."

Kole averted his eyes. He didn't want her sympathy. Feeling sorry wouldn't bring them back.

"That's how you got your scars, isn't it?"

Kole dipped his head, letting the hood shadow his jaw and mouth. "Yeah."

"How did you and Russé survive?"

"The trees helped us." He heard the resentment in his own voice. "They pulled me back to safety. I was injured, but Russé healed me."

"He must be a very powerful sorcerer to heal such wounds."

"He's not a sorcerer." The words escaped him. He shut his mouth tight, ashamed he had let it slip. He had to raise his guard. It wasn't that he distrusted the Liberation, he just didn't know what was what anymore. When it came to Russé, Kole felt just as confused now as he'd been two nights ago when his mentor revealed his true identity. "The trees gave him a tonic," he said, trying to backtrack. "That's what healed me. Mostly."

"Well, I've never heard of tree tonics," Piper confessed. "Maybe he could teach me a thing or two. Leo is boring me with the basics. 'We can't move on unless your incantations are perfect'," she mimicked Leo's deep voice. "I'd be thrilled to learn something worthwhile for a change. You were Russé's apprentice, right? Did he dull you with basics in your shepherd training?"

"Yes," Kole admitted with a half-smile. "Russé had me sitting in the middle of the forest, telling me I needed to 'familiarize' myself with the sounds of the animals and trees. He'd have me sit there until dusk. Make me find my own way back." He shrugged the memory away. "It went on like that for a few months until he finally thought I was ready for the next stage."

"Sounds as bad as Leo. He's had me making salves and reading runes since I arrived."

Kole noted the bitterness in her voice. "When did you join the Liberation?"

"Almost a year ago."

"And your parents, are they...?"

The tip of Piper's quill ripped the page. She set it down. "They died at sea."

"You're not from Socren, then."

"No." She leaned back in her chair, eyes fixed on Kole. Her gaze made him uneasy, as if she was scrutinizing his every move. "I lived in Rush with my parents and my little sister, Raya. It's a small city on the eastern coast. Heard of it?"

He nodded, grateful for Goren's geography lessons.

"My parents were fisherman. It was our livelihood. That last year hadn't been very good to us. We ran low on food and money, so they set sail a week before the winter storms for one last haul." Her shook as she continued. "We waited three weeks for them to return. I knew after the first that something terrible had happened, but I kept quiet for Raya's sake. Then she got sick. I took her to the healers in town, but they were no help. Rumors of the Liberation had circled town for years. If anyone could help my sister, it was them."

By her tone, he could sense a morose end.

"She died on the road the next morning."

Kole looked away. He knew exactly how she felt. It echoed him losing Niko, except she'd watched her sister suffer.

"I haven't heard word of them—my parents. They just disappeared without a trace. No bodies. No wreckage. That's why I want to know about the Black Wall."

"You think it killed them?"

"It would certainly explain the 'no trace' part. That's why I came here instead of turning back. I had nothing left in Rush, and I wanted answers. But Leo's knowledge is limited to sorcery." Piper shrugged. "I think he felt bad for me, so he offered me a place here. But I have to tell you," she said lightly, lifting the mood, "this wasn't what I expected when he promised to teach me sorcery. Runes?" She waved a hand. "What use are they? I want to get into the more exciting things like his 'seeing truth' spell. Now *that* would be useful."

"Is that what he's doing when his eyes turn black?"

"A bit creepy, huh?"

Kole nodded. His stomach tightened as a smile touched her rosy lips.

"Can you imagine me throwing a salve at Idris? I mean, really. Leo means well, but I need to be better equipped if we're to fight creatures that powerful. And the Red Cloaks... I wouldn't stand a chance." She sighed. "I think Leo is waiting until I turn eighteen to teach me anything else. He sees it as being cautious; waiting until I am 'mature enough to know the severity of using more powerful types of magic.' But his caution at a time like this could cost me my life." She tucked a fallen strand of auburn hair behind her ear. "I wish he would trust me. He's never said it outright, but I think Leo's afraid I'll be tempted to use blood magic, like his brother."

"His brother?"

"Savairo," Piper said as casually as if she'd said the sky was blue.

Kole's mouth fell open. "Savairo is Leo's brother?"

"You didn't know?"

Mouth still agape, Kole shook his head.

"Leo doesn't like to talk about it, but it's not exactly a secret."

Another thing Goren had failed to mention, apparently. At this point, Kole wouldn't be surprised if Piper told him the ocean was made entirely of purple sand. "How did Savairo end up warden?"

"After their father's death, Leo was next in line. But when time came to take the position, rumor has it, he was too distraught and fled the city."

Leo? Distraught? The Liberation leader had kept an almost too-calm demeanor when Kole first arrived. Leo never even flinched when he learned the Black Wall had wiped out the orphans.

Kole leaned back in the cold, stone chair, folding his arms over his chest. "That doesn't sound like him."

"Because it isn't. Savairo forced him out. I don't know the details, but I know he cheated him, and Leo's been trying to take back Socren ever since."

"And he can't because Savairo is more powerful," Kole said, connecting the dots. "Because of blood magic."

Piper nodded.

"What is blood magic? Why is it so strong?"

Piper glanced to the double doors, a look of caution on her face. She leaned in, voice quiet. "Sorcery is fueled by the ingredients you use. Plants, metals, gems—that sort of thing. But the more sentiment or emotion the sorcerer has with an ingredient, the more powerful the spell becomes. Blood magic is the same, except, as I'm sure you've guessed, they use blood in *their* rituals." Piper checked the door again before she continued. "Sacrifices. Torture. The pain—the emotional anguish—gives strength to the spell. Savairo uses the blood of his victims to fuel his magic."

"The town knows about this? That he uses this kind of magic on his people?"

"Everyone knows."

"How can they stand for it?"

"Fear is a tight leash. Many have stood against Savairo and have suffered because of it. They don't want to end up dead. Or worse."

"A Kayetan," Kole said. It started to make sense, if only just. The city folk were trying to save themselves and their families. The refugees and the people of Socren were one and the same. They both did what they needed to survive, letting others suffer to secure their own safety. For every orphan smuggled out of the city, away from Savairo's grasp, another citizen disappeared to replace the empty slot in his experiments. If the only options meant living under Savairo's rule or facing a life of torture—or worse, see your family go through it—Kole could hardly blame them for their choice.

"I'll admit, blood magic *does* have a lure." She squeezed the quill in her hand. "It's the highest form of sorcery. With the right intent, we could do a lot of good with it. But Leo refuses. He says once you use it, there's no coming back. The lust for power consumes you." The white light of the moonstone lanterns glowed eerily on her alabaster skin. Her caramel eyes found his. They were serious and unwavering as she said, "But I am *not* Savairo. I'm stronger than Leo thinks."

Her fiery stare kindled a warmth in his stomach. Kole broke from it and cleared his throat. Trying to fix his gaze on anything else, it landed on her open book. *The Fifth Escape*, written in fine scrawl, headed the page.

"What is that?"

She looked down. "They're the Escape Records. Leo is having me update the names of the dead after...."

Kole craned his neck to read the page. Piper had gone through marking *deceased* next to those who had perished in the Black Wall. A spark of hope ignited within him. "May I see that?"

Piper gave him an odd look before sliding the book across the table.

He flipped it around, dragging his thumb down the page as he scanned the names. His finger paused at his friend's name. *Niko: deceased*. Next to it was a record of relatives: parents, siblings, aunts, and uncles. All dead, just as Niko had told him. Further down, more of his camp mates graced the page, their families listed after them, all branded as dead. He turned the page: *The Sixth Escape*.

Flipping back, he reread the list of children, slower this time. Dread filled him as he finished.

His name was missing.

Keeping his face calm as to not alert Piper, he flipped through the rest of the records, hoping his name had been jumbled into one of the other Escapes by mistake.

"I haven't gotten past that page yet," Piper said, a hint of irritation in her voice as if he was messing up her work.

He slammed the book and shoved it back over the table.

Etta was right. Goren had lied to him. If he hadn't come to Solpate through the Escapes, where did that leave him? He chewed his lip. Every time it seemed he verged on an answer, he was met with more questions. It sparked a fear in him that this whole facade held more behind it than he'd initially thought. Goren deliberately hid this from him. He must have had a reason. Worse yet, Kole couldn't shake the feeling that something terrible was lingering in his past—something his mind refused to remember.

The stone chair scraped the floor as he stood. He made his way to the double doors without so much as a glance toward Piper. He felt too angry to play cordial. She called after him, but he ignored her. The only thing on his mind was Goren's journal as he stalked back to the bunk Felix had set up for him.

Snatching the book from its place under the column of stone beds, he flipped it open. It must contain something. A name. A place. At the last page, he stopped. The Seven Souls symbol stared up at him as if it were mocking him, saying, *I'm the only thing you've got!*

Kole slammed the book shut, cursing Goren. He chucked it across the room just as the door flew open.

The journal slammed into Felix's stomach, who grunted and doubled over as the book dropped to the floor, sprawled open to a random page. "Maybe I should've knocked."

"Sorry," Kole grumbled. He snagged the journal before Felix had a chance to notice the strange runes.

"What's got your knickers in a twist?"

"Nothing."

Felix pursed his lips, unconvinced, but he didn't press. Needing a moment alone, Kole pushed by him and plodded down the hall to the bath.

He shut the door behind him and leaned into the wood, head buried in his hands. His lower back stung on contact. Kole let out a grunt, more out of annoyance than pain, and pushed away.

Stripping out of his borrowed uniform, Kole unwrapped the bandage from his waist and gingerly reached an arm around his back to finger the wound. Slick with ooze. There was little he could do on his own, save for keeping it clean.

He turned his attention to the small stone basin carved into the floor at the center of the room. Water already filled the bath. Kole lowered himself in and washed the stink from his body, taking extra care not to agitate his sensitive skin. The dirt and grime from the mountain slipped away.

He focused on the silence as he washed. Thoughts of the Soul, the Black Wall, and Goren clouded his head. He pushed them down. It had been so long since he had a clear mind. The whirlwind of danger these past few days left him in a constant state of fear and rage.

All he wanted was a moment alone. Peace seemed too much to ask. Numbness. That's what he needed: a moment to forget—to be nothing and think of nothing. He sat in the water, drinking in the rare moment.

By the time he felt ready to face the world again, the skin of his hands and feet had wrinkled. He took a towel from a stack in the corner and dried. Not wanting to risk infection, he ditched the grimy old bandage and slipped into his borrowed uniform.

Felix was waiting on Kole's bunk, feet swinging impatiently.

"I need a bandage."

"Leo'll have something. That's where we're headed anyway. He's got news of your friend."

Kole straightened. "Russé? Is he ok?"

Felix shrugged. "I'm just the messenger."

Felix brought Kole through a short tunnel to a room he called Leo's laboratory. It was considerably smaller than the great room, or maybe it only looked that way because of the vast amount of stuff Leo had crammed into it. Corked bottles of brightly colored liquid, dusty old books, and rusted tools cluttered every flat surface in the room, sometimes precariously stuffed and stacked into places, where even the smallest bump would send them tumbling. The stone floor was barely visible under the thick layer of scribbled parchment and broken bottles.

Leo held the door open to his laboratory, hands and face smudged with black powder, and ushered them in as if completely unaware of the state of the room.

Walking by, he stole a glance at Leo. How could two people from the same bloodline end up so different? It extended far beyond one preferring the summer and the other winter. Leo and Savairo stood on opposite sides of morality: brothers turned enemies. Kole suspected quite a story behind the fallout.

He tiptoed over the papers, careful to avoid the steam rising from one of the broken bottles lying in the center of the room. Kole glanced from Felix to Leo. Their disregard told him the fumes were nothing worthy of concern. Still, Kole kept his distance as it filled the room with a sour odor.

"Blondie's wounded," Felix said.

"I'm not *wounded*." He waved a hand at Leo's worried gaze. "It's a little thing I got a couple days ago. It hasn't had the chance to heal with everything going on. Just need a fresh bandage."

Leo nodded and moved to a set of drawers, returning with a long strip of fabric.

Kole lifted his shirt at Leo's command. Though he couldn't see the wound for himself, the Liberation leader's frown gave him an idea of its festered state.

"I have something to help boost the healing process. And keep it from infection."

Before Kole could protest, something cold slid over his back. The wound sizzled, and he sucked a breath through his teeth.

"My apologies. I should have warned you." Leo laid the fabric flat across Kole's stomach and wrapped his torso. "Give it a moment. This little concoction of mine works wonders."

"Not too tight." The snug bandage, though soft to the touch, felt like sandpaper on his skin. Leo released the tension and continued his work.

A bird chipped. Kole's eyes followed the sound to the corner, where Fiona perched. She'd returned. He nodded to the bird. "What did the refugees say?"

"The refugees received our message. They are changing their plans to coincide with ours." After tying off the bandage, Leo pulled a scroll, no bigger than Kole's thumb, from his coat pocket and handed it over.

Kole shifted back and forth, testing out the tension of the band. Pleased, he pulled down his shirt and unraveled the scroll.

It was a letter from Darian. The refugees were making the trek over Poleer a day earlier to arrive at midnight. They were mass producing as many bows and arrows as time allowed, so most of the refugees could attack from the cliffs and use their hunting backgrounds as an advantage. Darian was bringing every trained forest mount in his possession, along with any melee weapons they had in camp. He also informed Leo that Idris had not been seen since Kole and Russé's departure.

Details of the Soul had been left out. Russé's secret seemed safe for now. Kole handed it back.

Leo slipped it into one of his breast pockets. "While you two were out causing a scene at the festival, Thomas returned with some useful information."

"How does he do it? Every time." Felix sulked.

"He found Russé?" Kole asked hopefully.

"We have confirmation he is being held in the prison, but...." His face darkened.

Leo's hesitance made Kole's stomach ache.

"The Red Cloaks have been questioning him."

"Shit." Felix slammed a hand on the counter.

Kole jumped at the noise and whipped his head between the two. "That's good, right? We know who we're looking for... where they are. And if they're questioning him it means he's alive."

"For now," Felix muttered.

Mouth agape, Kole looked to Leo for hope.

"We'll need to move quickly." The Liberation leader took a slow breath. "I have never heard of anyone lasting more than a day in their custody."

CHAPTER 15

Criz held a dumb look of excitement on his face as he stood atop the opposite end of the long, stone table. He was dressed in an extremely dented suit of armor identical to the ones Kole had seen Socren's on-duty guards wear. "Hit me! Hit me!" he yelled at Kole, his voice bouncing around the domed room.

Kole's borrowed sword shook, unsure in his hand, as he stood at the opposite end of the grand table. Leo had made plans to break into the prison at dawn, during the guard's shift change. Since Kole had no previous combat training, Leo only agreed to let him go along if he could hold his own against armored guards. He would need to convince Felix of his capability and he'd be in the clear.

"Yeah, hit him!" Boogy chorused behind his brother.

"Whoa, whoa, whoa!" Felix stepped onto the table and planted himself between them. "This isn't a willy-nilly, 'see-how-many-hits-ya-can-take-ta-the-head-before-passin'-out' brawl. We gotta train him right."

Criz hunched over in the creaking armor. Though the helmet concealed his face, the long sigh disclosed his disappointment.

"Maybe we can play after." Boogy consoled his brother with a pat to his metal-clad shoulder.

"No." Felix pointed a threatening finger at them as if scolding a misbehaving dog. "Leo wants you both in one piece for the battle. And besides," he motioned to the armor, muttering under his breath, "that's how we got it taken away in the first place."

"What are you guys doing?" Thomas entered through the double doors. Catching a glimpse of Criz's attire, he shook his head. "Not again. Didn't Leo hide that from you three?"

"Just *those* two," Felix corrected. "*I* wasn't involved."

"You might not have worn the armor, but you sure egged them on. I'd say that involves you."

"He *un*-hid it from us." Boogy donned a proud smile.

"He *gave* it to us." Felix rolled his eyes at him, then lifted his chin. "We're trainin' Blondie."

"Training?" Thomas asked. Kole frowned as Thomas cracked a laugh. "I thought you only knew how to steal, Felix."

Felix's freckled cheeks reddened. "Think you can do better, eh?"

"Well, let's see if he's learned anything." Thomas leaned his hip against the table and looked up to Kole. "Where are the weak points in a suit of armor? What is your best advantage against an opponent like this? And most importantly, what do you do if you find yourself outnumbered?"

"I–uh…." Kole's eyes glided from Felix to Thomas. He tried to think of something to say to ease the thickening tension between them. He drew a blank. "I don't know."

Felix's shoulders fell forward. "We've only just started."

"We got no time to waste. Put your sad excuse of a brain with mine, and let's give him some pointers so he won't die." Felix made a choking sound, obviously taken aback by Thomas' cooperation, until he added sharply, "Or worse, get *us* killed."

Kole's knuckles tightened around the hilt, determined to pass as a more skilled swordsman than he actually was. He told Leo he'd been trained in combat. A partial lie. He and Niko had spared since they were old enough to swing a stick. Informal training, but something. Armed guards offered a more difficult adversary. He risked more than welts and bruises if he made a mistake on the battlefield. The only problem he foresaw lay in his scars. He hadn't picked up a sword since the accident, but using Russé's staff on the guards earlier gave him a clue of how his range of motion had changed. *You only have to convince them enough to let you go.*

"All right then." Felix stepped forward with a new certainty, Thomas scrutinizing from the ground, and stopped next to Criz. "There's a few places ya gotta aim for if ya wanna do any damage to these blokes. Lift your arms, Criz." He obeyed. "The armpits. They'll be exposed when the guard swings. It's the easiest place ta hit flesh, but ya gotta position yourself right. Sword, Boogy." Felix held out his palm as Boogy handed over his weapon. "It helps that we're shorter. Makes all the difference in positionin'." Felix lowered into a stance in front of Criz.

Armor clanking, Criz readied himself.

"Slow strikes so we can show him."

Criz rattled his head up and down, and they began.

Felix did the opposite of what Kole would have expected and lowered the tip of his blade so it skimmed the top of the table. "Ya wanna wait for them ta strike first. Give 'em an openin'." Criz swung at Felix, a horizontal strike aimed at his torso. "Deflect it up." Felix lifted his sword, and it collided with Criz's blade. Flicking his wrist, he redirected the swing over his head. "Then duck under," Felix demonstrated, moving under Criz's arms, which were still locked into the momentum of his swing. "And make your hit." He touched the blade to Criz's exposed armpit. Then, they both relaxed and returned to the starting position.

"Don't hesitate," Thomas added, joining them on the table. "The window to make your move will be small. Miss your opportunity, and they'll know what you're up to next time. Stab strong and deep. Go for the kill."

Kole sucked in his lip. *Go for the kill.* He'd only ever killed animals. But people? Living, breathing people? His hands shifted nervously on the hilt.

"Go for the kill," Thomas repeated as if he sensed Kole's hesitance, "or be killed."

Felix went on to explain the next vulnerable spot—the inner thighs. He motioned to the place on Criz where the armor stopped and Criz's black uniform peeked out.

"Use your speed," Thomas commentated as Felix rounded Criz before he could recover from his initial swing. "And slice this time. You're aiming for the artery."

"If ya hit it, he'll bleed out." Felix stopped when his blade touched the inside of Criz's leg.

The boys reset.

"And lastly," Thomas said, "you can focus on the head. I wouldn't do this unless you're in a bind. It leaves you vulnerable no matter how you do it. The blade will slide off the curve of the helm. But a pommel to the skull?" Thomas balled his fist and tapped the top of Criz's helmet. "Even a dent will press into their heads. You'll disorient them after a few blows."

"That's my favorite," Boogy said from the floor. Criz's grunts of agreement resonated inside his armor.

"But the biggest rule when fighting, if you want to stay alive is...."

"Don't fight alone," all four chorused together.

"We stick together," said Felix.

"Keep close ranks," said Thomas. "Run when you need to, and most importantly, don't be a hero."

Now came Kole's turn.

He learned quickly. They talked him through each movement, slowly at first, until Kole repeated it so many times he was convinced he could do it in his sleep. Then, they sped up the movements.

The feet came naturally—he accredited his shepherd's training for that. Kole imagined himself dodging in and out of rambler roots instead of evading a sword, making it all too easy for him to duck under and sidestep Criz's blows. The sword, on the other hand, took time for him to master. When he had passed through the movements a few minutes ago at his own pace, his body hadn't bothered him. The faster swings proved harder to control, and the momentum of the sword twisted his arms and torso uncomfortably. Kole found himself holding back mid-swing so he could stop the blade before it could pull his skin. This weakened his attack, and he could tell by Thomas' frown that he wasn't happy with it.

The final blow gnawed on Kole's conscious. Sure, he could go through the exercises and pretend, but that was just what is was: pretend.

"What's wrong, Blondie?"

Kole pulled himself from his thoughts, realizing he was standing next to Criz with his sword resting against his arm pit. Who knows how long he had stood there, frozen in place. *Too* long by the odd expressions forming on Felix's and Thomas' faces. Even Criz held a curious stare from behind the slates of his helm.

"Nothing," he lied. If he told them the truth it would make him look weak. And if they thought, even for a moment, Kole would refuse to kill in the heat of a fight, he'd have no chance of joining the prison break tomorrow. "I'm getting too hot. I need a second." *That* wasn't a lie. His body was overheating from the exertion like it had when he had climbed Poleer.

"Let's call it a night." Felix took the sword from Kole and handed over the waterskin from his belt. "Drink up."

"Thanks." Kole chugged the contents, wiped his mouth, then sat on the edge of the table and handed back the waterskin. The cool stone alleviated some of the heat in his legs.

Criz shuffled to the edge of the table and stretched an armored leg. With only a few small slits to see through, he misjudged the distance and toppled forward. The clamor of armor echoed down the halls as he face-planted onto the stone floor.

They all stared at him in silence.

Laughter erupted from the suit of armor. "Didn't feel a thing," Criz wheezed.

They all joined in, laughing harder still when Criz tried to stand but only succeeded in looking like a turtle flipped on its shell as he rolled side to side on the curved breastplate.

Kole laughed until his stomach began to ache and his cheeks pained from smiling.

Boogy finally, after catching his breath, gave his brother a hand.

"Some of us are trying to sleep," Piper's voice bellowed from the doorway. Her usual sleek, auburn hair puffed in a frizzy mass atop her head, and she held a blanket tightly around her shoulders. Her pale skin looked more washed out than normal.

Thomas stifled his laughter. He cleared his throat and stepped from the group, separating himself from the chaos. "Sorry, Piper. I'll send them to bed." His cheeks flushed a bright shade of pink.

Her eyes flicked over to Thomas for a moment, pursing her lips disapprovingly, then landed on Kole. Piper stared at him a bit too long, and Kole felt his cheeks warm. A strange curiosity flickered in her eyes, something between concern and suspicion. He shifted under her gaze. Without a word, she turned on her heel and, bare feet slapping the stone, left them in an awkward silence.

Kole blinked as Thomas' stare burned into him. His expression morphed to his usual scowl, and he stomped from the room.

Felix rested his arm on Kole's shoulder. "Don't worry about him. He gets jealous when Piper gives anyone a bit of attention."

"Are they together or something?" Kole asked as the blood resettled in his cheeks.

"He wishes! Been followin' her around like a pup since she got here, but Piper doesn't seem to be interested in anythin' other than trainin'." Felix shrugged. "C'mon let's get outta here."

Boogy's grunts made Kole turn. His arms were wrapped around his brother's head in a struggle to pull the helmet off. "Your head is too fat! I told you I should've put it on," he wheezed. Criz made odd whimpering sounds from inside the armor.

Felix waved a hand at Kole's concerned squint. "They'll be fine."

As they returned to the bunks, he couldn't shake off the look Piper had given him. She had been so open about her past when they last spoke. Yet she regarded him with a coldness like she had when he'd first arrived. Maybe his abrupt dismissal earlier had upset her. He *had* left her right after she'd opened up about her family. It could have come across as rude, but after scouring through the records he—

Kole stopped in the doorway as a thought came to him. *She knows.* Piper went through the records same as he had. She would have noticed his missing name. His and Russé's.

"You all right?"

Kole blinked at Felix. His demeanor hadn't changed, which meant Piper had kept this new information a secret. Would she continue to? Worse, would she tell Leo? Did Piper even know what his absence in the records meant? Kole sure as hell didn't.

"Blondie?" Felix leaned in, scrunching his nose as he inspected Kole.

"Fine. Tired is all."

"Well, you're in luck. I got somethin' that'll put ya right ta sleep." Felix reached under his bunk and pulled out a bottle. "Have any of this back in Solpate?" He popped the cork with his thumb.

"What is it?" Kole sank into his bunk on the opposite wall. He eyed the darkened bottle curiously.

"Mead." Felix tilted his head back and guzzled the liquid. Bringing it away from his lips, he whistled, then offered it to Kole. "Go on, a swig is all *you'll* need," he said when Kole hesitated.

Kole took the container from him. The bitter smell wafting from it made him gag, but his body ached and his mind raced with guilt and questions. If mead was anything like ambrosia, his body would be grateful. Kole took a long swig.

The bitter liquid rolled over his tongue. He forced it down and pushed the mead away. A warmth tingled down his throat into his belly much like the ambrosia had done, but instead of reaching out to his limbs, it pooled in his core like he had stuffed himself full of Goren's rabbit stew. Slowly, his stiff muscles relaxed, and the mess in his head cleared. Curious to see what another drink would do, he tipped it back, but Felix pulled the bottle away and waved a cautioning finger.

"Just the one for you. It gets stronger, trust me." Felix took another sip, then stopped the jug and stashed it under his bunk. "It'll kick in soon. Helps me sleep when my mind gets ta racin'," he said as he crawled back into his bunk. "Just close yer eyes and welcome it."

Kole didn't protest. He climbed onto the flat stone ledge. Pulling the blanket to his chin, he sank his head into the pillow and stared up at the bunk above him. His mind grew calmer as the warmth of the mead in his belly and the soft blanket weighing down on him pulled him closer to sleep. Even the rock slab, hard and cold against his spine, began to feel comfortable.

His head felt free, as if he'd had a wall built up around his mind this whole time and with that small sip of mead, he'd finally burst through; all his thoughts and worries draining out... completely forgotten now. His eyelids anchored shut.

"You'd better have something."

"We have been unsuccessful thus far."

"What do you mean 'unsuccessful?'"

"We are not able to penetrate his mind. He is unlike anything we have seen."

"Move aside."

Kole's eyes flitted open. He lay on a table in a dimly lit room. Hunched figures draped in red cloaks, their faces hidden beneath long hoods, surrounded him. One of them stepped back as a man in a long, black coat approached. The man appeared a spitting image of Leo, save for a pair of deep-set wrinkles between his brows that could only have come from holding a constant grimace.

Savairo.

He pulled off his black leather gloves one finger at a time. A pressure built around Kole's mind as Savairo pressed his thumbs into his temples.

It felt as if his brain rested in the palm of a hand. Then, the hand closed. It squeezed until an energy burst inside of him.

By the smirk deepening on Savairo's face, Kole knew something bad had happened.

Suddenly, a fiery anger surged through him, and an alien presence in his head lashed out at Savairo. The anger – the energy – it wasn't Kole's.

Without warning, Kole shot his hand up to Savairo's cheek. Thin, wrinkled skin covered his arm where burn scars should be.

Savairo's eyes opened wide at his touch. A flash of metal at the sorcerer's neck. A mirrored brooch. He found his reflection in it, but it wasn't Kole's face staring back at him. It was Russé.

Russé was the one lying on the table. Russé was the one fighting back. His nails had dug into Savairo's cheek, making him scream, not Kole's.

Foam bubbled from Savairo's mouth as his eyes rolled back. Whatever power Russé set loose on the blood sorcerer seemed to be working.

A heavy exhaustion cut the assault short, and Russé released his hold. Kole felt a bite in his knuckles as the Soul's hand fell limp against the table.

Savairo stumbled into one of the red-cloaked men, who caught him before he landed on the stone floor. He pushed the acolyte away and lifted to his feet. Standing tall once more, he wiped the froth from his mouth. "Send word to Aterus."

The men silently looked to one another from under their red hoods.

"Is it him? Are you sure?" one asked. "A false report could — "

"I said send word!" Savairo roared. The men in red flinched, then bowed and left Kole's view.

Alone, Savairo pulled a vial of crimson liquid from his coat and downed it. A violent tremor shook his body. He inhaled. Forcing a breath through his teeth, he straightened. A new, more malevolent presence flickered in his bloodshot eyes. Savairo returned to the side of the table and bent down to Russé. Kole felt the sorcerer's humid breath on his ear as he growled. "Won't be long now."

CHAPTER 16

"Kole! Hey, Kole!"

Kole's eyes whipped open. His breath came in short bursts.

Felix hovered over him. "You all right, Blondie? Ya don't look so hot."

"Fine." Kole kicked the blanket off, welcoming the cool air on his overheated skin. "Had a dream."

"Eh? What kind of dream? You were screamin' pretty loud there, mate."

"I wasn't... I don't know. I saw Savairo and those people in red."

"Whoa, hold up. People in red? Ya mean the Red Cloaks?"

Kole nodded.

Felix's face grew hard and serious. "We need ta go see Leo."

"Leo? Why? It was a dream."

"It's never a dream if there's sorcerers, mate."

When Felix opened the door to Leo's lab, a wall of stench hit Kole's face. He covered his nose.

Leo hunched over a peculiar pike, half covered by a draped cloth, made entirely of white stone like the charged obsidian blades the Liberation carried. An odd pair of glasses with small telescope-looking pieces where the lenses should be, rested on the bridge of his nose. Leo looked up from his work and quickly pulled the fabric over the pike as if trying to conceal it.

"Kole had a dream. I think ya need ta hear this."

As Kole recounted it, the Liberation leader kept a stone face. "I see...." He tapped a finger on his chin.

"So... it's nothing bad, then?" Kole asked.

"It was not a dream, it was a mind-link. They can only be established by a trained sorcerer, used to get inside a person's head. Gain access to thoughts, memories.... But it is odd. Mind-links normally work with two people; the first being the sorcerer casting the spell, in this case Savairo, and the second being the target, which was Russé. It is odd that it pulled *you* in when it should have only affected the shepherd. Never heard of something like this. Mind-links do not jump from person to person. You are sure you were *in* Russé's body?"

Kole vividly remembered the feeling of Savairo's skin against his hands as he—well, Russé— fought back. Savairo's screams still rang in his ear. "I'm sure."

"Have you had any training in the arts?" Leo's demeanor changed. His voice became even, and he stared at Kole with unblinking black eyes similar to when he'd interrogated Kole earlier that day.

"You mean sorcery? No, I'm a shepherd—just a shepherd."

"But your friend has such training." Leo's eyes grew distant. "Russé faces grave danger if Aterus is interested in him."

Kole didn't know if it was the fog of the mind-link or the haze of the ale Felix had given him a few hours earlier, but the name finally registered in his head.

Aterus. He knew him as the Gray Soul: the one who'd birthed humanity. It looked like Russé wasn't the only Soul on Ohr. "What does Aterus want with Russé?"

"I was going to ask you the same question," Leo said. "What would a Soul want with a shepherd?"

Kole held his gaze for a long moment. Leo was luring him. "I don't know."

Leo's pupils retracted, breaking the spell, and he turned to Felix. "Grab Thomas." After Felix left, Leo returned his attention to Kole. He leaned against his work table and folded his arms. "Aterus is responsible for Savairo's reign. Do you know the story?"

Kole shook his head.

"Before that day, we all thought Aterus had ascended with the other Souls, as the stories told. I was a bit older than you when he first came to Socren. He called upon my father. We had our doubts, but Aterus proved very convincing. The magic he could do... we had no doubts of his validity. A Soul. One of the Seven." Leo motioned to the tattoo on his neck. "He seemed like a decent man—a bit proud, looking back on it— but he was kind to us. He only stayed for a short while. After he left, my brother," Leo caught himself. "*Savairo* was forever changed. He began exploring the dark arts: blood magic, sacrifices. Horrible things. Our father disapproved, but Aterus encouraged the practices. The Soul showed up every now and then, always calling on Savairo. Then, my father died." Leo placed his hands on the edge of the table. "After the funeral, I planned to take his place like he wanted, but that night my own guards expelled me from the city. Savairo had forced their hands. Bribed. Threatened. I still do not know how. But I was banished."

A pang of sympathy echoed through Kole. He remembered the utter betrayal he'd felt when Darian had sought to shun him for leading Idris to the southern camp. "Why are you telling me this?"

"Because I know Aterus had something to do with my banishment." Leo's clenched fist relaxed on the table. "I do not know what he wants with your friend, but it cannot be good. Just as he changed Savairo, he could very well change Russé. We need to get him back before that happens."

Something still confused him. Leo made it seem like Aterus might intend to hurt Russé. Why would a Soul harm one of their own? Kole chewed his lip. He was missing a big piece of the puzzle, and that piece might be the reason Russé had kept his identity hidden. Kole was tempted to find out what else Leo knew of the Souls, but he feared that showing too much interest would induce more suspicion. So he kept his mouth shut, promising himself he would find his answers once they got Russé back. Kole would *make* him talk. "How do we get him back?"

"By the description of your mind-link, they are most likely keeping him on the bottom level of the prison. Savairo likes to conduct his experiments down there. The screams are muted that far underground," he said, grimly. Leo set his onyx eyes on him and shifted into a more relaxed stance. "Kole, if there's anything I should know... I implore you to speak now. Do you know why Aterus would harbor an interest in your shepherd?"

So that's your strategy. Share a secret in hopes I'll spill one of my own. A lump formed in Kole's throat. He could tell him now. How easy it would be to speak the words. Even as they formed on his tongue, a sense of warning—alien to him—weighed on his conscience, as if someone else was there with him, monitoring his thoughts.

Her again. The voice from the basin. The same voice that emerged during his fight with Idris under the Great Red. The one that warned him of the Black Wall moments before it annihilated the orphans. He opened his mouth to speak. Her grip tightened around his vocal chords.

"No." The word came out on its own.

"Look who I found lurkin' in Pipes' room," Felix said. He wore an amused smirk as he strolled through the door, Thomas in tow.

Kole relaxed, grateful for the distraction. The presence hovering over his words eased.

"I wasn't lurking," Thomas snapped, then turned to Leo. "She's been gone too long. Something could've—"

As if reluctant, Leo pulled his eyes from Kole and shifted his attention to the boys. "She is on an errand for me. I am certain she is safe."

"I wouldn't be so sure. I found this under her bunk." Thomas held up a tome bound in black-and-red leather.

Leo paled. Then, quicker than he could blink, Leos' face darkened to an angry shade of maroon. It marked the first time Kole had seen him lose control of his poised demeanor. Leo snatched the book from Thomas, slammed it on the counter, and rifled through the pages.

Kole elbowed Felix. "What is it?"

"Hell if I know."

"It has dark spells in it," Thomas said.

"How do you know?" Felix asked.

"Because I *talk* to Piper," Thomas said, annoyed. "The cover has the blood magic seal."

Leo stopped on a page halfway into the tome. Kole raised to his toes to get a better look. Runes littered the page in blocked handwriting. A ripped edge sprouted from the middle seam where a page had been torn out. Leo slammed the book closed, and Kole spotted a skull symbol embossed on the cover. "She has taken it with her."

"What spell is it?" Felix asked.

"I do not know." Leo shoved the tome under a pile of books in the corner.

"How'd she get it?" Thomas asked.

Leo pressed his palm to his forehead. "I had it."

"I thought you never used blood magic," said Kole. The conversation he had with Piper earlier resurfaced. Her voice rang in his head. *"Once you use it, there's no coming back from it. The lust for power consumes you."* That's what had happened to Savairo. He had gone mad with power. Consumed by it. And it could happen to Piper, too. Even Leo.

"I would never use blood magic."

"Then why do you have it?" Kole snapped. The Liberation leader's denial sounded genuine. He wanted to believe Leo, but he needed more convincing.

Leo turned and looked each of them in the eye. "I have been trying to find something to kill Idris. Because he is made through blood magic, I thought I might find something in here to undo his power—weaken him. I never intended to use the spells, more... reverse engineer them. Get a better understanding of what he is. Replicate the spell, even, with different components."

Plausible. Kole knew too little of blood magic, or magic in general, to know if his explanation held truth. Glancing to Thomas and Felix, he relaxed. They seemed to buy it. "Would Piper use it?" he asked.

"She ripped it out, didn't she?" said Felix.

"She wouldn't," Thomas growled.

Leo shook his head. "No. She knows better."

He heard her voice again. *"I'll admit blood magic has its lure. With the right intent, we could do a lot of good with it."* Kole understood the pain she felt from losing her family and the lack of control and helplessness that came with it. They had both lost people close to them. But would she resort to torture to get what she wanted? He could guess the answer. If it meant erasing the last three days from his own life, Kole would be tempted to do the same. "Why would she take it if she wasn't going to use it?"

They all looked at one another, no answer to offer.

Finally, Leo spoke, "We have no time for this. We need to focus on Russé."

"What about Piper?" Thomas asked.

"I will deal with her."

"In the meantime, you want us to rescue some unknown shepherd who got himself locked up?" asked Thomas.

"He has a name," said Kole. *You'd eat your words if you knew you who you were talking about.*

Thomas glared at him. "We protect our own first."

Leo pounded his fist on the table. A wildness filled his eyes. "You protect who I tell you to!"

The way Thomas and Felix recoiled told Kole that the Liberation leader had never shown this side of himself before.

Leo closed his eyes and took a long breath. "Things have changed. They have summoned Aterus. We must retrieve the shepherd before the Soul gets to him."

"I don't suppose you have a plan," Thomas said with a hint of disdain.

"You three *are* the plan."

"We can handle this on our own," Thomas said, throwing a glare Kole's way. "He's not ready. He'll only slow us down."

Kole scowled.

"He did all right in trainin'." Felix shrugged.

"He was poor at best."

"I'm not staying behind this time," Kole said. He would sneak out again if he had to.

"This is no time to bicker," Leo scolded. The room grew silent. "He is being detained by Savairo's sorcerers. You will need all the help you can get."

Thomas crossed his arms. "I'd rather take the twins."

"We wouldn't make it five steps into that prison with Criz and Boogy," said Felix.

"At least *they* can fight," Thomas said.

"The twins are on the outskirts, recruiting the farmers to our cause. Kole will have to do."

Thomas rolled his eyes. "Fine, but I'm not going to be responsible for him. If he falls behind, I'm not going back for him."

"I can handle myself," Kole snapped. The reality of the break-in swelled inside him. His sole focus had been on Russé. The uncertain chance of death during this mission spiked his adrenaline. It very well could be the last thing he did, especially if no one watched his back like Russé. As much as he hated to admit it, Thomas was right: he wasn't very good at combat. But he'd learned many things from being a shepherd, and one of them was how to move undetected. That skill had made him one of the best hunters in camp. He only hoped his burns wouldn't get in the way.

Leo gave them all a sharp look. "Kole is a part of this Liberation as much as any of us. I am counting on you to work together." He looked from Kole to Thomas. "There is something much greater at stake than your egos."

Kole and Thomas passed scowls to each other.

"I know a way in, and I can tell you the layout of the bottom floor, but the rest is up to you. Listen well. There is an entrance through the sewers...."

"This is *disgustin'*." Felix's voice echoed through the sewer. His dim lantern gave off just enough light for Kole to spot the dark puddles of sludge dotting the floor.

"I've seen worse." Kole side stepped the slime as he crouched through the cramped pipe, bringing up the rear. The small space, along with the stink, made him breathless, but he would take this greasy, rat-infested sewer pipe over a basin full of corpses any day. His shoulder brushed the side wall. Thick grime smeared onto him. Maybe he spoke too soon.

Felix tilted his head at Thomas. "I've *smelled* worse."

"At least you're used to it, then," said Kole, holding in a laugh.

Thomas shot a burning look over his shoulder. "Can you two shut up? Going to get caught before we make it to the grate."

"Just tryin' ta lighten the mood, ya old humbug," Felix grumbled.

"The mood doesn't need lightening," Thomas said. "Have you not grasped what we're about to do in that tiny little head of yours? Savairo's prison will have guards crawling around every corner, and that's not counting sorcerers or Kayetans."

Kole squatted, trying to stretch out the black Liberation uniform Leo had made him wear, which clung to him like a second skin. The fact that it covered every inch of his scars made up for the poor fit. Kole had brought Russé's staff along. He remembered the Soul couldn't produce magic on his own and hoped once they found him, Russé could aid in their escape. "How do we handle the sorcerers?"

"Pray we stick a blade in them before they can get into our heads." Thomas stood, stretching his back where the pipe had elbowed, rising up nearly a dozen feet. "Bring the light." Thomas grabbed it from Felix and lifted it up. "Think I see a grate. Ten—twelve feet up."

Kole and Felix ducked into the pipe with him.

Setting the lantern down, Thomas nodded to Felix. "You up for it?"

"Be concerned if I ever say no." Felix smiled. "Watch out, Blondie."

Kole stepped back, trying his best to give them room while avoiding the walls of muck.

Thomas locked his fingers together, cupping them securely in front of his hips as Felix crept back into the tunnel. After taking a running start, Felix jumped up into Thomas' hands. A labored grunt and Thomas flung Felix into the air. He disappeared into the darkness.

A faint thud. "Got it."

Squinting to glimpse any sign of Felix, he faintly made out the outline of his feet pressed into either side of the pipe. The scrape of metal against stone filtered down to Kole's ears.

"No one's home," his voice came again. "Pipe is clear. Toss 'em up."

Thomas took his position again, waving at Kole. "You're next."

"Uh...." Kole stared at Thomas' hands in the dark, realizing 'toss 'em up' meant *him*. No way he could jump like that.

"I'll try not to throw you into the wall." Thomas sighed when Kole stood still. "I'm kidding. Let's go, we need to be quick. Just kick off my hands and jump. I'll do the rest. Leave the staff."

He gripped Russé's staff. "We need it!"

"I'll take it up. Calm down."

We're about to break into a prison, and he wants me to calm down. Kole held back an eye roll then propped the staff against the wall.

"Running start if you need."

If Felix needed a few strides, Kole needed a mile. *Still won't help.* He settled for a few meters. Trying to mimic Felix, he did his best run toward Thomas and clumsily hopped into his hands. A quick shove and Kole soared upwards.

Wind rushed past his face as he sailed up through the drain. A flicker of joy sprouted in his stomach. For a brief second he felt like his old self — the limits of his body forgotten as he soared uninhibited. He stretched his arms far as his taut skin would allow, ready to catch the lip of the pipe, but his momentum slowed. His stomach sprang into his throat. Blinded in the darkness with no hints at where to grab or how far he was from the top, hands seized Kole's wrists.

"Gotta work on that vertical, mate." Felix pulled Kole into the black room.

"What about Thomas?" Kole squinted down the drain. The lantern cast Thomas' shadow on the side of the pipe.

"He can manage."

Kole massaged the tender skin of his wrists where Felix had grabbed him.

A moment later, quick taps echoed up the pipe, growing louder. Kole craned his head and peeked down. Thomas leapt from foot to foot, kicking up the sides of the pipe. Each jumped gained elevation. A final kick off the narrow pipe and one hand caught the lip. Thomas pulled himself to his elbow and climbed from the pipe, the other hand easily gripping the staff and lantern. Even in his prime, Kole never had such strength or agility. Envy swept through him.

After taking the lantern from Thomas, Felix swung it around the room. "All right, from what Leo said, this is Savairo's old lab."

Cobblestone made up the floor, ceiling, and walls. No windows. The only way in or out of this room, besides the drain, was the wooden door across the way.

The lab would have looked normal enough if not for the hundreds of blades, tools, and strange devices mounted to the walls. Some had long, jagged teeth like oversized saws, while others were small and thin, with needle-like blades, which looked like they were designed to pierce deep into flesh. He could only imagine what Savairo used them for.

"A torture room," Thomas said, taking his feet. Kole offered him a hand, but he refused it with a scoff.

"These are...." Felix stood before a peculiar knife baring four jagged teeth. He flicked the blade with his nail. A bright note sang sweetly. " ...disturbing."

"Keep it down." Thomas shoved the grate back into place, then tossed the staff to Kole.

He wrapped his fingers around the wood. "He uses all of these?"

"No, they're for decoration. Doesn't it look nice?" Thomas scowled.

Felix motioned to the floor. "He uses them all right."

The cobbles beneath Kole's feet held deep, rust-brown stains. His palms grew clammy as he backed away from the residue.

"Whoa." Thomas wandered to a stone table at the far end of the room. "Look at this."

Kole and Felix followed.

Carved into the top of the stone were odd runes—sorcerer's runes—like the ones Kole had seen in Leo's lab back at the base. The carving took up the entire slab of stone. They coalesced into an odd shape. Upon closer inspection, he saw it formed the outline of a body. Tiny holes drilled deep into the stone along the line of runes.

He glided his finger over them. Thin metal blades shot up and sliced his finger. He snapped his hand back, wincing as he pinched the thin cut. Sucking the pain from his finger, he watched the blades rise up and bend; their razor edges curving in toward the center of the table as if inserting themselves into an invisible body.

"I've seen markings like this before." Kole backed away. "They were on all those bodies in the basin."

"Think it's how he makes the Kayetans?" Thomas asked dismally.

Kole backed into Felix's rigid body. He spun.

Felix stared at the contraption with distant eyes. "This is where they...."

"Let's get moving." Thomas ushered them away from the table. When Felix ignored him, Thomas grabbed his arm.

Felix ripped from the hold. By the strange flicker in his eyes, Kole could tell his mind had moved far away from the mission.

Thomas sighed. His jaw twitched impatiently, but his voice came soft. "Staying here will only get us caught. We have to move."

No response.

"Get it together, Felix. You have a job to do," Thomas said, more forcefully this time. Leaning in, he dropped his voice to a whisper, but it resonated in the small room. "They wouldn't want you to end up the same way."

Felix rolled his shoulders. His green eyes hardened as he wiped his nose on his sleeve, then shoved past them. "We go straight until the stairs."

Kole gave Thomas a questioning look. "What's that about?"

"Don't ask," he said, then moved to the door.

Felix gingerly turned the knob and pushed. The hinges squeaked. He poked his head out for a moment then, giving them a nod, pulled the black cloth over his face and slipped through the door, eventually signaling them to follow.

Thomas went next, while Kole pulled the mask in place over his mouth and softly closed the door behind them.

They stood at the end of a long, arched corridor. Rafters striped the ceiling, and torches mounted the walls, leaving the passage spotted in trembling shadows. Felix took advantage of this and led them from one dim patch to another until they came upon an intersection.

Voices echoed down the left hall.

Felix held up a hand and edged to the end of the cobbled wall, arching his neck around the corner. He snapped back and tugged the cloth from his chin. "Wait here," he mouthed and replaced his mask.

With a boost from Thomas, Felix climbed to the beam above. He hung, hands hooked over the thick rafter, and pumped his feet until he got enough momentum to swing himself up. After gaining his balance, Felix kicked off, sailing nimbly to the next beam where the two hallways connected. One more frog-like hop and he was in place.

Kole barely made out Felix's silhouette crouched in the darkness. Fumbling around his waist, he produced his slingshot. A ping sounded from the corridor as the pellet ricocheted off the walls.

The voices stopped. Kole's heart hammered.

When stomps of metal armor faded away, Thomas pushed Kole from the wall and they darted across. As they passed, Kole glimpsed two forms marching away to investigate the noise.

Felix jumped across the beams, following them overhead. Safely around the corner, he hopped down and took the lead. They followed the curving path until they spotted a line of windows on the right, just like Leo had said. The midnight breeze howled through the barred windows as they reached the stairs leading to the lower levels of the prison. One problem they hadn't foreseen: An iron gate blocked the way.

"Bloody Souls," Felix cursed. "Locked, too. Fantastic."

"Can you pick it?" Thomas asked in a hushed voice.

"Maybe." Felix examined the mechanism. He traded his slingshot for a ring of rusty tools from his belt. Each one looked like an unfinished key, bearing small prongs near the end. He jammed one in the lock and started tinkering.

"Why don't we just find the key?" Kole asked.

"Go looking for guards? That's the complete opposite of stealth." Thomas fixed his eyes on the hallway behind them. "Plus, we risk getting lost. Leo only told us how to get to the lower cells. We don't have a map of the entire prison."

Kole hushed him with a touch to the shoulder. "I hear something." He ignored Thomas' scowl and peeked around the corner.

Two tottering shadows neared.

"Guards," he whispered.

"We have to hide," Thomas said.

"Where?" Kole glanced to the iron gate blocking the way. Dead end. If they retraced their steps, they'd be seen. And he wasn't about to jump out the window. By the rising volume of the guards' footfalls, they'd round the corner soon. Kole hoped Thomas had something up his sleeve.

Thomas clasped his hands and nodded to the roof. "Into the rafters."

Kole jammed the staff into his belt loop, then stepped into Thomas' hold and grabbed the beam like he'd seen Felix do earlier. He tried to pull himself up, but his arms failed him. Thomas gave him a boost and Kole scrambled up into the darkness. Balancing on the beam proved harder than Felix made it look. Instead of perching on his feet, he lay flat on his stomach and wrapped his arms and legs around the wood for fear of falling.

After Felix helped Thomas to the next beam, he returned to the lock, jamming yet another half-key into the hole.

"What are you doing?" Thomas scolded in a hushed whisper. "Leave it be. Get up here."

"Wait, I might have it, gimme... one... second...." Felix twisted the tool clockwise, then waited as if he was expecting something to happen. When nothing did, he let out a huff.

"Give it up," Kole whispered down.

Felix slammed his fists against the bars in frustration.

"Did you hear that?" came a voice.

Felix climbed the gate and hoisted himself up next to Kole as a pair of guards came into view. Jingling on the side of one of the guard's belt hung a ring of keys. One guard went to the window while the other made for the gate, where Felix's tools still hung from the lock.

The guard pulled the key free. "Look at this."

The second guard turned from the window, and Felix unsheathed his knife. Thomas and Felix exchanged a silent look, then nodded. As the guard moved from the window and passed beneath Kole to join his comrade, Felix swung down, knees hooked over the rafter. He hung upside down behind the guard, his blade poised around the guard's throat.

The guard by the gate looked up in horror as Felix slit his partner's throat. He reached for the horn on his belt, but before he could pull it free, Thomas dropped from the beam and clamped a hand over the guard's mouth. With a quick pull, Thomas moved his knife across the man's neck. A thick coat of blood poured over the polished armor.

"Get down here," Felix called to Kole.

But Kole froze, eyes fixed on the slit flesh. A river of red. His head told him to follow orders, but his heart—his core—couldn't break the trance. Felix and Thomas went for the kill. An immediate response. A trained response. The same way Kole would treat his prey in the hunt. But these were no animals.

A curse from Thomas snapped Kole back to reality. "For Soul's sake. First Felix, now you? I should've come *alone*. Get down here!"

Kole slipped from the beam, landing hard on the stone.

"Get up, mate. Hold 'em," Felix ordered.

Kole raced over and took the guard's weight as instructed. He held on with shaking arms.

"Get his keys," said Thomas, whose hand still smothered the guard's mouth. Both were still alive, but their eyes had gone distant. It wouldn't be long.

It's just prey. No matter how many times he thought it, he still saw two dying men before him.

"Lean him back," Thomas ordered. "Don't let his blood get on the floor if you can help it."

The full weight of the guard on his chest, Kole tipped him back as much as he dared without dropping him, while Felix slipped the keys from the man's belt and then tried them on the gate.

The guard grew heavier by the second, and the blood, dripping down the breastplate, made his fingers slip. Kole tightened his arms around the bulky armor, but they fell short, and the body continued to sink toward the floor.

With a click, Felix unlocked the gate and swung it open. He hurried over to Kole, lifted the guard's feet, and they rushed the bodies down the stairwell.

Felix ran back to lock the gate behind them as Kole and Thomas dumped the guards on the floor.

"What do we do with them?" Kole asked.

Thomas waved a hand down the hall. "Stash them in one of those for now."

Kole peered into the darkness, allowing his eyes to adjust. Rows of barred cells stretched the length of the corridor. Quiet. A draft poured down from the stairs, and a wave of goosebumps crossed his skin. Kole fought back a shiver as Felix returned.

"Got a key for one of these?" Thomas asked.

Felix tried the first cell. A few keys and the lock clicked. Kole and Thomas dragged the bodies inside, across the straw-littered floor. After laying the corpses in the shadowed corner, the three boys scooped handfuls of straw from the cell floor and sprinkled it over the dead men.

"Someone is going to notice they're gone," Kole said as they returned to the corridor.

"Then we better make this quick," came Thomas' rough voice behind him.

Locking the cell behind them, Felix nodded to the hall. "Check the others for the shepherd."

Kole took to one side, peeking through the bars in search of the Soul, while Thomas did the same on the other. Felix ran ahead. Though Kole had done his best to describe the shepherd to his comrades back in the tunnels, he worried about their accuracy.

The first four cells lay empty on Kole's side. As he passed the fifth, a pair of hands shot out between the bars. They grabbed Kole's shirt and tugged him into the icy metal. Kole struggled against the hold, but the hands held firm. The culprit's face emerged from the shadows, the potent scent of urine wafting in with it.

A young woman, covered in filth, looked on him with desperate eyes. Something in her gaze dragged Niko's face to the forefront. Not a memory from when he was alive, but of Kole's dream of his old friend after his death. The same strange emptiness lived in her eyes.

She whispered two words, rank with the stench of rotting teeth: "Help me."

Before Kole could respond, Thomas pried her off. She folded her arms over her stomach. A soft hum reverberated in her cell. She closed her eyes, dancing to her own music like she had forgotten the boys' presence.

"Stick to the center." Thomas eyed the cells warily.

"Can't we help her?"

"We just killed two guards. We're in no place to 'help' right now. You said yourself someone's going to notice them missing."

"Just unlock the cell. She can get out on her own."

"There's probably more prisoners down here. You going to release them, too? The guards will sound the alarm as soon as they're spotted. You want to ruin our only chance at getting your friend back, be my guest." Thomas gripped the collar of Kole's shirt and dragged him away.

Kole shrugged his hands off.

"What's goin' on back here?" Felix emerged from the shadows.

"Nothing." Thomas shot a scowl to Kole and folded his arms. "Right, *Blondie*?"

Kole gritted his teeth. As much as he hated the thought of leaving her here, subjected to Savairo's twisted desires, he couldn't risk botching Russé's rescue. To deprive Thomas the satisfaction, he pushed on down the hall, blocking out the sneaking thoughts of what would become of her after they left. An experiment? She already seemed too far gone. Maybe because of the isolation of the cell... or maybe she had *already* undergone an experiment or two.

Weak pleas rippled from the cells as the boys passed. It took all of Kole's effort to ignore them. Reaching a bend in the hallway, they paused. Deep chanting penetrated the walls.

"Sorcerers." Thomas pulled out two stout swords. "Be on your guard. When you see them, strike. Don't be afraid to kill them. Else they'll get into your head... make you see things... do things...."

Kole remembered all too well. He refused to let those Red Cloaks meddle with his head again.

When Felix pulled out his dagger, Kole freed his staff from his belt. He slowed his breathing, gently eased each step on the stone floor, and crept around the corner. His nerves screamed and, although he was trying his best to stay silent, Kole grew suddenly aware of the faintest noise from his movements: the swipe of his pants as his legs passed, the slow gulp of his tightening throat. He swore he could hear the joints in his hands squeaking as they flexed around the staff. He prayed the sorcerer's chant drowned it out.

They found no cells down this leg of the hallway, only solid cobblestone save for one open arch on the left wall. Pulsing orange light radiated from the archway.

The chant continued.

"Russé's gotta be in there," Felix said, so quietly that Kole wondered whether he had actually heard his voice or read his lips.

When Thomas replaced Felix at the head of their group, fingers twitching around either hilt, Kole knew the time for stealth had ended.

They approached the archway.

Thomas pressed his back to the wall and leaned in, surveying the room. He nodded — Russé was there — then held up four fingers and slipped back.

Four sorcerers. Worry took hold of Kole. They were outnumbered, but the headcount troubled him most. Earlier he had seen six, which meant at least two more remained somewhere in the prison. Hopefully nowhere close. Kole sucked in a deep breath; a weak attempt to calm himself. The drum of his heart pounded louder — faster.

Thomas' knuckles paled on his sword. He took one hand off, raising his fingers for the countdown.

Three.

Felix lowered, ready to run.

Two.

Kole's stomach tightened as a shot of adrenaline burst through him.

One.

They pushed off the wall and charged through the archway.

CHAPTER 17

It was all slow motion to Kole. The sorcerers, engrossed in their archaic chant, stood around Russé, who lay still on a rock slab at the middle. They only seemed to notice Thomas once one of their brothers fumbled his part of their incantation. His gurgling noises stopped them as he choked up blood, one of Thomas' blades protruding from his back. Thomas tore out his sword and the sorcerer fell to the floor; a dark glistening stain spread as blood soaked through the cloth. The blur of a spinning dagger flew from Felix's outstretched arm. It sunk into the darkness of a hood, and a second sorcerer hit the floor before Kole could blink.

Staff shaking in hand, Kole lunged at the sorcerer hunched over Russé's head. He stopped at the sight of the Soul, bruised and bloodied. The wrinkles around Russé's mouth and eyes had all but disappeared due to the swelling.

"Russé," Kole called out.

An unseen force hit Kole's chest, knocking the wind from him, and swept him off his feet. He flew backward, a spasm flashing through his back as he landed on the hard cobbles. The slam re-agitated the already wounded skin, but he had no time to register the pain. He rolled to his feet, eyes darting back and forth to catch sight of his assailant.

One of the sorcerers stepped toward him, pulled up a draping red sleeve, and thrust out his bare palm. Not up for playing the ragdoll again, Kole dove under the table. He skidded to a stop at the hem of the sorcerer's billowing cloak and swung the staff into the Red Cloak's knee.

A terrible crunch. The sorcerer wailed in pain. He staggered back and hunched over, a hand clutching his knee. While he was distracted, Kole slipped out from under the table and lunged to land another attack. Before his strike hit home, the sorcerer looked up. Two golden orbs glowed from the depths of the hood.

Kole began to feel light-headed—dizzy like before. His swing slowed, and the sorcerer knocked the staff away with a hand. It clanked on the cobbles somewhere behind him. The room spun faster and faster until it blurred, save for two golden orbs. Those remained still and clear. Remembering their encounter outside the prison, Kole tore his eyes away and the dizziness waned. The cobble beneath his hands and knees felt solid, and he could once again hear Felix and Thomas' grunts of battle around the room, accompanied by the slap of feet to his left. Kole opened his eyes in time to see the hem of a cloak closing in on him.

Gaze fixed to the floor, Kole blindly punched the sorcerer. His knuckles hit flesh, and the sorcerer reeled back. Before the Red Cloak could recover, Kole tossed his arms around his opponent's waist and dragged him to the floor.

Fists raised, he hesitated. He wanted to kill the sorcerer for everything he had done to the Soul, but as he peered into the hood, he remembered it concealed an orphan beneath. An orphan like him. For a brief moment, he wondered if this would've been his fate if the timing had been different. If he had been in the orphanage when Savairo had raided Etta's home that night.

He couldn't kill a foe so near himself.

Taking advantage of Kole's hesitation, the Red Cloak grabbed him and forced his gaze to the gold eyes beneath the hood.

Like staring into the sun, it burned his eyes, but he couldn't look away. Something deep within him didn't want to stray from the light. No escape. When Kole thought of his last moments on Ohr, he'd always pictured coming to an end during an act of heroism. But this, a cornered animal at the mercy of the sorcerer, seemed fitting for his rashness. Now he'd pay the price.

"I got him," Thomas' voice rang out behind Kole.

Kole twisted away as Thomas drove his sword into the sorcerer's chest.

A final gasp, then the sorcerer fell limp. The red hood fell back, and a female face stared, blank-eyed, to the ceiling. Small features hinted to her youth, yet her skin held the vast wrinkles of an elder. A heaviness weighed down on Kole as he stared at her mutilated face. Her complexion held a ruddy hue, similar to his own, and drooped around her jaw. Long gashes scarred her brow and right cheek, hinting she had been on the wrong side of an angry blade more than a few times. Kole moved off her as Thomas retrieved the blade from her chest, then knelt down and closed her golden eyes. "Sorry, I-I...."

Thomas shrugged. "It happens."

"To you, too?"

"Yeah."

Kole sighed, relieved to hear his hesitation to kill was normal.

"You just gotta be more careful. It's natural to look into your opponent's eyes, but you have to train yourself around it."

"Oh." Kole folded his arms, realizing he had misunderstood him. "Guess I need more practice."

Better for Thomas to think that Kole had screwed up. If Thomas knew he had no intention of killing, he'd think him a coward, and Kole didn't need any more trouble from him. But as he stared at the girl draped in red, he found himself wishing she were still alive. Give her a second chance without Savairo's corruption.

"You did all right." Thomas held out a hand.

Kole took it. He found something different in Thomas' eyes; the arrogance had gone, though Kole wouldn't go so far as to call it respect, either. "Thanks." With a sharp pull from Thomas, Kole rose to his feet and gauged the scene. Three more bodies lay motionless on the floor, their mangled faces peeking out from the hoods. Kole felt a pang of guilt. Savairo had bent their minds so far that it had come to this. *Orphans killing orphans.* The thought weighed heavy on his heart.

"Kole?" Russé's feeble voice came from the table.

Kole retrieved Russé's staff, then dashed to the wooden table where Felix fiddled with the locks. After releasing the chains around Russé's wrists, he moved aside for Kole, making quick work of the ankle restraints.

Kole touched the distinct bruise on the Soul's neck. Five angry red lines swelled on his throat where a hand had clamped. "Are you all right?" he asked, but Russé had passed out.

"They're sorcerers, mate. The wounds ya really have ta worry 'bout are in here." Felix tapped Russé's temple.

"What did they do to him?"

"We won't know 'til Leo takes a look at him. No sense worryin' now." Felix moved around the table and slid Russé's feet to the edge.

Russé's eyes rolled in his sockets as Kole heaved him to a sitting position. He placed the Soul's arm over his shoulder and guided his feet to the floor. Kole's knees buckled under the weight. Felix caught the Soul's other arm before he fell.

"I'll carry him," said Thomas.

Kole eyed him. He had pinned Thomas for an 'everyone-for-himself' kind of person. "Thought you weren't going to help anyone who lags behind."

"That's just you." Thomas glowered back. "My mission is the shepherd. No point coming along if I'm going to leave him. Besides, Felix needs to lead, and your scrawny ass can't lift him without falling over."

Apparently Thomas had returned to his normal, unpleasant self. Though annoying, his words struck true. Kole would buckle beneath the old man eventually.

Thomas wrapped Russé's arms around his neck and heaved him to his back. A few shaky steps forward, testing it out, and he seemed satisfied. "This'll work. But we'll have to take it slow," he warned them as they turned down the celled hallway.

"Now who's lagging behind," Kole said under his breath.

"Sure, mate. I'll let the guard know we get a head start before he can go runnin' us down," Felix muttered.

An irritated growl answered him, but Thomas saved his retort.

They ran past the cells and rushed up the stairs, Kole and Felix leading the way while Thomas trailed after, bogged down by Russé's limp weight.

Halfway up the staircase, Felix halted mid-step and shot out his arm to block the path. Kole opened his mouth to question him, but he put a finger to his freckled lips, then pointed out the shadows flickering on the top step.

Muffled voices sounded from the landing. Felix dropped to all fours, his stomach skimming the steps as he moved to get a better view. When he returned, his brows hung low in frustration.

"What's going on?" Thomas breathed as he caught up.

"Five guards," Felix said.

"We can catch them by surprise like we did with the sorcerers," said Kole.

Thomas shook his head. "It's the main hall. They'll be more coming around on patrol. They'd see the bodies."

"Then we drag them down here. Put them in a cell with the other two," Kole offered.

"Too risky," Felix said as he crossed his arms, fingers tapping his biceps. "They'll see us comin' and we're outnumbered. Only takes one ta sound the alarm."

Kole rattled his brain for another solution. "Is there another way out?"

"Maybe." The side of Felix's mouth twitched.

"We *aren't* going another way. What if we run into guards? We can't pull his dead weight into the rafters." Thomas jutted his chin to the shepherd on his back.

Felix huffed and shook his head. "We got no chance with Russé like this. We might have to wait until he comes to."

"Wait down here?" Kole asked. They couldn't stay here. There were four dead sorcerers down the hall, with at least two more unaccounted for.

"You gotta better idea, Blondie?" Felix snipped.

Kole moved his attention down the stairwell. He could make out the cell bars in the darkness. *The keys.* His eyes fell to the ring of keys dangling from Felix's belt. He snatched them and bounded down the staircase.

"What do you think you're doing?" Thomas snapped.

"Keep it down," Felix said. He followed after him, yelling as loud as he dared, "For the Seven Souls, Blondie! Are you crazy?"

When Kole reached the first cell, Felix grabbed his arm.

"We have the keys. Why not use them?"

"If you set them loose, they'll stampede the place."

"*Exactly.*"

His grip lightened around Kole's wrist. "What are ya gettin' at?"

"A diversion."

Felix titled his head. "I'm listenin'."

"You said yourself we can't hide with Russé in his condition, and we certainly aren't going to outrun anyone." He gestured to Thomas, who was trotting down the steps, trying to keep Russé from sliding off his back. "Think about it. If the guards see a group of escaped prisoners, they'll raise the alarm, sure, but they won't know to look for *us* until they discover the bodies."

After stroking his chin for a moment, Felix turned to Thomas. "Hate ta say it, but Blondie's got a point."

"I think you're forgetting these people have been tortured by sorcerers," Thomas said. "No telling what state they're in. They could be a danger to us, too."

"I didn't say they'd do what we ask. I just said they'd be a distraction," Kole answered. "I imagine they won't object to a chance at escape."

"The guards can't chase us all." Felix released Kole's arm.

"We have to risk it," said Kole.

Thomas studied him skeptically.

Kole took his silence as approval. He tried a few keys before one clicked. The metal groaned as he opened the cell. A young man, who looked no older than twenty, eyed him from the corner. He watched

Kole warily for a moment, then lugged himself from the floor and limped over. He moved to the next cell and tried the same key. It clicked open. He scrambled down the line, doing the same.

Cries of joy filled the hall as the prisoners realized what was happening. They shuffled from their cells in a daze, as if unsure whether this was reality or a wondrous dream. Women and men flooded the tight corridor and made for the stairs. A guard's voice echoed from the top of the stairwell, and the rusty gate whined.

"They're coming," Felix half-whispered, half-yelled from the bottom of the stairs.

"Go, go, go." Kole hurried the lagging prisoners down the hall. He pocketed the key ring and stepped ahead of Thomas as they followed the crowd.

They let the prisoners go first. Shouts of warning came from the guards as sounds of the gate slamming into the stone wall reached Kole's ears. Felix nodded and slipped in with Kole and Thomas. They rushed up the steps.

When they reached the top, the scene was as chaotic as it sounded. Half of the guards stumbled over one another, tackling the passing prisoners, while the other half stood at the window, dumbfounded at the sight. One fumbled for his horn and drew a long note.

Kole rushed a guard who had grabbed a woman and pinned her to the wall. He pushed the guard backward, sending him rolling into the foot path of the stampeding prisoners. Kole lifted the woman to her feet, and she bolted down the hallway after the others.

The prisoners dispersed and sprinted in every direction as the guards trailed after them. Felix knocked one of the guards to the ground to clear a path for Kole and Thomas. The building echoed with screams as guards tackled and beat prisoners into submission. Kole wished to save them all, but they were on their own.

Get Russé out. That was their goal.

He tailed Felix, glancing back every few paces to make sure Thomas kept up, more out of concern for his cargo.

Felix led them back the way they came. With each new corridor they passed, their group dwindled, as prisoners split down the different corridors, taking their chances alone. Only a dozen or so still followed them.

The drain was close now. One stretch of hall stood between them and Savairo's torture room.

Then, all at once, the prison resounded with bloodcurdling screams.

Kole's veins ran cold at the sound. He had heard cries like that before. They held the same raw edge as the ones he'd heard the night the Black Wall overran his camp. Something horrific had happened. He could feel it rippling under his skin.

Even Felix flinched. He cast a troubled look back at Kole and Thomas. Rounding the corner, they found the cause.

Felix whistled a low warning. The boys skidded to a halt, taking safety behind the bend.

Kole leaned past Felix. At the far edge of the hall, four guards stood shoulder to shoulder in the middle of the corridor, creating a human barrier. Black smoke billowed past their armored boots.

They'd called the Kayetans.

Feet stampeded behind them. Kole snapped around. The prisoners ran full speed around the bend toward them, unfazed by the small squadron or the sight of the Kayetans. As they ran past, Kole recognized the spark in their eyes: desperation.

The woman Kole remembered from the first cell ran ahead of the group and smashed into the guards. She bounced off them like a pebble hitting a tree trunk. One guard moved from the line and slapped shackles around her wrists. She shrieked.

The rest of the prisoners slowed.

"That's right. You're all going back to your cells. If you resist, the Kayetans have orders to kill," a guard said from the line. He swept his broadsword through the air, daring them to make a move.

The prisoners looked at one another as if debating whether to fight or flee.

"What do we do?" Kole's eyes darted from Felix to Thomas.

Thomas warily eyed the scene. "Wait for someone to make the first move."

The Kayetans' lingered behind the guards like trained dogs awaiting a command. Still struggling against her restraints, the woman kicked the guard off and lunged at the broadsword. It caught her in the ribs, but she kept going. She rushed the guard, knocking him to the floor, and kicked him with such ferocity that his armor dented. Her naked toes bent unnaturally, but she kept up her assault as if the pain never registered.

Before the other guards could come to his aid, the bystanders behind the woman charged. The prisoners pulled the guards to the ground and savagely stomped their armor.

Kole watched the scene in horror.

"Kill them!" a guard yelled from beneath the dog pile.

Smoke swirled around the mound of bodies on the floor. Tall, human forms took shape. And those claws, long and sharp, came down on the prisoners. Fresh blood sprayed the stone walls, and screams pierced the air.

Kole started forward.

"Don't interfere," Felix snapped. "Our only chance is ta slip by 'em. Make for the drain, Thomas. We'll make sure they don't follow ya."

Thomas grunted as Felix took the lead, weapon in hand, ready to strike if the Kayetans noticed them. Desperately trying to push his long legs into a jog under Russé's weight, Thomas waddled down the hall, barely keeping up. Instead of following, Kole's head swung back to the prisoners. He couldn't take his eyes off the massacre.

The Kayetans showed no mercy, slicing through arms, legs, and torsos. Those lucky enough to escape the onslaught ran, but they didn't get far before the Kayetans struck them with sweeping claws, bringing them down like game.

Kole gritted his teeth. It took every ounce of restraint to stand his ground; to watch them die, slaughtered like pigs.

Felix called his name down the corridor. A cry of anger escaped Kole's lips as he tore his eyes from the scene and retreated in a daze. He turned the corner after Thomas and Felix. His feet moved him, but his mind stayed on the prisoners.

A screech pierced the hall, growing near. Kole allowed a quick glance over his shoulder. A Kayetan had veered from the pack in pursuit.

Kole roared as he spun on his heel and took up Vienna's borrowed blade in a shaking fist. Smoke swirled and the Kayetan loomed over him, a claw directed at Kole's head. He ducked. Slipping behind the shadow, positioning himself like Felix and Thomas had taught him, fingers coiled around the sunstone blade, he plunged it into the Kayetan's heart. A flash of light filled the corridor, and the creature pitched backward, wailing. When the light faded, the Kayetan had vanished.

Glancing back, Kole caught Felix's gaze. He nodded to Kole, then returned to Thomas, who was approaching the wooden door, Russé's body slipping further down his back with each step. Kole moved to catch up, but as Thomas yanked the door open, he froze.

A shadow loomed in the doorway.

Idris floated into the hall. He pointed a claw at Thomas. "Put the shepherd down, and I will spare you a lifetime of torture and kill you where you stand."

CHAPTER 18

"Your negotiatin' skills ain't very good. Ya see, one option has ta entice us. Yours—well—they're both pretty bleak," said Felix. "Don't know about these guys, but I'll gladly hand over the old geezer if ya make me—say, King of Ohr?"

"What are you doing?" Kole hissed under his breath.

Felix didn't bother to keep his voice down. "Oh come on, Blondie. We're either gonna die or escape. Might as well have an epic story ta tell if we survive," he said with a wink.

Idris' dark form shot forward.

Diving out of the way, Kole bumped into Felix. They both hit the floor. Felix immediately rolled onto his back, pounced up, and darted for Idris as his funnel of smoke changed direction and sped toward Thomas. Felix stepped in the Kayetan's way and raised his sunstone blade.

"It doesn't work!" Kole shouted. He scrambled to his feet and raced to Thomas.

Felix ignored Kole and jabbed the knife at the gray stream of smoke. But his attack sailed straight through. Like a charging bull, Idris hit Felix in the chest, sending him reeling, and continued for Thomas.

"Move!" Kole called.

Thomas dropped Russé, letting him hit the floor like a ragdoll, and jumped from the Kayetan's path.

Idris' smokey form swirled into the rafters.

Kole crawled to Russé. A splotch of blood stained the stone wall where Russé's head had hit. Taking the old man's arms, he tried to tug him to his feet. "Come on, help me out. This isn't the best time to be unconscious," he said to the Soul.

A groggy moan came from the old shepherd, but he didn't stir. If he could just get him to the grate... *then what? Drop him in so he hits his head again?* He needed something to hold Idris off.

The staff! Russé had used it against the Kayetan back in the basin. It kept the creature at bay then; maybe it could do it again. He held up the staff, squeezed his hands, and swung it in an arc toward Idris' form encircling the beams.

No spray of roots. Not even a creak. He tapped the top against the stone floor.

"Come on," Kole cursed. "Work, dammit."

Nothing.

Fighting seemed hopeless, so he chose flight. Ditching the staff, Kole hooked his arms under Russé's armpits, then leaned back, using the strength of his legs to drag the old man into the torture room.

Felix and Thomas guarded the door while Kole hauled Russé to the drain. He laid the Soul down. His fingers curled around the metal grid and yanked the grate free. As the metal screeched over the cobbles, the door slammed shut behind him. He spun. Instead of Thomas and Felix standing at the door, he found Idris.

Muffled shouts and pounding fists sounded behind the wood.

"You escaped me the first time," Idris said coolly. The hiss of his voice reverberated off the torture tools, filling the room with the deep hum of metal. "Now you have no barrier to protect you."

Before Kole could blink, Idris had crossed the room. A shadowed claw clenched his throat and lifted him from the floor.

"You will die in the very room I was born," Idris hissed.

Kole's face grew hot—numb. Instinctively, he clawed at the hand tightening around his windpipe, but his fingers passed through the Kayetan's hand. His scream came out as a guttural moan, and his vision blurred; mind thickening with a disorienting fog.

Then he saw red.

Bright auburn hair flew from the drain. Piper impaled the Kayetan with a gleaming white pike—pure sunstone. Kole remembered seeing it in Leo's lab a few hours earlier, yet the surface of the weapon churned like molten lava, different from the blades the Liberation normally used which only emitted a soft light. This weapon seemed overcharged—bursting with power. Piper held it firm in her bare hands, twisting it as she jammed it further into Idris. Flames licked out from the weapon, popping and crackling at the edges of Idris' swirling body. White light flashed from the wound. Idris let out a deafening screech and dropped Kole.

Kole landed on Russé, who still lay unconscious. The room spun as the blood rushed to Kole's head, but he managed to stumble to the door and lift the wooden latch.

Felix and Thomas burst in. They instantly ran to Piper's aid, who stood over the whimpering shadow with a sneer.

"No!" she growled. Piper jerked her chin toward Kole and Russé. "I'll hold him off. Get them out of here."

Felix raced over to Kole. "You all right, mate?"

"I'll be fine," Kole said through gritted teeth.

Hunched in the corner, Idris probed his new injury. The wound shimmered, and a handful of ash drifted to the floor, leaving a gaping hole where the pike had pierced.

"I'm not leaving you," Thomas said.

Idris lurched at Piper. She sidestepped his attack, spun, and stabbed him in the back. Another shriek and the Kayetan dropped to the floor, cowering like a cornered animal.

Rage swept over her features. "Have you forgotten your mission? Or do you think I can't handle him myself?"

"No, I—"

"It would do you well to remember *who* trained *who*." Piper bared her teeth and ran at Idris' lumped form in the corner.

Felix grabbed Thomas' arm and steered him to the drain. "Don't argue with a girl holding a flaming stick." Felix pulled a rope from his belt and tied it around the grate. "You first, Blondie."

After snatching the staff, Kole swung his legs over the opening as a chorus of screeches sounded from the door. Black smoke billowed at the far end of the corridor like a growing fog. It appeared the Kayetans had finished slaughtering the prisoners and had come to aid Idris.

Piper peered down the hall. "Shit." She sent another strike at Idris, but he zoomed up to the ceiling, away from her reach. "Go," she said, crossing to the door and slamming it shut. "I'm right behind you."

Kole wrapped his legs around the rope and slid down into the darkness, feet slapping the damp floor of the sewer tunnel. Next came Thomas with Russé slung over his shoulder. After they landed, Felix sent Piper down, then cut the rope and dropped the dozen feet on his own. A chorus of shrieks echoed above, and they sprinted into the tunnel.

At the first fork, Piper turned and stood her ground. "Go, I'll hold them off."

Felix pushed Thomas past her before he could react, saying, "Kole and I can't carry the shepherd on our own. If she wants ta stay, let her."

"She'll be ok, won't she?" Kole asked between breaths, struggling to keep pace with Felix and Thomas. A quick glance over his shoulder. She stood firm, the pike tucked under her arm as her darkening silhouette faded from view. He felt guilty abandoning her. She had saved him, and now they were leaving her behind.

Felix cast him a look but didn't answer.

"Won't she?"

"Shut up and run," said Thomas.

Once the trio safely made it out of the sewers and entered The Cobwebs, they slowed their pace. Either Felix, who led the way, bided time, hoping Piper would catch up, or the maze-like mines really did provide enough protection that they could risk a more relaxed pace.

They returned to find Leo pacing at the head of the table. "Thank the Seven Souls!" He rushed over and helped Thomas lay Russé on the table. "You took longer than I anticipated."

"We ran into Idris," Kole said, pulling off his mask.

Thomas stood in the tunnels as if he expected Piper to turn the corner at any moment. "If it wasn't for Piper and that weapon of yours, we'd all be dead."

"Piper? Where is she? What weapon?" Leo rummaged through the many pockets of his coat, then pulled a chair next to Russé.

"You know," Felix said, "that flaming stick she had. She showed up with it when Idris had us cornered."

Thomas rolled his eyes. "It was a pike."

"Fine, a pike. Ya gotta make more of those, Leo."

"She stole the damn—" Leo cursed. "Stupid girl." His face turned an angry shade of red. *"Where is she?"*

"She held them off while we escaped." Kole rushed to the table where Leo hunched over Russé.

"Shut that door," Leo snapped at Thomas.

Thomas lingered a little longer, then slammed the tunnel door and plopped onto a stone chair.

"His head is bleeding." Kole pointed out the wound on the back of Russé's head.

Leo's fingers prodded the injury, but the Soul didn't flinch. "I'll have to stitch it." He produced a needle and string from his coat and got to work. "Let us hope Piper will not be so stupid as to return now— even through the tunnels. She will blow our cover if any Kayetan steps foot down here."

"*If* she makes it back. She could be bleeding out in a prison cell for all we know," Thomas said.

The Liberation leader's hands paused for a moment at Thomas' comment, then resumed sewing the torn scalp. As he worked, Russé's eyes opened. Kole called to him, but the Soul didn't respond. His eyes rolled, drool dribbling from the corner of his mouth.

After dressing his head wound, Leo examined the bruises on his temples. "What foul things were you up to, Savairo?"

"Is he all right?" Kole asked.

"He has been through hell, that is certain."

Kole pushed from the chair and shuffled around the table. "Can you help him?"

"I am not sure." Leo's jaw set. "Physical ailments are easy enough to mend. The mind is a different beast. I will do what I can, but if Savairo used dark magic on him, I will not be much help. The only instant remedy is magic of the same nature."

A new worry crawled through Kole. If Leo's magic couldn't snap Russé out of it, they'd not only be down a shepherd, but a Soul in the battle to come. He *had* to recover in time. The refugees had no hope of winning the rebellion without him.

"There is something I could try, but I need to enter his mind to do it." Leo pursed his lips, fingers twitching tentatively over Russé's face. "It is an act of hostility to enter a mind without consent, I—"

"Do it," Kole said. He could only guess the risks of what Leo would need to do, but Russé was useless to them like this.

Though Leo still seemed reluctant, he nudged Kole out of the way and took his place near Russé's head. He lowered his hands to the shepherd's temple and closed his eyes.

Kole, Felix, and Thomas, whose attention had finally moved from the door, watched in silence.

Eyes rolled beneath Leo's lids. The muscles in his jaw tightened. His body went rigid, and the blood vessels in his neck swelled, pushing against his skin with such force that Kole thought the Liberation leader's veins might burst.

"Leo?" Felix snapped his fingers in front of his face. "Ya there?"

Kole stepped back as Leo's mouth snapped open in a silent scream. Froth spilled from his mouth. The same thing had happened during Kole's mind-link when Savairo had tried to breach Russé's head.

"Is this normal?" Kole stepped back. His jaw quivered, worrying he'd unintentionally encouraged Leo to his ruin.

Thomas pushed from his chair and rushed over. "Piper would know."

Russé was doing this to Leo. Kole was sure of it. The Soul might still think he was imprisoned. He probably didn't recognize the strange presence in his mind and went straight for the attack. From the looks of it, the Soul held nothing back.

"Stop him," Kole said. When no one moved, he reached for Leo's hand.

"No." Thomas stopped him and shoved him aside.

Kole stumbled and fell on his backside. "What are you doing?"

"Don't interfere. We don't know the repercussions for stopping the spell short," said Thomas.

"This isn't a spell." He looked back to Leo, whose face stretched and contorted unnaturally. *What have I done to him?* "Look at him. He's in agony. You don't need to know sorcery to see it. You have to stop him." Still, Thomas didn't budge. Kole turned to Felix. "Please."

Felix's hands twitched at his sides, eyes darting between Kole, Thomas, and his leader, who convulsed.

"Do it!" Kole yelled.

Felix ripped Leo's hands from Russé. Leo collapsed, but Felix caught him by the arm before he hit the floor. "Boss? You all right?"

A violent gulp of air and Leo leaned against the table, catching his breath, then hobbled from Felix's grip. "Fine," Leo grunted. Slicking his hair in place, he slumped into the nearest chair.

Kole returned to Russé's side, who still lay peacefully on the stone table. "What happened?"

"His defenses are strong. His mind overtook me," Leo said. "Savairo likely met the same obstacles and with as little luck. I now know why he called upon Aterus." He shook his head and gestured to the shepherd. "I surmise Russé's current state is of his own doing. A defense mechanism. He needs time to come out of it on his own. I cannot help him."

"You sure yer all right, boss?"

He nodded. "I need rest."

Kole found little relief in his words. Though Leo seemed convinced Russé would be all right, *he* wasn't so sure. He'd never seen the Soul like this. Not only that, but a god in a comatose state could prove a bad omen. More concerning was the way Leo looked at the shepherd now. And the way he looked at *Kole*. The Liberation leader's expression was guarded, like it had been when Kole had first walked into this hideout.

He gripped Russé's shoulder tighter, wondering if the episode had merely shaken Leo, or if he had seen something in the Soul's head that he shouldn't have.

"I'll put him to bed." Kole held Leo's gaze, searching for any sign that he knew Russé's true identity.

Eyes softening, Leo gave a warm smile and said, "That would be best. Felix. Help him, will you?"

"Yessir."

They lifted Russé's limp body from the table. Felix ended up taking most of the weight.

Thomas reluctantly moved to hold the door. "Don't put him in my room," he said sourly as they passed.

"Don't be a bugger." After the door closed, Felix spoke again. "He's bein' rude cause his *girlfriend* isn't back yet."

Kole grunted in response. He had more important things to worry about than Thomas' mood swings.

Halfway down the hall, Felix veered left. "The shepherd can go in our bunk." He kicked the door open and backed himself in, careful not to drop Russé.

They were both sapped of energy and strength for the night, so they heaved Russé onto the bunk below Kole's. He snagged his blanket and pillow and tucked it under Russé's head. The Soul's body seemed frail. Blood pooled under paper-thin skin around his neck and wrists, presumably where he'd been choked and held down. Exhaustion had paled Russé's complexion, making the bruises appear more severe.

Using his mask as a cloth, Kole cleaned the dried blood around the Soul's face. The bandage came loose after a few swipes.

"Might be easier with a wet cloth. I'll bring one from the washroom."

Kole murmured his thanks as Felix closed the door behind him. Hoping the gash wasn't too serious, Kole unwound the cloth. The bandage fell free from Russé's head. Kole paused, unsure of what he was looking at.

The surrounding hair was soggy with blood, but the gash which had been there moments ago, sewn with neat stitches, had vanished. A thin, silvery patch of raised scar tissue, as long as Kole's finger, ran down the side of Russé's skull. An old wound, one that looked as though it'd had weeks to heal. Wrong wound? Kole probed the Soul's gray, matted hair in search of the source of blood. Nothing but smooth scalp.

He returned to the scar. Was this it? Couldn't be.

"Here," Felix's voice came behind him.

Kole laid a hand over the scar.

"It's warm, too. Should feel good." He passed the cloth. "Bandage came off?" Felix asked, peeking around Kole. "I'll go get—"

"No!" Kole shot. "I—uh, I can do it. I'm sure Leo's busy anyway."

"He won't mind."

"I can take care of him," Kole snapped a bit too harshly.

"All right, mate." Felix held his hands up defensively. "Just tryin' ta help. Anyway, I gotta go check in. See what we're gonna do about Pipes and all." He turned for the door. "If ya need anythin', holler."

Kole waited to move until the door clicked shut. Once Felix's footsteps faded from the hall, he locked the door and lifted Russé's shirt, exposing his gaunt chest. Nothing. No visible wounds. Kole rolled him on his side: unblemished. Idris had stuck the Soul clear through the chest little more than twenty-four hours ago, and not a trace remained. He replaced the shirt. *Souls heal freakishly fast.*

"Would've been nice to know," he mumbled into the empty room. "Could've saved me a world of panic back in the basin."

He frowned. Savairo would have noticed it, too. The thought made his stomach ache. It flipped again when he remembered Savairo calling for Aterus in the mind-link. The Warden knew.

So much for keeping your godhood a secret.

CHAPTER 19

Kole woke, shivering without his blanket. He sat up and caught a glimpse of Felix's empty bed. Russé, though, still lay in the bunk below, unmoved from where Kole had placed him the night before. One eye on the door, he hopped down to inspect the Soul. Still unconscious. His neck had healed during the night, leaving no evidence of the nasty bruises. Kole checked the bandage around his head, making sure it held securely; he couldn't risk it slipping off again.

At a glance, Russé looked the same. *Good enough for now.* Eventually someone would notice the disappearing wounds. *How am I going to explain that?* He hoped Russé would wake before then. Deeming nothing else he could do, Kole pulled up his hood and headed for the door.

He caught an intoxicating aroma as he stepped into the hall. His stomach answered with a gurgle. The scent led him to the domed room.

The Liberation sat around the table, chowing down on breakfast, their lively chat bouncing off the stone walls. As he entered, his eyes went to Piper.

She made it back.

Her flaming auburn hair stood out brilliantly in the gray surroundings. Thomas sat next to her, too busy shoveling his breakfast in his mouth to notice Kole as he walked in. Across the table, Criz and Boogy looked as jolly as ever.

"There he is. I was wonderin' when you'd wake up," Felix said through a mouthful of food. "C'mere, Blondie. Ya gotta try this."

"He *stole* it fresh this morning," said Piper. She winced as she moved to grab another biscuit. A fresh bandage encased her torso. Remnants of her diversion last night. She hugged her side until she caught Kole's gaze, then dropped it as if nothing was wrong. Thomas snagged a biscuit for her. After a long side eye, she reluctantly took it.

"Stolen food always tastes better. Besides, I don't see you complainin'." Felix helped himself to the pile of biscuits at the center of the table.

"They're still warm, too!" Criz stuffed an entire ball of dough in his cheek. Boogy groaned next to him, leaning back in his chair and rubbing his plump belly with an expression that told Kole he'd eaten too much.

"Come in, Kole. Eat." Leo stretched his hand toward the empty seat beside him.

Kole peeked over at Piper. "Idris, is he...?"

The table fell quiet at the name.

"Dead?" Piper pursed her lips. "Badly injured is more like it."

"Probly licking his wounds," said Boogy.

"We miss out on *all* the fun," Criz said. "Wasted our time out in the farmlands."

"I would not call protecting our people a waste of time, Criz." Leo raised his eyebrows and glanced between the twins.

"No, sir," they said, dipping their heads.

Felix chucked a biscuit at Kole. It bounced off his chest and fell to his lap.

"How'd you escape?" Kole asked.

Piper paused before taking a bite. Her eyes moved to Leo, whose jaw twitched behind his beard. "I gave them the slip."

He wanted to ask for more details, but she'd gone back to her breakfast. Kole studied the rest of the Liberation. They held their heads down, eyes away from Piper and Leo. Something must have gone down when she returned. Probably the fallout for taking the blood magic spell from Leo's book. He wondered what the spell was, or if she even used it. She must have by the silence in the room. The pike was another factor. Leo must have been furious. Kole couldn't deny his curiosity, but he had his own problems.

Leo leaned in. "How is Russé?" he asked, changing the subject.

"He's still out. Not much to tell."

Leo passed Kole the jar of jam. "I have some balms in my repertoire that can speed up the healing process."

Kole ripped open the biscuit, steam rising and warming his hands, then slathered it in jam. "I don't want to risk waking him. Isn't rest the best remedy?"

Leo nodded. "Very well," he said, seemingly satisfied with Kole's answer. "In that case, eat up. You will all need your strength today."

Kole glanced at Felix, who gulped down a rather large bite of chewed dough before saying matter-of-factly, "Leo's finished the traps."

"I have. The refugees are arriving tonight, so they require set up before sundown." He turned to Kole. "I think it is best if you stay with me. In case Russé wakes."

A nod and he took another bite.

Shortly after breakfast, the Liberation left with sacks full of Leo's traps. Kole watched them leave, then returned to his bunk. He sat next to Russé, jostling him gently every few minutes hoping he'd wake, when a knock came at the door. He gave the Soul a quick once over before he answered. "Come in."

Leo stood in the doorway. "Any change?"

"No," Kole sighed.

Leo's mouth scrunched to one side. "It will take some time, but he will pull through, I am sure of it. If anyone can, it is him. I have never encountered such powerful defenses."

He stared at Leo, searching for a twinkle in his eye, a twitch in his mouth—anything to hint at the Liberation leader's thoughts.

"You have been in here all morning. Take a break. I have food in the lab."

Kole's stomach growled. His appetite had increased substantially since he'd been scarred, like anything he put in his body evaporated the moment it hit his stomach. He glanced back at Russé.

Leo must have sensed his reluctance, because he dipped his head, saying, "The base is quite secure. If he wakes while you are gone, we will only be a short walk down the hall."

After a deep breath, he hopped to the floor and followed.

Leo motioned to a parcel of jerky and fruit on the table upon entering the lab. "Help yourself."

He grabbed two handfuls of the dried meat and dug in.

The Liberation leader chose an apple from the pile and bit into it. As Kole ate, Leo moved to the table and gathered the various empty and half-used bottles of colorful liquid, replacing them neatly on the shelf in the far corner. His fingers swayed back and forth, following the line of bottles like he searched for one in particular. "Piper has informed me of the records."

Kole stopped chewing. "What about them?"

Back still to Kole, Leo continued. "There is no need to feign ignorance. I do not pick the Escape groups from a hat. Each decision takes weeks of research before I write their name in that book. I weigh the risks. The consequences we face for taking them over. I can recite every name, and yours is not in there."

Kole swallowed his bite. It went down rough against his dry throat. He eyed the door.

"Worry not." Leo turned, following Kole's gaze to the exit. "You may not have traveled to Solpate in one of my Escapes, but it does not mean I trust you any less. And I think I may have an inkling as to how you got there." His dark eyes narrowed. "That is why you wanted the records, is it not?"

Kole stayed quiet for a moment, wondering if he should keep up the charade, but his curiosity got the better of him, and he blurted, "What do you know?"

Another crunch into his apple, then Leo set it on the table. "I started the Escapes a little over ten years ago. I knew Savairo was up to something. He would send guards out in the night and raid homes for easy targets: the homeless, orphans — anyone whose disappearance would be less noticeable. You can imagine how hard he hit the outskirts of town. I did not know it at the time, but he was taking them to serve as lab rats. Fodder for his experiments as he perfected his Kayetans. I saved who I could in the orphanage, but it was not enough. Some were murdered. Others, like you have seen, became the Red Cloaks: Savairo's slaves."

"You think he took me in one of those raids?"

"Not exactly. We have accounted for every disappearance, even from Etta's orphanage. I have reason to believe you were born into his custody."

"In the prison."

Leo nodded.

Suddenly, Kole lost his appetite. He pocketed the jerky warming in his palm for later. No matter how plausible it seemed to Leo, Kole rejected it. A small shred of hope harbored inside him that he still had a family here. That he had been Niko's childhood friend. He cursed himself. *A fool's hope.* Though his heart wanted to keep up the fantasy, his mind wandered into the unknown. "If I was born in his custody, how did I end up in Solpate?"

"There could be a number of explanations. Most likely someone from the inside smuggled you out." A knowing look in Leo's eyes said he was holding something back.

"Who?" Kole pressed. He held Leo's gaze, not giving him a way out.

"Goren."

Somehow, Kole wasn't surprised. Everything involving his past linked back to Goren. Unless Leo knew more than he let on, Kole had no way of unearthing the truth. He couldn't question a dead man. More than ever, he yearned to decipher the camp leader's journal. "You knew, didn't you? From the moment I walked in. You knew I wasn't from your Escapes."

Leo gave an apologetic smile. "I just needed Piper to check and make sure before I said anything."

"Why didn't you tell me?"

"Would you have believed me if I did?"

Kole thought about it for a moment. Only the hard proof of seeing the records would have swayed him. Even still, after reading it himself, his heart wanted to deny it. "I guess not."

A final bite and only the apple's stem remained, eaten just like Kole had been taught out in the refugee camps: nothing left to waste. Though the lab seemed well stocked with ingredients, the stolen biscuits this morning, Leo's eating habits, and the depleted numbers hinted that the Liberation had truly fallen on dark times. They remained close to the city, but they were as much refugees as the people in Solpate. Kin fighting for the same cause.

"We doubt the word of a stranger no matter how much certainty it holds. That is a good thing, Kole. Never believe someone who has not earned your trust. And even then, be wary of believing those who have."

"You sound like Russé."

A smirked edged his beard. "Must be a wise man."

"Kole?" came a small voice from the door.

Russé stood under the archway.

In that moment, Kole didn't see a Soul. He didn't see Risil. He saw his old mentor, hunched and weak against the door frame. He rushed to Russé's side and slipped an arm under his shoulder, taking some of the weight.

"Shepherd Russé." Leo gave a small bow. "I am glad to see you awake."

"How long have I been out?" Russé mumbled.

"Nearly two days since the basin," Kole answered. "The battle is tonight."

Russé's eyes, an earnestness behind them, stayed glued to Kole. "I need to speak with you."

"And I need to speak with you, shepherd," Leo interjected. "It is of utmost importance, but I can wait for the time being." He strode to Russé's opposite side and guided the shepherd's arm around his neck. "Let us get you back to your quarters where you can rest."

Kole and Leo led him back to the bunk and sat him down. Relief washed over the old shepherd's face as he leaned into the stone.

"Once you are through, meet me in the lab," Leo said, then closed the door.

"Lock it," Russé wheezed after the door clicked shut.

Kole obeyed, then returned to the edge of the stone bed.

Russé's blue eyes appeared unusually dull, made even more so by the dark bags weighing heavily beneath them. He looked rough—tired mostly—but awake, nonetheless.

"You're all right," Russé said.

Kole didn't know if his mentor intended it as a question, or if he was merely reassuring himself. After a curt nod, Kole sat on the bunk. He kept his instincts in check, the ones concerning his injured mentor and reminded himself the man laying before him was a god.

"What did they do to you?"

Russé tapped a long, bony finger on his forehead. "They tried to get inside my mind."

"Did they?"

"No. It took four sorcerers just to keep me unconscious. Even if they did break through, I could squash them like the parasites they are." Russé waved a hand over his worn-down body. "*This* is my own doing. I have exhausted myself. Nothing a little rest can't cure."

Kole noticed new creases on the Soul's forehead and around his eyes. He looked like he'd aged a decade since Idris had dragged him from the basin.

"I am not important right now," Russé said at Kole's scrutiny, and he readjusted himself on the stone slab. "There is something I must tell you—something I've been keeping from you. All these years I have been going back and forth, questioning when to do it."

Kole flexed his jaw. "About you?"

Russé shook his head. "About *you*... and the others."

"Others? The Souls?"

The silence confirmed his question.

"Any time would've been the right time." Kole didn't care to hide the pique in his voice. Now, seeing Russé alive and well, Kole found his worry quickly dissipating, replaced with the anger and frustration he had felt the night Russé revealed himself a Soul. He took a long, slow breath, keeping the festering rage at bay.

"I know. I should have. And here we are, on the brink of it all. You have no clue what's going on. I never thought it would get to this. Not so soon." Russé's eyes burned into Kole's. A desperate gaze. "I know you don't trust me. I've seen the doubt grow in you, and I... I'm sorry. But please understand, I only wanted to protect you."

"Why do I need protection? *You're* the Soul. Idris was after you, not me."

"Because you were the one who released me from the Great Red."

Kole leaned back. "What?"

"The old, massive tree in—"

"I know what the Great Red is! What are you going on about, releasing you?"

"You released me from that tree ten years ago."

"I heard what you said, I just don't...." He shook his head. "How?"

Russé closed his eyes for a brief moment, then continued. "It's hard to explain. But I can show you." Russé extended a shaking arm to Kole. "Come here."

Kole studied the god, leaning in. As his forehead inched closer to Russé's hand, the image of Leo's contorted face, silently screaming in pain, surfaced. *Russé won't hurt me,* he reminded himself. *Right?*

The moment Russé's trembling hand brushed his temple, the room vanished.

Kole tossed his head back and forth. He was alone. Darkness, blacker than a starless night, surrounded him, pushing against his body with a growing pressure so strong, he felt as if his ribs would collapse.

Like a whisper on the wind, leaves rustled in the distance. He focused on the sound, tried to walk toward it, but the darkness held him in place.

Crunching boots came to his ears, and he knew exactly where he stood: Solpate forest.

By the crisp sound of the crushing leaves, he guessed it was fall. He pictured the yellowing trees just beyond the darkness, though he couldn't see them.

A strange sound emerged between the footsteps. No louder than a soft murmur at first, but as it grew, he could tell it belonged to a child. A boy. Laughing.

The footsteps rushed up beside him, and the laughter ceased.

Silence.

Then, an explosion wrecked Kole's ears.

The pressure alleviated. Color flooded his vision. Jagged pieces of wood and splinters flew away from him, and the golden forest he knew so well revealed itself. Just as he remembered it.

But the boy.... Where was the boy?

With the darkness gone, so was the hold on his body. Kole stepped into the lazy afternoon sunlight. His legs shook with each step, as if he'd forgotten how to walk. He urged on, desperate to find the boy.

Something stirred in the corner of his eye. A lump lay still, face down on the carpet of leaves. Kole rushed over to the body and fell to his knees, trying to shake the child awake, but he wouldn't rouse. He flipped him over. A glimpse at the young face made him fall back.

Round cheeks, rosy pink, and a small, narrow nose. Kole would know this face anywhere.

It was his own.

But the hair was different. Dark brown. Then, as he watched, white sprouted from the boy's scalp. The color spread down the strands, draining the dark pigment away.

From the child's frame, Kole guessed him no older than five, around the time Kole had first arrived in Solpate. He had no memory of this scene. Where had he come from? And why was he here alone? He was so small. Where was Russé? Goren? Niko? No one ventured the woods alone, especially not a child.

A leaf floated down from the canopy, landing on Kole's knee. Red — blood-red.

Kole spun.

The Great Red towered over him. Its massive trunk was freshly mangled from the explosion, leaving behind a deep cavity where he guessed he'd been trapped a moment ago.

In a swirl of color, the scene vanished. Darkness clouded his vision, and the familiar stone room of the Liberation hideout returned. Gone was the forest. Kole sat on the stone bunk next to Russé like he'd never moved.

"You released me," Russé wheezed, his face even paler than when he'd first awoken.

The image of Kole's younger self branded into his mind. He moved to touch what was left of his hair since his encounter with the Black Wall. In the vision, it changed color after releasing the Soul. "How did I get there? Where was Goren? The other orphans? What's going on, Russé?" He looked back to his mentor, remembering the hold of the darkness. "Was that you? Trapped in the tree?"

Russé nodded.

"Who put you there?"

"Aterus."

CHAPTER 20

Aterus. The Gray Soul. Creator of Man.

"Leo mentioned him earlier. He's alive, then? Here on Ohr like you?"

"Yes. Me and my kin were supposed to ascend before...." Russé shifted uncomfortably against the wall. "We had one rule set in place to protect ourselves and our creations. Aterus broke that rule."

"What did he do?"

"He interfered with one of his creations."

"Interfered?"

"He fell in love."

It wasn't the answer Kole expected. He would have guessed that Aterus killed someone. But love? The same Aterus who introduced Savairo to blood magic had fallen in love? Kole found it hard to believe someone with the stomach for dark sorcery was capable of such things.

"If only it had stopped there. Souls are immortal. Our creations are not. As Aterus' lover moved closer to death, he grew more rash in finding ways to prolong her life. His solution was to use his own blood to sustain her. It worked for a time. But soon the humans found out. Word spread around Ohr about the god who granted eternal life. The humans changed then. They worshiped Aterus with archaic rituals and offerings in hopes that he would bless them, too."

"Did he?"

"Some. Aterus thought it would make his creations happy, but the blood of a god has terrible consequences when mixed with a mortal's. While some were blessed with long life like his lover, others were instead cursed by his touch. Unbeknownst to him. Only so much life can be given before nature corrects the balance. A black death spread from the cursed. It seemed to be in the air, killing men and beast alike. When the other Souls and I discovered what Aterus had done, we gave him a choice: cut ties with his lover or ascend. He rejected both. Once mortals discovered

Aterus, the rest of us soon followed. The sick sought us out. Begged to be saved. And others wanting the same gift of extended life Aterus had granted. It was beyond what humans were designed for."

"Aterus fed people blood?" The thought disgusted Kole. "Wait, like blood magic?"

Russé's eyes went glassy. "Yes. The birth of blood magic."

"And you just let it happen?"

"Of course not!" It was Russé's turn to sound disgusted. "We gave him the ultimatum. When he refused, we decided to forced him out. We had no choice. Things had gone too far. Humanity was growing mad. It wasn't only them. Somehow, the sickness mutated. It started poisoning the animals and earth, too. Another decade and everything would've been destroyed. On the day we confronted him, Aterus betrayed us. He imprisoned us."

"That's how you got into the Great Red."

Russé nodded.

"How long were you in there?"

The Soul shook his head. "I don't know. Centuries. A millennium? Perhaps more."

"What happened with the black death? The plague Aterus put on Ohr. You said a decade more would destroy everything, but if what you say is true, we'd all be...."

"I don't know what happened while I was confined. He must've restored balance. My guess is he *revoked* his blessings."

"Murdered," he whispered. *What kind of person can grant life and steal it away?* The balance of Ohr weighed into everything.

Kole thought back to the scene Russé had shown him, trapped in darkness, unable to move or speak. A thought came to him. "The ramblers. They were your doing. Goren said the Great Red gave the forest its magic. It wasn't the tree at all, was it? That was you." It all made perfect sense. The red tree had been Russé all along—the source of it all. His power was why the trees roamed at night. Russé had influenced everything within the forest, including the animals.

"I wasn't aware of my effect on the forest until you released me. My powers seeped from my prison. Something Aterus failed to foresee when he put me there, I imagine. One of many things...."

"Like what?"

"The Black Wall."

Kole fidgeted uncomfortably with his sleeve. Only a few days had passed since the wall of fire nearly consumed him and his camp had burned to ruin. All for what? Aterus' lover? He had heard the refugees talk of love. It was supposed to be unselfish and kind, or something. Kole could only guess what *that* meant, but it seemed far from black walls of destruction and imprisoning your own kin. How could one person put their desires before the entire world? Was that what love did to a person? *So much for unselfish.*

Russé must have noticed the hurt on Kole's face. He reached out, gently patting his back. Kole flinched and leaned away, ignoring the sting of pain in the Soul's eyes as he did. He didn't need Russé's comfort; he needed the truth. "So Goren was right. The Soul's created the Black Wall."

"Not entirely. The wall was more of an effect of our imprisonment. The Souls are not individuals. Remember what Goren said? We are seven pieces to one whole. He was right in that. If one piece is missing, our powers falter. We all knew this, including Aterus. I believe he thought he'd found a way to bypass it by imprisoning us *on* Ohr. If we remained on the planet, we would stay connected, and the world would go on as if nothing had changed. But he made an error. The magic it took to keep us detained locked us in another dimension. The Seven Souls became disconnected, and the world began to unravel. Our *imprisonment* birthed the Black Wall."

"And if the Souls are released?"

"The Black Wall will disappear."

"Sounds simple enough." A bud of hope bloomed within Kole. The Black Wall was no all-powerful entity, after all. It had a weakness like everything else.

"I wouldn't call it simple. All these years and I am the only Soul to be freed. I have no idea how to find the others. That's why I need you."

"For what?"

"I believe you can find the others like you did me."

"I didn't find you. I was *five*. More like I stumbled by a weird red tree and... I don't even remember how I got there. How do you expect me to find them? You're the Soul. Shouldn't you know where they are?"

"My connection to the others broke when you released me."

"Hold on. Is that what you meant the night at the basin? You said I'm the only one who can take down the Black Wall."

Russé nodded. The Soul leaned in, the tip of his index finger tapping Kole's temple. "You have a connection with them." Kole gave an unconvinced frown, but Russé continued. "You've been hearing voices."

Kole drew back. Sliding from the bunk, he folded his arms self-consciously. No way Russé could have known about that. Kole had never said a word to anyone. Not even Niko.

"I know you heard them that night at the basin."

A small wave of relief took him knowing he might not be going crazy after all. He swallowed. "I've heard it other times...."

"When you are in dire need of help?"

Kole gave a curt nod.

"After all of this talk, you haven't connected the dots?"

Kole frowned. Of course he'd guessed, but the idea seemed too outlandish to say aloud—to confirm. Knowing who spoke in his mind only made it more real, and he was still trying to pretend that he had imagined her. Her powers, though, were harder to ignore. "She didn't just speak to me. She *controlled* me. In the basin... she took over my body." The helplessness he had felt that night crept up again. No control. No way to move. He loathed that feeling: being someone's puppet. "I couldn't help you. I couldn't do *anything*."

"None of it was your fault," Russé dismissed.

His tongue pressed into his check. "Which one is it?"

"Issira."

"The Blue Soul."

Russé peered at him as if he expected Kole to suffer some sort of mental breakdown. "She was protecting you that night. She will keep you safe at all costs because you are the key to her freedom."

Pulling back the tight sleeve of his uniform to expose his burns, he snorted. "Where was she then?"

"She warned us, remember? Our fates would've been much worse if she hadn't broken through when she did."

"It made no difference with the others."

Heavy silence swelled in the small room. Tension so thick it dried his mouth. He paced to keep his rising fumes at bay.

To think, Kole had put his faith in these beings: a lying old shepherd, a lovesick man, and a terrifying puppeteer. *And* there were four more Souls he had yet to 'meet.' He didn't want to imagine what they would be like. Hopefully they were more god-like than the others—or at least more what he imagined a Soul to be: divine, all-knowing, wise. If Issira showed a little less aggression, he might not fear her. Paralyzing someone wouldn't be Kole's first choice if contending for freedom. It only made him more reluctant. "How did she get into my head?"

"The day you freed me, a bond formed between us. When you bonded with me, you bonded with all seven of us. That's why you can hear their voices. They are connected to you. If you talk to them—"

"No way. She *won't* do that to me again."

"It's the only way we'll be able to find them."

"Wait," Kole stopped, mid-step. "The day I freed you... I don't remember anything before. It's the same day you lost your connection, right? Does the bond have something to do with my lost memories?"

Russé shrugged. "Possibly. The bond could be blocking them. I'm not entirely certain. I wish I could tell you more. You were alone when I found you. The memory I showed you came straight from my head. From there, the trees guided me to the northern camp, where I met Goren. He recognized you immediately. Said you had wandered off." His voice lowered an octave. A desperate tone. "Please believe me. I don't know anything beyond that."

If his late camp leader recognized him, it meant Kole had already been living in the forest at the time. But what of before? He hunched over. So badly he wanted to believe the Soul, but after all the lies, how could he? Just when the old man finally seemed willing to offer answers. Why did it all have to be so confusing?

"Don't give up on your past. Only Goren knows the truth."

"But he's—"

"I know." A pain hid behind his eyes—a vulnerability unsuitable for a god. "His journal. It may hold a clue. You did take it, didn't you?"

Kole snatched the book from the hidden spot under the bunks and passed it to Russé. "I couldn't read it."

"I tried the night after the Black Wall came." Opening to the first page, Russé dragged a thin finger over the text. "It's not a language."

Kole peered over his shoulder, taking in the odd designs. "What is it?"

"A code. One only Goren can read, I reckon. He always showed such caution. Quite the clever lad."

Kole scoffed. "More like two-faced liar."

Russé closed the journal. "He only said those things to protect you."

"How was that, in any way, protection? He lied about *everything*."

"Kole...."

"Don't. You have no right to defend him. You're both the same."

Kole rubbed the burn scars on the back of his neck. Russé's deceit had made him paranoid. If he had only told him the truth from the beginning, maybe things would be different. Sure, Kole hadn't always been obedient. He'd twisted his mentor's orders on several occasions — and admittedly, he was quite stubborn — but he was *loyal*. Always. "Why couldn't you trust me with this?"

"We thought you would blend in with the other children if you thought you had the same past. We didn't want you to be an outsider."

"Enough with the half-truths. My past is gone because of the two of you. Haven't you done enough damage? Now Goren's gone, and there's no way to ask him. Or to read his *damn* journal." Nothing could reign in his anger now. He promised himself he'd make the god talk. Whatever it took. "Whatever you know about me, just spit it out!"

His voice echoed around the room and no doubt filtered into the hall despite the heavy door.

A pause. Whatever wall Russé had been holding up seemed to crumble. The Soul took a long breath. "Word couldn't get out about you. If Savairo or Aterus got wind, even a rumor, about a mortal capable of speaking with the gods, they'd come after you."

"Kill me, you mean?"

"Possibly. Aterus may not hold enough mercy for that. I know it's hard for a mortal to understand, but imagine. Imagine Savairo. What's he's capable of. His experiments forced you and the refugees into hiding. Killed thousands. Created monsters out of your people. He is blind to anyone but himself." Another shallow breath. "Imagine that same blindness in a god."

Kole knew the pieces of the puzzle. For the first time, they all aligned. He could do more than imagine what Aterus was capable of. He *lived* it. The Black Wall had wiped out nearly the entire planet just as Savairo did to the people of Socren. Same crime, different scales. Suddenly, keeping Russé's secret sounded like the best option. Now he had his own to keep, too.

Seconds ticked by as Kole let it all sink in. The Soul made no move to speak, only waited.

Did the Soul want an apology? A sign Kole finally understood his and Goren's choices? Kole *did* understand, but he refused him the satisfaction of forgiveness. Instead, he lowered himself on the edge of the stone bunk, hard-faced, and said, "Okay."

Russé tucked the journal into his belt loop. "We may have a way to recover your memories. It's only a theory."

He couldn't bring himself to look at the Soul.

Russé continued, "If the connection between you and the Souls *is* obstructing your memories, perhaps breaking the connection would bring them back."

"Let me guess." Kole peered at him. "The only way to do that is to release them."

"Yes."

Kole's gut twisted. He'd have to let *her* in again if he wanted his past back and the Black Wall eliminated. The mere thought of those dark flames made his skin crawl.

"It's a chance, but that's all we have to go on for now."

A chance. Kole pursed his lips. All these answers, yet his past eluded him. He wanted those memories. After all he'd lost in the last few days, he needed the truth now more than ever. Something good to focus on. To hope for.

What a mess that old man had made. Kole cursed the camp leader in his head, wishing he could talk with the dead man. Five minutes was all he needed. Since there was no way to resurrect someone—as far as he knew—he'd have to rely on the journal. Kole crossed his arms. "I'll do it. I'll help free the Souls. On one condition: you decipher Goren's code."

"Agreed." Russé held out a quivering hand.

He extended his own, then paused. "One more thing. No more lies. You tell me *everything* from here on out."

Russé's tired eyes lingered on him.

As the moment passed, he got the feeling Russé would refuse. Then, the Soul dipped his head and grabbed Kole's hand. "Deal."

He watched Russé carefully as he released, trying to read the god's expression for a sign he would hold true to his word. "If we are done here, we should leave."

"But the battle is in the morning."

"Which is precisely why."

"We can't leave," Kole said firmly.

"The Liberation has been warned. We have fulfilled our promise to the refugees. Savairo and his Kayetan know what I am, and Aterus is on his way. We need to put as much space between us and this city before the Soul arrives. You and I are in more danger every moment we linger."

"Since when do you run from danger?"

"I'm not running from anything."

"It sure sounds like it. Don't you want to meet Aterus in battle? You can end this."

"I'm not strong enough to face him."

"What are you talking about? I saw what you did back at camp—the plants moved at your will. Take Aterus out and we can end all of this tomorrow."

"You don't understand, Kole. I can't do it."

Kole's brows drew together, skeptically. *I can't do it.*

Aterus had betrayed Russé. He had trapped him in the Great Red for years. That alone would make Kole want revenge. But Russé was different, as he continued to prove. Surely, he would want to make things right. To save what remained of Ohr. That's the whole reason they'd free Souls in the first place. A thought washed through him.

Maybe Russé was not after Aterus at all. They were kin. Did Russé still feel some kind of connection with him? One which would make him want to spare his life? Kole would have done anything to save his own family. Was Russé bent on doing the same? Would he put Aterus' life above the lives of their creations? In Kole's eyes, Russé had made his stance on human life pretty clear when he neglected to save Niko and the others. He may have only saved Kole because he held value to the Souls. Thinking on it, every choice Russé had made thus far had benefited himself and the Souls. "You can't do it? Or you won't?"

Russé's jaw set.

Kole growled at his silence. More than willing to hold up his end of the bargain, he needed to know Russé would do the same. "You said no more lies. If you won't be honest, the deal is off."

"Both," Russé said quietly, his gaze straying from Kole. "It's not what you think."

Coward, liar, traitor, he wanted to scream. "Are you sure? There's a lot going through my mind right about now."

Russé stared at his wrinkled hands. Rounding his back, he leaned forward. "I haven't been the same since I broke out of that tree. I am weak." Kole opened his mouth to protest, but Russé lifted a finger at him. "Those things I did before... it took me years to build up that power. I stored it up in case I needed it one day. And need it, I did. My reserves have dwindled. I have a puddle at my command when I need an ocean. If there's any chance of subduing Aterus, I will need the others. Assuming they share my shortcomings upon release, the only way we can take on our brother is to combine our strength."

"What about the refugees? The Liberation? The people of Socren? They'll help in the fight. You don't need to do it all on your own."

"Their strength will not be enough." Keeping one hand firmly on the bunk for support, Russé struggled to stand, but his body had other plans. His legs wobbled and buckled beneath him. It was the first time Kole saw Russé's body act its age, or rather act as old as it looked.

Kole reached out to steady him. The shepherd had always been strong beyond his means, now Kole knew why, but what really bothered him was the thought that something held enough power to weaken Russé—no—weaken a god. It had only taken Savairo and a few of his sorcerers to quell him. A shudder took him at the thought of Aterus' capabilities.

"You're not well enough to travel anyway." Kole rolled the staff off the bunk and tucked it under Russé's arm.

He took it gratefully and leaned into it. "I will have recovered enough by tonight."

Oh, right, the whole super healing thing. Kole gently pushed on Russé's shoulders, trying to get him to sit down, but he refused and instead forced his feet, one in front of the other, attempting to walk.

"We can't abandon them, Russé. Their numbers are low as it is."

"It's not worth the risk." Russé massaged his temples. "If Aterus finds me, he will return me to my prison."

"The refugees are on their way here as we speak. Everyone I have ever known is about to go to war. They're risking their lives to see this through. This was *your* idea. We can hold off for one night," Kole argued. No matter what Russé told him, Kole had made up his mind.

The old man shifted weakly, all of his body weighing down on the staff. "The future will be far worse for them should something happen to you. If you die, who else can find the Souls? Ohr might be consumed by the Black Wall before I figure out another way."

Kole turned away. "And if *they* die... just like everyone in the northern camp... what then?" He clenched his jaw. "It's a sacrifice you're willing to make?"

"I don't like it anymore than you do."

Kole spun around. "*Then stay.*" Russé's head tilted forward, clearly exhausted, but Kole only grew more angry at his silence. "You're going to let them die!"

"You know that's not what I mean," Russé said quietly as he moved back to the bunk.

A tinge of guilt loomed over Kole for pushing the old shepherd this far, but how could he allow himself to be dragged off in the wake of the rebellion? He helped Russé onto the stone ledge, then took the staff and placed it within reach in case the Soul needed it.

"I've seen what Savairo's done to these people. They're skeletons, Russé. I can't—" He chewed his lip and sat on the ledge. "I'm not going to turn my back on them. Go if you want. I'm not leaving until this is over."

"Always the hero," said Russé, his lips curling into a sad smile.

"It doesn't take a hero to want to see our people live through the night." Kole felt Russé's eyes on him, but he refused to meet his gaze. This was the right thing to do. Russé had to see that. There were too many lives at stake to go searching for Souls. Kole wasn't even sure how to find them.

"I was a little too ambitious to think I could convince you otherwise."

Kole turned, his eyes curiously searching his mentor's.

"We will stay." His voice turned harsh. "But don't expect to be in the battle."

Before Kole could challenge him, a noise came from the hall. Kole's head whipped around as the doorknob rattled.

Felix's voice carried through the keyhole. "Hey! What's the deal, Blondie? You can't take away a man's room—let me in!"

Russé raised an eyebrow. "Blondie, huh? I can see that."

Cursing under his breath, Kole shook his head and strode to the door.

"C'mon, mate, don't make me sleep in the twins' room." Felix lowered his voice, trying to whisper through the opening. *"That place stinks of armpits and gas."* Felix stumbled into the room, profusely thanking Kole as he opened the door. His eyes landed on Russé. "Hello." Holding out a hand, he went to the bunk. "I'm Felix, Leo's right hand. Kole's probly told ya all about me, eh?"

Russé shook it, the corner of his mouth twitching in amusement. "A pleasure."

"Leo wants ta see ya," Felix said, motioning to the door.

"I thought you came in to sleep," said Kole.

"I needed ya ta open the door, didn't I?" Casting a wink at him, Felix then turned his attention back to Russé. "Ready, Gramps?"

"He's still weak," Kole protested.

Russé silenced him with a raised hand. "I'll be fine. Help an old man up, won't you?" he asked Felix, who then offered an arm. Russé grabbed his staff with a shaking hand and hobbled out the door with Felix.

Kole ran to catch up.

Rounding the corner, they collided into Piper.

Felix kept Russé firmly on his feet, but Piper was knocked to the floor.

Kole could tell straight away she was in a rage; her face a deep shade of maroon and the vein on her forehead exposed. She didn't care to conceal her curses as she climbed to her feet and dusted herself off.

"Hey, Pipes," Felix said.

"Watch where you're going," she snapped. After noticing Russé, her demeanor changed. She averted her eyes to the floor, arms stiff by her sides.

"Someone's in a mood," Felix grumbled, then patted Russé on the shoulder, who clung on his staff, body braced under the force of Felix's hand. "This is Ru—"

"I know who he is." She stared back with such ferocity, Kole expected flames to shoot from her pupils. "Any other pleasantries I need to sit through, or may I take my leave?"

Before anyone could respond, she shoved past and continued her rampage down the hall.

Kole's eyes trailed after her. "What's gotten under her skin?"

Leading them down the corridor, Felix said, "Leo really gave it to her about stealin' his spell. And the pike. And—well, she's gotta long list of things, really."

"Spells?" Russé asked.

"Leo's been teachin' her sorcery stuff." They slowed as they reached the laboratory door. "She's got a pretty good knack for the basics, so I've heard. Never seen her do nothin', now that I think on it, but Pipes has a short temper. If she slips up, she's a jug of sour milk for the rest of the week."

"Patience is the key to anything worth learning, especially sorcery," said Russé.

Felix raised a dark eyebrow. "Know much about it, Gramps?"

"A bit."

Holding a suspicious gaze, Felix opened the door to reveal the Liberation leader hunched over the molten pike Piper had used on Idris in the prison. Leo grimaced at the weapon, whose pale flames lashed out harmlessly at the table, not making so much as a curl to the ends of the parchment pinned beneath it. The pike seemed a bit more restless than Kole remembered. Beside it sat a torn page: the stolen spell.

Leo's eyes flicked up from his work when they entered. He bowed slightly at the waist, not bothering to hide his frown, and greeted them.

"Leonardo, so I'm told," Russé returned the bow.

"Leo is more than fine, Shepherd Russé."

"What happened to it?" Kole jerked his chin to the pike.

Leo examined it once more. "Piper tried to strengthen it on her own. Thought she could make it strong enough to kill Idris." He sighed and pulled up his sleeves, muttering a language Kole couldn't understand, while he waved a hand over the weapon. The molten surface regressed to a gentle smolder, like the glowing coals of a dying fire. It hardened to a sleek white sheen, but to Leo's frustration, tiny veins remained, running along the entire length of the pike; a hot, orange glow pulsing beneath the surface. "That might do the trick."

"You're snuffing it out?" Kole asked.

"Taming it, rather. The girl is reckless. This kind of magic is dangerous, especially for an amateur. Done improperly, it could destabilize at any moment." Leo clicked his tongue disapprovingly. "She is lucky it did not melt in her hands. She has the Souls to thank, I suppose."

Kole flinched when Leo mentioned the Souls. A casual glance to Felix to see if he noticed. Thankfully, Felix was too distracted, tip-toeing around the table to get a closer view of the strange weapon; his eyes twinkled mischievously and flicked from the pike to Leo and back again, as if repressing the urge to swipe it from under his nose.

Russé wore a stone face. Perfect control over his expressions, as usual.

He forced himself to relax.

Setting the pike aside, Leo said, "I will have to deal with this later. There is much I wish to discuss with you, Shepherd Russé." He turned to Felix, who's face drooped when the pike moved out of reach.

Kole half hoped Felix would've swiped it. It seemed an utter waste to undo Piper's magic. So what if it was dangerous? *Idris* was dangerous.

"As for you, get some sleep," Leo said to Felix. "You'll need your full strength tonight."

"I fetch Gramps for ya and ya send me ta bed?" Felix's shoulders fell forward.

"It's probably for the best if you go, too," said Russé, looking to Kole.

Kole crossed his arms and leaned into Russé. "I thought we had a deal."

"We do." Russé pulled away.

CHAPTER 21

Kole waited, staring into the dark room. Felix had fallen asleep long ago. Despite his stomach, stuffed with leftover biscuits from breakfast, and his body miraculously warm under his thin blanket, he couldn't do the same. Conditions seemed perfect for a deep, slobber-inducing sleep like Felix had achieved so easily across the room. Yet Kole's eyes remained open and anxious.

If Russé really intended on keeping his promise, then why insist on speaking with Leo alone? Kole would make him honor their deal as soon as he returned.

In the meantime, though, his mind ran wild, thinking of the swiftly approaching battle. He walked through Felix and Thomas' battle techniques. Making a fist, he waved his arm about in his cramped bunk, mimicking the motions. After a few dozen times, he grew bored and sat up.

Light from the hallway poured in beneath the door and stretched along the floor until it completely succumbed to the darkness within the room. It reminded him of the first time he'd heard the Soul's voice. Russé's words rattled in his brain. *You are the one person who can speak with them.*

Kole glanced to Felix. Still asleep.

He closed his eyes and dared a whisper. "Hello?"

The seconds ticked by.

No answer.

"Hello?" Kole tried again, a bit louder. Felix stirred in his bunk.

Still nothing.

Kole sighed. "So much for saving the world." He twisted his blanket in his hands. "You are the only one who can speak with them," Kole mocked once Felix's breathing returned to its normal cadence. He felt stupid for even trying. What if Felix had caught him talking to himself? He would never live it down. Bad enough being called Blondie; he didn't need to be Batty, as well.

Kole wasn't sure if he wanted to talk to them anyway. Seven all-powerful gods swimming around inside his head next to his most private thoughts? No thank you.

Kole had only ever heard *her* voice in his head. When he'd tried to reach out to her before, she didn't hear him. He had yelled and screamed, pleaded to her to let him save Russé that night at the basin, but he might as well have been yelling to himself. She couldn't hear him. Or maybe she did and she just didn't care.

That was it! He had been yelling, yes, but what if Issira couldn't hear him because he had been doing just that—speaking. She couldn't hear his voice, only his thoughts. He'd need to communicate using *her* way: through his mind. It was worth a shot, and it seemed a lot less embarrassing than being caught talking to himself.

Closing his eyes, he thought of what to say to a god. He settled for something basic and concentrated on forming the words in his head. They formed clearly in his subconscious.

"Hello? Can you hear me?"

He waited.

Biting his tongue to keep his bubbling impatience from surfacing, he tried again. The words crept back into his head.

Nothing.

Kole fell back in his bed so hard that the air gushed from his pillow, flattening as a handful of feathers zoomed free of the seams and floated to the floor. He turned toward the wall, yanked the blanket to his chin, and squeezed his eyes shut, hoping sleep would find him.

Then he heard it.

A whisper grew deep within his mind. Foggy at first, as though calling to him from atop a mountain. Then the voice rushed closer, chanting his name.

Kole opened his eyes, expecting to see someone floating above him, shouting into his ear.

It stopped as suddenly as it came.

A chill crawled over Kole's skin, raising the hairs on the back of his neck. His heart pounded with the foreboding rhythm of a war drum as five distinct words whispered, *"They know. They are coming."*

"What?" Kole shook his head, realizing he said it aloud. He formed the words in his head. *"Who knows? Who is coming?"* he asked desperately, but Issira's presence had faded.

Alone again.

They are coming? What does she mean? The refugees? Of course they were coming. He already knew that.

Kole hopped from his bunk. Just as his feet touched the floor, his knees buckled at a piercing screech, penetrating the stone walls of the base.

A flash of movement and Felix bolted up. He squinted at Kole through the darkness. "Blondie? Why are ya awake?"

"Something's wrong." Kole tiptoed to the door and placed his hand on the knob.

"Was someone screamin'?"

Feet pattered up beside him. The sound must've put Felix on edge too, because he palmed his sunstone dagger. Kole cracked the door enough for one eye to glimpse the hallway.

Empty.

Easing through the gap, he slipped into the bright hall. His eyes took a moment to adjust.

Felix followed closely behind. With light feet, they crossed the corridor. The door on the left burst open with a brisk wind. Deep in the shadows lurked a bulky form. Kole reeled back as Felix lunged and pinned it to the wall.

"Whoa! What are you doing?" Boogy squealed, cheek pressed against the stone.

"Boogy?" Felix squinted at his comrades face through the darkness. "Heh, I guess this *is* your room."

Criz appeared in the doorway looking from his brother's concerned face to Felix, whose twitching arm was still outstretched, a mere inch between the tip of his blade and Boogy's throat.

"Was he sleep-fighting again?" asked Criz.

"Sorry, mate." Felix dropped his arm. "Kole got me all riled up. We heard a scream and—"

"So did we," said Boogy, rubbing his neck.

"Where'd it come from?" Kole asked.

A shrug from Boogy. "Maybe it was Pipes. She was in a mood last I saw her."

Kole, Felix, and Criz gave him a skeptical look.

"So ya think she'd scream in the middle of the night?" Felix asked. "'Cause of a mood swing?"

"I dunno." Boogy's eyes shifted uncomfortably between Felix and his brother. "Girls are weird."

"Maybe we should check on her," said Kole.

"Right. Nothin' wrong with that." Felix put on a cheesy grin as he knocked on an invisible door, acting it out. "Sorry ta wake ya, Pipes, but we heard a scream and thought it could *only* be you."

Criz shook his head. "That'll put her right in a frenzy."

"What do you suggest, then? Go back to bed?" Kole hissed.

The screech came again.

"Over there." Felix pointed to the closed double doors of the vaulted room.

Black smoke slid through the crack. It rose, taking a humanoid shape. The featureless head directed its gaze at them.

They know. They are coming. Kole played her warning in his head.

Another screech, and the Kayetan charged.

Kole's hand went to his belt. Empty. A curse slipped from his lips, and he pushed past the three boys. Nothing but dead weight without a weapon. *Now who's the damsel?*

"Bring it on, Smokey!" Felix taunted, twirling his dagger in his palm. As the Kayetan neared, Felix gave an odd gesture that must have been for the twins. The brothers immediately moved back-to-back behind Felix.

Once the Kayetan came within range, Felix lashed out with a reckless blow, missing by a good foot.

This is no time to play games. Felix wasn't even trying to hit the creature. Kole fell back, pressing into the stone wall.

The Kayetan swerved left to avoid Felix's sad excuse for an attack, which forced the creature right in front of Boogy, who stabbed it clear through the heart. It vanished in a spray of light.

"Good work," Felix slapped Boogy on the back. "Now let's find out how the hell this bugger found us."

"What in Souls' name is going on out here?" Leo turned down the corridor, Russé hobbling close behind.

"Kayetan," Felix reported with a nod to the double doors. "Think it came in through The Cobwebs."

Leo froze mid-step. "Here?"

Kole pulled Russé aside as Piper and Thomas ran down the hall to join them; apparently the noise of the fight had alerted everyone. From the look on his wrinkled face, Russé must have seen the concern in Kole's eyes. After making sure the Liberation was distracted, Kole said, "I talked to her."

"Issira?" he asked in a hushed whisper. "What did she say?"

"A warning. *'They know. They are coming.'* I think she means the Kayetans."

Russé nodded. His lips parted to speak, but the Liberation's discussion had taken a harsh turn.

"Maybe they're smarter than we thought." Boogy swung his head side to side, fervently watching the halls, as if expecting another Kayetan to pop out of the shadows.

"The Cobwebs ain't the only thing keepin' this place hidden, y 'know." At Leo's presence, Felix tucked his dagger away. "Leo has magic mumbo jumbo and stuff protectin' it. There's somethin' weird goin' on here, I tell ya."

"Leo' ll take care of it," Criz chimed in, clapping a firm hand on his brother's shoulder. It seemed to calm him for the moment.

"If one Kayetan knows about our hideout, they all will," Leo said grimly. "I imagine that one was a scout. It is only a matter of time before more follow."

"How did they find us?" Piper asked.

"They would not have come across us by accident. The Kayetan could have followed any one of us in." Leo turned to Piper. "Perhaps you were not as sly returning from the prison as you intended."

Her eyes sharpened at the accusation. "I was careful," she said, venom in her voice, as if she had reassured him a thousand times already.

Thomas waved a hand at Leo's insinuation. "She knows better than that."

Her eyes snapped to Thomas. "Don't talk about me like I'm a child."

At that, Thomas lowered his head. Even his long hair couldn't hide his face turning as red as Piper's curls.

"If anyone's to blame, it's them," Piper pointed a finger Kole and Russé's way. "They've drawn more attention from Savairo and his Kayetans in the last two days than any of *us* have in a year."

"Enough." Leo massaged his temples. "We will get to the bottom of this. Everyone take a seat." His hand motioned to the double doors.

Piper, her bed-head making her look like a ruffled bird, directed a toxic glare at Kole and Russé. Kole held it. He refused to back down from her. Though he couldn't blame her. New blood always drew suspicion. It would be Kole's first instincts, too.

The Liberation quick on her heels, Piper marched into the domed room.

Every pair of eyes went to Kole and Russé as they walked in, Thomas and Piper's being the most scrutinizing of the group; they even moved to the opposite side of the table as if to keep their whispering private.

Everyone took a seat around the gray stone table while Leo waited at the head.

The Liberation leader turned to his left, lowering himself eye level with Kole. His eyes stilled—unblinking and black. A Seeing Truth spell, Piper had called it.

"Have you given any information about our whereabouts to Savairo or his men?"

"No," said Kole.

With a nod, Leo moved to Russé's chair and asked him the same question.

"No."

Silence. Then, Leo's jaw twitched. "Have you given any information about our whereabouts to Savairo or his men?" he repeated.

"I have not."

What was Leo getting at asking Russé twice? The Liberation leaned into the table, their stares on Leo, awaiting his confirmation.

"You are lying."

"I knew there was something off about him," Thomas sneered. "I bet they are both in on it. Are they even from the refugee camps?"

"They could be Savairo's spies," Piper said.

"What? We aren't, I swear!" Kole said, but Russé stayed silent—stoic.

"Quiet," Leo boomed. Piper and Thomas reluctantly leaned back in their chairs, their eyes like daggers on Kole and Russé. "He did fail the question, but... something is muddling the spell. I sense magic within him."

Kole opened and closed his fists beneath the table. His eyes shifted to Russé in the chair beside him. The Soul's fingers curled around his staff: the first sign Kole had seen hinting at nerves.

"It's familiar...." Leo cocked his head, extending an arm toward the Soul.

Russé grabbed Leo's wrist before he could touch him. Leo blinked, the curiosity in his dark eyes replaced with surprise. The Liberation stood from their chairs, hands on their weapons.

"What are your intentions?" Russé asked, his fingers wrapped tight around Leo's arm.

"I sense a peculiar presence within you. One absent just yesterday."

"You wish to inspect my mind?"

Leo's breath faltered a fraction of a second. After foaming at the mouth the last time, Kole wasn't surprised by his hesitance. But Leo's answer came firm. "Yes."

Releasing his hold, Russé allowed him to continue and gave Kole a reassuring nod.

Leo placed his hands on the Soul's temples.

No screams this time. No spasms or rolling eyes. The sorcerer remained calm and relaxed, as if meditating. After a moment, Leo stepped back, clutching the Seven Soul's pendant hanging around his neck and cursed. "He has a tracker."

"What?" Piper's fists pounded the table "How is that possible?"

A motion to the bandage around Russé's head. "His injury." Leo let out a low, melodic whistle. Flapping wings rushed from the hall. Fiona landed gracefully on Leo's shoulder, the grip of her needle-like talons wrinkling his clothes. Using his finger to delicately stroke the back of her head, he said, "Poleer mountain. Return when the refugees near the peak." Fiona clicked her beak, lifted off, then disappeared through the hole in the dome ceiling. "When you were wounded in the prison, you left behind your blood. Savairo is using it to track your whereabouts. If he was unsure of our location before, he knows now. We must leave before he sends more Kayetans."

"Let 'em come. We can take 'em," Felix bellowed.

"I will not risk it. Our battle is on the mountain, not here. The refugees will arrive shortly. They need our guidance."

"Break the spell." Piper demanded. Sloppy red curls plastered to her forehead. "Reverse it, Leo."

"The only way to do that is to —"

"Use blood magic," she finished.

A shadow fell over Leo's face. His words came short and sharp as he spoke, "*I will not use blood magic.*"

Hardening her gaze, Piper scoffed.

"Even if I did, it would change nothing. By the laws of sorcery, I would need the user *and* the victim's blood to reverse the spell. Do you happen to have a vial of Savairo's blood?"

Ever so slightly, the side of her mouth lifted. With a glint in her eyes, she said, "We have yours."

"Family blood is not exact. I would need time to figure it out." Leo shook his head, dismissing her. "We escape while we can and make for Lilith's pass before they learn our plans. The best I can do is create a diversion. Gather your things and meet back here. We leave in five minutes."

The Liberation parted without argument, save for Piper. She glared at Leo until Thomas pulled her from the room.

Leo turned back to Russé. "I am going to need your blood."

"No way." Kole said.

"How much?" Russé asked, ignoring Kole's protests.

"Quite a bit, I am afraid. Enough to confuse Savairo. Make them think you are still here while we escape. A pint, maybe more." Leo knelt down, pulled a blade from one of the many pockets of his coat, then turned Russé's forearm, tender side up. "I will pull from here. You will be weakened—dizzy for a time—but I have stimulants to keep you on your feet. Are you up to it?"

"Whatever is needed."

"But, Russé—" Kole cut off when the Soul gave him the side eye. Sure, Russé probably knew his own limits better than Kole, but it still seemed like a bad idea. Though if Piper had her way, it could've been worse. At least this wasn't blood magic. So claimed Leo.

Russé never so much as winced as Leo pressed the blade into his forearm. Red streams flowed down the Soul's arm and dripped from his skin into the expanding puddle below. Leo wiped the blade on his coat and put it away. He let Russé's wound flow freely for a solid minute, rubbing the tender area often to quicken the process. It felt odd, seeing his blood spill out onto the floor—to see Russé wounded like that—and stranger still that he'd willingly weakened himself. The sight took Kole back to the moment in the prison when Russé laid unconscious—helpless—on Savairo's wooden table. A helpless god felt a bit unnerving.

"Elevate it and apply pressure." Leo pulled a cloth from his coat and handed it to Russé. "How are you feeling? I can give something for the pain." He produced a wad of herbs from a jacket pocket.

"I'm quite fine, thank you."

Leo replaced the rejected herbs and rose as the Liberation returned, garbed in their black uniforms; masks hung idly around their necks.

The familiar jingle of Felix's pellet bag, cozied up next to his slingshot, drew Kole's attention to their belts, which were cluttered with weapons of all sorts: knives, short swords, maces, and a few odd contraptions he couldn't place. Leo's inventions, he guessed. The abundance of weapons made it glaringly evident that Kole had nothing to fight with save for Vienna's dagger.

Leo pulled on his mask, his nose poking into the thin fabric like a sharp beak, and crossed to the tunnel door.

"Are you—" Kole began as Russé pulled the blood-soaked cloth away from his arm. Smooth, untouched skin lay beneath. No trace of a cut. Not even a scar.

"As I said. I'm fine."

A hint of jealously washed through Kole. He wished his own body could heal like that. His scars would never worry him again.

As Felix approached, stepping around the pool of blood, Russé pulled down his sleeve.

"I've got somethin' for ya, mate." Felix held out a rough-looking bow—one that, by the dullness of the wood, might have been as old as Kole. "Thought ya might be able ta handle this a bit better than a sword. It's not much ta look at, but it does the job. Any good with one of these, Blondie?"

"Very good." Kole grabbed the belly of the bow. Its worn wood felt comforting in his hand. A smile tugged at his mouth. Even if it wasn't his own, it felt amazing to hold a bow again. Maybe he could prove useful in the rebellion after all.

Giving it a quick test, he brought the bow to the ready position. His shoulder tightened under the pressure. Kole flinched and let the weapon fall back to his side. Since the burns, his arms had lost flexibility, but he could manage. He'd have to. Shouldering the bow, he thanked Felix.

"That's not it, mate. See these?" Felix swung a quiver from his back. "They're sunstone tipped. Leo's enchanted 'em. I'm not much with a bow, so I never really used 'em." He tapped the arrowhead with his finger. "They'll take out Kayetans just as well as any of our blades. 'Course twelve is all ya got, so try not ta waste 'em."

"I won't," said Kole.

"We move swift and silent to the lift." Leo's voice pulled everyone's attention. He opened the door leading into The Cobwebs. "There is no telling if more Kayetans have followed the first. Be on your guard and stick together."

They all funneled into the abandoned shafts of the mine.

"Where's Piper?" Thomas called, head snapping side to side after a few steps into the passageway.

Kole looked back as Piper slipped through the doorway and took up the rear. "I'm here." A sheen of sweat weighed heavy on her brow. Kole relaxed a bit knowing he wasn't the only one nervous for the battle.

A hint of aggravation glazed Leo's voice. "*Stick together.*"

CHAPTER 22

Kole, Russé, and the Liberation squeezed onto the rickety platform. The chains groaned under the heavy load, but Leo seemed confident in his contraption. He hurried them up one by one and pulled the lever. The floor shot up with a jerk.

Kole was unprepared for the quick movement. His knees buckled, and he grabbed the nearest shoulder to steady himself. Piper, her hair peeking out from the edges of her black mask, turned a narrow gaze at him until he released her. Scooting away, his eyes caught sight of a vial poking out of a pouch at her hip. A red drop stained the cork. Blood? The light shifted from Leo's lantern, and the liquid gave off a sheen. It was fresh. Her chin moved in his direction. Kole snapped back. In his peripheral, he saw Piper push the vial deeper into the pouch, then pull the hem of her shirt over it.

What are you up to, Piper? He avoided her eyes and thumbed his new bow on the ride up to the surface, hoping it would soothe his nerves. It didn't.

In a matter of hours they would battle Savairo's soldiers alongside the refugees Kole had sworn to protect. It wouldn't be a happy reunion for Kole, though, knowing many of them would die in the fighting. Would he? The thought crept up from the depths of his consciousness. He shook it away. Thinking like that would do no good, only make him more on edge and mess with his focus. Above all else, he needed focus. A steady hand. A calm mind. He'd need all of it else his bow would be of little use.

Leo grunted and tilted his head so his ear pointed toward the surface. "Does anyone else hear that?"

Everyone quieted and shifted their attention to the still air above.

A low, hollow whoosh sounded from the hatch overhead. Kole would've dismissed it if not for the dull, scraping noise accompanying it. Something slithered in the shadows above.

"There," Kole said, pointing to it as it darted down the walls of the shaft.

Felix instantly drew his twin blades, but they all stood so tightly packed, he couldn't so much as swing without hitting his comrades.

The Kayetan lingered above them, just out of sword's reach as it took its humanoid form. From the soft curves of the outline, Kole could tell this shadow had been cut from a woman. Her eyeless face stared down at them for a moment before turning to the rattling chains of the over-burdened platform. She raised a claw and struck the chain. Sparks flew, and the platform pitched forward.

The platform collided into the rocky walls of the shaft, and Boogy fell into Kole's chest. Splintered wood sprayed up around them as a rotten plank broke loose and fell, spiraling down into the darkness. The Liberation huddled closer to find solid footing, further cramping their already tight quarters.

The chain had held but for how long?

Kole tried to wriggle his bow free but kept bumping into the others.

The Kayetan swiped again, and one of the four chains snapped.

The corner of the platform gave way, and the wood under Kole's feet rocketed up. He grabbed onto the rock wall of the tunnel as gravity slammed his feet back onto the rickety platform.

From the corner of his eye, he spotted Felix stumbling backward and, in an instant, he dropped out of view. Leo dove and caught his wrist. Felix dangled above the open void below, green eyes wide with fear.

The Kayetan screeched. One more swing and they would all be falling to their deaths.

Kole focused back on the Kayetan as Leo pulled Felix up. Someone had to kill the damn creature, or at least distract it. Unsure if it would work, he lifted one foot briefly, then the other. He smirked. Using the cramped space to his advantage, Kole lifted both his feet, his torso suspending between the pressure of Boogy and Piper as they leaned into him. He pulled his knees up and anchored his boots on his neighbor's hips, then pressed up. Kole felt vaguely like a butterfly wriggling from its cocoon as his chest rose over the group.

Catching on to what he was doing, Piper and Boogy wrapped their arms around his legs and held him steady. Kole snagged an arrow from his quiver and pulled back the creaking bow string.

The Kayetan squared her face to him as if daring him to shoot. Her claw drew back for another attack.

Kole squinted. He took in a deep breath and released.

A flash ignited the shaft as the arrow struck true. Her form burst, and she disappeared.

"Nice shot, mate," Felix said as Leo lugged him back onto the platform.

Piper and Boogy lowered Kole to the floor.

"We are likely to encounter more where that came from," Leo warned, holding the lantern up.

They neared the hatch above. The platform jerked to a stop, and Leo tossed open the splintered slat of wood, sending in a wave of fresh air. One at a time, they stepped onto the mountain, their weapons drawn; eyes searching for unwanted company.

Kole helped Russé find his feet on the loose rock carpeting the mountain. The Soul took his hand gratefully and leaned in to his ear saying, "Don't think I'll let you be on the front line. With or without a bow."

Kole pursed his lips. He hadn't expected Russé to relent. Picking up the stray arrow where it landed on the platform, he noticed Russé stood taller, stronger; merely using the staff as a prop now. Color had returned to his face. He looked very much like his old self. His unnaturally strong self.

After Kole returned the arrow to his quiver alongside its brothers, Leo kicked the hatch closed, and they hiked up the valley to the top of Lilith's pass.

A mass of shadows huddled together at the cliff's crest. Kole braced his bow as one broke off and came to meet them. "We serve the Lion," Kole recognized the voice and the frail frame in the moonlight.

Anna was dressed in borrowed leather armor, which sagged low on her chest, and trousers with a thick belt wrapped around her waist. The bulky leather made her look like a child playing dress-up.

Leo pulled his mask down and touched her shoulders in greeting. "How many have shown?"

Anna frowned. "Maybe fifty, sir."

"Fifty?" Leo lowered his voice as to not alarm the villagers behind her. He leaned in. "Why so few?"

"Most are too weak to fight. Or they're too scared of what Savairo'll do to 'em if they do. If we lose, there'll be hell ta pay." Anna shrugged. "Ain't much different than what we got now, I say. We only got this many 'cause of the rumors spreadin' 'round town that there was a break-in in the prison last night. I got the feelin' I'm starin' at the culprits."

Leo nodded.

"Well, tell ya the truth, that's the only reason I joined. It changed me mind... did theirs too," she said, tilting her head back at the group.

"Have you encountered any Kayetans up here?"

"No, sir."

"Well, be on guard. We have seen a few tonight, and we cannot give our position away before we strike."

"Yessir, I'll let 'em know to keep good and quiet."

Anna hiked up the incline to the villagers. Even from afar, Kole could see their sunken eyes and bony necks. The silver moonlight only emphasized their thinness, resembling skeletons. Kole couldn't fathom how they planned to fight in a state like that. They looked too weak to lift a weapon. He bit his tongue, eyes falling to his bound shoulder, and realized he was barely better off.

"Once Fiona returns, it won't be long," Leo said, his gaze cast toward the distant peak. He slicked a hand over his smooth black hair and turned to the darkened city. "That's odd."

Everyone followed the Liberation leader's gaze to the city as Leo climbed a few more meters to a better vantage point.

"What is it?" Thomas called after him.

Leo squinted toward the city. "The streets are empty. The lights... no one is out."

"So?" Piper shrugged. "What did you expect at this hour?"

"He's right." Felix reached for the hilts of his daggers hanging on his belt. "Look at the prison. It's completely snuffed out."

Kole dug his nails into the wood of his bow. "What does that mean?"

"It means the guards aren't at their posts," Thomas said, his voice cracking into a higher pitch than normal.

"Where are they?" Kole looked from face to face. They'd all turned as pale as the full moon floating overhead, their jaws held slightly ajar, waiting for something.

As if answering Kole's question, a deep horn sounded from the base of the mountain. It held long and pure, sinking through Kole's skin; rumbling his bones. A tingle climbed his spine, pausing on each vertebra like a step on a ladder until it reached his neck. Kole didn't hold back his violent shudder as the city gates below began to rise.

"This... cannot be." Leo stepped back from the ledge of the cliff. Like the crack of a whip, his head snapped at the Liberation, eyes blazing through the darkness. "They know." His fists clenched at his side. He turned to Anna. "Did anyone follow you here?"

"No... I don't know," she said. "Word has gone around the outskirts. Only the people we can trust. I haven't told no one."

"They got it from the shepherd's head," Thomas said.

"It matters not." Leo's jaw flexed in the darkness. "Dwelling on it will not deter his army. They are coming no matter who slipped."

They are coming. The familiar words rang in Kole's head. *This. This is what Issira was trying to tell me.* It meant more than the Kayetan finding the base; it meant Savairo. He *knew* about the rebellion, and he was coming for them.

The horn bellowed again. Lines of soldiers marched out from the gates, their armored boots hitting the ground simultaneously, like a war drum.

Kole's lips parted, his jaw loose in horror. Rows of soldiers moved out: five–ten–fifteen. Still they marched out, their lines forming a massive dark rectangle as their formation pushed further beyond the wall and curved toward the wide mouth of Lilith's pass.

"There's so many... " Piper breathed next to Kole. Thomas moved closer to her, silently placing a hand on her back.

"I will not die here tonight." Leo drew his sword. "Kole."

Surprised, Kole tore his eyes from the soldiers, marching ever closer in the distance.

"Stay on the cliffs. You are in charge of the boulders. When the army gets in range, push them over the cliff-side. I'll leave you with three people, the rest will come with us into the pass. Understood?"

Kole pushed down the growing lump in his throat and nodded.

Leo turned. "Russé, I want you with me if you are strong enough."

"I am."

Leo whirled around and descended into the valley. The Liberation trailed behind, pulling their masks over their faces.

Mid-step, Felix stopped and looked back over his shoulder. His expression alarmed Kole–brows pressed down over eyes, and his mouth, normally built for a smile, scrunched to the side. A look of uncertainty. "Watch my back, will ya, Blondie?" Kole gave a sharp nod then Felix lifted his mask into place and quickened his pace to catch up with the others.

Kole turned to face Russé, who had lingered behind, no doubt to give him a lecture about how he needed to stay safe.

"Keep to the cliffs. Even if it the battle goes sour, you are to remain out of harm's way. Risking your life jeopardizes our chances to release the Souls. If they get past us, you run. Run back to Solpate. The trees will protect you until I can find you."

Kole's eyes drifted to the Liberation. He could never do what Russé was asking of him. It meant running while his friends died. The thought seemed unbearable.

"I need you to promise me this." Russé's words edged on desperation.

Kole clenched his jaw. He could not make that promise. He wouldn't.

The Liberation had moved halfway down the slope now. Savairo's army marched up the valley only a mile from their position. Still, the Soul waited. He would stay there until he got his answer. Kole used everything he had to keep his muscles from twitching, from giving himself away. If Russé was unconvinced, Kole worried his mentor might pull him from the battle that very moment.

"I will run."

Russé held his gaze. A sad smile spread over his face. "We both know you won't."

Kole's throat tightened.

"I'm not the only one who needs you safe." Russé brought a finger up to Kole's head, tapping his temple. "*She* will hold you to your word, whether you mean it or not."

CHAPTER 23

Kole took his place atop the cliffs next to the first boulder in line. The two villagers he had sent across the narrow pass had just finished their climb. They huddled around their first boulder, leaning on it as they clutched their sides. Seeing their exhaustion, Kole began to question picking them for the job.

He waved to Kross, the man he'd put in charge of the other line of boulders, grateful for the distance between them to hide his deepening frown. Kole had no time to change his mind; those two would have to do. They only had to watch Kole and wait for his signal to release the boulders from the eastern cliff. Surely they could manage that.

Kross gave a short wave back in response.

As for the other man leaning next to Kross, well, Kole didn't remember his name, but he looked as hardy as they came in Socren, which wasn't saying much. Kole only hoped his bulk, however slight, would measure up when the time came.

Kole crouched next to Anna. "They're in place."

Russé and the Liberation had reached the deepest part of the valley and were climbing the mountain, following the curve of the pass. How small they looked compared to Savairo's army, which inched ever closer like a storm cloud on the horizon.

Out of the sky whizzed a blur of brown.

Fiona swooped down and circled Leo until he held out his arm for her to land. Kole's heart drummed as he glanced to the peaks. Far up the mountain, a dark mass crested Poleer.

The refugees. Would they make it down before Savaior's army reached the Liberation?

Anna shifted beside him, pulling something hefty from her belt. A horse shoe, rusted and dented. She closed her eyes and pressed it to her lips, whispering something inaudible, then hooked it back on her belt.

"Is that Honey's?" Kole recalled her sickly yellow horse.

Anna patted the horseshoe thoughtfully. "Took it from her 'fore I left. My lucky charm."

"I'm surprised to see you here," Kole said, remembering her affections for the animal. "Didn't think anything could part you from your horse."

"That's what I thought, too. After I heard 'bout ya guys breakin' inta the prison I thought, well, if a couple boys can do that, I can do what I can to make Socren a better place for Honey... for everyone."

"Where is she now?"

"Gave her to a friend."

"They'll keep her safe, I hope."

"As best they can."

"You'll be back tomorrow to retrieve her, won't you?"

Anna's fingers clasped around the horseshoe. "'Fraid I won't be around to." She paused for a moment, letting Kole absorb the words, then she flicked her sunken eyes to her comrades shuffling along behind the Liberation in the valley. "None of us expect ta make it through the night."

"Don't say that." His hardened gaze remained on Savairo's army. "You have to have hope. We can win this."

"Look at that army. Those shiny suits of armor aren't to make'm look pretty. These are Savairo's soldiers — all of 'em by the looks of it. He's got sorcerers, too, you can be sure of that. And they're terrible, they are. We all know the odds here. We fight not 'cause we think we'll win but 'cause it's the best chance we got at changin' somethin'."

Kole dipped his head. How could Anna already count their defeat?

As if sensing his thoughts, she gripped his hand. "Ya don't think I know what stares back at me in the mirror? I'm only a shell of what I was. Growin' crops like a trained pet can't fill my emptiness. This isn't livin'. As much as I love Honey...." She swallowed. "If my life can save any of those poor souls... well, then I think I lived to do somethin' worthwhile." Anna fell quiet. Her fingers slid from his and caressed the nicks in Honey's shoe.

Kole pulled Goren's chain from his shirt, letting the seven-stoned symbol dangle in before his face. He couldn't lose hope. "We're going to win this, Anna."

Her bleak stare lingered on the marching soldiers. About to tuck the pendent away, he paused. *If I'm to instill hope, I have to have it myself.* He let the symbol rest open over his uniform for all to see.

A loud boom rattled the air. Kole looked down the mountain.

Large clouds of soil sprayed into the valley at the front lines of Savairo's army. Terrible cries of agony cut through the still night, followed by another thunderous clap. *Leo's traps*, Kole presumed.

The haze cleared, revealing a gaping hole in their ranks. It shrank as soldiers replaced their fallen comrades, and they pressed on like nothing had happened. The army continued despite three more explosions, each time the soldiers filled the massive holes in their formation.

Silver flashed as, handful by handful, soldiers were launched into the air, only to fall back onto the mountain with a crunch that echoed up the valley. Still Savairo's army marched toward the Liberation and the fifty or so townspeople Criz and Boogy had recruited from the farms. And as they did, they came closer to the line of fire—closer to the boulders.

Kole sucked in a breath and put down his bow. Even though they marched a ways below him, he could make out the large insignia etched into each breastplate. Their helms gleamed in the light of the full moon. His targets.

He waited. They came closer.

Adrenaline flooded his bloodstream. His wrists tingled; hands grew clammy. If he didn't get his anxiety under control, he would send them out too soon and miss the army completely, ruining the element of surprise.

He could do this. He could wait.

His fingers tapped the boulder.

In the valley, the first few rows marched past the boulder.

Yet he waited.

Two more rows. Three. Four.

Finally, they were in place. Kole waved his hand to Kross on the opposite cliff.

"Now!"

Kole and Anna clawed at the small rocks surrounding the base of the boulder and pushed with all their might. It rolled to the edge. They gave it one last shove, and it plummeted down the cliff, crashing into the flanks of the unsuspecting army. Outcries orbited the valley, cut-off prematurely as the barreling chunk of stone flattened its targets.

Kross' also hit its mark: both rocks rolling to a stop in the middle of the formation, a trail of crumpled bodies in their wake. Kole grabbed his bow, and he and Anna raced to the next boulder a few meters away.

Kole kicked the rocks from the base and heaved, his heart thumping in his chest. The boulder sailed off the cliff. A few of the soldiers jumped from its path, but their comrades weren't so lucky.

As they tipped the third rock, a horn sounded, and an ear-splitting shrill cut through the night.

Dark shadows burst from the ranks and split into two groups. The first went east toward Kross, surging up the cliff like a black tidal wave. The second group came for Kole and Anna.

They sprinted to the next boulder. Kole nocked a sunstone arrow as he tailed her, his boots slipping on the loose gravel underfoot. Once at the boulder, he leaned his back into it, readied his bow, and waited for the Kayetans to show themselves. Anna shoved the small rocks away from the boulder's base, wheezing through the effort. Her body was weak like the other villagers. She would only have the strength to help him a little longer.

Out of the darkness, a cloud of smoke shot up from the lip of the cliff.

Kole aimed and fired. A flash lit up the sky like a shooting star as the arrow hit its mark. The demon shrilled and disappeared. *One down, two to go.*

Screams echoed from the other cliff between the explosions, and he knew Kross and his companion were dead. Kole and Anna were on their own now. They had to topple the last boulders. The Liberation was counting on them.

"Ready," Anna gasped, holding her side to steady herself.

Together they pushed. The boulder creaked, tilting toward the cliff, then the rock grew heavy and tipped back against his hips. Kole stumbled forward from the shifting weight. Regaining his balance, he found Anna sinking into the gravel.

"I can't," she coughed.

Before he could respond, two shadows slithered in the corner of his eye. As the Kayetans emerged from the cliff, Kole slid another arrow in place and pulled back the string. He bit down hard on his tongue, hoping the new pain would distract from his skin pulled taut across his chest.

The swirling trails of smoke crisscrossed above his head. He let his arrow fly.

It missed.

They moved fast, and the darkness made it harder to get a clear shot. He eyed the remaining sunstone arrows in his quiver. He'd have to use them sparingly if he wanted to last through the night. He tried again, following their forms with his arrow, his head tilted against his hand, waiting for the right opportunity. But they didn't slow... and they didn't attack.

He'd never seen them act this way. They were always aggressive — unyielding.

"Stop playing around," he hissed through his teeth.

That was it. They were toying with him; distracting him from the boulders. Kole growled. He knew better than to play their games. He had to get this stone off the edge, even if it meant doing it alone.

Kole dug his heels into the ground and lowered into a squat, bow still aimed at the Kayetans. When his feet felt secure, he pushed.

It refused to budge.

Kole cursed and pushed again, his legs straining underneath him.

No use. He wasn't strong enough.

War cries came from the north. He took a chance and tore his eyes from the Kayetans to peek over the boulder.

A wave of Kayetans broke off from the army's tight ranks below and surged ahead to meet the Liberation head on. Kole prayed they could survive until the refugees arrived. They had a Soul on their side, after all. Hopefully Russé had a few tricks of his own.

Kole glanced back to the Kayetans overhead. Taking a risk, he lowered his bow and tried his luck with the boulder again, this time using his hands to grip the rough stone, all while keeping an eye on the clouds of smoke soaring above.

The rock tipped. It inched closer to the cliff. His heels sunk further into the earth. He gripped with his toes, his fingers, every muscle in his body. His taut skin screamed at him, but he gritted his teeth and pushed.

The Kayetans dove, whizzing through the air like black arrows. Kole gave one last heave. Surprisingly, the boulder inched forward.

Anna stood next to him. Kole had been so concerned with the Kayetans, he hadn't noticed her rise from her slumped spot on the ground. Her legs slid in the gravel, creating shallow trenches as she tried to find leverage. She thrust her body into the rock and added her strength to his.

The boulder rolled.

His lips parted in relief. He prayed the ledge was near. Then, he felt the stone drop — roll on its own. He fell into the gravel, landing on his back. His fingers automatically readjusted and tightened around the grip of the bow. He sat up and set an arrow.

The demon's smoking forms blocked out the moon.

Kole pulled back the string. His fingers slipped and he released prematurely.

A flash told him he had hit one, but his triumph was short lived as the second still charged. Kole reached for another arrow, but he was too slow.

The claw slashed.

At the last second, a flood of mousy brown hair dove in front of the swooping claw bound for Kole. The soft sound of ripping flesh met his ears as Anna took the full brunt, then collapsed on his torso.

Kole's mind went blank.

Smoke spiraled to his left as the Kayetan took its shadowy human form. The shadow strode over to Kole, pinned helplessly under Anna's body, and bent down, lowering his featureless face inches from Kole's skin as if inspecting him.

Kole held his breath. His body trembled as he stared into the hollowed eyes of the last face he would ever see.

A force broke through the dam in his head. Issira. He didn't fight her this time when she took control. The Soul pried his jaw open and a ray of blue light emitted from his mouth. It shot through the Kayetan who screeched and backed off.

Then, the Kayetan did something Kole did not expect. It straightened up, walked to the rocky ledge, and dropped down the cliff.

Confusion soared through Kole. After a few moments to ensure the creature had truly gone, he reached for Anna. He sat up, and her body rolled to his feet. Kole slipped his boots out from under her and cradled her head. "Anna?"

Her youthful eyes took in his face and smiled. She fumbled for the horseshoe looped on her belt. Kole pulled it free and set it on her chest. She clasped her hands over Honey's horseshoe and closed her eyes as she began to hum.

The song filled his body with a strange sense of peace. Then, the notes wavered and faded, replaced by the sounds of Leo's traps detonating in the valley below. Kole's blood boiled. The Kayetans had taken enough. *Those abominations will die—all of them.* He would kill every last one.

He snapped the chain from his neck and eyed the symbol doubtfully. "Help me! Help *us!*" he yelled. "How can you let this happen? Do something!"

The moment passed in silence.

Kole cast the necklace into the dirt. It bounced, landing next to Anna's arm. As he glared at it, another horn blew. The sound was low and hollow, a familiar pitch he'd know anywhere. It was a scout's horn—one he had used many times before.

He turned. The refugee army had split; those on forest stags ran ahead, while the ones on foot trailed behind, flanked by a dozen full-grown ramblers. For a fleeting moment, hope overtook him. No amount of armor could resist the swipe of a rambler's root. The trees dwarfed Savairo's army—made them no more than insects fresh for stomping. It would only be a few more minutes until the trees and mounts caught up to the Liberation. The ramblers may solve the problem of the army, but they held no threat to Savairo's Kayetans. As long as the army of shadows stood, no victory would come to the rebels. Maybe Anna was right. This fight was doomed from the beginning. He stepped away from Anna and glared at Goren's necklace resting beside her.

"*Help us,*" he tried one last time. Kole let the thought flow through him to the ends of his fingertips and down to his toes. He squeezed his eyes shut and repeated it over and over again in his head, hoping Issira would hear him.

His head hung low. "Please."

Then, just as he was about to turn away, a presence bloomed within his thoughts. Her voice rang inside his head like the chime of a beautiful bell.

"*Kole,*" she answered.

"*Help us! My friends are going to die. The Kayetans—you have to destroy them.*" Kole squeezed his eyelids tighter and forced himself to hang on to the words.

"*It is not... that easy....*"

"*Please! Can't you do something?*"

"*My powers cannot go beyond you.*"

Her words struck him like a punch to the gut. Opening his heavy lids, he forced his eyes to the battle. What were they going to do? They had no way to even the odds. Only dawn would rid them of the Kayetan army. No way the rebellion could last until then It was hopeless.

"*The burden will lay solely upon you.*"

"*What burden? I'll do it. Anything. I'll do anything. Just tell me.*" Kole blinked back the welling tears. Had he heard her correctly? After what seemed like minutes with no response, Kole grew worried she had abandoned him. "*Please come back to me.*"

When her voice came again, it was distant as though she was calling from the top of a hill.

"*There is a way... kill... K-Kayetans,*" Issira managed. Her next words scrambled together. Kole held his breath, catching each drifting sound as they came to him and deciphered her message. "*Destroy the hearts....*"

She spoke of what he already knew. Defeat touched his core.

"*Host... destroy.*" Her voice was barely a whisper now, like she was being dragged away.

"*Wait! Don't go!*" Kole urged, his eyes frantically darting to the sky as if he expected to see her floating away from him.

She was gone. And he had never felt so alone.

"The hosts...." He collapsed to his knees, his chin resting on his chest as he stared at Anna's body. He repeated Issira's words over and over again in his head.

Destroy the hearts. Destroy the hosts. *Destroy the hosts' hearts?* Kole peered up to Poleer's dark peaks. He jumped up and pushed himself into a sprint. He had to reach the basin.

CHAPTER 24

Kole's nose was numb—icy cold, as the chill night wind rushed over his body and penetrated the thin fabric of his Liberation uniform. The hammering of his feet against the mountainside under his long, labored stride was nowhere near as fast as the pounding of his heart, which felt as though it would explode from his chest at any moment.

Hope filled him as he neared the rumbling stampede of refugees. While he stayed hidden, darting between boulders and crags, he could see them clearly, some masked in war paint with spears and bows as they bounded down the mountain atop their mounts. They rode fast down the slope; the vibrant mossy skin of the forest animals' unnatural against the barren mountain.

Kole veered from the refugees' path then started uphill once more. His legs burned and ached, tempting him to stop and rest, but seeing his kin gave him new energy. He clamped his jaw and forced his feet faster.

A sleek blue-and-green blur came into view. Kole glanced over as it rushed past him. A glimpse of pearly white fangs offered a dead giveaway: a forest wolf. Atop him sat Lucca, the old, wiry-haired leader of the eastern refugee camp. Behind her followed a pack of forest wolves, dozens of stags, and the shepherd-charged ramblers, whose trunks hovered low over the mounts like giant shields. They charged down the mountain, oblivious to Kole's ascent, for which he felt grateful. If they spotted him, someone would stop and question him, or worse, bring him back down the mountain. He could spare no time for that, so he hunkered low to stay out of sight.

Soon the last of the mounts ran by, and he was in the clear. He lifted up and focused all his attention on the hike. Between his shaking legs and the exhaustion creeping up, he was unable to recover when his foot came down on an angular rock. He stumbled. Kole reached out and stopped his face from slamming into the mountain. As he scrambled to his feet, rocks crunched behind him. Someone approached. And by the overlapping footfalls, he could tell they didn't travel alone. Kole kept low. If he stayed still, he hoped whoever it was might overlook him in the dark.

A pair of antlers appeared over the top of the rock.

Kole lifted his head to find a forest stag.

Blonde curls fell down the rider's back, stopping short of the stag's vine-twisted rump. He hadn't seen her since she saved him that night in the forest. Felix's sister, Vienna.

She pressed her heels into the animals' side, and the stag stopped. Vienna looked directly at him despite his best efforts to hide, her angular brows furrowing as she took in his black uniform. "Get on."

"I can't go back down. Not yet," he said through his mask.

Vienna studied him, then held out her hand. "I'll get you where you need to go."

Their unwavering eyes met. Her fierce green eyes shone brightly like her brothers, but they held none of the happy-go-lucky sense in them. Once Kole swung his leg over the animal's back and took a seat behind her, Vienna tapped her heels again, and the stag sprang up the slope with a giant leap. Kole surged back and would've fallen off if not for Vienna's quick reflexes. She pulled him back, then guided his arm around her waist for support. Kole grew so entranced by the feel of her hand holding his in place over her stomach that he'd missed what she said.

"Where am I going?" she asked again, impatiently.

Kole shook the lightness from his head. "The basin. It's at the—"

"I know where it is." Her voice was quick and low, as if she were restraining a deep anger. "Hold on."

Vienna redirected the stag. It opened its stride, and they flew up the mountain. Vienna leaned forward into the animal's neck, pulling Kole along with her. He felt the rise and fall of her stomach under his hand. The breaths came slow and even, unlike Kole's. He had been wheezing since moving the boulders. The run up the mountain hadn't helped. His body needed to slow down—*cool* down—or he would overheat. He focused on his breathing and let it fall in time with Vienna's.

Did she know who he was? Surely she was helping him because she recognized his uniform. But did she know? Could she? He doubted it. His face was covered, after all. And even exposed, she wouldn't know his new face—his scarred face.

The horn-like peak of the Poleer mountain enlarged until they finally closed in on the rim of the basin.

"Tasil, slow." The stag dropped into a trot and halted a few meters from the rim. She slipped from Tasil's back, her dark cloak swinging behind her.

Kole dismounted. When the full weight of his body touched down on the rock, his legs buckled. He took a step, trying to hide his exhaustion, but she saw straight through his act. Vienna looped her arm around his, encouraging him to use her as support.

"What are we doing here?" Her boots stopped at the ledge of the basin and, although the stench was just as bad as Kole remembered it, she never so much as flinched. Her eyes found his. This time her gaze was less confident.

Kole scanned the basin. "I have to destroy the hosts' hearts."

Hundreds of corpses stared up at him. The eyes didn't frighten him as they once had. Instead, their blank stares seemed to call to him, as if begging him to end it.

Disgust flashed over her face. "What will *that* do?"

"Kill the Kayetans for good." After he said it, he realized how ridiculous it sounded.

Her green eyes darted from the corpses back to him. She raised one brow. "How do you know this?"

"Someone told me."

"Who?"

"Doesn't matter. Just—" Kole was forced to take a breath. "Trust me."

Vienna's mouth scrunched to the side. "last time I trusted you, I woke up alone with a major headache."

His heart skipped a few beats. So she did know. "I-I'm sorry, Vienna, I—"

She raised a hand. The tug of a smile flashed over her mouth, only to vanish within a blink. "I've been through worse." Then, to his surprise she asked, "How do we do it?"

"I'm not sure."

"Destroy it...." Her grip tightened on Kole's arm. "But they're already dead. The heart isn't pumping. Doesn't that mean they're already destroyed?"

"There's no time to think it through. We have to go at it trial and error." Kole tugged his arm loose from her grip and stepped toward the basin.

Vienna blocked him with a hand. "You think I'm letting you go down there like that?" she said. "You can barely stand. How do expect to climb back out?"

"I just need to rest." The uphill run had sapped him entirely, only more evident now that he'd reached his goal.

"Then rest." With her help, he sat on the rocks, feet swung over the ledge of the Basin wall. "What do you plan on doing anyway?"

"Stabbing them like we do the Kayetans."

"Even if it works, there are too many to stab them all."

"We can't waste time thinking on it."

Her hands moved to her hips. "Thinking is never a waste of time. *Mistakes* are a waste of time."

"Then what do you suggest?" Kole held back the aggravation in his voice.

"Burn them."

"The fresh ones won't burn. There's too much moisture."

Vienna tilted her head. "Don't you smell that?"

"How can I not?" The thick scent coated his tongue every time he opened his mouth.

"Besides the rot. It's… turpentine. I recognize the smell. Leo has some in some in his laboratory."

"What is it?"

"A chemical. He repurposes it as medicine but soaked into the corpses like this… these bodies are embalmed. If you're right about the hearts, Savairo would want to preserve them for as long as possible. It makes sense." Vienna flicked her cloak behind her shoulder, revealing a thick brown belt at her waist. It sagged in places, bogged down by the sheer number of items strapped to it. Vials, flasks, a tightly wound rope, and hefty pouches shifted as her fingers grazed over them, like she was trying to remember what each one contained. It reminded Kole of Leo's workshop, only portable. "Turpentine is flammable. Even a small fire will catch." With a pull of a string, Vienna opened the mouth of a small pouch and pulled out a piece of flint and a starter. She pushed them into Kole's hands for safe keeping, then turned her attention back to her belt. Finally, she plucked off a heavily stained pewter flask and uncorked it. "Oil," she said, answering Kole's curious stare. "It'll keep the flame burning. We need something to soak."

Kole took in the barren mountain. He hadn't seen a single tree on either side of Poleer as he'd climbed. "Wood isn't an option."

"Then we use our clothes." Vienna unhooked her long cloak. Now crumpled in a pile on the ground, she tipped the flask over it. The oil disappeared as it soaked into the fabric. Vienna bent down and, starting from the top, she twisted the cloth until it looked like a thick rope. done, it resembled a large, coiled snake. Vienna stepped back, examining her handiwork. "Your mask," she demanded.

He stood there, reluctant to follow her command and expose his face. He was afraid of... of... *of what?* A war raged down the mountain, and he was scared to show his scars? *Selfish. Coward.* He scolded himself. *There are far greater things to worry about than his disfigurements.* He ripped the mask off. Nose free to the air, the potent stench hit him full on. He gagged.

When he handed over his mask, Kole noticed the edge of Vienna's mouth twitching as she looked upon his face.

"Etta told me what happened to the northern camp while I was comatose." Her eyes didn't linger. "I'm sorry it couldn't be stopped."

At his silence, she took the two ends of fabric, crossed them, and made a knot. She repeated this process, over and over again so it formed one dense ball of cloth, then placed it at the center of her coiled creation and doused it in oil like the last piece. Picking it up, Vienna scooted to the lip of the basin and let her feet dangle over the edge.

"What are you doing?" Kole asked.

"I have to go down there."

"Light it up here. You can throw it over."

"And take the chance of it getting caught on the rocks? It will be hell to move it once it's lit. I'll take it down myself." She opened and closed her hand at Kole, and he handed over the flint and metal starter. "Besides, I want to get some of the oil on the bodies. Give it a nudge in the right direction."

Kole watched as she corked the flask and held it between her teeth. One more scoot and she slid down the curved wall. Kole stood and craned over the lip to watch her go. Her feet flexed and stretched out in front of her to control her speed.

She descended quickly. Kole could barely make out her small frame in the dark as she reached the bottom. If not for her bright hair, he would've lost sight of her the moment she left the ledge.

Vienna held the cloth above her head as she tiptoed further toward the center of the basin. Her steps seemed careful and calculated, sticking to broad backs and chests to use as stepping stones. Once in position, she set the cloth down and a glint of silver shone as she dumped the remaining oil over the surrounding bodies, trailing it out and away from her cloak so the blaze would expand.

The click of metal rapping against flint echoed around the basin. A warm light emerged under Vienna. The fire swiftly overtook the oil-drenched cloak.

She backed away, keeping a safe distance from the blaze as it grew into lofty flames. The trails of oil ignited over the bodies, their clothes turning black as they burned.

Vienna hurried back to the basin wall and climbed. "How do we know if it worked?" she asked, pulling herself over the rim.

Shifting his gaze to the valley, he frowned. "I'm not sure...."

"That seems to be a running theme with you." She called for the stag.

More and more bodies flared up as the fire moved outwards. Their hair burned first, fizzling away like a snuffled-out candle. The fire took the skin next. Kole couldn't keep watching. He felt guilty for what they had done to the dead. Being turned into a Kayetan and dumped into a basin enough seemed awful enough.

Vienna must have seen the guilt on his face because she nudged his arm. "An honorable funeral." Her lips curled upward slightly with what could hardly pass off as a smile. "Now their souls can be at peace."

Tasil's warm breath puffed on the back of Kole's neck.

Vienna scratched the animal's nose then mounted the stag in one seamless motion. "Let's go see for ourselves if it worked. Ready?" She reached down to help him on.

Kole swung up behind her. He welcomed the earthy smell of the animal. It reminded him of Solpate. Of home. Of times before....

He let Vienna guide his hand around her waist. She looked over her shoulder at him saying, "Try to stay on," then leaned into stag's neck. "Swiftly, Tasil."

He squeezed Vienna and braced himself as the animal bolted down the slope. They headed for the two dark blobs halfway down the mountain. He watched as the mounted refugees joined the Liberation to fight the Kayetans, while behind them, the glow of flames inside the basin burned brighter as it overtook the dead. Yet the Kayetans remained. Panicked trembles coursed through his hands at the realization they'd done something wrong—misinterpreted Issira's clue. What else could he do?

"Look there!" Vienna called, her voice faint in the wind.

Kole looked east to the dark mass of Kayetans surrounding the Liberation. Their forms grew more detailed with every passing second, but he saw nothing but the terrible, inevitable end for his allies. Before he could question her, a burst of brilliant orange lit the night.

It faded.

"One of Leo's traps?" he yelled into the wind.

"I don't know."

Vienna rode Tasil hard and fast, whispering words of encouragement in his moss-laden ears when the cadence of his hooves, hammering against the rock, slowed.

The ride was brutal. Kole felt every bump and shift of Tasil's stride, but it offered his body enough time to rest.

Soon, they caught up to the refugees, who ran on foot down the mountain. They passed a few ramblers. Shepherds braced on the ledge of their trunks—roots in hand as if steering a horse rather than a giant tree. Tasil bounded from side to side, navigating the narrow passages between the refugees and the walking trees whose arachnid-like legs stabbed into the earth as they crawled down the slope.

War cries bellowed below. Kole squinted for a better look. Dark shadows broke off from their onslaught on the Liberation and dashed up the slope, toward the refugees. Kole's heart sank. What had they done wrong? *They had done what Issira asked. Why are they still alive?*

The Kayetans infiltrated the refugee army. They made quick work of the unarmored front line, slashing through their fleshy torsos like a finger dragging through the current of a stream. The shadows struck down anyone in their path. No remorse. No guilt. Only slaughter.

The refugees fell en masse, their bodies rolling down the mountain like ragdolls. Then a shepherd entered the fray, tugging on his rambler's roots. The tree whipped its mighty limbs at the shadows, but it had little effect but to distract the creatures.

After pulling his arm from Vienna's waist, Kole reached over his shoulder and grabbed his bow. He pressed his thighs harder into Tasil's belly to keep his balance and prepared an arrow. "Keep him steady," he said. Vienna leaned into Tasil's neck.

The bow string whined next to his ear as he took aim: a Kayetan gliding up the left side of the valley. He let fly. Kole lost sight of the arrow in the darkness, but a flash of light told him he had hit his mark. He took down several more like this, but his killing spree didn't go unnoticed for long. Two nearby Kayetans, slithering up the valley, abandoned their slaughter of refugees and changed course for the stag.

"Kole," Vienna warned.

"I see them."

As his aim swung to them, the Kayetans hovered low to the ground, moving ever closer to the stag. They must have known Kole would not risk a shot for fear of hitting the refugees.

He cursed and lowered his bow.

Tending to the wounded, the refugees were oblivious to the Kayetans lurking at their feet. The creatures blended in with their own shadows under the radiant moonlight. The demons closed the gap to the stag. Kole impatiently tapped the arrow sandwiched between his fingers, waiting for the right moment.

The first Kayetan sped under Tasil. A large claw formed from its smoking body. One smooth, quick reflex and Kole struck it down. Kole rolled his shoulder to release the tension in his skin. Then he moved for another arrow, but his hand shook so badly, the arrow wouldn't nock. The second Kayetan leapt. Its claws came mere inches from Kole's face when a brilliant beam of orange light erupted from the Kayetan's chest just like they had seen from the mountain top.

Vienna gasped as the light engulfed the shadowy body, disintegrating it.

Kole stared, slacked jawed, at the empty space where the Kayetan had been seconds before. Excitement in her voice, she yelled back, "It worked! It's dead. It has to be." She turned in her seat. "I can see the glow from here. Once the whole basin burns, they will all receive the same fate."

As she stared up to the peaks, Kole turned his gaze down the valley. Savairo's army drew dangerously close to the Liberation. He didn't want to ruin Vienna's blissful moment, but this battle was far from over.

She followed his gaze and tightened her hold around the stag's mossy neck. "I have to get down there." The victory in her voice had slipped away.

A horn sounded next to them. The refugees split like parting waves before them; those with bows climbing either side of the sloping walls of the valley, encasing Savairo's army. The stags and boars carrying large loads of arrows climbed, too; their only purpose to replenish the refugees' empty quivers.

"I must go to the Liberation. My brother needs me. I think it's best if you stay up here with the archers."

Kole looked to the refugees preparing to fire from the slopes. Staying here would mean watching the battle, not fighting in it, just as Russé had wanted.

Vienna spoke again at his hesitation. "Decide."

This battle wasn't about Russé; it was about the refugees. About revenge on Savairo and his Kayetans, for his entire murderous reign. But for Kole, it was purely about Idris. He heard Russé's warning replay in his head. *She will hold you to it.* Issira alone could stop him now, but her presence had long faded.

"I'm coming with you."

Kole refused to stand by and watch his friends die. He figured he would be more useful fighting by their sides than sitting behind some rock. He had already done that job tonight.

Vienna tapped her heels into the stag's belly and called into the wind. "Take us down, Tasil." With a burst of speed, the stag headed for battle.

CHAPTER 25

Tasil carried Kole and Vienna to the Liberation. They both flung themselves off the stag's back and dashed to the Kayetans swarming around their friends. Kole emptied his quiver, clearing the path as Vienna led him to the center of the battle. Out of arrows, Kole pulled his sunstone dagger, which reflected a dull, pulsing gray instead of the brilliant white he remembered. The stone's spell was fading. He landed two more strikes, then, on the third, his attack sailed straight through the Kayetan. Without a force to stop his momentum, his skin stretched and a jolt shot up his shoulder. Kole winced and snapped his arm to his stomach to alleviate the pain, but his hesitation gave the Kayetan an opening. Peddling back, he dodged the swing and ran into something solid.

"Duck!"

Kole recognized the voice and dropped to the gravel. Out of the corner Kole's eye, a pair of long, black claws sliced the air above him where his head had been a second earlier.

Felix stabbed the Kayetan, and it vanished with a deafening wail. "Hey, Blondie! So much for stayin outta the thick of it, eh?" He yanked Kole up and led him to the center of the Liberation.

They all stood in a circle with their backs toward the center, each member in their own dance of battle. After every kill, they retreated back, closing the circle once more, keeping their ranks tight.

Felix guided Kole into the circle between him and Russé as Vienna joined ranks between Thomas and Criz on the far side. The new group of refugees mimicked the Liberation's strategy, ditching their mounts as they trickled into the battle and formed new circles of their own, swiping the Kayetan with lit torches. The fire did little to hurt the Kayetans, but the light acted as a deterrent and painted the abominations as easy targets for the others.

Russé shot Kole a look of surprise that morphed into a grimace. Luckily for Kole, a Kayetan darted at them, forcing his attention away.

Russé ran up to meet it. Before the clawed strike made contact, the Kayetan disintegrated in a flash of fiery light.

Like a spreading wildfire, the circling Kayetans burst with light. Kole and the others shielded their eyes as, one by one, the Kayetans burned to ash like the one Kole and Vienna had encountered on the ride down.

The battle fell silent save for the marching army.

Next to Kole, Felix still held his fighting stance, but his eyes widened. They darted around as if he expected the Kayetans to reappear at any second.

Leo lowered his weapon and stepped forward, glancing around, just as bewildered as the others.

"They won't be back," said Vienna.

The Liberation turned at her voice; an array of surprise and expressions of relief filled their faces.

"But how did—" Leo stopped as he crouched down, taking up a handful of ash the Kayetans had left behind.

Vienna glanced at Kole. "We handled it." She pointed at the glowing peak.

Everyone's heads swiveled to the fire raging on the mountaintop.

"You burned the corpses..." Leo said, shaking his head slowly.

"Get rid of the host, and you kill the Kayetan," Kole said.

Leo squinted curiously at them. "How did you discover this?"

Kole looked around. Everyone's eyes, including Vienna's, rested on him, waiting for the answer. Russé's expression, though, held more anger than curiosity.

Another horn sounded.

"The story will have to wait for another time." Vienna pointed her dagger down the pass at Savairo's oncoming army. She locked eyes with her brother. They shared a brief moment and a smile before the camp leaders barreled through the cloud of ash left behind by the Kayetans.

"What's happened here? We agreed to march at dawn," Darian barked, his beard bouncing as his stag slowed to a halt.

"Word got out about our plan." Leo wiped a dribble of blood from his lip, looking around the Liberation.

Savairo's army loomed less than a hundred meters away. Their boots stomped in unison, making the ground shake. Adding to the vibrations, the refugee army and the giant ramblers slowed behind their mounted camp leaders.

Kole's stomach dropped when he eyed their numbers. Even with the refugees waiting to shoot from the slopes and the power of the shepherds, they were painfully outnumbered. An outbreak of sharp whispers and shifting feet from the refugee army told Kole they saw it too.

"What is the plan? We can't survive a head-on attack," Darian said, clenching his chubby hands around the stag's reins.

"I... I may have a plan...." Leo patted his coat and pulled an object from his pocket. It was small, smooth, and as white as bone.

It *was* a bone.

Leo held it carefully in his palm. "I am not sure if it will work... or how potent the spell will be if it does."

"What is it?" Piper asked, circling around Leo for a better look.

"It belonged to my father. At least I think it is him," Leo admitted. "The only thief who would take the job was not what you might call trustworthy."

Piper's lifted brows revealed her surprise. "A patriarch bone."

"What's a patriarch bone?" Kole whispered to Felix.

"Hell if I know."

"Aye." Leo answered Piper, twirling the tiny bone between his fingers.

"But Leo. If it isn't a piece of him—"

"I know the consequences." Leo pulled out a vial, a pouch, and a small quill from his pockets. His father's bone went into the pouch first. Then the contents of the vial. Kole could only guess the contents, but it smelled awful. Finally, Leo tied the pouch shut and took up the quill. He scribbled on the leather, then pulled the cord from his neck and placed the iron symbol of the Seven Souls over the bag. Kneeling to the ground, he closed his eyes, then brought the pouch to his mouth and whispering into it. After his spell was done, he stood. "I need to get this as far as I can into their ranks." Leo looked from face to face, jaw flexing.

Darian shifted in his seat when they landed on him. "Don't be a fool. That is a sure route to death."

"Maybe." Leo held his chin high. "But it is worth the risk."

"We'll give you a lift," Lucca said behind Darian. She kicked her heels into her wolf, who growled and slinked forward. "He's fast. We'll have you there and back in no time."

Leo nodded.

"You can't get through their ranks with a beast like that! You need strength and heft to charge through. We'll go." Harlow smiled confidently as he pat his boar on the rump. Its long, wooden tusks curved up toward the sky; no doubt one swipe of his head could send a handful of armored men flying. "We'll clear the path for you," he said.

"Yes, all right. Take them both, then," said Darian. "I'll need to signal the archers anyway."

Kole rolled his eyes. *Coward.*

"Leave your weapons here." Leo tucked the pouch away and climbed up behind Lucca. "Iron will be the victim."

"Leave our weapons?" Harlow took his giant axe from his back, cradling it in his arms.

"We have no time to spare," said Leo.

Harlow stared at the sorcerer, jaw hanging open in disbelief. Then, after seeing Lucca comply, he dropped his ax. He reached down to his ankle and pulled two daggers from a strap above his boots, a sword from his belt, four throwing knives from up his sleeves and, from his hands, a set of spiked knuckles.

"Borrow what you'd like," Harlow said, eyeing the Liberation's sunstone weapons. "'cept for the ax. I'll be back for that." He grabbed the reins strapped to the boar's tusks then slapped the animal's rump. It squealed and charged off, the emerald wolf fast on its heels.

Kole collected two arrows from the ground. Since they'd only been used on the Kayetans, they remained in good shape. Though the sunstone might be too fragile to penetrate a soldier's armor, he'd rather have something in his quiver. As he searched the gravel for a third, Russé caught his shoulder.

"What are you doing here?" Russé whispered harshly in his ear. "I thought I told you to stay on the cliffs."

His hands tightened around the bow. "I can still fight."

"Close ranks!" Darian bellowed. "Mounts and shepherds to the front. Soldiers fall in. Wait for my signal." The refugees cleared a path and the shepherds urged their ramblers to the front lines.

"I can't *believe* she let you leave your post." Russé pulled Kole by the arm and led him away from the forming lines of the refugee army. Kole would've jerked free if it wasn't the same arm he'd overextended minutes ago. Already he worried it might compromise his ability to use a bow.

"Keeping me there wasn't in the rebellion's best interest. Even *she* could see that. Why can't you?"

Russé pulled him to the edge of the formation. "Stop focusing on one battle and see the war, Kole. Your survival decides Ohr's fate."

The Soul no longer slouched. He looked strong, like his old self. Kole would have expected the opposite from someone who had endured a fight with a swarm of Kayetans. It seemed the battle itself had empowered him.

The formation quieted. Their eyes stayed on Leo, Lucca, and Harlow's receding forms as they closed the small gap between the armies. A collective gasp came as Harlow's boar thrust its tusks into the front line, ripping the soldiers from the ground. The beasts vanished as the ranks closed in behind them.

"Ready yourself!" Darian shouted to the Liberation.

A horn blew and a chorus of stretching bows surrounded them.

"Ya can't fire yet, Leo's still in there!" Felix's cries carried over the wind.

Darian blew again, ignoring the protest. A sea of arrows arced over the valley, plummeting down like deadly raindrops. Loud clanks echoed in the pass, as most ricocheted off the soldiers' armor.

"Retreat to the cliffs," Russé told Kole, his eyes moving back and forth from Kole to Savairo's approaching army. "Remember the plan if things go wrong."

"Charge!" Darian yelled.

The ground thundered as the ramblers stampeded the frontlines. Kole lowered his stance, keeping his balance as best he could as the refugee army shot by.

"But—"

"Go! You must go! If you truly wish to save your friends, you need to stay safe. It's the only way, Kole. Ohr is counting on you!" Russé's blue eyes flashed. *"You have to trust me."*

A clank came as the two armies collided not far ahead. The ramblers swept their roots from side to side like the armored guards were nothing more than a swarm of insects at their feet. Handfuls of soldiers flew into the air, some crashing into the side of the cliffs while the others rained back on their comrades. Quickly, the soldiers began hacking at the roots in hopes of crippling the trees.

Kole looked back to Russé's pleading eyes.

"Go," Russé said, then turned and fell in stride with the others as they charged Savairo's men.

Kole stared after him. The refugees passed by in a blur of color and battle cries. His gaze swung to the frontline. Though the ramblers seemed to making easy progress, Kole caught sight of a refugee impaled through the stomach with a sword. Another had fallen on his knees, a shield bludgeoning him into submission. The ramblers couldn't protect them. *He* couldn't protect them.

His throat tightened. Gritting his teeth, Kole shouldered his bow and turned. He ran past the refugees, eyes fixed to the ground. Kole couldn't look at them. Not now. Not when he was abandoning them. His heart screamed with every stride. *Coward! Coward!* The wind dried the tears on his cheek as he stumbled up the cliff.

This was bigger than him. Bigger than Niko and all of the people the Black Wall had taken. It meant more than just revenge. This was about Ohr. About survival. And he had made a deal with Russé back in the Liberation hideout. So he obeyed.

Smearing his hand over his wet cheek, he ducked his head, blocking out the cries of war fading behind him. As he climbed, the sound of shattering glass stopped him. Kole risked a peek over his shoulder. His eyes widened.

Kole repeated Leo's words. "Iron will be the victim...."

Silver dust shimmered on the wind like a dense fog, hovering over the middle of the battle. Both armies stopped as they, too, digested the scene. A large chunk of Savairo's army, once adorned with plated metal armor, now stood plain-clothed before the refugees. Leo's spell had destroyed all trace of iron. As Kole peered through the darkness from the edge of the battle, he saw that their armor wasn't the only thing to suffer. The soldiers now stood weaponless — their swords and maces reduced to their wooden hilts.

A wolf howled from the army, bringing the battle back to life, and everyone whose weapons had shattered resorted to throwing punches.

Leo's spell had affected both armies, and the rear half of Savairo's army seemed to have been too far out of range for it to work. Once his armed men made their way to the frontlines, the ramblers would be the deciding fate between victory and slaughter. Yet as he watched, one great tree tilted forward, most of its roots cut clean off. The shepherd atop dove from the trunk before it toppled and smashed a few dozen soldiers, ally and enemy alike.

"Kole!"

He heard his name clearly over the grunts and heated growls of battle.

"Kole!" It came again — louder.

He scanned the battlefield, searching for Russé. Maybe he'd changed his mind.

A figure draped in a red cloak stood motionless at the edge of the battle. Chills flooded him. Kole turned to run. As soon as he did, another sorcerer appeared, blocking his escape. He towered over Kole. Red hood low over his face, the sorcerer lifted a hand.

Kole backed away.

Three more appeared out of nowhere, flanking him like they'd been there the entire time. They circled him. He eyed for a way out, but they moved forward in unison, closing the gaps in their ranks.

Each one lifted a hand, palm open to Kole, and a low hum filled his head. His vision blurred — thoughts jumbled. The hum made him forget his name. The mountain. The battle.

Then.

Red.

A flash of red swept past him. Another sorcerer?

No. Not red. *Auburn.*

Piper tackled the sorcerer in front of him. With a swift pull of her blade, she slit his throat and pounced to the next one.

With the sorcerer's concentration broken, clarity hit him like a slap to the face. He blinked, taking in his surroundings once more.

"Get out of here!" Piper yelled to him. Blood dripped from her dagger as she moved to her next victim. The sorcerers swarmed her like an agitated beehive.

Kole raced to climb the cliff while Piper held them off, but his scar tissue fought against him with each stride, slowing his pace. He only made it a few steps before a pair of arms pulled him back. Hot pain erupted from his shoulders as the arms squeezed tight around his fragile skin.

"Follow the trail," a slithering voice said in his ear. A tendril of smoke reached around forming a long claw.

Idris. He was alive. But how? Kole had watched the bodies burn — watched every Kayetan turn to ash. His shock turned to anger.

"Quite clever you were to set a decoy. All that blood spilled on the floor of your hideout... and for what? A waste of power. You and the Soul should have run while you had the chance."

"Let me go."

"Not until I get the Soul. Where is he? I doubt he'd leave his pet behind."

When Kole didn't answer, Idris swung him around, bringing Kole's face to his own.

Blinking back the whiplash, Kole barred his teeth. "You should be dead."

The Kayetan gurgled a laugh. The hollow where his mouth should be fell deeper into his shadowed skull. "I'm surprised you figured it out. Did Leonardo tell you how to do it? How to destroy a Kayetan? Did he finally manage to solve his brother's puzzle? No matter. The real question is why I'm still here, isn't it? Can't you figure it out? The host bodies are destroyed and along with it, the parasites they left behind. Figure it out, runt. Why was I not consumed in the fire?"

Kole thought back to what Leo had said about Savairo's new breed of Kayetan. He was a special creation. Savairo's best yet. And for that, he would prize him more than the others. He would take precautions. Kole shook his head as the truth weighed on him. "Your host wasn't in the basin."

"Very good. Now, if you are an obedient hostage, I'll let you live long enough to watch your beloved Soul die."

"Find him yourself," Kole snapped.

Idris hissed. "Oh, I won't need to find him." The smoke of Idris' body funneled into Kole's nose. "I know how to make him come running."

His ghost-like form dispersed into a cloud of smoke. It swirled around Kole. He gagged on the thickening air as his feet lifted from the floor, suspended in a sphere of smog. Kole knew what was coming. The same thing Idris had done to Vienna back under the Great Red. He took in a deep breath while he could, expanding his lungs to the limit. He wanted to call out, to fight against him, but it would only deplete his strength. Instead, he stayed completely still, hoping someone would notice him before his oxygen ran out.

He spotted Piper a few meters away. She knelt between three sorcerers. Her head fell slack against her heaving chest.

At first he thought she was catching her breath, tired from the battle, but when she didn't move, he cried out.

They had her subdued. The sorcerers inched closer, blocking her frame behind a wall of red fabric.

A fire sprouted in his lungs. He clamped his mouth, conserving what little air he had left. His eyes burned from the smoke. *Help us! Please, help us! She's going to die! Please!* The words scrambled in his head as he reached out to the presence within him.

The Soul didn't respond. He cursed. Just when he needed her most....

The battling armies before him blurred. He sucked in the smoke, hoping to bring the world back to his eyes, but it only made it worse. As his eyes rolled back, the sphere of smoke burst into flames. Idris shrieked as Kole landed on the gravel.

He gasped and lifted to his elbows.

Piper stood between him and Idris, who slowly re-materialized above. Clutched in her hand was a sword. The blade's surface churned with molten fire, exactly like the pike she had wielded back at the prison.

"Where did you get that?" Kole asked, one eye on the weapon, the other on Idris, who had almost fully reformed.

Without taking her eyes off the sky, she said, "I was bored with the basics."

Piper reached for her belt and pulled out the same vial Kole had seen her hide earlier. She clamped the cork in her teeth, tugged it free and spat it into the rocks. Raising her sword, she dumped the red contents onto the blade. Even in the darkness, Kole could tell it was blood. The sunstone absorbed the blood on contact and the glowing blade shifted to a deep red hue. Her voice came softly, speaking a language Kole didn't understand.

His eyes widened. *Blood magic.* He shuddered, wondering where she got her hands on the blood fueling her spell. Was it her own? Or had she taken it from some poor soul? *Soul? Soul.*

Then, all at once, the events of the night replayed in his head. Piper was the last one out of the base. The blood on the cork had been fresh when he had glimpsed it on the platform, meaning she could've only gotten it beforehand. He recoiled as he took in her blade. "Is that Russé's blood?"

The chanting stopped. Piper's gaze locked onto Kole. "He wasn't using it."

Fully reformed, Idris shrieked and dove for Piper. She took up her blood-infused sword and met him head on. Swing after swing, he blocked her attacks with his claws. Idris and Piper danced along the edge of the valley, neither one able to land a strike.

Kole shot up, grabbed his bow, and chased after them. He nocked an arrow. As he followed them, he realized Idris wasn't fighting at all. The Kayetan whirled out of her sword's reach, blocking when necessary, but he never retaliated with an attack of his own.

He's luring her. But where? He looked ahead. They were nearing the edge of the battle. If she entered the fray, Idris would get the jump on her.

"Piper!" He called out in warning, but his voice carried away in the wind. Grunting between shallow breaths, he locked his elbow and pulled back the string in one swift motion. He adjusted his arm, keeping his eye on Idris, and followed the two as they spun around each other.

The Kayetan rose up, avoiding Piper's next swing. It was the opening he needed.

Kole released.

The arrow disappeared into the night. He chewed his tongue, hoping he had aimed properly. With a flash of light, Idris reeled back.

Piper thrust her sword into the smoke, but Idris proved too quick.

The Kayetan zoomed around her blade and hit her square in the chest, knocking her face-first to the ground. Her sword flew from her hand and soared over the rocks until it came to a clanging stop a few meters from Kole. Before Piper could get up, Idris stood over her, claw raised to strike.

Kole ditched his bow and sped for the sword. Mid-stride, he scooped it up.

Piper flipped to her back, her eyes wide as they locked onto the daunting claw.

Just when Kole thought he wouldn't make it in time, she reached out, sunstone blade in hand, and stopped Idris's arm mere inches from her throat. She gritted her teeth and strained against the Kayetan's strength, the claw lowering ever closer to her neck.

Dread filled Kole's stomach. The same feeling he'd had the night Niko had slipped from his grasp. No. No one else would die by Idris' hand.

Squeezing his stiff fist around the hilt, he picked up speed. The skin at his hips tore open when he lengthened his stride. He staggered, nearly tripping from the sudden burst of pain, but his next foot came down in time to keep him upright. Warmth oozed from his side. He only pushed faster.

Felix and Thomas' lessons echoed in his head. A growl escaped him as he forced the sword into position. Idris was much faster and cunning than any soldier. Kole needed to do this carefully—adjust his strategy to the opponent. But he wasn't as skilled as Felix or Thomas. Wasn't free to move like they were, so he would alter to his own limitations. *Use your scars. Make them your advantage.* He lurched at Idris, shoving the blade wildly at the shadow. The Kayetan shot away, freeing Piper from her hold.

Kole didn't know what Idris would do next, but he had a hunch. Trusting his gut, he passed the blood-infused sword to his other arm and flipped it so that the blade pointed behind him. He covered the pommel with both hands and lifted the sword until his skin screamed at him and threatened to split apart. Then he thrust back, using the tension in his skin to add speed to the blow.

A deafening screech blared at his back. He whipped around.

Idris had appeared behind him as he had hoped. The blade stuck in his shadowed form; a darkening circle emanating from the wound.

"Again!" Piper yelled from the ground.

Kole swung with all his strength and sliced through the middle of Idris' torso. A gash appeared where the blade had passed, and the shadow around the wound disintegrated. Idris let out another shrill scream as his body turned to ash, cutting his cry short.

A cloud of dust floated in the empty space. Kole stared as the wind carried away the remnants of Idris' body and scattered them onto the cliff. A shuffle behind him made him turn. His eyes trailed from the glowing red sword clutched in his hand to Piper. He had killed Idris with blood magic. What did that make him? What did that make Piper? A blood sorcerer?

Still, he held out a hand to her. "Are you all right?"

Piper gestured to the darkening spot on Kole's pants where his skin had torn. "Are you?"

Kole meant to nod, but he stopped himself. She had used Russé's blood. Had she seen the puddle in the hideout, then acted? An act of opportunity. Was it coincidence that she got her hands on the blood of a Soul? Or did she know more than she let on? His head spun. Whatever the truth, the edge of battle seemed a poor place to discuss it. Idris was dead. For now, that would do.

"I shouldn't be here," he said.

"I'd be dead if you weren't." Piper lifted to her feet and held an open hand toward the sword.

Kole stared at it.

"Get yourself safe, I can manage from—"

The thunderous clatter of hooves rose from the noise of the battle. Piper looked past Kole's shoulder and paled. "Run!"

He followed her gaze. A white stallion bearing a thick, muscular man draped in gray burst from the side of the army.

Sleek black hair. Piercing eyes the color of coal. The resemblance was uncanny, as if Leo had betrayed them all and turned sides. Savairo.

Pressing two fingers to her mouth, Piper whistled. A bird screeched in response somewhere above the battle. "Go!" She snatched the sword from his hand then pushed him away.

Kole stumbled. He managed a few steps up the cliff before the ripped skin of his hip stopped him. The hooves ceased somewhere behind him. He crawled as best he could up the steep slope. Red fabric clouded his vision as he bumped into something.

Another red-hooded figure peered down, two golden globes shining from the depths of the hood. Kole scooted back but lost his balance and rolled down the slope next to Piper's feet.

"Bring me the one who killed Idris." Savairo's voice was rough and jagged like the sheer cliffs of the mountain.

Kole fumbled to his knees, eyes snapping back and forth as more sorcerers appeared, popping out of thin air, and closed in on him and Piper. *He'd* killed Idris. They were coming for *him.*

Piper raised the sword up. "I killed your beloved parasite."

Kole looked up at her. "Piper—"

"Quiet," she snapped, then stepped forward.

Savairo waved a hand at her. Eyes rolling back in her sockets, she fell limp and collapsed to the ground. "Take her."

The sorcerers advanced.

"No!" On hands and knees, Kole clambered over the rocks, the jagged pieces cutting into his scarred hands as easily as glass. He threw himself over her body, ignoring the nearing sorcerers.

One waved a hand toward her. As if lifted by invisible hands, her body floated up from the rocks. He clung to her, but his strength was no match for the magic. It dragged him along with her, drifting toward Savairo, who sat impatiently atop his steed.

The rocks tore through the skin of his legs. Unable to bare the pain, he released, bringing his bloodied knees to his chest as she drifted to the horse.

With a hand, Savairo guided her body across the animal's back like she was nothing more than hunted game.

"Piper," Kole called, but he froze as Savairo's head turned to him. His coal-like eyes bore into him, sending an involuntary spasm through every muscle. As Savairo steered his horse toward Kole, a manic cry pierced the air and Thomas burst from the battle. He pushed his way through the line of sorcerers, tackling two to the ground.

Russé and the Liberation rushed in behind, distracting the remaining sorcerers while Thomas climbed to his feet and sprinted toward Piper's unconscious form atop the horse.

Savairo sneered. With little more than a shift in his saddle, he lifted his hand. A tendril of smoke shot out from his palm. It hit Thomas in the gut, propelling him so high, the outline of his body faded in the dark sky.

Kole watched helplessly as Thomas fell back down to the mountain. Eyes clamped shut, he waited for the crunch. But a snarl sounded next to him. He opened his eyes.

The long, billowy tail of Lucca's forest wolf swept pass as the beast vaulted off his hind legs. Lucca and Leo hunkered down, desperately hanging onto the wolf's fur as they soared up. The wolf caught Thomas between his canines and landed with a soft thud.

While Vienna and Felix rushed to Thomas' side, Russé hunched over Kole, pulling him to his feet. "I thought I told you to get out of here," he said, but he never took his eyes from Savairo.

"I tried," he mumbled through the throbbing pain of his tattered skin.

After a quick look of horror at Kole's wounds, Russé ducked under his arm and dragged Kole behind the Liberation.

From afar, Kole watched Leo slide from his mount. He pulled the black mask from his face. "Release her."

Savairo turned at Leo's voice and swung off his horse. "How are you, dear brother?" His smile sent shivers down Kole's spine.

Leo flinched at the greeting.

"I see you've learned a new trick." Savairo gestured to the portion of his army affected by Leo's spell. "Was that a Patriarch Bone? I wonder how you got your little hands on something like that." He leered. "The spell was quite beautiful. A bit showy. But that's always been your thing, hasn't it?"

"Release her," Leo repeated steadily.

Savairo unhooked his gray cloak and let it fall onto the rocks. "Come and take her."

Kole gasped. Even Russé shifted uncomfortably next to him at the sight.

The warden's body, clothes and all, rippled like a mirage, as if he were something between flesh and ghost.

Leo backed away. "What have you done to yourself?"

"I have become stronger. Something you have always been too cowardly to pursue."

"So the rumors are true." Leo shook his head. "How could you use *his* blood? I never thought you'd stoop so low."

The way he'd said it stuck out. *'His blood.'* Like it meant something stronger than what he'd used before. Stronger than a sorcerer.

God's blood? Did he mean Russé? But Leo didn't know Russé was a—

No. Leo only knew of one Soul: Aterus.

"Stooping? *I* am the one who is stooping? You have been hiding underground like a rat in a hole," Savairo spat. "You think because you've destroyed my Kayetans that you have shifted the tides here?" He nodded to the refugees still locked in battle with his men. "Don't worry, I will have plenty of bodies to experiment on and with which to replenish my army."

Leo glowered at his brother; jaw tight, fists clenched.

"Look around you, dear brother. Your allies are dying. All because you are too weak to make the sacrifice."

"Blood magic is dan—" Leo said.

"Blood magic is power!" Savairo's shoulders broadened, making him look half a foot taller. The shadows under his eyes deepened with rage. Then, something flashed across his dark eyes, and he leaned back. Calmer this time, he said, "There is still a way out for you, if not for your friends. I could use your skills, brother. Let me teach you." He held a hand out.

Leo didn't move.

"Don't be a fool like Father," Savairo threatened, venom dripping from his every word.

Kole leaned around enough to see Leo held his hands together, a small chain hanging from his clasped fingers. At the bottom, swinging like a pendulum, was the Seven Souls pendant.

The red cloaks lifted their hands at Leo, but Savairo strode forward, waving at them to stand down. "Still playing with trinkets?"

Leo's voice carried on the wind. An incantation, Kole realized. The words were rushed. Leo sped through the strange tongue as Savairo closed in on him.

Despite Savairo's ghost-like appearance, his boots thudded heavily into the gravel. "Let me show you *real* power—forces you could have at your beck and call!" Long tendrils of smoke rose from his back like the tentacles of an octopus.

Russé dragged Kole back as Vienna and Felix raced to Leo's side. Kole could make out their silhouettes, weapons held high, ready to strike.

The smokey arms lashed out at Leo.

"Ulfric!" Lucca commanded. Her wolf dove for the tentacle, but his fangs sank through the smoke. Howling in frustration, the wolf nipped at them, each one failing like the first. Lucca threw her head back, gave a throaty war cry, and charged in after her wolf.

Once Savairo came within swinging range, Lucca brought down her sword. Savairo moved at the last second. He didn't sidestep or duck. His body just... vanished. Kole thought the blood loss was playing with his head, because in the next moment, Savairo reappeared two feet to the right. Kole squinted through the darkness. Had he seen that right?

Lucca swung again.

Savairo evaded in the same fashion. It seemed whatever power he had allowed him to move like one of his Kayetans.

A smokey arm lashed at Lucca. Her wolf leapt in its path, shielding the camp leader from the blow. But the force behind the strike slammed the animal's body into his master, and they both skidded along the rocks.

Criz and Boogy ran after them and pulled the wolf from Lucca's body.

Kole swung his head back to Leo, who had finally looked up from his hands. An orb of white light burst from his palms. It hurled toward Savairo at lightning speed.

Savairo smashed a tendril into it and sent it flying back into Leo's chest, who let out a gut-wrenching cry and collapsed.

"What a shame." Savairo tutted his tongue as Felix and Vienna checked on Leo.

"Stay here," Russé said to Kole.

"What are you doing?" Kole called, but the Soul had already left.

Russé gripped the middle of his staff. The wood cracked as he snapped it in two. Long branches sprouted from the splintered edges, morphing into two wooden blades. Russé stepped before Savairo, his strange weapons hanging at his sides.

Kole dug his fingers into the gravel. This is what he had wanted: Russé to fight. But as the Soul stood before him, dwarfed in Savairo's hulking form, Kole began to wonder if Russé had been telling the truth about his exhausted powers.

Savairo gave a sadistic smile. He opened his mouth as if he were about to say something, but Russé gave him no chance. The Soul sliced through the nearest tendril; his wooden weapon cutting it clean off.

Savairo recoiled and sneered. Squaring to Russé, he whipped his remaining shadowed arms at him.

Russé whirled, eluding each one. Then he lashed out, chopping another off. He stuck one of his wooden swords into the gravel, using it as a lever to propel himself into the air, while the other slashed through a tendril. After an easy landing, he crossed his weapons over his face to block Savairo's next attack. Russé pushed forward as the tendrils caught his wooden swords, coiling around like constricting snakes.

Savairo was overpowering him.

The Soul strained. His boots slid in the gravel.

Someone had to help. Kole shifted his weight forward and leaned on his hands. The open wounds stung as they hit the dirt. He flinched but pushed on and managed to take his feet.

Russé sunk further into his knees, his eyes locked onto Savairo's.

Kole took a step with his good leg. It held. He tried his next, easing into it. Pain shot from the tear in his hip. His knee buckled, but he steadied himself. He limped closer, catching the Soul's eye.

With a flick of his wrist, Russé pulled one of his weapons free and chucked it to Kole's feet.

Thinking the Soul was offering him a weapon, Kole reached for the blade. When he grabbed the wood, roots sprayed out, entangling him like a fly caught in a web. Kole staggered back and tripped. His back throbbed from the rough landing. Vision spinning, he lifted his head to Russé's blurry outline.

The Soul dove to the side, letting Savairo's smoking arms spring past him. With a swift pull, he severed the outstretched tendrils.

Shock flashed in Savairo's black eyes. He retreated to his horse.

Russé stalked him. The blade of his wooden sword reshaped, lengthening like long ropes, and wrapped around Savairo's neck.

Savairo wheezed, purple-faced as the root tightened around his neck. "Do it!"

The circle of sorcerers lifted their hands and placed them on their chests. With a swift word, they crumpled to the floor. No bodies. Just piles of red fabric. Clouds of smoke seeped from the folds and siphoned into Savairo's gaping mouth.

The warden breathed it in, and the edges of his once-quivering mouth curling into a wicked smile. He braced his hands around the wooden ropes. With new strength, he pried them from his throat.

The wood shuddered and reverted to its original blade-like shape, but Russé seem unfazed. He crouched low, a fierceness exuding from his frail body as he waited for Savairo to make the next move.

Savairo's black eyes narrowed. Instead of attacking, he placed his hand over the stallion's chest. The horse whinnied as a gust of thick, ashy wind burst out in every direction. It hit Kole, knocking the air from his chest. Lifting his head, he caught a glimpse of the horse.

Its pure white hair burned red hot. Kole shielded his face from the intense heat as the stallion's flesh melted away. Within seconds, all that was left of the beautiful beast were the broad, ivory bones of its skeleton. A nauseating crack echoed through the night as the horse's ribs broke from its spine. The bones lifted, growing out into long skeletal wings. They gave a windless flap, and the horse moved its head to Savairo, black orbs glowing from the empty eye sockets.

Russé swung as Savairo jumped to his steed's back, behind Piper's unconscious body.

The horse reared. Its hooves clipped Russé's staff, knocking it from his hands. Then the beast charged.

Russé leapt from its path.

Kole's eyes widened as the skeletal horse swerved toward him. He scrambled back, but Russé's vines kept him rooted. His eyes barely focused on the scene as his vision blurred from blood loss. He did the only thing he could and buried his head in his hands.

The thuds grew louder—nearer—until the drumming of hooves fell in time with the beat of his racing heart.

A whoosh of wind and the pounding stopped.

Kole peered up. The underbelly of the skeletal horse launched over him and set off into the sky. The image swirled. His eyes rolled back in his head.

CHAPTER 26

It had been one day since the battle. After Savairo's grand exit, Kole had been told that most of his soldiers had fled. The rest surrendered. Many of the rear ranks were newly drafted guards, not hardened soldiers and were forced to fight under threat of Savairo killing their families.

Refugees and soldiers alike joined the Liberation in burying the dead. With such great numbers, the shallow graves had only taken a day to dig. The following morning, it was time to bring peace to those who had fallen.

Kole welcomed the warm sun on his face. He closed his eyes and pulled his hood down, making the most of this rare moment of silence. He missed the calm — the serenity — of Solpate. Breathing in deeply, he remembered the smells of the forest: rich soil, fragrant flowers bursting into bloom, crisp fresh air....

His stomach sank.

It might be a long while until he stepped foot into Solpate. As much as he hoped, he knew things would never be the same. *He* would never be the same.

"Kole!" Felix called in the distance. "Hey, Blondie, you up here?"

Kole opened his eyes.

With most of the bodies already in the graves, Kole had slipped away from the group and hiked up the pass. He knew the danger of going off on his own, especially since Savairo was still out there, but he couldn't leave her up here to be forgotten.

He stared at the horseshoe clasped in Anna's cold hand. "I'll make sure it stays with you always," he whispered.

"There you are. You could've answered, ya know. What are ya doin' up here?" Felix crested the slope, huffing. The sounds of his crunching feet slowed when he saw her. "Anna... how'd she —"

"She saved me from a Kayetan."

Felix knelt next to Kole.

Kole shrugged against the stiff new bandages over his hands and legs. The pain was gone for now, though he'd need another dose of Leo's concoction soon. Still, he was lucky compared to so many others. Thomas had gotten away with a few broken ribs, and Criz had suffered a few lacerations from the fight. Both, Leo assured, would heal in time with bed rest. Lucca, though, wasn't as lucky. Her body had been crushed under her wolf. Leo could only do so much for her, but her spirit was strong. They had hope.

It was Piper he worried about most. She was with Savairo now, and they had no way of knowing where.

It should have been him on that horse's back. *He* had killed Idris, not her. She had saved him time and time again. He couldn't help but wonder why. He was a stranger to her. And now.... now she was gone, because he'd been too slow. Too weak.

Kole's hand trembled as he placed it over Anna's. Another unfair death. One that could have been avoided if only he'd been stronger.

He was tired of all the death around him. Tired of being helpless — of being the one who needed saving. Back in Solpate, before the fire, *he* had been the strong one. Out here he was weak. Naive. A burden.

"I should've done better," he whispered to Anna.

"It's not your fault. There's nothin' ya could've done."

"After he killed her, he looked at me — *really* looked at me — like he recognized me. Then he left. He let me live."

Felix frowned. "Have you told Russé? Leo?"

"Not yet."

"It sounds kinda important. Maybe they'll know what it means."

"Yeah, I guess." Kole blinked back the welling water in his eyes.

"I'll take her," Felix said, waving him aside. "Just don't go wanderin' off while my back is turned or Russé'll have my head." He lowered his voice, peeking around nervously. "I never wanna be on his bad side, if ya know what I mean."

Felix lifted Anna's small frame. The horseshoe slipped from her hands. Kole picked it up and turned to follow. He paused.

Something glittered between the fine layer of rocks where the shoe had been. He nudged them aside with his boot. Goren's necklace reflected in the bright morning sun.

Kole eyed it as Felix's footsteps receded. He picked it up and held it in his palm.

He hadn't heard Issira's voice since the battle, but he didn't need to hear her to know that she was still somewhere, in the depths of his mind, watching over him like the others he had yet to meet.

Kole closed his hand around the symbol. "I will find you. All of you. And put a rest to this."

"C'mon now," Felix said when he discovered Kole was lagging behind. "You might not be afraid of Russé, but I am."

"You don't know the half of it," he muttered under his breath, then hurried to catch up.

"There you are," Russé said as Kole and Felix reached the valley. Worry lingered on the edge of his words. He leaned against his staff, which had returned to its familiar form. Seeing Anna, he cleared a path through the hundreds of people huddled around waiting for the ceremony to begin and led them to an empty hole.

Kole helped Felix place her in the shallow grave. He arranged Honey's shoe on her stomach, then looked at her one last time and thanked her.

Russé stayed back with Leo while Felix led Kole out of the crowd and up the slope to where Vienna, Thomas, and Boogy stood, waiting silently for Leo to begin his speech.

Vienna gave him a weak smile as he approached, her face and clothes covered in dirt and grime—as they all were—from helping dig the graves and transport bodies.

Thomas' eyes were blood shot, and his normally tanned skin looked pasty. Kole had heard him crying all night. Thomas' distant gaze remained on the bodies piled in the grave as Kole and Felix took their places next to the Liberation. Boogy fiddled with his hands, shifting uneasily from side to side as if he didn't know how to act without his brother next to him.

Lilith's Pass was spotted with fresh-turned soil; a grid of open graves, each one headed with a small stone as their markers. There were too many to count.

Leo began his speech.

Kole didn't hear a single word. His thoughts lingered on his conversation with Russé the previous night. They were to leave quietly after the ceremony, while everyone was preoccupied giving their final farewells and prayers to the fallen. They'd already packed their bags and hidden them between the rocks at the top of the slope.

Nothing remained for them here or in the north, save for the Black Wall and an empty forest, so they would head south over the hills in search of the imprisoned Souls.

No goodbyes. No hints as to their destination. No explanations.

They would simply leave behind everyone and everything Kole cared about. It was better this way. If he became too attached, he would never want to leave. And Leo was already growing suspicious of Russé since the battle.

'*It's for the best*,' as Russé would say, and, finally looking out over Lilith's Pass, Kole found he agreed.

Wherever they went, death seemed to follow, and he would only feel worse if something happened to his new friends because of him.

He finally understood what he had to do. Even though Russé was a Soul and had been living a lie ever since his liberation from the Great Red, they'd made a deal. Kole wanted to rid the world of the Black Wall as much as Russé, and he wanted answers to his past. It was their common ground for now. Despite his lies and deceit, Russé was all Kole had left.

Kole thought of Niko as he looked over the graves. He imagined the ceremony was for him, too, along with the orphans. Now that Idris was dead, they could all rest in peace, at least a little.

His mind felt a bit of relief knowing the Kayetans were dead. Though the Black Wall remained, and Savairo and Aterus were still out there, today was a victory as much as it was a loss. He had to believe that.

The smell of honey passed under his nose. Kole glanced at Vienna from the corner of his eye. Her blonde curls swayed back and forth in the wind as she listened to Leo's speech. He was glad she was safe. Glad they all were. They would stay that way as long as they didn't get any more involved. There was enough to do in Socren now anyway, what with recovering the city and leading them into a better future. That would take a great effort on all of their parts.

He shifted his eyes back to Leo and Russé, who were shoveling the first patch of dirt over the dead.

Russé held his palm to the sky, his voice carrying over the crowd, "May the lost find their way."

He lifted his hand with the others and repeated the words.

The shovels were passed down the lines as everyone stepped up and took a turn pouring dirt over the bodies.

Russé glanced up to Kole on the slope and gave a slow nod.

It was time.

He sighed.

"Are you all right?" Vienna's emerald eyes glittered at him.

He gazed back at her, wishing he could tell her the truth, but instead said, "Yes."

"Death is always hard. The pain will pass in time." She took up her brother's hand. "It helps when you have someone to lean on."

He couldn't muster the strength to smile, so he let his eyes drift to the open graves.

"I never got the chance to thank you," she said.

He glanced back. "For what?"

"The forest." She held his gaze. In that moment, he knew she was looking at *him*, not his scars. "Thank you, shepherd."

He swallowed and dipped his head.

Vienna gave him a soft smile then descended the slope with the Liberation.

Kole made a few slow steps after them, feigning to follow, then turned and climbed.

The longer he lingered, the harder it would be to leave. And he had to leave. He had struck a deal with a Soul, and he wasn't about to turn back now. Ohr was counting on him.

He crested the cliff and didn't look back.

THE END

ACKNOWLEDGEMENTS

Thank you to my earliest beta readers Sarah Chavez, Andrew Hartz, and Madison Wells for helping me sort out my vision. Your feedback was invaluable for figuring out my story. To my writing critique group, I can't say enough to express my gratitude for your keen eyes. You all went above and beyond, finding ways to improve this manuscript and help me hone my craft. A special shout out to Stephanie Horton, who dove in for a final readthrough before my submissions.

My Mother, Amy Maxwell, and Dad, Michael Maxwell, who encouraged me to follow my dreams no matter how out of reach they seemed. That 'summer writing vacation' sparked it all.

Thank you to my sister, Bianca Ehrler, for being a relentless wave of encouragement.

To Darren Todd, editor extraordinaire, writing teacher, and friend: I am so thankful to work with you, and even more so, learn from you.

Sam Keiser made my visions of the ramblers come to life. Such an exquisite artist. The book cover is more than I ever hoped for.

And thank you to David Lane (aka Lane Diamond) who gave me a chance. I am forever grateful to be a part of the Evolved Publishing team.

ABOUT THE AUTHOR

Parris lives in Mesa, Arizona with her husband and two golden retrievers. She discovered her love for reading when a middle-school reading assignment led her to the fantasy section of the library. This passion sparked stories of her own imagination, yet she never put pen to paper until after college. When she's not consumed in her writing, she enjoys Olympic weightlifting, playing Dungeons & Dragons, and coaching color guard.

For more, please visit Parris online at:
Website: www.ParrisSheetsAuthor.com
Facebook: @AuthorParrisSheets
Twitter: @Parris_Sheets

WHAT'S NEXT?

CHILDREN OF THE VOLCANO
Essence of Ohr – Book 2
(Coming Spring 2021)

*With the people cursed by a god—forever doomed—Kole enters their
stronghold to seek the heart of the volcano.*

Peace has returned to Kole's city, yet day by day, the world dies.
Only the gods can return balance to Ohr. Kole has already found one,
Russé, his mentor. Together they decipher the cryptic map in Kole's
head to locate the others, but they aren't the only ones searching for the
gods.

Tailed by the enemy, the trail leads to a volcano in a forsaken land,
with winds of swirling ash, toxic fumes, and creatures of living stone.
Kole and Russé will discover why the grounds are rumored to be
cursed, why no human has set foot near the volcano in centuries, and
just how much grit they'll need if they hope to reach the god first.

BEYOND THE FLAME
Essence of Ohr – Book 3
(Coming Spring 2022)

*When old scars open—wounds that never truly healed—can Kole find
the courage to stand against the deepest fear he's ever known?*

MORE FROM EVOLVED PUBLISHING

CPSIA information can be obtained
at www.ICGtesting.com
Printed in the USA
LVHW092113101120
671306LV00008B/1763

9 781622 536535